MW01488151

# TESTIMONY

JASON BOND

This is a work of fiction. All of the characters, names, incidents, organizations, and dialogue in this novel are either the products of the author's imagination or are used fictitiously.

WestBow Press books may be ordered through booksellers or by contacting:

WestBow Press
A Division of Thomas Nelson & Zondervan
1663 Liberty Drive
Bloomington, IN 47403
www.westbowpress.com
1 (866) 928-1240



ISBN: 978-1-9736-2369-4 (sc)
ISBN: 978-1-9736-2370-0 (hc)
ISBN: 978-1-9736-2368-7 (e)

Library of Congress Control Number: 2018903519

Print information available on the last page.

WestBow Press rev. date: 04/10/2018

*This book is dedicated to that voice that whispered in my ear to "stop talking about it, and do it" not just once, but at least 831 times. This one is for you, my muse. Thank you for waking me up, and helping me to dream.*

*And of course, to my Lord and Savior, Jesus Christ.*

# CHAPTER 1

What is your testimony? You know, the story of how you finally made that big decision and came to Christ. The story about how Jesus became your personal savior. All Christians have one. Most people have never sat down and told it to anyone but other Christians. You know just to play it safe, the people that will just nod their heads in agreement as you tell your story. And I bet on top of that, you couldn't even name one person who has taken the time to write it all down.

That is what I plan to do. But I'm not doing this so you will read it, and then make a life changing decision. Look, either you are going to believe me or not. That is all up to you. I don't even know you, but I hope that after you read this, you will know a little something about me.

Most Christians have basically one of two stories about how they came to Christ. The first one is what I like to call the "Rock Bottom Way to Find the Lord." This is the person who lives a life of sin. Sometimes they have made a series of wrong choices and have even gone to jail or something, or maybe through some tragedy of no fault of their own, they lost everything that they love, or maybe they just have nowhere else left to turn. This to me is the most sincere way to find Jesus. These people are down on their hands and knees begging Jesus above for forgiveness. But the more I think about it, are they really that sincere, or do they just have no other options? Anyone will embrace broccoli if they are hungry enough. Did I just compare Jesus to broccoli? Don't tell Him, ok? This type of "Rock Bottom Christian" puts the *save* in Savior.

The second type of Christian is what I like to call the "Been There –Done That" Christian. My best friend until the third grade was one of these. His dad was a Baptist preacher, and so he spent almost every waking moment when he wasn't in school, at the church. Basically, if the doors were unlocked, you could find my friend, Jim, somewhere inside. He was a follower by default. Sure, when he was old enough, he was supposed to make his own decision about Jesus, but come on, what were his options really. Jim wasn't one of those problem children of the preacher-type kids. Nope, he was smart and funny, respectful and kind. So when he was baptized, everyone was happy, but no one was surprised. I think that the "Been there-Done That" Christians have an advantage that most of us don't have. They were born halfway saved. All they have to do is not mess things up.

So, that begs the question. "What type of Christian are you, Peter?" I'll tell you what. What if I just write all of this out, and I'll let you decide. I mean, if I was just to come out and tell you, where is the fun in that. Plus, you wouldn't get to hear about the ghost, now would you?

# Chapter 2

When my family first moved to this town, I knew the moment that my parents saw that bright red and white sign that read: "Shaping Minds – Saving Souls – St Thomas Christian Academy – Enroll Now" that that is where I would be going to school. You see, my dad got transferred here for his job, and so it was either move to this backwards little town, or find a new job. Looking back, I bet he would have chosen to look around a bit longer. Now, because we didn't know anyone, and therefore didn't know what neighborhoods were considered "safe," both my mom and my dad agreed that St Thomas sounded like the best option for a boy entering the fourth grade. I mean, come on, it's a Christian school, what could be safer than that right? *Ha!*

So, after I was officially registered and with less than a week before school was scheduled to start, my mom and I were frantically flipping through whatever was left of the racks and racks trying to find me a set of school uniforms that would fit, not to mention the required school supplies from the school supply list that didn't have puppies or kitties on the cover. I guess the good news that was to come out of all this was that I would be walking through the doors on day one instead of in the middle of the semester. I have done both, and believe me, it is ten times worse being the new kid after everyone has settled into a routine.

What was even better news was that I wasn't going to be the only new student in the fourth grade. How did I know this? It just so happened that on the day my mom brought me down to the school office to fill out the last bit of paperwork and visit my new classroom, there was another kid my age with his dad doing the exact same thing. As mom and my new teacher, Mrs. Anderson, talked about our move here to town and if my mom had indeed discovered the antique stores tucked away downtown, Brady and I didn't talk to each other at all. We didn't have to. We both had the same look on our face. You have probably seen the look before. It is the same look that the newbie prisoner has on every cop show. You know, the look on his face as they are escorting him to his new cell.

Brady and I both looked around the room at the desk in perfectly straight, uniform rows and the "reading corner" complete with a thick rug and fluffy, brightly-colored pillows. We both tried not to make eye contact. It seemed to me, that Mrs. Anderson, our new teacher, was also *really* into rainbows. Now, I totally understood the rainbow theme when I saw the pictures of Noah and the ark, but why would Jesus have his hands behind His head leaning back on one? When I overheard my soon to be new principal, Mrs. Ramirez, tell my mom that Mrs. Anderson had been a kindergarten teacher for the last thirty years and had just recently "graduated" to fourth grade, I was no longer the least bit surprised.

So after a tour of the empty cafeteria, the tiny chapel that sat in the corner of the property, the huge sanctuary complete with a cross that hung over the pulpit like a jet plane flying over, and the gymnasium that smelled of sweaty socks, my mother could not have been more excited. She told me that although the family finances would be a little tight, St Thomas Christian Academy was so wonderful that she and Dad were going to make it work. It was settled. I would be one of the newest kids at the school and church that is the ancient St Thomas Academy, In fact, I wouldn't doubt it if St. Thomas himself probably attended at some time or another.

The next five days were a blur. Mom spent every waking moment unpacking boxes and making home repairs. My dad spent every waking moment at his new office trying to make a good first impression on all of his co-workers. I spent mine helping mom the best that I could and trying to keep my baby brother Aiden, from putting anything that he could reach into his mouth. Somehow, we all came together at dinner to share our daily adventures and to plan what movie we would watch after Mom put Aiden to bed. When I think about it, I don't even think my dad asked me about my visit to St Thomas, or what I thought about my new school. All he was concerned about was whether or not Mom thought it was safe, and how far away it was from his office in case he ever had to pick me up.

The first thing that I noticed as my mom walked me to class that first Monday morning, was that no other moms walked their fourth grade sons, or daughters for that matter, to class. Even Brady struggled to walk in with his arms full of school supplies, and dropping his Kleenex box three times, rather than being seen needing his "mommy's" help finding his desk. I could tell you that I have never been more embarrassed, but that would be a lie. (You don't know my mother.) And yes, she even pulled out my chair as I found the desk that had my name on it in the upper left-hand corner. Looking back, I don't know if every single kid in class stopped what they were doing to memorize this moment for future ammunition, but it surely felt like it then. After what seemed like an eternity, I was finally alone behind the security of my desk and ready for the morning to be over with.

The second thing that I noticed on my first day at school, was that this school was much, much smaller than my last school. There was only about twelve kids in my class, and by the look of it, all but three of us knew each other. So, without saying a word, Brady found his desk next to mine. Although I felt uncomfortable and awkward, and this was only the first few minutes of the first day of school, and I was already better off than Frances Maggie Lingersham. She was the other new kid in our class, and as if that name wasn't bad enough, she came in wearing thick bottle-bottom glasses and a sweater that was a combination of Joseph's Technicolor-dream coat and my Grandma Nina's favorite argyle. As you can imagine, she sat in the back of the room, and every single girl in class snickered at first but was then quickly ignored her. After the initial embarrassment that was my mother, it was easy enough for me to blend in with only the occasional glance until everyone had settled themselves in, and Mrs. Anderson began her introductions.

"Class, as most of you know my name is Mrs. Anderson, and I will be your homeroom teacher this year. I will *not* tolerate any interruptions or misbehavior in my classroom." she bellowed. Her balled up fist pounded the table as she spoke to emphasize each syllable.

For some unknown reason, she seemed really angry, and her voice was way too loud and aggressive for 8:00 o'clock in the morning. Did someone make her mad or something? This was not the same bright-eyed and positive teacher that my mom met earlier last week. I would soon learn that the nice happy-go-lucky, wouldn't-hurt-a-fly teacher that my mother fell in love with was the mask that Mrs. Anderson put on to trick my mom, and I am assuming every mom that walked into her classroom, into enrolling their child here in the first place. As the school days ticked by, I would learn that Mrs. Anderson could slip on the "Princess Sunshine" mask in the blink of an eye. Once, she was red-faced and on the verge of murdering Donald Finkleman because he had accidentally left the water faucet on in the back of the room. In the middle of her tirade about the oceans drying up and millions of fish flopping around helplessly because Donald left the faucet running, Principal Ramirez opened the door and walked in the room. Instantly, Mrs. Anderson went from evil Hyde back to timid Jekyll. Principal Ramirez smiled her peaceful smile, and Mrs. Anderson just smiled back and continued our math lesson without missing a beat.

The first thing on Mrs. Anderson's agenda was to humiliate the new kids in class. She did this by calling the whole class to attention and then having the three of us take turns telling the class all about ourselves and what brought us to St Thomas Christian Academy. Brady was called first. He started to speak from his chair and was immediately ridiculed and told that students in Mrs. Anderson's class, "stand and speak properly and loudly when addressed."

Brady stood and began again. "My name is Brady."

"Brady what?" Mrs. Anderson interrupted. This made Shane and a few others start to giggle. Mrs. Anderson shot the class a look of daggers that stopped them suddenly.

"My name is Brady Heath." Brady, clearing his throat, continued, "My family and me..."

"My family and I" Mrs. Anderson interrupted again.

I didn't even know the guy, and already I wanted to rescue him. The whole time I remember thinking that if she wanted him to share his story then she should just shut it and let the kid speak. For what seemed like a lifetime, Brady stood in front of his desk, gripping the corners until his knuckles turned white and shared the travels of the Heath family from Kentucky to Florida to now, Texas.

Be careful what you wish for because before I knew it it was now my turn. I could feel the heat rising from my sweaty palms to the flush of my reddening cheeks. My heart beating so hard that I make a promise to you that I could hear it echoing of the whiteboard in the front of the classroom.

All I had to do was tell the class my name and where I was from, and maybe a story or two. I could do this. I looked toward Brady who had made it through this interrogation and now had a new hero. How could Brady have survived this? Now I know how the Jews felt during the rising of the Third Reich. *"Where are your papers? Your papers are not in order!"*

As quickly as I could, I relayed all of the information that was needed to send me safely on my way. "My name is Peter Gentry. I am originally from a small town near Atlanta, but my dad got a new job, so we moved here about a week ago. I have a little brother that isn't old enough for school. My mom stays home and takes care of him. I like games and t.v." I said all of this as fast as I could. Before Mrs. Anderson could ask a question, I was back in the safety of my seat looking at Frances as if to say, *beat that!*

Mrs. Anderson rolled her eyes and motioned to Frances that it was her turn at the inquisition. Of course, Frances got the sleeve of her sweater caught on the corner of the chair. Of course, her whole body jerked forward suddenly when it did. And of course, this caused every school supply on her desk to go rolling across the floor. This time the class did more than just giggle. Most of the class was laughing uncontrollably and pointing at the pencils and other school supplies making their way across the tiled floor. Mrs. Anderson did not offer to help Frances. Instead, she slammed her stapler down with a hard *smack*. The room went dead quiet. Frances stared at the ground in horror and shock as the tears welled in her eyes. I can still remember her voice as it squeaked out inaudible sounds that were barely heard above the whispers from the rest of the class. I wouldn't find out until much later just how loudly Frances could scream.

This was also the day that I was introduced to Shane Wilkerson. Although Shane was in the same grade as me, he had to have been at least half a foot taller. Also, I have never before or since seen a fourth grader with a five o'clock shadow. Like any school bully, Shane had his minions. But more about that later. I found out later that Shane had been coming to this school since he was old enough to walk; therefore, he knew every teacher by both their first and last name. You see, his parents owned the local car dealership, so not only did his mom and dad give heavy to the church and to the school, but also almost everyone in town drove a car or truck from the lot of Wilkerson auto. Some kids said that the principal even went over to Shane's house for dinner sometimes. At the time, I wasn't sure that that was true, but now after everything that has happened it would make a lot of sense.

I really couldn't tell you what I did the rest of that first day. You know how it is. You think that the first day in a new school will never end, but it does. You think that you will never make any friends, but eventually you do. You think that the staring and leering that you get throughout the day from your fellow classmates will scar you for life, but that usually doesn't happen until later.

The only real friend that I had made that first week was Brady. You see, all of the other boys in my class got along just fine with one another, but for some reason that neither Brady nor I could figure out, we were left out of everything. At first, I just chalked it up to us being the new guys, but after a few days I started to get the feeling that they wanted us to join them, but for some reason, we just couldn't.

Also, Shane Wilkerson was feeling and acting less and less like a bully. You see, because my dad had us moving around a lot, I had seen my share of school bullies. Once, when I was in second grade, a fifth grader made one of my classmates eat a wad of wet toilet paper while we were in the bathroom. The poor kid was so afraid, that he didn't say anything to anyone. None of us did. No, Shane didn't pick on anyone and most of the kids seemed to actually like him. It was almost as if Shane and the other boys in my class were actually told not to include us in anything that they did.

Here, let me give you an example. In P.E. one afternoon, the boys and the girls were separated from each other, as usual, and Shane along with Darrick Henderson were picking teams for kickball. Well, everyone in our class got picked by one side or the other until there was just Brady and me. I mean it's a no-brainer right, you either pick me or Brady. Shane instead looks around the field for the coach, and the coach just lowers his head so all you could see was the brim of his worn-out Astros cap. The next thing you know, everyone is playing kickball, and Brady and I are sitting cross-legged all alone under a tree wondering what had just happened. I mean, why didn't the coach stand up and say something?

Wait that is not the whole truth. I told you that I was going to be honest as

I told you what happened, so I better not leave anything that I can remember out of it. On the other side of the field in a corner that I could barely see, sat Frances Maggie Lingersham. Looking back, I can't believe that I was such a jerk. This whole time that I was griping and complaining about my first week at St. Thomas, Frances was doing the same thing. Only she was having to go through everything that I was. Only, she was having to do it alone. When I look back on all of this now, I have to wonder if, in fact, she was the strongest of us all.

Anyway, like I was saying. It wasn't as if Shane and the other guys were picking on us. It was if they were not *allowed* to like us. But, that all changed the first week of October.

Every day a little after noon, after we had finished eating our lunch, we were allowed to walk around the semi-grassy concourse area just outside of the cafeteria doors, and we could spend that time soaking up about fifteen minutes of freedom before we had to make our way back into the classroom and tackle the pile of work that Mrs. Anderson tried to get in before the 3:30 p.m. dismissal bell. The outdoor concourse area consisted of a hand full of tall Oak trees that over shadowed almost the entire area. There was even a few times that I looked out the cafeteria and thought that it was night or a solar eclipse or something because the shadows of those Oaks covered so much of the sun above. There were also a few cracked concrete benches that had pencil marks and elementary school graffiti. And right in the center of it all was a five foot statue of St Thomas that no one was allowed to touch. Most of the older kids claimed the benches way before any of the fourth graders could get there, so we mostly spent our time either walking around in circles or leaning against one of the Oak trees.

That particular Tuesday I was talking to Brady about the Dallas Cowboy game that was on the night before, when Shane Wilkerson called us both over. Although it was a bit strange, it wasn't that unusual for him to call us over to his gaggle of friends. Given that most of the time it was just to ask about an assignment that he and his pals didn't do the day before, or maybe just to verify a "nerd" fact. A typical conversation between Shane and us would be brief and go a little something like this:

Shane- "Hey guys, come here." (He would motion with his finger.)

Us- (after walking slowly over to him) "Yeah?"

Shane- "Was the math practice homework numbers 7-11, or 7-14?

Us- "7-11"

Shane- "See told you." (He would say to his friends.) "You can leave now," (He would say to Brady and me.)

Like I said, that was just one of two in depth conversations that we shared. The other one was a little more intense. It is what I like to call the "nerd" facts conversation that went a little something like this:

Shane- "Hey guys, come here." (He would motion with his finger.)

Us- (after walking slowly over to him) "Yeah?"

Shane- "What was the name of the guy that trained Obi Wan Kenobi?"

Us- "Qui-gon Ginn"

Shane- "See told you." (He would say to his friends.) "You can leave now," (He would say to Brady and me.)

You know, now that I think about it, I don't see how Shane thought that Brady and I were the nerds if it was *Shane and his friends* that were the ones talking about Star Wars. Anyway, on this particular Tuesday afternoon, this was neither one of those conversations. It has been a while, but I can almost remember this one word for word. It went something like this:

Shane- "Hey guys, come here."

Us- (after walking slowly over to him) "Yeah?"

Shane- "It looks like you guys are going to be here a while so you might as well know what is going on."

Us- (both looking at each other and then slowly back at Shane) "Ok, so what's going on."

Shane- "We want you to be part of our class. You know, be one of the guys. All of us here have each other's backs, and we know that we can count on one another no matter what happens. That is because we have all been through it. " All of Shane's friends nodded in agreement. I could tell by the look in their eyes that they were not just kidding around. Whatever they had planned for us was serious. As serious as something could be to a bunch of nine and ten year olds. Shane continued, "But to be one of us here at St. Thomas is not just something that you get to be. It is something that has to be earned. You see…." Shane stopped talking and looked at his friends. He patted Darrick on the shoulder and continued, "We all made it through."

Now, I had no idea what Shane was talking about when he said that. I mean, "made it through," could he possibly be more cryptic? Don't get me wrong, I know exactly what he means now, but at the time it was just strange. Shane and his friends barely said more than two words to me the first six weeks of school and now this. Plus, you have to realize that Brady and I were getting desperate. It had been almost two months of the silent treatment, so both of us were willing to do whatever it took to be finally be included. And I am not just talking about being included in Shane's little clan of friends. No, I'm talking about being included at St. Thomas Christian Academy.

Before I tell you about what happened next, I wanted to tell you about something that happened between Mrs. Anderson and I. Remember when I said that the coach didn't seem to mind that Brady and I were never picked for any of the games or the fact that we seem to be excluded on all the teams, well it wasn't just the coach. Mrs. Anderson was probably the meanest teacher that I had ever had, but there was something subtle in the way she would phrase things when she talked to Frances, Brady, or me. She always treated us as if she was the ticket taker at the movie theater, and she had just caught us sneaking in to watch the show. Don't get me wrong. She was doing her job and she still taught us everything the rest of the kids in the classroom were learning, but I noticed that the only time she ever called on any of us was when no one else in the class had their hands up. Not that Frances ever raised her hand. There was even a time when Mrs. Anderson asked a question to the entire class, and Brady must have known the answer because he had his hand raised well above his head to the point I could hear him straining. We were talking about the Native Americans of Texas, and instead of calling on him, Mrs. Anderson just shook her head in disgust at the lack of knowledge in her classroom and instead was forced to read the answer from the textbook. Now, I know what you are thinking, "Peter, that has happened to everybody." But I am telling you, it was the way that she did it that still creeps me out.

For the next few minutes out there in the warm, October sun, Shane told us exactly what one had to do to be a member of the Mrs. Anderson's fourth grade class, and for that matter, to be considered a real student at St Thomas Christian Academy. And for the next few minutes both Brady and I couldn't believe our ears.

What I didn't know at the time, was that Frances Maggie Lingersham was getting almost the exact same talk from Betty Schwartzman on the girl's side of the cafeteria. If I had known then what I know now, I believe that Frances would have been in on our plans from the start. Instead, just like Brady and I had done all year, we let Frances deal with St. Thomas on her own.

St. Thomas Church for Godly Patrons was established in the arguably the hottest part of Texas in 1906 by a man named D.B. Smith. D.B.'s plan was to not only find like-minded individuals who loved the Lord the way that he did, but also to have a safe place for his children and other families in the area to raise their children too. So, on a blistering August afternoon, the St. Thomas Home for Godly Patrons broke ground. The St. Thomas Home for Godly Children didn't follow too far behind and was established in 1913. Over the next few decades, hundreds of boys filled the hallways of the young church and school. They were raised "properly" by the church. I stress boys because although the name on the signs read "Godly Children," girls were not admitted until 1952.

If you search the archives of the church library, you could actually find some of the yearbooks and photographs of long dead students whom were educated in the same classrooms as the students today. Now that sounds a lot creepier than it really is. Tradition and history sometimes do. I mean think about it. How many students sat in the same classrooms, maybe even at the same desk that you sat in as a kid? And now that kid is no longer around? He or she is long dead. That is just the way it is with old buildings. In fact, in the halls on the way to the sanctuary, there is row after row of long dead pastors and other prominent leaders of the church in their Sunday best. All of them now resting in their graves. Even our gymnasium was even named after one of the first Pastors to ever allow women to wear pants in the building. What a rebel!

Because our elementary school is also a working and functioning church there are always dozens of faces of church members that we don't recognize in the hallways, and dozens of locked doors that are never opened down each walkway. Most of the people are just harmless, church members and old ladies who greet each student as if he or she was their own grandchild. As a student, you get used to it. And if you were to ask anyone about the locked doors around the place, you would always get the same answer, "supplies." I personally didn't know what that meant, but I always assumed it was just stacks of bibles and hymnals. Maybe, if you were lucky, you might run across the room where the stash those dry, saltless, little crackers that they save for the communion. Yep, I'm talking about shelves and shelves stacked with boxes of the body of Christ. So every Monday and Friday, as Mrs. Anderson lined everyone up to make our way down the curved hall to the library, our class would walk by at least ten doors that none of us had any clue as to what was on the other side.

Let me get back to the story. You see, Brady and I were standing there dumbfounded when we found out what we were expected to do to be part of the group. I mean this had to be some sort of joke, right? It had to be some kind of hazing trick that they pulled on all of the new kids that came in. I mean there is no way that we were going to be allowed to do it. Before we had a chance to ask any meaningful questions or find out what exactly was going on around there, the bell rang ending our lunch break, and we all drudgingly headed back to the classroom. I tried asking Shane a few questions that I had along the way, but he just started ignoring me again and instead went back to talking to his pals.

Before the end of the day dismissal bell, I did something that afternoon that I had rarely done before. I asked someone for their phone number. You have to remember that this was back in the days of landlines, so no one had a phone in their back pocket. So when you asked someone for their phone number, what you were really saying was, "I am going to call your house, and everyone in your family will know." Then you will have to answer questions like, "Who was that?" and, "What did they want?" But that afternoon I asked Brady Heath for his number. He didn't have to ask what it was for, he knew exactly why I was asking. We had to get to the bottom of all this, and we had to do it together. So, for the rest of the afternoon, we both tried to concentrate on Mrs. Anderson's lessons about math facts and times tables and then later more social studies, but those five words that Shane had shared with us during lunch echoed in our every thought and were the only things that we could hear.

"You have to spend the night."

# CHAPTER 3

"What do you think that Shane meant when he said that we gotta spend the night?" Brady asked me later that night as we talked over the phone.

I sat at my kitchen table with the twisting and turning yellow, phone cord stretched out as far as it would go, making it look like a tight rope across the room. I balanced my bologna and cheese sandwich, which dripped in mayonnaise, in one hand and the kitchen phone in the other.

"I think that Shane means exactly what he said. You and I are going to have to spend the night at the school." I said, taking a bite and letting a small piece of the cold thin bologna fall to the floor so our scruffy dog, Oliver, could snap it up.

"But don't they have like alarms and stuff all over that place?" Brady tried to reason. "I mean the second that we open the doors or even move, the alarms would go off. I saw in this movie once where the whole entire hallway was filed with these bright green lasers, and the lady that was breaking into the place had to bend in all these weird shapes just to get by them."

"Come on Brady," I said with a mouth full of sandwich. "It's not like they are housing the Ark of the Covenant in the school. Why on Earth would they have lasers in the hallways?" A blob of mayo landed on my t-shirt, so I scooped it up with my pinky and licked it clean.

You see, that is the thing that you have got to learn about Brady, not only is he the first one in a group to start worrying given any given situation, he also believes everything that he has ever seen on television or in a movie.

"I'm not dumb, Peter. I know that the Ark of the Covenant isn't in our school; it's in a warehouse. Not only that, it would be far too dangerous. I mean can you imagine our entire class with our faces melting off just because Mrs. Anderson opened the wrong door?" Brady said.

I tried as hard as I could to just keep my mouth shut. I'm not lying when I tell you that I don't think that Brady was kidding. If Steven Spielberg took the time to put it on celluloid, then it's the gospel according to Brady. To this day, he does not step foot into the water when his family goes to the beach.

So getting us back to the topic at hand, I asked him, "What do you think? Are you going to do it?"

And he said, "What choice do you think we have? It is either spend the night at the school, or be ignored for the rest of this year and probably the next."

Now looking back at everything, all the good and bad that went happened that night, I might have just been better off being left alone for the next few years. I mean, St. Thomas only went up to eighth grade anyways, so what was another three and a half years. Okay, maybe a lot of good came of it, so that wasn't such a good idea. Instead I answered, "I guess you are right. We really don't have much of a choice. It is not as if we are going to have to be all alone, right? I mean they will let us both go inside together? You know, on the same night and all."

It is kind of funny, and a little stupid, when I think about it all now, you know the peer pressure of being part of a crowd when you are just a little kid. At the time, it is like the worst thing on Earth to not be included. I once knew a kid who let the entire school call him Lucifer Lawrence the entire school year, just so he wouldn't be left out, and so he didn't have to eat lunch all by himself. I mean now, I would kill for just an hour or so to be left alone and maybe have a little time to myself. You know what I'm saying?

"How hard could it be, Brady? I mean we go inside, we find a place somewhere to hole up, and we crash out with our sleeping bags, flashlights and a bag of junk food." I told him.

"That's true. It might even be kind of fun." Brady told me. He didn't know it at the time, but he couldn't have been further from the truth. Unless you find yourself hanging by your fingertips about to fall to your death "fun," but wait, I am getting way ahead of myself. There is so much more that happens between the phone call that night, and Brady on the verge of death.

"That's the spirit!" I reassure him. I popped the last bite of bologna and cheese in my mouth to Oliver's dismay. Then I remember our conversation being interrupted by my mom yelling at me from across the house.

"You aren't eating again, are you? You just had dinner, Peter." My mom shouted from the living room.

"No!" I lied. It wouldn't be the last time that I would lie to her, that's for sure.

"Good!" She answered. "Now tell your little friend that you need to get off the phone now. I need to call your Aunt Barbara."

You have to understand something about the way my family worked back then. We had no problem with yelling across the house to get our point across. It didn't mean we were necessarily mad at anyone or upset at anything. It just meant that we didn't have the patience to walk all the way into the other room to have a normal human conversation. It was really all about just saving steps.

"Ok, Mom!" I yelled through the kitchen. Then I turned my attention back to Brady, "I gotta go. We will figure out the rest tomorrow, and don't sweat it. I mean it is only one night, right?"

"Yeah, I heard your mom." He answered. "I'll catch you tomorrow." And with that he hung up the phone, and I got up to put my empty glass of milk in the sink.

Now, here is something kind of strange. I don't really remember most of my dreams very often. I mean every once in a while I will wake up and be weirded out about falling out of a plane, or maybe drowning in the Atlantic Ocean, but for the most part, I wake up every morning, and have no idea about what it was I was dreaming about the night before. But to this date, I remember exactly what I dreamt that first night after finding out that I was going to have to spend the night at St. Thomas Christian Academy.

I dreamt about a beautiful flowing river of color. It was grey at first. Just a sea of grey swirling and swirling below me. Then it changed slowly and wonderfully. The blues and reds and yellows and greens all flowed under me in an endless fast moving river. I remember hovering above it, and how I gasped for one final breath as I finally let go and began to fall, but right before I hit the rainbow of colors, a hand grabbed me and pulled me back upward.

And for some reason, I remember that I felt both very depressed that I wasn't taken by the swirl of color and very relieved at the exact same time.

I'm doing it again. I am leaving Frances out of this story. You see, this whole time Brady and I were talking on the phone and trying to put our minds at rest about this whole situation. In a weird fourth grade way, we both were making sure that we knew that we would be there for each other no matter what a night at St. Thomas might entail. Meanwhile, Frances was alone. I don't know if Brady was thinking about her being a new kid in class too, and that maybe she would have to spend the night to be accepted too. You would have to ask him about that, but as for myself, Frances never even crossed my mind. Just like every other student in Mrs. Anderson's class, I just shoved her off into the corner of the classroom and pretended that she didn't exist. I wonder what went through her mind that first night we were told about the sleepover of our nightmares. I wonder if she had any dreams.

Now, here is something that I did notice about Frances. She was absent for the next three days after we found out about our little initiation. Normally, it wouldn't have even been on my radar as to whether she was at school or not, but I noticed because all the girls in the classroom would look at Frances's empty desk and then look at each other with worried faces. They would then exchange inaudible whispers each morning as Mrs. Anderson called her name during roll, then marked the attendance book. Maybe they thought that the pressure was just too much, and she had her parents check her out of school or something. I know that that thought had crossed my mind. Or maybe they thought that she went to the principal's office to tell Mrs. Ramirez about what all the girls in the fourth grade class were trying to make her do. Neither one of those two things were true. I know that now. The truth was she was planning.

You see, what no one, including myself, knew was that Frances was a watcher. She was one of those people in life that no one ever notices, but she noticed everything. You know, the ones that are in the darkest part of the gymnasium leaning against the wall at the high school dances. The ones who then go off to a college that no one has ever heard of before. They drive a brown car. You know the kind that no one can identify by the make or model, they just know that it is brown. They never wear anything too flashy or bold, and heaven forbid if they ever say anything out loud at the office staff meeting for fear of being ridiculed. But don't be fooled. They see everything. That is why I say that Frances was a watcher.

All this time that everyone, including the teacher, thought that she was just in the back of the class trying to melt herself into the teal paint of the classroom walls, she was really taking thousands upon thousands of mental notes and remembering every little thing that she could that went on not just in the classroom, but in the entire school.

Here is an example. I loved the Frito pies at school. There was something about the warmness of the canned chili meat and the crunchiness of the Fritos connected by a stringiness of the imitation cheddar cheese that made my mouth water. But Frances never bought one. Every other kid in our class loved them, and most of us would even circle that day on the monthly lunch menu so we could let our parents know that we would *not* be needing a sack lunch that day. Like I said, everyone but Frances.

It was because one day the school lunch lady was stirring and serving the chili from a huge aluminum pot. She was happily ladling out scoop after delicious scoop of meaty warm chili over crunchy salty sweetness. What Frances noticed one Thursday at noon, that no one else seemed to see, was that the Band-Aid that the lunch lady was wearing around her pinky finger was there one second and gone the next. It had fallen silently off her finger and was soon lost in the vat of delicious meat sauce.

So, you are thinking fine, that's gross, but so what. Just wait until next time they serve Frito pie and try again. I mean that is what most fourth graders would do in that situation. But you see, here is the deal. Three weeks later, when everyone in class was gathered around the lunchroom tables laughing it up and scarfing down spoonful after spoonful of delicious Fritos and chili, Frances didn't say a word. Instead she quietly opened up her Hello Kitty lunch box and ate her peanut butter and jelly sandwich with the crust cut off. Not only was Frances not willing to take the risk of biting into a used Band-Aid coated with imitation cheddar cheese, but she also noticed that the orange ring around the inner part of the pot was still there from three weeks ago. What I'm saying is that the lunch lady didn't empty and clean out the pot from week to week. She would just replenish it with more canned chili when it started to run low. I mean why wash out a pot of chili meat, just to add more chili meat, right? So to this day, there is probably a small school lunch lady pinky Band-Aid waiting to be scooped up into some poor sap's Frito pie. That is what I mean when I said that Frances was a watcher.

"Friday." was all Shane said when he called Brady and I over to him and the rest of the guys at lunch the following Monday. A whole week went by and nothing, but then out of nowhere, with one word, the game was on. Brady and I then had a major decision to make. But there was something in the way that Shane had said it it didn't sound like we had a decision to make at all. It sounded like it was just a stone cold fact that Brady and I would be spending the night in the church.

"We doing this?" Brady asked me later slightly under his breath as we sat there listening to Mrs. Anderson drone on and on about the life cycle of a frog. Brady looked at his shoes.

"I think so. We gotta, right?" I said to him. We were both talking to each other, but neither of us were making any eye contact. I remember that I was focused on the third button from the top on my school uniform and that Brady seemed to be preoccupied by the tip of his black Converse. You see, the truth was that we both knew that we really didn't have a choice in the matter. If fate said that we were supposed to spend Friday night in the church/school, then that is what we were going to do.

I tucked my hands in my pockets and looked up at Brady. "I will call you tonight, and we can go over stuff that we should bring." I said with a false bravado.

"Peter, I'm scared. I don't know why, and I know that I am just being some kind of wimpy baby, but....I just wanted you to know." Brady said under his breath as if somehow if the words got out into the open air it would make things much worse.

And the truth was, so was I. But did I tell him that? Of course not, admitting you are scared of anything when you are in the fourth grade is just not something you do. So instead, I said, "Don't be. It's nothing." I couldn't have been further from the truth. It wasn't "nothing", just the opposite, it was everything. But I didn't know that at the time.

So that night after homework, dinner and a bath, I grabbed a pen and a blank page in my notebook. I made my way into the kitchen. My brother, Aiden, was putting away his sippy cup like a "big boy," so I told him that he was doing a good job and waited until he left the room. Then I called Brady. I remember sitting at the kitchen table for almost an hour going over our notes and our plans before my mom called out from somewhere down the hall for me to say it was getting late and I needed to say goodnight to my "little friend."

But before that happened we needed to be on the same page. We needed to compare list. "So, I am definitely bringing a sleeping bag. There is no telling where we will be or what floor of St. Thomas we will have to sleep on." I told Brady.

"I was actually thinking about that part, Peter. All we have to do is make our way upstairs." Brady mentioned.

"Why would we have to go all the way upstairs?"

"Think about it. All we have to do is make it to the adult study area in the far corner of the church. They have couches that we can use to relax on and even a few tables. In fact, they even have a soda machine up there, and it is close to a bathroom. All we have to do is make it to that area and then we can set up our camp. It will be just like sleeping in our own living rooms. I was even thinking about bringing some change so I can sit back and sip on root beers all night." Brady said with a sense of pride.

I had to admit. That was a great idea. You see, the whole time I was thinking about the cold tile of the classroom floor or maybe one of the long dark hallways of the school. I hadn't even thought about the fact that the whole entire church would be available to us. Well, as long as the doors were unlocked we could pretty much go anywhere we wanted.

Also remember that this was before cell phones and hand held tablets and games. We would have to find a way to kill some time too. It isn't like the way it is today. Back then we couldn't just plug in somewhere and watch movie or play games until dawn. No, we were just going to have to find some way to entertain ourselves for hours. "Maybe I will bring some cards or something." I suggested.

"That's a great idea. We could play poker or something." Brady said. Keep in mind that neither of us knew how to play poker.

"I was thinking about not only bringing a flashlight, but maybe one of those flashlight lanterns. We could put it on the table and pretty much light up the whole room. My neighbor has one, and I could borrow it." I added. We had come to the conclusion that it might not be a good idea to just go into

St. Thomas and start flicking on all the lights. After all, we were breaking and entering.

Brady and I talked about the games we could play that night, and if we were brave enough, even a little exploring we might want to do. We made of list of snacks that we would pack being careful not to overlap and bring the same things. The longer that Brady and I sat there and hashed out the plans for Friday night, the more and more fun the whole thing was sounding like it might turn out to be. In my head I could see the whole thing. We were both laying back on the huge leather sofas like kings eating fistful after fistful of Cheetos and drinking root beers, laughing at each other's jokes until the carbonation stung our nostrils. Like I said, that is the way I had it playing out in my head. Come to find out, that whole conversation was a waste of time. Of course, we didn't know that then. How could we have known?

For the rest of that week it was all I could think about. There was even one time on Wednesday afternoon that the custodians were busy shampooing all of the carpets in the church hallways, so Mrs. Anderson had to take our class the long way from the sanctuary back to the classroom. That meant that we had to walk around the church and upstairs right past the adult bible study rooms. As our class snaked our line upstairs, I eyeballed the comfy soft sofas in their rich, dark leather. I could almost smell it. There was even a fancy glass lamp on the end table that would be perfect for lighting up the area at night if we decided that we were brave enough to turn on the light. I shot Brady a look from the front of the line and then did my best to point with my eyes to the larger of the two sofas against the wall. And with that silent gesture, I called "dibs." I could tell by the look on Brady's face that he knew exactly what had just happened, and although he was probably a good six inches taller than me, I would be sprawled out on the longer couch while he would have to hang his feet over the arm rest of the shorter one. But what I failed to notice at the time, and wouldn't find out until much later, was that Frances had seen our whole little exchange. Like I said, she was a watcher.

I guess that I should tell you about Shane and his best friend Derrick before I start to tell you about what happened Friday night. Like I said before, Shane and his buddies were not too crazy about letting Brady and

I play in any of their reindeer games. That was until that week before our initiation.

At first it was the little things that I noticed around the classroom that were different. On Tuesday, Shane and Andrew were in charge that week of passing out the school supplies as needed. Mrs. Anderson didn't trust us to keep it in our desk without touching them. So the two of them began to hand out the glue and scissors for a science activity on the growth cycle of a bean that the entire class was working on. Now for the first two months of school, whoever passed out the classroom set of supplies always happened to give me the Elmer's glue that leaked from the side of the bottle just underneath the pointy bright orange cap and the safety scissors that were made for a left-handed kid. I mean that might happen once, but every time? Anyway, on Tuesday, Shane comes walking around to my desk to hand out the scissors and instead of just handing me the lefty pair, he grabs another pair, tries it out to make sure the thing is sharp and smooth, and when he is satisfied, hands me the pair. I remember crinkling my nose at that and then looking at Brady to see if he caught it too. But when I looked over at his desk, Darrick is taking the leaky, glue bottle out of Brady's hand and replacing it with a newer one.

Whatever right? "But wait," as the salesman says, "there's more!" That same day at P.E., I was picked first! That's right, somehow I went from sitting in the shade of the overgrown Oak trees to now being picked first. Oh, and for the record, Brady was picked second. You know what, I didn't even think about this until just now, but coach didn't seem to have a problem with it. Hmm, that's strange if you stop to think about it. That afternoon when we had P.E., we both went from being the invisible twins to being the star players, the number one draft choices for each team, and the coach didn't even flinch. By the way, there is something else that I totally remember about that afternoon, but you can leave it out of your notes if you really feel like it. I struck out three times that day. What did you expect? It was my first game!

Now, if I was a watcher like Frances, I probably would have noticed that the exact same thing was happening on the other side of the P.E. class. But unfortunately, I don't notice those types of things. But if I did, I would have noticed that the little girl in the grandma sweater was the first one chosen for softball that afternoon. So it wasn't just Shane and his pals that were acting differently that week, it was everyone.

The next time that Mrs. Anderson had a question about the different types of landforms during geography class, she called on Frances first! Now, keep in mind that Frances didn't even raise her hand. You see, Frances had been trained over the first two months of class not to even try and answer questions any more. Every once in a while, at the beginning of the school year, she would timidly raise her hand if she knew the answer to a question, but just like Brady and me, Frances learned pretty quickly, why bother. It wasn't like Mrs. Anderson was going to choose you anyway. But Wednesday right before lunch, it happened. We were learning the difference between a lake, a sea, and an ocean. Mrs. Anderson asked what you would call a piece of land that had been totally surrounded by water. The room was silent. As an unfortunate reflection on our education system, most of our class didn't know the answer. Some students that did know the answer were afraid of Mrs. Anderson's wrath if they answered incorrectly. That is when out of nowhere, Mrs. Anderson asked, "Frances, what about you?"

Frances stood. She shrank down and hid as much of herself as she could behind her tiny plastic chair and her overgrown granny sweater. "I think the answer is an island?" she said barely above a whisper.

"Speak up dear!" Mrs. Anderson demanded. Wait that is not right. She didn't say it in the mean overbearing tone that she usually said everything else. No, there was hint of humanity in the way she said it, dare I say friendliness. "I not sure the rest of the class could hear you." Mrs. Anderson smiled.

"An island" Frances repeated a little more confidently.

"That is correct." Mrs. Anderson confirmed. She motioned to Frances to now take her seat. I couldn't believe what I had just witnessed, and I fully expected every other kid in class to be just as astonished as I was, but they weren't. Well, I take that back there was one other person who was just as amazed, Brady.

The rest of the week went exactly like that first few days. There were just a thousand little things that you couldn't quite put your finger on. For the first time, I felt as if I was truly a student at St. Thomas and not just a witness to whatever was going on in the classroom. It was as if everyone had a super-secret meeting or something and decided that Brady and I had made it through the first two months of school and were now scheduled to be inducted into the fold; therefore, we now deserved to be included. I'm not going to lie to you, it was awesome. A guy could get used to it, and in fact by the next Monday after Brady and I had spent the night inside the walls of St. Thomas Christian Academy, that was what I thought every day would feel like. All we had to do was spend one Friday night. Easy.

It wasn't until Thursday at lunch when Brady and I found out that our best laid plans were not going to happen the way that we had wanted. As I said before, we had made a list, and just like Santa, we checked that bad-boy twice. I had my bases covered and asked my mom and dad if I could spend the night at Brady's house, and he did the same with his parents and mine. Because we had never even been over to each other's houses before, our parents made sure to talk to each other over the phone. To this day, I don't know how we pulled it off. Like I said, different time. And because it was a different time, my mom and dad allowed me to pack my own bag and ride my bike down the block to Brady's house. But wait, hold on, let me tell you about what happened on Thursday at lunch before I get into all that.

Brady and I were still inside the cafeteria finishing our sloppy joes when Shane motioned and called us over to his table. The cafeteria was buzzing with the sounds of elementary school gossip and the smell of tater-tots lingered in the air. I remember that I rushed across the cafeteria to throw my trash away and head straight over to Shane's table while Brady shoved the last three bites of his sandwich down his throat in one big gulp.

Darrick and Andrew got up from their seats and offered them to us. Then the both of them went to the nearby table and pulled themselves two new chairs and rejoined the group. After getting over the initial shock of that friendly gesture, I was ready to hear what Shane had to say.

"Ok, so here is the way that this works." Shane looked over each shoulder cautiously and began. "Show up at the back gate by the gym at 10:00. Don't be late."

Now, notice that he didn't ask if we were going to do it or if we had any questions. No, Shane just assumed that we were perfectly fine with the whole thing. As if breaking and entering school and church property in the middle of the night was no big deal. That is the first time I really thought about it that way and said it out loud before. We were, in fact, breaking and entering. That is a crime. I don't know if they even throw nine-year olds in jail, but I bet you anything we would have been looking at 5-10 years in juvenile hall if we had been caught, but thank God, we weren't.

"I have a key to the back door. Don't ask me how I have it. I just do. We will unlock the doors and let you in. We will come back for you at 7:00." Shane said.

"Sounds good." I lied.

So that was it. Nine hours of being locked inside the school. It didn't sound too bad. Now, I didn't like the idea of being locked inside without a way to get out. I mean what if there was an emergency like a fire or something. How would Brady and I get out of there? I guess we could have smashed a desk through a window or something if we needed. But that wasn't the problem, it was the next thing that Shane said that stopped both Brady and I in our tracks. Like I said, all of that planning and list making was a waste of time.

"Don't bring anything with you." He said.

There was no long drawn out explanation, or a long list of excuses. Shane said that like he said everything else that day. I don't know if he even knew that he had shattered all of our planning and packing with those five words. Brady looked at me dumbfounded, his eyes saying, "What were we going to do now?"

"Of course." I answered. "Why would we bring anything?" Now, you have to remember that on the inside my heart was racing like a thoroughbred that had to take a quick pit stop before making its way on to the track, but meanwhile on the outside I tried to remain as cool as I could. Of course I was panicked, but I mean I was in fourth grade, and that is right when you start to realize that everyone is cooler than you. You have to do your best just to keep up. And also, by this time I had experienced four solid days of finally being treated like a normal human being at school, so there was no way I was going to do anything to jeopardize loosing that. I looked back at Brady and raised my eyebrows as if to say "Don't be a nerd. Agree with me." But of course he didn't.

"What do you mean don't bring anything! We are going to be there all night. I mean what if we get hungry or thirsty or something, and you do know it is going to get pretty dark in there, and it will get cold in the church at night." Brady told Darrick, Shane, and the rest of the boys. "I mean, we need to bring some stuff, right?"

"Nothing, just the clothes on your back. In fact, the best thing to do would be to even empty your pockets before you go inside." Shane added.

"I wish I had." Darrick said.

"Quiet. You can't tell them too much." Shane cut Darrick off before he could say anything else. Immediately Darrick stopped talking. "Just take my word for it. Don't bring anything with you. Ten o'clock and remember don't be late."

I know, I know, I called Shane a bully before, and even though the kid was huge, there was something in the way that he shared all of that that made it sound as if he was really trying to help us. He no longer looked and sounded like some kid that just wanted to punch me in the stomach and make me cry in front of all the girls, no instead he looked like a kid that was trying to protect me from whatever Friday night had in store.

That Thursday night I remember unpacking everything from my bag and putting everything either back into my dresser or back in the pantry where I had found it in the kitchen. My dad walked in while I was putting away the Zebra Cakes and almost scared me to death.

"What happened?" He said. "I thought you were going to spend the night at your new friend Grady's house and sleep in his tent in the back yard?" My dad asked.

"Oh," I said startled. "I'm still going over and all, but we aren't going to be sleeping outside in the tent. He said that it….smells like pee. So, we are just going to crash out in his room instead. And it's Brady, not Grady." You see, I told my parents that the plan was to campout in the backyard so they wouldn't ask me about why I was bringing a back pack full of supplies and snacks, not to mention a flashlight.

I still had no idea why we were not allowed to bring anything the following night, but after the serious way that Shane had talked to the two of us in the cafeteria, Brady and I agreed, it would be best to not take any chances. I talked to my dad a bit about his day at work and my day at school, and then I said goodnight to him and gave him a little guy hug. As soon as he walked out of the kitchen, I grabbed the phone and quietly dialed Brady's number. I think I must have tried off and on to call Brady three times that night, but every time I did, the line was busy.

So there I was in the quietness of my bedroom, just lying there on my bed, staring at the crack in my ceiling that started in the left hand corner of the wall by the window and ran its jagged tail serpent-like up to the middle of my room where the ceiling fan steadily rocked itself back and forth. The sound of the little motor inside was squeaking a steady rhythm.

I am amazed that after all this time I can still remember what I was thinking that night before everything happened. I remember that the Houston Astros were playing the Los Angeles Dodgers in the rubber game of the series on the radio. Mike Scott was on the mound for the Astros. Like almost every game, I listened to as much as I could before falling asleep.

But that Thursday night was different. As the baseball game droned on the radio filling my room full of the sounds of Milo Hamilton doing the play-by-play, I thought about the pictures that hung in the halls on the way to the chapel. I thought about the way that a few of the still framed pictures that gathered dust seemed to stare at you as you walked quietly by. The long dead pastors and leaders of our church and the long gone principals that shaped the school were now just ghostly images shoved in an 8x10 black wooden frame. Each one begging to get out. I remember thinking as I drifted off to sleep about whether or not they ever had to spend the night at St. Thomas Christian Academy. Right before I fell asleep for the night, I think it was sometime late in the eighth inning, I thought about the dream that I had had a few nights back, only this time no one caught me.

# CHAPTER 4

The wind was howling that Friday night. I can still remember the sound of the leaves blowing and the branches battling overhead as the north wind rustled through the trees. Brady and I lived on different sides of the school so as I was riding my bike from the west, he was riding his from the east. I think that the hardest part of the night from the time I left my house was waiting until 10:00 o'clock. I was in the fourth grade, so being in the fourth grade meant that you couldn't just leave your house at 9:30 at night and not get a "And where do you think you are going at this time of night young man?" from at least one of your parents.

So I pretty much had to leave my house right after dinner was over. And although I was starving, my stomach was in nervous knots. I only ate a little bit of my fried chicken and picked at my food, because I told my mom earlier that Brady's mom was going to have a ton of snacks for us to munch on all night long. After a warning not to get sick just eating "junk" all night, Dad passed around the plate of fresh, hot, crispy fried chicken. My mom was and still is the best at making fried chicken. The aroma wafting throughout the kitchen made my tight stomach growl. But I had a role to play that night, so I was tempted to pile up my plate for show, but I only grabbed a leg and passed the rest to my mom. Listen closely, I was then on the verge of making one of the biggest mistakes of my life right after that. You see, my baby brother was diving face first into his mashed potatoes like some kind of barnyard animal, so as Mom and Dad were distracted and were trying to keep Aiden under control, I stuck a fried chicken wing into one of my pants pockets. I remember I was wearing one of my favorite pairs of cargo pants, so the pockets on each thigh were huge and deep. They fastened with a little metal snap that I would catch myself playing with all the time just to keep my fingers busy. I slid the fried chicken wing inside carefully and snapped the pocket closed. That was the first in what was sure to be a series of embarrassing mistakes.

After dinner I helped my mom, after a short protest, clear the table and pack up the leftovers for Dad's lunch over the next few days. I had hours to kill before I had to be up at the school, and mom must have noticed that I wasn't in much of a hurry to head out. I must have been moving pretty slowly around the kitchen table and maybe I was checking the kitchen clock a bit too much, because my mom finally made a comment about my pace.

"I'm sure your little friend must be getting worried about you, Peter. I can take care of the rest of this mess and finish this up if you want to go ahead and get your stuff together to head on over there." she said.

"Thanks, Mom. I guess I am running a bit late." I answered as I put the stack of dirty dishes that I was holding in the sink. After a quick hug, I grabbed my black overnight bag that was sitting on the edge of the staircase and headed out the front door. You see, now I was kind of between a rock and a hard place, because here it was only a little bit before 7:00 p.m. Because I had to leave my house so early, I now had to figure out a way to kill the next three hours before I had to make my way back up to the church. I also had to figure out what I was going to do with my overnight bag. You have to understand that although I wasn't supposed to bring anything with me into St. Thomas that night, I still had to pack a bag as if I were heading to Brady's place to spend the night. Not only that, but my mom insisted that she needed to go over the things that I packed in my bag just in case I had forgotten to pack anything.

"Did you remember to pack your toothbrush?" my mom questioned. She gave me that mom look and put her hands on her hips.

"Yep, I sure did." I answered.

"Show me." My mom raised one of her eyebrows and waited for me to prove that I had packed my toothbrush. My mom loved me, but she fully believed in the Ronald Reagan form of parenting. "Trust but verify."

So I dug through my overnight bag and whipped out my tooth brush. I waved it sarcastically in front of her. "Got it."

"What about your toothpaste?" She added.

"Mom, I am pretty sure that Brady has toothpaste at his house that I can use." I said and shoved my toothbrush to the bottom of my bag.

"Peter, you know as well as I do that you have what the dentist said are sensitive gums." She said. Her hands went quickly back to her hips. For the record, I do in fact have sensitive gums.

Then about ten minutes later, as I was almost done packing, my mom walked by with a basket full of clean laundry. "Here. Grab a clean pair of underwear and put it in your bag." She said, as she leaned the white plastic laundry basket in my direction.

"Why do I need to bring underwear? I'm coming home first thing in the morning." I questioned.

"You never know. What if you have an accident?" Mom answered.

You see, those are the kinds of things that only moms think about. I could have left the house that night wearing nothing but a poncho over my head and a pair of flip-flops on my feet, and my dad wouldn't even think twice. It would just be like, "Have a good time, Peter."

"I'm not two!" I protested. "I'm not going to have an accident." but as I was saying this, I was grabbing an extra pair of plaid boxers from the top of the clean clothes.

I distinctly remember riding my bike down Mulberry Lane because that street had more trees growing over it than any other in our neighborhood. I was trying to find a safe place that I could stash my overnight bag until the next morning. That was when I spotted old lady Owens' tool shed. She lived near the corner in a beautiful blue and white ranch style home and had gotten too old to mow her own yard about a year ago. Although she fought to the bitter end to hold on to that piece of her independence, she now had Jeffery Duggers come by every other Saturday to mow it for her. The only reason I knew this was because old lady Owens still sat on the front porch on her rocking chair and yelled at Jeffery as he worked. "You make sure that those rows are even, Jeffery!" She would shout from the porch. Those two were hilarious. Sometimes I would ride my bike and stop in front of her house to pretend to fix my chain, but in reality I just liked hearing them go back and forth. "Yes, ma'am" Jeffery would say loud enough for her to hear over the grumbling of the lawn mower. Then he would mumble something about her being an old bat under his breath. Well I knew that her yard was just cut last week, so I knew that no one would be opening that shed for at least another eight days.

I pulled my bike around to the side that was not directly facing old lady Owens' house and quietly opened the shed door. The strong smells of cut grass caked to the under carriage of the mower mixed with the bags and bags of fertilizer on the warped wooden shelves on the wall to create a wonderfully pungent smell. I unloaded my overnight bag and shoved it deeply inside a clay pot that hid itself carefully in the cob-web filled corner. There was no way that anyone would find it. You know, looking back at that moment I am not really sure why I tried that hard to hide my used tooth brush and a clean pair of boxer shorts. Oh, well.

After I felt that my belongings were safely hidden from whatever evil robbers that might be lurking in the suburbs, I hopped back on my bike and started peddling toward the school. Ok, I did it again. I am not being totally honest with you. I didn't head directly to the school. You have to understand that there was a big part of me that was scared and didn't want the night to start. I didn't want to have to be close to the St. Thomas until I absolutely had to be there. The last thing that I wanted to do was park my bike and stare at the grey stones of the church as the shadows of the trees lurked slowly at first like a cat creeping up on a broken bird, then covered it in darkness like a thick blanket. The butterflies in my stomach were already turning into huge vampire bats, so the last thing I needed to do was sit in the playground outside the main building for three plus hours scaring myself half to death.

So, what did I do? You would think that I would have headed to Brady's neighborhood and looked around for him, because I assumed that he had to leave his place just as early as I had to leave mine. But unfortunately, I couldn't do that because he was supposed to be spending the night at my house. So he and I couldn't just bike around his block and accidently have his mom or dad see us, not to mention his older sister would just love to catch Brady breaking the rules so she could hold it over his head for the next few years. No, instead I made my way to the little man-made lake that was only a few miles from the house, and there I just hung out on the nature trails and amongst the trees waiting for the sun to start and set. I was only in fourth grade so I really couldn't go into a department store like Target or anything, because my luck some nice lady would see me wondering the aisles all alone and just assume that I was lost. The next thing you know, they would be announcing my name over the intercom and eventually, I would have been brought back home in the back of a police car with my bike strapped to the rear bumper. So I was forced to spend the next few hours that Friday night in hiding, waiting until 9:45 or so. Looking back at all that time I wasted, I should have headed directly to the school so that way I could have helped Frances. While I was picking up acorns and seeing how far I could throw them into the lake, she had been at the school for hours.

What I know now and what I didn't know that Friday night could fill an auditorium. In fact, the first ten rows would be filled with just what I didn't know about Frances. You see, while I was riding in circles and watching the weeds grow in the nearby nature trails and while Brady was throwing rocks at the cockroaches behind Al's Discount Tire waiting for the sun to go down, Frances was at the school.

She had gotten to the church not long after school had gotten out. My theory is that she just went around the corner and waited for the cars to leave the parking lot. She has got the patience of Job, because there is no way I would have been able to just sit there and wait until even the custodians left for the night. But once the coast was clear, she went to work.

Frances must have unlocked one of the cafeteria windows earlier in the week, because the first thing she did was carefully slide open a window and boost herself up through the opening. She told me that she used a milk crate to get herself up high enough. Once inside, she pulled her pocket flashlight from her coat pocket and began to make her way down the halls. She stopped every once in a while to unzip here backpack and take something out. Months later, someone would find the pocket sized pen and paper notebook under the seat cushion of the fluffy orange and grey chair that sat at the bottom of the wooden staircase that she had hidden. She had also flicked the lamp that sat on the end table beside it off so it would no longer light up that end of the long hall.

As she made her way to the area of the church were the classrooms were, she must have tried every door knob, giving every one of them a half turn just to see which ones were locked and which ones weren't. How else would she have known? Now, I'm not sure what else she took the time to hide around the church that night, and to tell you the truth, I wouldn't be surprised if someday a student or maybe some poor janitor runs across something that Frances Maggie Lingersham took the time to stash away all those years ago that no one since had ever found.

Like I said, if I was smart I would have tried to help her, but because I never took the time to even consider that she would be involved in this whole ordeal, and I never took the time and asked her after Brady and I were told about it, she was on her own as always. And looking back, I'm not sure that she needed my help.

With her backpack empty, she slowly made her way back through the quiet deserted hallways, through the cafeteria that echoed every step she took, and finally back out through the open window. She exited just in time to see Shane and his buddies walking hunched through the faculty parking lot toward the back entrance to the church. I should also mention that Elizabeth Penny was there too. She was the female version of Shane Wilkerson, and she too had her little group of minions.

So the group of seven to eight fourth graders waited outside the back entrance to St. Thomas Christian Academy for Brady, Frances, and I to show up.

Like I said, at the time I had no clue that Frances had already broken into the school and done a little reconnaissance work of her own. Who knew that she had that in her to begin with? As far as I knew, when I pulled into the back lot of the school that I was just the second kid to show up at the school. Or is "victim" a better word? I didn't have a watch on my wrist or any other way to tell time, but after a while I knew that it had to be getting close to 10:00 pm., because everyone that had gathered around the rear entrance to the church was starting to get a little anxious. There were at least eight of us hanging out waiting to get started. Some of the girls had formed a circle and sat on the curb, while most of the guys stood around and fidgeted with the stones that landscaped the grounds or stood with their hands in their pockets. The air was cold, but not cold enough to see our breaths. I looked down the long abandon street as far as I could using only the street lights as my guide, and still no Brady.

At first I thought that maybe he had chickened out and decided that the whole thing wasn't worth it. I mean I wouldn't have blamed him. But there was no way that that was true. He would have called me and told me that he had changed his mind. Then I thought that maybe his mom and dad somehow found out about our plans, but if that ws the case either he and his parents would have shown up by now, or the police would have pulled up telling us all to get off the property and to go home. Shane was the first one to break the silence.

"We will give him just another few minutes. It's not quiet 10:00 o'clock yet. If he ain't here soon, we will have to start without him. It has to start at ten." Shane said. He wasn't wearing a watch either, so I don't know how he planned to start at exactly 10:00 o'clock. But I guess everyone trusted him, because everyone, including Elizabeth, assumed he was in charge and knew what he was talking about.

"He'll be here." I said reassuringly. I don't remember to be honest if I said that more for Shane, or for myself. Meanwhile the whole time in my head I was thinking, "He better be here."

Shane reached into his jeans pocket and pulled out an old rusted key. As he did so, Brady came peeling his bike around the corner as fast as he could. It was dark, but you could still see the dirt flying from the back of his bike tires as he sped under the lights of the parking lot. Everyone stopped watching Shane and turned around to watch Brady's grand entrance.

"I'm here! I'm here!" Brady yelled.

Everyone, including myself, quickly motioned for him to keep his voice down and to stop yelling. I don't really know why. I mean we could have been as loud as we wanted to there was no one around for what was probably miles. I guess it was the whole idea of a bunch of kids doing something they were not allowed to do and being somewhere they were not allowed to be just made it the perfect atmosphere and a perfect opportunity to whisper. After what sounded like basket of snakes "Shhhhhhhhh," Brady finally got the hint.

"Ok! Ok!" Brady repeated. Then he whispered, "I just didn't want you guys starting without me."

"Well you're here now, so let's get this started. It's actually pretty simple. The rest of us don't have much to do. We are going to open this door and let you in. Then we are going to lock the door and go home." Shane pounded on the door a few times. The thick banging made my heart jump into my throat. He continued, "Then, at 7 o'clock, tomorrow morning we will come back up here and unlock the doors and hopefully let you out."

That's right you heard correctly, he said "hopefully." I know that a lot of time has passed since that night, and because of that I will probably leave some things out, but I will never forget the fact that Shane used the word "hopefully."

"Now, you guys on the other hand. You are on your own." Shane continued, "What you decide do inside all night is totally up to you, well maybe not all up to you, but you will figure it out."

Elizabeth turned to the three of us. "Remember don't bring anything inside with you." Elizabeth focused her words on Frances. "You told the guys the same thing, right Shane?" she turned and asked him.

"Yeah, yeah, I know what I'm doing Liz." Shane told her. "I was the one that helped you get through it remember, so don't worry about me. This isn't my first time." he reassured her.

In the stress and confusion of the moment, I couldn't really tell you everything that happened next. I remember Frances taking a few small things out of her pockets and hiding them behind a few little pink flowers and thick green bushes that lined the bricks of the building. But I couldn't tell you what it was exactly that she was hiding. I remember Brady talking to one of the guys. I don't remember which one. He was trying to get as much out information out of him as he could, but I couldn't tell you exactly what the two were saying at the time.

I can tell you what I do remember though, I remember the clicking and shuffling sound of the lock as Shane turned the rusted key. The key that Shane used to unlock the back door looked like any old key that your dad might have on his keyring, and the lock that fastened the chain around the heavy double doors of the church was not the original, so it looked like any back entrance to any other school in the city, but for some reason that night they both looked and sounded differently. The key that Shane struggled to hold still in his hand looked heavy, and the way that he was fumbling around with it, I wondered if the biggest, toughest guy in our class was actually afraid to unlock the door. But, he did eventually get it unlocked. The lock snapped open with the key still sticking out, and the weight of the iron chain pulled away.

The rest of the kids in Mrs. Anderson's class were just as mesmerized as I was by the whole ordeal. Looking back now, it was almost comical the way all of us were staring at Shane as if he was performing the most amazing magic trick that we had ever seen, instead of just turning a key and unlocking a door. I will also never forget that when the door was finally unlocked, and

Shane slowly opened the door, everyone took a step back. We didn't jump backwards like we were scared or anything like that. No, it was different. It was as if something or someone gave each of us a gentle push on our shoulders. Some kids just leaned backwards, while others actually had to take a half step backwards to catch themselves.

My mouth was desert dry and my tongue was sandpaper. For some reason, I couldn't seem to catch my breath, and the ones that I did manage to catch were small and shallow. I had no reason to be this scared. You have to remember, I had been going to this school five days a week, seven hours a day, for over two months. But for some unknown reason, seeing it in the pitch black darkness on this particular Friday night, and the fact that in just a few seconds, I along with Brady and Frances were about to be locked inside without any realistic way of getting out until we were let out, changed everything. I mean what if it was all just a big joke and they didn't come back the next morning to let us out? What were we supposed to do then? We would be in so much trouble and there was really no way out of it. We could either start breaking things until the police arrived, or sit tight and wait until 6:00 a.m. Sunday morning. Neither of those options sound like a good idea to me.

That is because the pastor and his wife usually didn't come in until around 6:00 a.m. every Sunday morning to turn on the lights and unlock the church doors. How did I know this you may ask? Well I'll tell you. You see, not only was I newly attending St. Thomas Christian Academy, but also because students and their families were "Strongly Encouraged" to attend Sunday morning service, our family started to wake up early almost every Sunday to hear Pastor Martin preach.

And I have to tell you that on more than one occasion, Pastor Martin made sure to let everyone know that no matter how tired you were as you walked in, or what time you woke up and got yourself to church that morning, the doors to the sanctuary were already open and friendly people were there to welcome you inside. And as Pastor Martin was always quick to remind us," You know that the doors don't just unlock themselves." *Wrong!*

So the idea of being forgotten and locked in the church until Sunday morning was always somewhere hiding in the darkest corners of my mind. Not only the thoughts of what would we eat over the two long days stranded inside, but also what would Pastor Martin's wife do when she opened the doors and walked in Sunday morning and found three pre-teen skeletons that had died of malnutrition leaning against the wall right inside the back exit? Like I said, it was always in the back of my mind.

As I peered down the long dark hallway that lead into the bowels of the church, I was amazed about how dark it really was in there. I mean I couldn't even see the end of the long hallway. I had only been attending St. Thomas for a while, and I had to admit that I wasn't familiar with every nook and cranny of the place yet. But this I did know, that hallway led from the back of the building to the main entry of the church if you followed it to the end. The first set of doors that I would run into would be the double-door entrance to the gymnasium. It would be my first set of doors to the left. I should have been able to see it from where I stood easily. But all I saw that night as Shane pulled the door open was darkness. How were we three supposed to find our way around St. Thomas once the doors were closed? Unfortunately, we didn't have to wait long to find out.

"Well, what are we waiting for? Let's get them in there, we need to get this started." Elizabeth told Shane. I remember that after she said that, she reached over and somewhat violently grabbed Frances by the arm. She took Frances and almost started to physically push her through the doorway. The reason that sticks out in my mind to me was because Frances didn't seem startled at all. I mean, there was no way that I would have wanted to walk in first. As it was my feet were lead weights that were securely anchored to the concrete. I couldn't move forward even if I wanted to, but not Frances. Not only was she not startled by the little shove that Elizabeth gave her, but she seemed to use it to begin what can only be described as a casual stroll through the school. I'm talking full on bravery.

"She's right. You need to get in there. It's 10:00 o'clock." Shane said to Brady and me.

Before Shane could reach out and grab me to start to push me inside, I said, "Yep, let's get this little thing over with." My false bravado didn't fool anyone. Most of the kids could read right through it, because all of the guys and even some of the girls started to laugh.

"Go ahead. I will be right behind you." Brady's voice shook as he reassured me. Yeah right!

So there we were slowly walking into the church, the three of us. With, who would have ever guessed, Frances leading the way. Now, the whole thing reminds me of Scooby Doo and the gang looking for the Creeper in those old cartoons. Not those super lame remakes that they had made years later, or when they gave up and started putting in Scrappy Doo. No, I'm talking about the good ones when Scooby and the gang actually solved mysteries. There was Frances with her glasses as Velma leading the way and not a fear in the world. She just wanted to start finding clues and get this mystery solved. If Frances was Velma, then Brady would have to be Scooby, no reason other than I wanted to be Shaggy, because he was always the coolest. And let's face it, the two were inseparable.

The three of us, with not even a flashlight to guide our way, all turned around once inside the building to face Shane and the rest of them just outside the open door. I remember that it was only probably a few feet between the asphalt of the parking lot where my class was standing and the Saltio tile of the church floor where the three of us stood, but the distance seemed like miles. The bright white moonlight peeking through the clouds high above and the dull yellow of parking lot lamps sprinkled here and there cast long shadows on the gaggle of fourth graders huddled around that back door. I wouldn't have even been able to tell which one of the shadows was Shane if his hands weren't still on the door handle, and the shadow of Elizabeth didn't still have her hand on his shoulder. This whole scene is still so vivid in my memories. You have to remember that in fourth grade, any and all physical contact with the opposite sex just didn't happen. So the fact that Elizabeth was touching Shane, and Shane didn't seem to mind stuck out to me. Even in this surreal setting, I noticed.

"Don't forget. I will open this door at exactly 7:00 am, not a second earlier. So don't even try to get out before then. I don't care how hard you are banging on the door. I don't care how much you are crying to get out. I don't care how much you beg. Not one second earlier." Shane's shadow told us.

Yeah, like I wasn't already scared enough as it was, so why would there possibly be any situation at all where I was banging on the back door of the school and begging to the people on the other side to be let out? They say that ignorance is bliss. Man, I had no idea what was in store for us as we entered the church and started our little adventure. After all, this was just the beginning. There was so much I didn't know yet. But hey, let me tell you about what happened when the doors closed and the real fun began.

# Chapter 5

*Slam!* The door that I had never heard slam shut before, slammed shut leaving Brady, Frances, and me in the dark. I was frozen stiff, and although I couldn't see Brady in the instant darkness, I knew that he was the block of nonmoving ice standing right beside me. Of course, it was Frances that broke our silence.

"Touch the wall." She whispered to us. "Use your left hand and reach out as far as you can for the wall. Brady grab hold of my belt loop with your right hand. Peter, grab Brady's belt loop the same way. I will lead us to the end of this hallway. From there, we should be able to find our way around the church." Frances reassured us with an unheard of confidence. It was the most I had ever heard her say at one time. After two months of school with nothing more than a half sentence here and there, here she was when we needed her most. Not so much with the voice of a drill sergeant, but more in the lines of a mother duck leading her ducklings.

So we did just as baby ducklings should, and did what our mama duck told us to do. Shuffling our feet down the hallway, I could hear every deep panting breath from Brady who was just a few feet away. And to tell you the truth, to this day, I swear that I could hear our heartbeats beating like a high school drumline. There was a pounding and pumping in my chest that a nine year old just shouldn't feel. I was much too young for a stroke. My uncle once told me about the heart palpitations that he could feel in his chest right before he had his attack, and thank God, I never had to go through that, but I think that the closest that I ever came was that night in St Thomas.

There was a familiar comfort that came over me like a wave when I got to the heavy double-doors of the gymnasium. There on my left were the cold metal chrome of the handles and the echoing click as I pushed on it. It was open! Immediately through the minute crack I could smell the decades of pre-teen sweat that emulated from the overly waxed wooden floor.

"Hey Frances, the gym door is open. Maybe we should go inside and check it out?" I said to the darkness in front of me.

"I know it is. I'm the one who made sure it was unlocked and the end of the day. I'm not sure yet, but we might need to go there later." She answered back.

Now, how exactly did she manage to do that? When did she do that? I wondered to myself. But as I was thinking it, Brady said it.

"How did you get in here and unlock the gym door? When did you do that?" He asked.

"Shhh! It should be just a few more feet ahead." Frances ignored the question and continued on. "Yes!"

Frances was right, and she had lead the three of us down to almost the end of the hall and to one of the many grand entrances to the front of the church. This particular entrance had a huge circular staircase made of dark, incredibly intricate Oak wood works and brightly detailed Italian marble. It was always the church's belief that the first thing that visitors and parishioners alike should see as they walk through the doors is a grand welcome. "It should be nothing short of the Pearly Gates!" one long dead pastor once said. The ceiling was highlighted by a beautiful crystal chandelier. Well, at the time I thought it was crystal. The last time that I was there I noticed that what I thought was once the dark, incredibly intricate imported Oak wood could be found at any Home Depot and the Italian marble staircase was more of a polished porcelain. And as for the crystal chandelier, let's just say that sometimes glass in the early light of a Sunday morning can look just as beautiful as the finest crystal.

Frances plopped herself down heavy and sat on the bottom step of the staircase. She looked up and out through the stained glass image of Christ walking on the Sea of Galilee. Although there wasn't much of it, the light that filtered through filled the room with dark shades blues and greens. In the dark, Brady tripped over the bottom step but caught himself with the handrail and carefully sat himself beside her. I remember that I was sitting on the floor cross legged and faced them both. Brady's face was glowing a soft aqua blue from the rough seas of the window, while Frances's face was paler as the image of Christ Himself shone through the glass and on to her cheeks. Although we were comfortable and safe, and it had only been a few minutes, already I was wanting this whole night to be over.

"I think we should just head up to the adult study rooms and settle in to the reading area. We can take turns on the couches and maybe even turn on one of the lamps. That is what Brady and I were thinking anyway." I shared our brilliant plan with Frances.

"Yeah, Pete and I were thinking that instead of walking around the entire church in the dark all night and running in to who knows what, it would be better just to maybe, you know, set up a little camp by the adult study rooms and just wait it out. The plan was to bring some snacks and games and stuff, but well, you know what they said about that." Brady agreed. He stood up and started to motion toward the steps hoping that Frances would take the hint and follow him.

"No." was all Frances said. She got herself up and started to make her way down the opposite hallway in which we came.

Brady and I really didn't have much of a choice on what to do at that point, I mean what were we supposed to do, leave Frances alone in the church all by herself to wonder around aimlessly and probably end up getting herself hurt? I mean all it would take is to get tripped up over any little thing, even a snag in the carpet would do it, and you would end up face first on the floor with a busted nose. After all, there was no way to call for any medical help. Even if we used the church secretary's phone, then we would once again be caught breaking and entering. I was too young to go to jail and carry around a criminal record. No, it was just a better idea to stick together and stay safe. Brady and I weren't much protection I admit. We were probably a hundred and sixty pounds combined, but we were her only protection. The problem was, not that we knew it at the time, Frances wasn't the only one that needed the protection that night.

So, there we were once again feeling our way down the pitch black halls of the church. Frances had us heading for the offices of the pastors and their secretaries. It was so hard to see, and our eyes had yet to get adjusted, so we kept at a slow pace. We also did our share of bumping into one another. I remember that one time Brady was hugging the wall so closely that he knocked down one of the posters announcing the annual Fall Fling and Carnival. That was like St. Thomas's version of a Halloween party.

Don't even get me started about that one. Let me just say that private Christian schools don't believe in Halloween, because of all of the evil devils and demons that it supposedly promotes, but during the Fall Fling and Carnival, all of the kids in the church are not only asked, but encouraged to dress up as their favorite characters. So, although Satan and ghost are not allowed (too spooky), ninjas and lions are perfectly fine. You know now that I think about it, I wonder if I had went to the Fall Fling and Carnival as the Holy Ghost if they would have been cool with it? Oh well, too late now.

Anyway, I am getting way off track. I'm chasing rabbits, at least that is what my ninth grade teacher used to call it. So, if I do that again, tell me. Now, I was a pretty well-behaved kid in school, which meant that I rarely found myself in the office of the church's pastors or their secretaries. So it goes without saying that I didn't know my way around that part of the church. That meant that even if all the lights were on, I wouldn't know which office belonged to which pastor. And as far as I knew at the time, the same could be said for both Brady and Frances, but somehow, someway, she knew every twist and turn of those back rooms as we felt our way down the hallway still moving Scooby Doo style.

"Frances is going to get us lost if we keep moving around here in the dark. Where do you think she is taking us?" Brady whispered. I say he whispered, but in reality the place was so eerily quiet that you could hear a roach fart. So, there is no doubt in my mind that Frances heard every word.

"I have no idea." I whispered back. "Just keep moving before I trip over your shoes again."

"I'm just saying that if there was one place in the whole entire building that would get us in the most trouble for being in here after the doors are locked, this is probably the place." Brady answered. "We can't just break into the pastor's office."

"Ok first off, we would be in trouble no matter where we were in the church after the doors were locked for the weekend. It really doesn't make any difference to the police as to what part of the building you were trespassing through. Second, we are not breaking into the pastor's office, we are breaking into his secretary's office." Frances said.

Well that cleared it up.

With her last remark Frances stopped abruptly in front of Mrs. Hanson's door. "I know for a fact that she never locks her door. There is really nothing worth taking. All of the important church paperwork and all of the petty cash gets locked up in the pastor's office at the end of each day." she continued. Remember, she was a watcher.

Now, you have to know that at the time I didn't question a thing that Frances was saying or doing. Sure at the beginning when she first started I was a little skeptical, but as she guided us from one part of the church and then later through the school, there was a confidence in her voice that was very, very un-Frances like. I hate to admit it, but if we weren't in the dark both figuratively and physically, Brady and I probably would have ignored her like we had done every day before. I mean think about it, how exactly did she know whether or not Mrs. Hanson locked her door at the end of every day? How could she possibly know where the church's petty cash and the important papers were locked up at the end of each day?

"How do you" Brady began, but before he could finish the thought, the door to Mrs. Hanson's office clicked open.

"Wait here." Frances said and grabbed Brady's hand. She placed his palm on the wall by the light switch. "Don't turn on the lights and don't move." she ordered.

It wasn't as if Brady and I had much of a choice. All we could do was stand there and wait for her to return. The hallway and the office were both filled with absolute darkness. To this day, I don't know how Frances was able to maneuver herself around the room without banging her shins or stubbing her toes. The next few minutes waiting there in the dark seemed like an eternity. In the darkness, I still had my index finger wrapped tightly around Brady's belt loop. Let me just say that I am glad that at that moment the lights in Mrs. Hanson's office didn't come on and reveal that the room was filled with my classmates with cameras, because I am sure that it would have been the end of my life as I knew it if anyone had seen me cowering by the doorway with my fingers tightly looped to Brady's pants.

I remember myself doing the best that I could to look around the room and down the hallway struggling to focus on any little speck of light that I could find. I was squinting in the nothingness. The only light I could find was an exit sign at the far end of the hallway that hung blood red over the back door, and on Mrs. Hanson's desk sat a small Dollar Store clock that had a fading soft green tint, but from my angle I couldn't see the time.

"What do you think she's doing in there?" Brady asked. He leaned back against the wall and the sudden jerk almost broke my wrist.

"I have no idea. What could she possible need in the secretary's office? Pens?" I added.

The rattling sound in her hand as she walked back to us answered my questions for me. The master keys! Of course! With the master keys to St. Thomas anyone could open any door in the entire church. The master keys could be used to open anything, and now every room in the entire place was ours. "Frances, you are a genius!" I said with a new optimism.

"What? What's going on? I can't see a thing in here. How am I the only one that is blind as a bat and can't see what is going on?" Brady said. I could tell by the way he was pulling my fingers back and forth through the loop of his belt that he was getting frustrated.

"Calm down, Brady." Frances said. "What Peter has figured out is that we now have the master keys and that means we now have access to every room in the place. So where do you want to go first?"

"What difference does that make? We still can't see a thing." Brady said, and with that he flipped the light switch both blinding us, and filling the room with florescent light at the same time.

All three of us were instantly blinded and squinted our eyes shut to keep out as much of the bright light as we could. The only thing that I remember from that half-second of light was Frances diving across the room arms first toward the light switch. I let go of Brady's belt loops to cover my eyes from the overhead light, and the next time I safely opened them the room was dark again.

"What were you thinking? Are you trying to kill us?!" I shouted to Brady as I covered my eyes, still temporarily blinded.

"*No!!!*" Frances was yelling at Brady. With one hand she was turning off Mrs. Hanson's light and with the other hand she was slapping Brady's arm out of the way. "You don't know what you just did! Why, Brady, why?!" Her voice was so angry.

But here is the funny thing, now that so much time has passed since then, and I think about that instant. I don't think that she wasn't yelling at him because she was angry, as much as she was upset and more like crying at him. Sure she was mad that he had turned on the light after she told the both of us not to touch anything, but there was something else behind it.

"We need to get out of here, now!" Frances said.

Without a care in the world, Frances ran back through the dark and ripped open the top drawer of Mrs. Hanson's desk and papers went flying. She grabbed a brochure and stuffed it in the pocket of her jeans. Although it was dark in the office, I could hear the papers rustling and the panic in her breath. As we were leaving, the three of us crashed into one another like a scene from those old Three Stooges shorts where they all try to walk out of the door at the same time. Finally Frances made it to the front of our little line, and she once again began to guide our way through the chaos.

"Come on, we don't have much time. They know where we are now." she said.

I know I shouldn't have done it, but I grabbed her by the shoulders and turned her around to face me. There was a look of terror in her eyes, but not because of the way that I had spun her around. No, she didn't care about that. It was deeper, darker. But I no longer cared. I wanted answers.

"What are you talking about? Who knows we're here? Shane? Darrick?" I yelled. I took a deep breath to calm down because I knew that I was starting to scare her.

"Look Frances," I said. "Brady and I have this all planned out. Just follow us. All we have to do is chill out on the couches upstairs and wait for sunlight. Then all we have to do is head back downstairs in the morning, open the doors and it's all over. Victory." I continued. "So whatever big plan that you think you are doing, just relax. We got this all figured out."

I'm was so stupid. We most definitely did not "have this all figured out." But you know what they say about hindsight and all.

The words coming out of my mouth did absolutely nothing at all to calm her. Her eyes were still saucers. Luckily Brady was there to help my cause. "It's true, Frances." he added with an unusual calmness in his voice. "Look I know I might have messed things up and turned on the light. I don't know exactly how I messed it up, but I did. And for that I apologize. Pete's right. We have this all planned out. I know that I never talked to you during school, and maybe I should have. You know what, I know I should have, but that doesn't mean that I don't care about you now. We are all in this together, so we might as well get through it all together. They just want to scare us. They just want to see if we are going to cry and bang on the doors begging to get out because we want our mommies. Well, Peter and I have a way that we can make it through the night and maybe even have a little fun in the process. So what do you say, Frances, want to join us?"

"No!" Frances said and grabbed his hand. "Come on. We are going to the library."

She shoved the master keys in her other pocket and began to make her way back through the dark hallways toward the main entrance once again. You have to remember that up until this point of the school year the only thing that I had ever heard coming from Frances's lips were a whispered answer or two when and if she was ever called on in class. I don't think that I had ever heard her put more than two or three sentences together at once. In fact at one time, I thought that maybe she was one of those foreign exchange students from Russia or the Ukraine or something and "Didn't know English too good."

Now, here she was barking out orders like a drill sergeant in full command. Also, I thought that maybe something was wrong with her spine because usually when she wasn't hunched over walking down the halls, she was propped up against a corner somewhere either in the gym or the cafeteria. Now, here she was leading the way like the guy with the biggest most ridiculous gun in all those Alien movies. But you know what, I have to admit that I was loving it, and I was totally following her. I didn't exactly know why back then, and I still don't know why now, but for some strange reason, I trusted her.

So before I got lost in the pitch of the tar black halls, I reached out again and instead of grabbing Brady's belt loop, I took hold of Brady's shirt tail. The maze that was the twist and turns of the administrative offices of the church were immediately confusing, and although we were heading back the exact same way that we had just come, I was lost after just the first few turns. The wood paneling that covered the walls and the eye catching posters advertising the next big events were just a blur of greys and blacks. My eyes wouldn't focus. They couldn't adjust to the lack of light. It wasn't until we reached the hues of blues and greens from the stained glass near the entrance that I was able to gather my bearings. That was when I began to feel safe again.

We stopped suddenly right before the light of the stained glass window of the entry. I bumped slightly into Brady's back and noticed it was sweaty. Was I sweating too?

"What are you?" Brady said, but his words were cut. I don't know if he was talking to me for bumping him, or to Frances for stopping short.

"Shhh! I will explain more when we get to the library. But for now, be as quiet as you can, and stay out of the light. I don't know why I didn't think about it before when we were in here. They can see our shadows." Frances whispered.

Although I know we were both thinking it, Brady said it first. "Who? Who can see our shadows?" He looked down at his feet to see if he was in fact casting a shadow.

"Boys!" she said. "Come on. I think we should try and find another way to the library."

"But all we have to do is go up these stairs and head to the left. We have come this way thousands of times. Even I can make it to the library from here in the dark." I added. "I'm willing to listen to you for now, but why go tripping over who knows what in this stupid dark if we don't have to. Let's just go up the steps and get there the way we always do."

"Fine." Frances said exasperated. And with that, she put her hand on the faux oak railing and carefully made her way up each step. "Don't say I didn't try to warn you."

"Wait up, Frances." Brady said and followed closely behind her. The clumping sound of his sneakers pounded each step and it echoed down the deserted halls. "And Pete, you don't have to hold my pants. You can make it on your own." he joked.

"Ha, ha!" I laughed sarcastically. "Very funny." I took a few steps up the staircase and then something made me look back. I don't know if it was the reflection of the stained glass on the stairwell, or the vast openness I felt as I ascended, but something made me stop and look behind me. When I did, I remember looking at stained glass Jesus as his reflection walked on the water and I had never noticed it before, but in the distance you could barely make out a boat-load of disciples waving at him franticly. To me, they didn't look very happy to see him as some of my teachers tried to convince me. No, to me they looked panicked. They looked like they were shouting at Jesus to get off the water and back into the boat. Don't walk on water, Jesus! You're going to drown! Run, run to safety! Oh ye of little faith.

When I finally snapped out of it and turned back around, both Frances and Brady were at the top of the staircase and already turning left down the hall. Neither of them looked back to make sure that I was with them. Neither of them checked to see if I was still lagging behind. "Wait up!" I yelled and started to take the blackened steps two at a time.

"Maybe this wasn't the right way to go after all." Brady said as he stared at the mountain in front of us.

Sure enough, it looked as if the custodial staff had done some renovating that Friday afternoon since we last left the school. In what was once just an empty hallway filled with signs on the walls that reminded students that "Jesus Put Others First" and that "God Loves Good Manners," were stacks upon stacks of cardboard boxes that smelled of decades old mildew and rat droppings. Long ago smudged out dates decorated the lids of the wet cardboard, and the corners bent inwardly soft with age.

One of the games that we loved to play in the halls when Mrs. Anderson wasn't looking was called "Blind Man's Steps." The way you played the game was pretty easy. All you had to do was take your index finger and barely touch the wall. Just touch it enough so you could feel the millions of tiny, little bumps that textured the sides. As you closed your eyes and attempted to read this painted braille, you would count the amount of steps in your head that you took before you couldn't take it anymore, and you had to take a peek. The walk from our classroom to the library was one of the best places in the church to play this game because the walk was pretty much one long curve. My personal best was almost thirty steps before I was too afraid that I would run into something, and I had to open my eyes. I will never forget the way Mrs. Anderson shouted at Willie Schultz when she caught him walking down the hall with his eyes closed and his hand straight out trying to beat his personal record. He tried as hard as he could to keep his hand touching the wall. He probably wouldn't have gotten caught except the fact that Willie had the habit of counting out loud.

Needless to say, I was relying on this skill to get us from the top of the staircase around the curves of the hall and eventually to the library, but now that they had the whole thing blocked with boxes and trash, it was going to be close to impossible to "Blind Man's Step" my way past this one.

"Told you." Frances said.

"Why didn't you say they were cleaning out the rooms this way instead of being all weird about it?" I remarked.

"I didn't know that they were going to throw everything in the hall. I had no idea that this way would be blocked." She answered back. "In fact, this had nothing to do with why I didn't want to walk this way." She snipped. "And I'm not weird." The last part of her words were under her breath.

"Fine! What are we supposed to do now? Do we head back?" I asked the others. "I mean why do we even have to go to the library in the first place?"

"I agree with Peter. I mean the whole hall is crammed to the ceiling in junk, and it smells. Let's just go back the way we came and figure something else out. We tried to do it your way and go to the library, Frances. It just didn't work." Brady said. He reached out and grabbed her hand to motion back to the stairs. But before he could grab it, she pulled away and got down on her hands and knees. Frances had found a crack in the cardboard wall and began to crawl her way through the piles of boxes like a dog in a gopher hole.

Brady looked at me and didn't say a word. He just lifted his shoulders as if to ask, "What do we do now?"

I shrugged my shoulders back and headed in after her. I mean what else could I do, right? Before I knew it, both Brady and I were on our hands and knees trying to keep up with Frances as she wove effortlessly through the ancient stacks of moldy paperwork and the teetering mountains of useless information. Most of making our way through was an act of trying to balance our way as not to collapse the boxes and not running over the person in front of us.

"This is ridiculous. One of us is going to twist an ankle or something." Brady said from behind me. He pushed a box under him and used it to propel himself to the next stack.

"Just shut it and try to keep up." I said back. I caught the corner of Frances's Converse sneakers right before they dove down below another pile of wet cardboard. "Slow down, Frances. How are we supposed to follow you if you won't slow down long enough for us to catch up?" I said to her.

"Will you two idiots keep your voices down? How many times do I have to tell you to keep quiet, and I will explain why when we get to the library?" Frances said in a voice slightly above a whisper. "It can't be much further."

Well, she was right. It couldn't have been much further. Looking back now at the stacks and stacks of paperwork, I can tell you that there was no way that that many boxes and stacks of garbage was all stored in one room. The labyrinth was never ending, and no matter how many times the three of us tried to climb our way to the top to see if we could see the ending through the pitch black, the way the boxes were piled up and curve of the hallway always made the end just out of reach. And there was more than one time that I made a few too many right turns and knew that I would smack myself head-first into the wall, but I didn't. In fact no matter how many times I turned and twisted my way through the chaos, there was always one more move I could make and one more stack of cardboard to traverse. To this day, I have no idea how Frances led the way and how the three of us aren't still trying to make our way out of that mess. I can imagine Brady and I stopping every once in a while to catch our breath and maybe Frances even stopping to do some light reading as she flips through those yellowed pages. But we were in too deep to turn around and head back out the other way. That was also when Brady screamed.

"A*aaahhhh!*" Brady yelled at the top of his voice. "It grabbed me! Something grabbed my ankle!" He scurried through the boxes not caring if he knocked anything over in the process, including me. He pulled at my legs pushing me downward and tried as hard as he could to crawl over me.

"Brady, cut it out!" I said, and I pushed him back the best I could in the tight maze. "What's your problem?"

"Something grabbed my ankle! I was crawling through just like you were trying to keep up with Frances, and when I turned to my left a bit, something or someone touched me. No, they did more than just touch me. They grabbed me by my ankle and pulled me backwards." Brady's voice was panicked. I can still remember the fear in his words. "We need to get out of here."

"That is what I'm trying to do. Are you sure you didn't just snag your shoelace on something?" I asked.

"I'm not stupid, Pete. I know the difference between getting your shoelace caught on something and someone grabbing me and pulling me back." Brady said. "Whatever it was, it was trying to stop me from crawling through. It was pulling me backwards toward them."

"I don't know. Maybe Darrick or one of the other guys are here and following us, and maybe they are just trying to scare us. If that is it, then we will see them sooner or later trying to hide." I said to try and reassure him that everything was cool. But in reality, even then I knew that there was no way that Shane or any of his minions would have been able to follow us quietly through the dark of the church without flashlights and not be seen or heard by one of us.

What made things worse was that I could feel Brady shaking. Up until that moment I had never seen or been around anyone that scared. I'm talking so scared that they can't even think straight. Someone with so much fear that they are physically shaking, but Brady had reached that point and all it took was something, or someone, tugging on his ankle in the dark. Maybe it was the twist and turns of the hallway. Maybe it was the way that Frances was acting that was spooking us both out. Who knows, maybe it was just spending so much time whispering in the dark. I think to myself that maybe it was all of those things and probably a lot more that I can't even remember, but what did I know. All I knew then was that I had never in my nine years of life here on this planet ever seen anyone that terrified. But like I said before, up until that moment. Believe me, we all had no idea just how scared we could get. A little squeeze on the ankle was nothing.

"Come on, man. Try to get around me, and I will take the back. It can't be too much further, can it?" I whispered to Brady. I flattened myself out the best I could on my stomach in such a narrow crevasse of moldy cardboard allowing Brady to jab and poke his way over me in the process. By the time he was able to get himself over me, I was sure that after all of the climbing, kicking and pushing, we were both coming out of there bumped and bruised.

"Thanks." he said as he made his way forward and finally over me.

"What was all that about?" Frances questioned and peeked her head through a tiny opening. To both Brady and my delight we could not only see Frances at the end of the box maze, but we could tell that she was standing up. "What part of keep it down do you not understand?" She no longer looked afraid or angry. No instead, she looked like my mom did when she has totally given up on me taking out the trash or any other chore that I promised I would do a thousand times. "I mean it sounded as if you were screaming in there."

Brady came to the end of the maze next and fell more than climbed down from the pile. His shoulder bounced off the carpet and with a small grunt, he stood up. "For your information, I was in fact screaming. And not on purpose either. For your information, I was attacked!"

"What do you mean attacked?" Frances questioned. But I could tell by the tone of her voice that she totally believed him.

"I was making my way through the boxes when someone or something grabbed my ankle and started pulling me back. It was a good thing that I yelled and was able to fight back, because if I didn't that thing probably would have killed me." Brady's enthusiasm grew as he continued the story.

"If that's true, why on earth did you come out before Peter? Shouldn't you have been behind him?" Frances questioned.

It was right about then that I stumbled out of the stack of junk and heard the last part of Frances's inquisition. "He was behind me. I let him pass me up." And then I did a terrible thing. The kind of thing only a real jerk would do. I sold out my friend. "He snagged his shoelace on the corner of a box or something and just started screaming for no reason at all." To this day I don't know why I said that. I mean did that remark somehow make me look braver in Frances's eyes? And if it did, who cared?

I could tell right away that Brady was upset with me. Although he didn't say anything at the time. Instead all he said was, "I think we better get to the library." Then without making eye contact, he turned his attention toward the door to the library.

"Whatever. Let's just get inside so I can show you two what I am talking about." whispered Frances. She reached wrist deep into the front left pocket of her blue jeans and began to try and dig out Mrs. Hanson's master keys. After what seemed like forever, she pulled out the cross shaped key ring that read, "Knock and it shall be opened." Which even today doesn't make much sense to me, because if all you have to do is knock and the door will be opened, than why would I need to carry around this huge keychain?

The three of us huddled around the door to the library as if it was a campfire, and we were all trying to stay warm. As if the tighter we closed our little circle the faster she would find the right key.

"Got it! Come on, come on." Frances said frustrated at herself as she jammed the key into the lock. You have to remember that we were doing all of this in the dark, so the fact that she even found the right key at all was pretty impressive. "Ok, let's get inside." And with that, Frances slowly turned the key and opened the library door.

# CHAPTER 6

To this day, I still love the smell of old books. Yeah, I know that I had just literally crawled through a hallway full of old papers and cardboard boxes. But there is something different about the smell of old books. The library at St. Thomas had been there since the beginning. We are talking about over a hundred years of knowledge and reading on the shelves. Sure most of the books had been replaced or repaired over time, and the library itself had gone through multiple additions and facelifts over the decades, but the smell of the shelves upon shelves of books still lingered in the air.

One of the blessings that I noticed right away as the three of us made our way inside the library was that there was a little bit of light leaking through the windows. Most of the landscaping outside the church grounds had a thick canopy of branches, so sunlight even during the brightest part of the day barely made its way through, but the windows outside the library overlooked the faculty parking lot. This meant that through the openings the moonlight was able to slyly peek through the window panes.

Through that moonlight Frances pointed to one of the large wooden tables that some of the older students used for studying their schoolbooks or working on group projects. One of the coolest things about coming to the library as a fourth grader was that the displays on the tables constantly changed depending on what the older grades were studying. I can still remember the seventh grade Viking ships that sat on each table, or the eighth grade dioramas highlighting scenes from World War II. But tonight the tables were bare. Brady and I pulled out two chairs that made a loud scraping sound as the legs scratched the floor.

"Sit there." Frances whispered. "Don't turn on the light." Frances gave us a stern look that even I could make out through the multiple shadows.

Every wooden table also had a little lamp that plugged into wall right beside it. The little lamps never did give off much light because the green lampshade was way too dark, and the librarian never put a decent watt bulb in them, but the librarian thought that it made our church library look more professional. So on every table there was a lamp that only looked nice when all of the lights in the whole room were on in the middle of the day.

"What do you think this is all about? Why do you think that Frances brought us in here?" Brady asked.

"I have no idea." I answered.

I remember looking around the room at the endless shelves of books and the posters on the walls encouraging all inside the joy of reading. During the daytime our church library wasn't much to see. There was a special section to the left that was set off especially for the school. That was pretty much the only part of the library the students were allowed to use. But for the most part, the library was used by church members and their families. There was shelf after shelf of Bible studies and devotionals. There was even more Christian Fiction to choose from, because the older ladies of the church loved to buy novels at the local Mardel's in the clearance racks and then after they read them, they would donate them to the church. You see, if you donated a book to the church library, and the librarian decided that it was worthy of shelf space then she would take a little sticker and put it on the inside front cover. "This book is donated by:" The sticker also had the date and a purple cross on the right hand side. And although none of old ladies would ever admit it, there was indeed a contest to see which one of them would die with the most books carrying their name, leaving a literary legacy.

I looked at Brady from across the table and said, "All I know is that this is the most light we have seen all night, and this is the most normal I have felt since they locked us in." I leaned back in my chair, "In fact, I say we just forget the adult study rooms altogether and just camp out here."

"That's not a bad idea. If you-know-who lets us turn on one of these lamps, then we can even read something." Brady replied and pointed to Frances.

The two of us just sat there quietly waiting for Frances to get back from whatever it was she was doing. I could see her hunched over by one of the bookshelves near the floor, but I couldn't quite make out what she was trying to do down there. Every once in a while through the darkness, I could hear the sound of scuttling or scraping. I told myself over and over that it was probably just a stupid mouse in the walls or maybe a roach crawling toward the trashcans. After all, the library was so quiet that we could hear each other exhale. I'm sure that if Ms. James was behind her desk, she would be smiling in her own personal librarian heaven enjoying the absolute silence. Like I said, mice or roaches.

That was until I looked over at Brady. He looked absolutely terrified sitting cross-legged in the wooden chair in front of me. His eyes kept darting from one shadow to the other trying to catch whatever it was that seemed just beyond his vision. Like I said, his feet were tucked tightly under him. There was no way that he was letting whatever grabbed his ankle in the hallway take another crack at him in the shadows of the library. Oh no, Brady was perfectly happy with my feet being the only ones dangling like bait under the library table. I'm also sure that he had just heard the same noises that I was hearing, but as you know, if either of us acknowledged them that would make them all too real. So we sat there in almost complete silence waiting for Frances to return.

"Move over." Frances said and placed the pages of the books in front of us. Well, at first I thought they were pages torn from books that maybe she had pulled from the shelves and torn them out, but they weren't. "Let me show you what I know, and maybe you two can help me get us through tonight." she finished.

There before us on the long wooden table that once displayed one of the most awesome dioramas that I had ever seen of the Allies storming the beaches of Normandy sat what looked like to me to be just pieces of random scraps of paper. All of the pages were hand written, some of them neat and some nothing more than scribbling chicken scratch. Some of them were written over the pages of real books (Oh, I bet Ms. James would blow a gasket if she saw that!), and some were written on pieces of torn out notebook spiral paper that still had the paper spaghetti noodles dangling from untorn holes. One of the pages wasn't even a page at all, just a napkin with scribbles that I couldn't make out.

"What is all this?" questioned Brady. He started to help Frances spread out the pages.

"Hold on. Let's get all the pieces out and in order, then I will tell you." Frances's voice changed. It was no longer the aggressive demanding tone that she had been using all night, first in the church's offices and then later throughout the box maze. It was also not the scared frantic sound that she made when Brady turned on the light switch. No, this was a voice I had heard before. Sometimes when Mrs. Anderson was in a particularly good mood, which wasn't very often, she would let us work in groups of two or three to help each other with our math facts. More than once I had been paired with Frances. Sure she didn't say much, so working with her in your group was not much different than working on your own, but when she did help this was the voice that she used. It was the voice of a teacher. Not Mrs. Anderson the Nazi instructor that I had this year. No, I'm talking about that loving tone that only caring teachers have as if they really want you to understand whatever it is they are teaching.

Now, I have to admit that I can't remember every little thing that Frances said around that table, but I will do my best to tell you everything that I do remember. After she was finally satisfied with the way that all of the pages and scraps of paper were laid out, she began to go over what I can only to this day call some kind of research.

"You see," She began, "ever since I found out that we were not the first group of kids asked to have to spend the night in the church, I started to wonder why that was so. I had to find out. I mean think about it. Why would it be so important for every new kid that comes to St. Thomas Christian Academy to have to stay overnight?"

Frances continued. "At first, no matter who I asked, no one would talk about it or tell me why. I mean every year there is a whole new set of kindergarteners, so why don't they just have some sort of field trip lock-in sleep over with parents and then everyone who came to the school would be set for the rest of their career here? But they don't do that. And even if they did, how would they handle late comers like the three of us?" she whispered. I could see the intenseness in her eyes.

She had only just begun, and already Brady and I were speechless. This whole time that Brady and I thought that this was all some kind of popularity test and thinking about what type of snacks we should smuggle in, Frances was doing an in depth investigation. She was so far ahead of us.

"You see, the three of us are no different from any of the kids that came in before. Well, hold on let me straighten that out a bit." Frances said and adjusted her glasses. "No different from any of the kids that came in later in the school year. As far as I can tell, if you started school here from the beginning, let's say kindergarten of even before in the pre-school, then what we are doing tonight you would never have to go through, but let's say if you came from another school, or you moved here from another city and started late, then you were made to stay the night." That is when Frances pointed to the first little piece of paper.

"This was the one that I think comes first. Not the first one that I found, but the one that comes first." she said and placed it at the far left hand side of the table. I could barely see the words written on it and I had thought about turning on the little lamp, but I guess because Frances didn't turn it on, I decided just to leave it alone. Immediately, Brady grabbed for the paper and tried to take a closer look, but Frances gently slapped his hand and put the piece at the beginning of what I found out was a time-line.

"It talks about staying here after the sun goes down, and then later mentions that it is better in the dark. But that is not the only one." Frances shuffled through the wads of crumpled and folded papers, and she spread them out trying to find the exact ones she needed. Brady and I could only sit there and watch because neither of us knew what she was looking for. "So does this one, and… …this one." Frances placed two more pages on the time-line. "This one just says to turn off the lights."

"Where did you find all of these?" Brady asked.

"Wait, before you answer that, answer this. Did you always know that Brady and I were going to be with you tonight?" I asked.

"Of course." Frances said. "Didn't you know that I would be with you guys too?" she asked back.

Now, there was no way that Brady or I knew that she was going to be involved with tonight's activities. Remember that we thought that this was just Shane and Derrick's way to somehow initiate the new guys into the class. We both wanted to be included, so we never even thought about the fact that Frances might want to be included too. But with her sitting there across from me and the light of the moon coming through the window, I could still make out the hurt on her face. So I did what every other red blooded American boy would have done in that same situation. I lied.

"Sure we knew you were coming with us, Frances. We were even bringing some snacks and a few games for us to play too. Well, until they told us not to bring anything." I smiled.

"My family calls me Franny. My friends do too." Frances smiled. The sullen look on her face disappeared and was replaced with a thin smile. Then it faded, and she whispered something I don't think we were supposed to hear, but Brady and I both did. "If I had any."

Trying to change the subject, Brady quickly caught on. "Anyway, how did you get all this stuff?"

"It wasn't easy." Frances said collecting herself. "I know I didn't have much time, and no one was willing to help me." Frances continued. "But I will tell you what really helped. What helped the most was talking to Ms. James. She may be the sweetest librarian in the history of librarians, but she *cannot* keep a secret. All I had to do was ask about the history of the church and the school. Mix in a little question or two about what happens here after dark, and before you knew it she was pulling out books. But here is the thing, she would pull our books that had to do with local history and the church, but the whole time she kept staring or at least trying not to stare at the paneling under the picture of Pastor O'Leary over there."

Although that side of the library was still too dark to see, both Brady and I knew exactly what painting Frances was referring to. Pastor Patrick O'Leary was the pastor of the church right around the time that the school started to allow girls and other minorities into its hallowed halls. So needless to say, at the time he was hated by at least half of the parishioners of the church. When the controversy hit an all-time high in the wings of St. Thomas, his oil painting was shamefully taken off the wall of fame, and later moved into the library, and replaced with a painting of Jesus gathering a bunch of children to sit at his feet. And although everyone noticed, no one complained, even the followers that were on his side, because no one wanted to be anti-kid.

Not a single parishioner was willing to say, "Hey could we get that picture of the guy who tried to ruin the school back on the wall and take down the one of the guy in the robe and sandals hanging out with the kids while their parents look lovingly in the background." So although the times changed and what Pastor O'Leary did would now seem brave and innovative, back then it wasn't. A few years later, Pastor O'Leary quietly moved away, but his impact on the school remained. The little girls in the classroom didn't bring about Armageddon as some of the church elders believed, and in fact, a few of the parents actually liked being able to drop off all of their children at the same school and the idea that maybe, just maybe it was good for girls to have a Christian education too.

But that is not the reason the Brady and I and every other student at St. Thomas knew about Pastor O'Leary. Or as most of us called him, "Pastor O'Creepy." He had what some people call "beady eyes" The kind innovative pastor's eyes would follow you around throughout the library no matter what part of the Dewey Decimal System you were using. If you didn't look at him first, you would be ok. But if you did make eye contact, then his eyes would follow you as you perused the shelves looking for your next chapter book. There were whole classes full of students that refused to check out any books on the shelves that sat under his picture. Walter Simmons refused to pass his reading comprehension test, because if he did, he would have been moved up to the next reading level and that meant that he would have to start reading books under the pastor's portrait. It was not a risk that he was willing to take.

"Yep, you see that little strip of paneling underneath the shelf. Ok, maybe you can't see it too good now in the dark, but under that picture of O'Creepy is a shelf, and under that shelf is a strip of paneling. So, I knew that Ms. James was staring at it, so I just waited until she finished helping me find the books I was looking for. When she went back to her desk, I popped it open and found all of this." Frances said.

"Is that where you found out what to do tonight, Frances?" Brady asked.

"Franny." I corrected. And then I gave Frances a smile.

"Yes, most of it." Frances smiled back at me, and then she turned her attention back to the pages to continue her story. "These, as far as I can tell, are notes that kids just like us wrote out over the past I don't know how many years."

"Is that how you learned about the lights?" I asked.

"Exactly. This one says, 'The lights make them come'." Franny held up a slip of paper that had obviously come from a page from a Dr. Seuss book. "And this one is a lot less scary and just says, 'They love the lights'." Frances added the paper to her time-line.

Brady asked the question before I could get to it, although I am sure that neither of us really wanted to know the answer. "Who are they? Who loves the lights?

"I'm not sure." Frances flipped a few of the notes over so the writing was on the top. Then she picked up a few more and let them drop to the table.

"None of these things say. But from the way that they are written, I don't think they are good, and I don't think they mean to be our friends."

"Do you think that is what grabbed my leg?" As Brady said this, I remember him reaching under the library table and grabbing his ankle. "Do you think that whatever likes the lights was the same things that tried to get me?"

"Come on, Brady. If anything grabbed your leg, and I'm not saying that anything did, but if something grabbed your leg, it wasn't whatever this is." I told him.

"How do you know that?" he asked.

"Because, don't you get it? All of this is just a joke. Something that the other kids put here to try and scare us." I picked up a few of the pages and lightly crumpled them in my hands. "This is just papers that Shane or Elizabeth put here so we would find it."

I could see the look of disappointment on Frances's face. "Peter, why would they go through all that trouble? And why would Ms. James be in on it? And how would that explain this?"

Frances pulled out a paper that had been torn out of a yellow notebook. The top of the page was jagged, and the creases of the folds had been used so many times that they had begun to rip. Before she could tell me who had written it, I already had a good guess. I had been staring at that handwriting since the first day of school, or at least the adult version of it. Mrs. Anderson's note filled every corner of the yellow notebook paper that Frances held in her hand.

"What is that?" Brady questioned.

"It's our teacher. Well, not yet she wasn't. Shannon Egress came to St. Thomas Christian Academy when she started the sixth grade. As far as I could tell, she was told to spend the night here at our lovely church just a few months after that." Frances told the two of us.

Brady gently took the yellow paper from her hand and examined the handwriting. "Well, it does look a lot like her S's and her T's. But our teacher's name is Anderson, not Egress."

Frances rolled her eyes. "Boys!"

"Hey, hey, don't include me with him. Brady, think about it. Was Mrs. Anderson married in sixth grade?" I tried to explain.

The look on his face was priceless. Brady was actually sitting across from me trying to figure it out.

"It was her maiden name. You know, her last name before she got married and changed it." Frances said, trying to help me out. "What was your mom's name before she got married?"

Brady thought about it a moment. "Nancy!"

"Her last name, Brady." Frances said exasperated.

"Oh," Brady sat and squelched his face. "I don't know."

"Forget it, Franny." I said. "Just take our word for it that this was our teacher before she was our teacher. This was a note that she left here in the library back when she was in sixth grade."

"This is what she wrote." Frances said and flattened out the yellow page the best that she could and pushed up her glasses. "It is hard to make out because I think she must have been writing on her lap or something. But this is what I can make out."

- *What time is it? It has to be daylight by now. Why haven't they come for me? I hope Sally is ok, I didn't see her breathing. Why haven't they come for me? God please help me! Make sure someone reads this and tells my mom and dad that I love them and that I'm sorry. I'm so sorry.*

"That was as much as I could get at least." Frances looked into our eyes to try to gage what we were thinking. She looked back down at Mrs. Anderson's note. "There is some more on the side over here." She turned the page sideways and pointed to another part of the letter, but the smudge had worn the writing down to the point that I agreed with her. It was illegible.

"What does all that mean?" Brady asked. I could hear him fidgeting under the table as he rocked his chair back and forth. There was a shaking in his voice. He was getting more and more frightened by the events of the whole night, and he wasn't the only one.

I could always count on Brady to ask the questions that I was too afraid to ask. I stretched my neck and squinted my eyes to try and focus in the crude writing in the faint light of the moon. But as far as I could tell, Frances had read the letter exactly as our teacher, Mrs. Anderson, had written it so many years ago.

"Well I don't know about you two, but as far as I can tell Shannon here was scared out of her wits and wanted to go home and be with her mommy and daddy." I said.

"Who's Shannon?"

"Mrs. Anderson!" both Frances and I said.

"Anyway," Frances rolled her eyes and continued, "As you can tell by what she wrote, she was not alone that night. And I don't mean her friend who ever this Sally girl was either. Mrs. Anderson was sure there was something else in the church that night with them. And if these other pages here are right, whatever it was that was with them didn't like the lights. That is why I have been telling the two of you to keep the lights out."

"Surely you can't believe all of this, Franny?" I asked. "I mean, you are like the smartest one in our class. Everyone knows it. You can't really believe that there is something in the dark with us in the church tonight? Something that loves the lights."

"Something grabbed my ankle. I didn't imagine that." Brady interjected and reminded us.

"And I think that Brady is right. There is something out there, and that something grabbed his ankle." Frances said. Brady smiled in satisfaction, and Franny continued. "We have to stick together and never let each other get out of sight. We have to stay close together. Now, we need to make our way back downstairs to the cafeteria." Frances said.

"Why do we need to head down there next? Are you hungry or something? Because my stomach feels like it's been punched. My knots have knots." said Brady. Which was saying a lot because Brady was always hungry.

I knew exactly how he felt though. I have always been able to eat too. I mean no matter what the situation, I always have room for a cheeseburger. But that night, in that library, after all of the things that Brady and I had just heard Frances share, there was nothing that sounded tasty. So when Franny suggested that we make our way from the library all the way down to the cafeteria at the opposite end of the school, it just didn't seem like it would be worth the journey. "I'm kind of with Brady on this one, Franny. The cafeteria is super far away. It feels pretty safe in here. Why don't we just stay here in the library until morning and then make our way to the back door right before dawn? Sure we may be starving by then, but if there is something out there, wouldn't it just make sense to stay here?"

"Two reasons." Frances said and slid another slip paper to Brady. "Read this."

Brady un-wadded the paper the best that he could. The tight little ball was by far the smallest note in the bunch. Brady tried to smooth it out with the edges of his thumbs. The whole time that he was struggling with it, Frances leaned in and shifted her eyes from Brady to me and then back to Brady. Her uneasiness made me more nervous than I already was.

Brady held the note up and read the words. "Keep moving." They were the only two words on the paper.

Brady read those little tiny wrinkled up words exactly the way it had been written. The letters were shaky and melted. Each letter looked as if it had been harder to write down than the one before it. Those letters were scared. And that is exactly the way Brady read it. He dropped the note on the desk as if it was on fire, as if it burned his fingers to hold it.

The library walls were silent for what seemed like hours, but looking back was only a few seconds, either way Ms. James would have smiled. It was Frances that was once again brave enough and broke the silence. "That is why I don't think it is a good idea to just stay here and wait until dawn."

Brady and I didn't need to be convinced that sticking around might not be the best of ideas. For some reason the multiple crumpled notes and chicken scratch letters warning us about keeping the lights out and the yellow notepad scribbling of our fourth grade teacher weren't half as chilling as the two words that Brady had just read. To this day I don't know why Frances handed that note to Brady to read, but I have never been more grateful for it. Handling that note would have been like being handed a dead rat. It would have been something you would never forget touching.

"You said there were two reasons." I reminded Frances.

"You're right, Peter. I did. Do either of you have anything in your pockets?" Franny asked.

"You know we don't. Shane told us not to bring anything, remember." Brady said. He untucked his legs and as carefully as he could, let his feet touch the worn green carpet of the library floor. Brady reached into the front of his jeans and inverted the pockets proving to the both of us that they were indeed empty.

"Yeah, Franny, me too." I added. I reached into the pockets of my cargo pants and pulled out the piece of fried chicken. Embarrassingly, I held the chicken wing in my hand.

"What is that? Is that a chicken wing?" Frances asked with a snicker.

"I forgot that was there." It was a good thing that the room was dark, so the two of them couldn't see how red my face was. I got up to throw it in the garbage.

"Wait!" Brady said.

"It's just a piece of chicken from my dinner." I told him.

"I know. I'll take it." Brady said and reached out motioning for the cold chicken wing.

I guess his stomach wasn't as knotted as he thought it was. I handed him the chicken, and Brady took a huge bite dropping bits of crust all over the library floor. Ms. James would have totally wigged out. Mice and roaches.

"Gross." Franny said.

She tried to take the focus away from Brady's eating habits by getting back to the subject. "Well, Lizzy told me the same thing too. She stressed that I was not allowed to bring anything at all inside the building when I went in tonight. I tried to look for something, anything in all of this to see if I could find out a reason why, but there is nothing written about it at all." Frances shared with us.

Frances began to gather the scraps of paper and organize them into one big pile. She even took the time to carefully refold Mrs. Anderson's not the exact way that it had been folded over before, and then she wadded up the horrible note that Brady had had to read. She was trying to put everything back the way that she had gotten it out. I thought for sure that she was going to stuff them all in her pocket or even ask us to hold on to a few of the more important ones so we could go back and read them later if we needed, and if that was the case there was no way on Earth that I was going to put that little wadded up ball in my pocket. I already knew that was *not* going to happen.

Instead, Franny got up from the table and went back to the place under the picture of O'Leary where she had pulled out all of the notes and crumpled pieces of history in the first place. The picture of Pastor O'Leary leered at her with his beady eyes the entire time as she carefully bent down to remove the faux wood paneling at the very bottom of the book shelves.

That was when I made the mistake of looking directly into the portrait. Pastor O'Leary's eyes locked onto mine like a steel trap snapping tight to the little mouse's tail, and he watched me unblinkingly as I silently sat there waiting for Frances to come back to our table. I could see it in O'Leary's glare that he was not only watching, but he was listening to every single word that we had said. The eerie smile that haunted every grade school student for generations had become a devilish sneer. The ghostly portrait of Pastor O'Leary knew what the three of us were planning to do even before we ourselves knew it ourselves. "It won't matter. It will never work. Soon your little friends will be with me. So say goodbye to your little friends, Petey." O'Leary whispered in my head.

"What was the second thing?" Brady asked again, repeating my question. His words broke the silence of the room and seemed to snap me out of it and rescue me from O'Leary's gaze.

Frances either didn't hear him, or was just choosing to ignore him. Instead, she finished replacing all of the pages, and popped the panel back into place with a snap. "As far as I know, Ms. James doesn't know anything about me opening this up, and that is kinda the way I want to keep it." Franny said.

That brought up a good question. Let me ask you. If Ms. James was so set in Frances not finding out about all of those letters hidden under the bookshelves, then why did she keep looking at them? And for that matter, how did Ms. James even know that they were there in the first place? Unless of course she was one of the kids that stashed something under there too. I never found out much more about Ms. James at my time at St. Thomas. When I was finally brave enough to go back into the building and do any looking, the church records showed that she was still the librarian for quite some time after I left. And later she married a man in the army, and the two of them moved to Phoenix, Arizona.

Frances stood up slowly and walked back to Brady and me. "Stop repeating yourselves. I heard you both the first time. Well to start, we got the scariest note in the whole world that I or any of us has ever read with a message that said we needed to keep moving. Second, the reason that I picked the cafeteria is not so we can make ourselves a sandwich and have a little picnic. It's for something else we might need."

For the life of me, I couldn't think of any possible thing that the three of us might need from the school cafeteria. There were just long foldable tables and cheap plastic chairs in all of the school friendly primary colors.

There were a few smelly trashcans tucked into the corners, because we were supposed to be old enough to throw our own trash away when we were done eating. I bet if we were hungry and brave enough, and we wanted there was even a nice hefty helping of chili in the walk in coolers. But I didn't know how any of those things might come in handy, and how any of it would keep whatever or whomever it was from following us around the church all night. And just the thought of that scab chili made my already knotted stomach do a few extra summersaults. Of course before I could ask, Brady had beat me to it.

"That is really a long ways from here. What could we possible need all the way down in the cafeteria, Frances?" Brady asked.

"Weapons." Frances said and started walking with her back to us and towards the exit of the library. "Oh, and it's Franny."

# CHAPTER 7

Neither Brady nor I said a word. We both just silently tucked our chairs under the thick wooden table and made our way out the door following Frances closely behind. I'm sorry, following *Franny* closely behind. Brady led the way, and I pulled up the rear. I carefully let the library door click shut. I remember now thinking about how careful I was, and that I didn't want the door to slam shut. Why? Because, whatever it was would hear us leaving. Enough time had passed that I can say that now, but that night I would have never admitted to a thing like that. And for the record, I also knew why Brady hurried to follow Frances. There was a part of him that was still petrified to be in the back of the line when it came to our little group. He was still afraid that whatever it was that reached out for him in the maze of letters, papers, and boxes might be out there, and could reach out for him again. Only this time it might not be so quick to let go.

At least Franny had the same frame of mind that I did. There was no way that the three of us should try and make our way through that pile of wet cardboard boxes and decades old stacks of record keeping, so the only real choice that we had to make it down to the cafeteria was to make our path the long way, all the way down the halls and past our classroom.

Most of the elementary school classrooms were down the same hallway. As the school grew over the years, many of the classes that started on the first floor were moved up to the second floor. Only the kindergarten classes were still on the bottom level. I once heard that that had to do with the statewide fire codes. You see, the fire department thought that if there were ever a fire, the kindergarten kids couldn't make it down the stairs and out the doors in time, and they would all get burned up tripping over themselves. But I don't think that is the reason. I think the truth is if there was ever a real honest to goodness fire in the church, the older students would spas out and in the panic of trying to get out of the building, they would be the ones to trample the kindergarteners as they tried to save their own hide. So for "Safety Reasons" the kindergarten classes were the only ones still on the first floor.

"We should see if our classroom is unlocked." Brady said.

He had clearly already forgotten that Frances had the set of master keys in her front pocket, therefore it didn't matter if the classroom door was unlocked or not.

"If it is, we can get some stuff out of our desk that we might need. You know in case we want to write a note later and put it in the library with the others." he added.

"We will worry about that stuff later." Franny whispered. "Let's just focus on getting to the cafeteria."

If you were to look up the definition of the word "dark," it would have the reference: See St. Thomas elementary school hallway. If I had thought that the other parts of the church were dark that night, it was only because I had not yet tried to make my way down our school hallway. Without asking, I reached out in front of me and grabbed the loop of Brady's jeans as we made our way down the hall blindly. He didn't make any smart aleck remark or for that matter, I don't even think he even bothered to look back. Not that I could have seem him if he did. In fact, I wouldn't doubt that Brady was grabbing on to Frances's belt loop at the same exact time I was grabbing his.

Although I had only been attending St. Thomas for a few months, I knew this hall like the back of my hand. Like most of the halls in the church, this one had a slightly rounded curve to it. The classroom order followed the progressive age of the students, so the first grade classrooms were the first ones that you would walk past and then the second grade classrooms and so on and so on until you got to the sixth grade classrooms at the far end of the hall. Now, the older students had classrooms on almost the opposite end of the church. The only things that the lower and upper grades shared were the gym, the library, and the cafeteria. But the church did a great job of making sure that the older students and the younger students never really saw each other. Even the library and gym days would alternate with our class going only on Tuesdays and Thursdays, and the older students getting Monday, Wednesday, and Friday. And the times the older kids ate lunch was at least an hour after we had eaten and had left to head back upstairs to our rooms.

I assumed this was done to try and cut down on things like bullying and other types of mischief. Yes, even at a super Christian school like St. Thomas there were problems with things like that. But who was I to talk about being bullied, if forcing three new kids to break into the church, and steal keys, and spend the night trespassing wasn't some extreme form of bullying, then I don't know what was.

"Man, this is some serious dark." Brady joked.

"Shh! The faster we get through this hallway and down to the cafeteria, the better." Frances whispered. "Remember to stay together and whatever you do, try to stay as quiet as you can."

"How can you see where you are going?" I asked. I tried to whisper as loudly as I could so Frances could hear me, and it still be considered a whisper.

Franny took a few more steps down the pitch black hallway, and then she stopped suddenly causing a small and silent pile-up. "Tell Peter that I can't see where I am going, and that I am trying very hard to count my steps so he needs to stay quiet." she turned and whispered in Brady's ear.

See, what I didn't know was that Frances had been doing something else while all the other kids in my class were playing "Blind Man's Steps." She was not only a watcher, but she was also a counter. I think some people might call that OCD, today. All of her classmates were trying to get from the classroom to the library by just touching the walls with their finger tips and trying to take the most steps they could without opening their eyes. Meanwhile, Frances was counting. She knew exactly how many steps there were from the front entrance of the church to the library, from the library to the classroom, from the classroom to the girl's bathroom, and how many steps up and down the stairs to get from the top to the bottom.

"What are you doing?" Brady asked.

"I'm counting." Frances answered.

"Good, because we are counting on you too." Brady whispered back.

Now, although no one could see it in the pitch blackness that passed for a hallway, I just know that I could hear Frances rolling her eyes at Brady and turning once more to begin our trek down to the cafeteria.

"I heard her." I whispered back in Brady's ear. "She must have counted how many steps it takes to get from one end of the hall to the other. So just don't lose her in this dark, and let her keep walking."

The three of us passed by one locked classroom after another. The artwork that hung outside each room reflected the grade inside, not that we could see much of it in the darkness. The first grade class hung their homemade paper plate clocks that had paper hands so each student could move them around to tell the time. But the metal brad in the center had been worn lose from so much spinning so that now all of the hands of the clocks hung low and every clock read 6:30. Brady's shoulder bumped the wall knocking a few to the floor. "Watch out, Pete." he warned.

The third grade classroom was the one that brought us to our knees, literally. I knew that the third grade classes had spent the last few weeks studying the solar system. You know, all of the planets and stuff, but what I didn't know was that Ms. Munoz's class had finished their mobiles and Ms. Munoz had taken the time to hang them by the ceiling tiles before she left for the weekend. So in the darkness that made the elementary hallway feel like the vastness of space, there were twelve cut-out solar systems complete with all of the planets and a Styrofoam sun. Frances was the first to scream.

"A*hhh!!* Help, it's got me!" Franny, instantly forgetting our pact to remain silent at all cost, yelled as she ran forward flailing her arms and entwining herself in the hanging fishing line.

She ripped at least three of the mobiles from the ceiling tiles overhead throwing the paper planets and the Styrofoam suns behind her. The first one made by Emily Castillo hit Brady square in the face. This caused Brady to lose his grip of Franny's waistband, and he began to pull violently at the web-like strings entangling his face.

"*No!!!* It's on my face! It's on my face!" he yelled. Brady started twisting and turning trying to get himself free of the solar system attacking his face and working its way down around his neck. But when the Styrofoam sun touched his nose, he let out a blood piercing scream that was so high pitched that every dog in the surrounding neighborhoods turned their heads slightly wondering where it had come from. "*It's biting me! There's a spider, and it's biting me!*" Brady screeched.

Now, keep in mind that I still had no idea what was going on at the time. As far as I knew, something evil had just attacked the three of us. Frances was running down the hall yelling that something had her and was pulling her back. Was it the same creature that had grabbed Brady by the ankle earlier? How could I know? And yes, I did believe that something had grabbed him.

I just didn't let him know that. And as for Brady, well he was obviously being attacked by spiders that were so large that they were biting his face. His twisting and turning caused me to let go of his belt loop, so all of us were now lost in the dark being attacked by the unknown forces of Ms. Munoz's third grade class.

That was when I felt it too. It started out as a tickle behind my ear that I quickly swatted away. That swat caused the paper Uranus to swing back and not tickle but full on touch my ear. It must have been the sharp edge of the paper that did it too because right there and then, I knew that whatever had bitten Brady was now biting me. "It's got me*!* I've been bit*!*" I yelled. Now, I'm taller than both Franny and Brady, so when I raised my hands above my head and started to run, all of the fabulously decorated solar systems, that Ms. Munoz couldn't wait to display and that had gone unmolested, quickly wrapped around my arms. Each one pulled and tugged at me. I felt as if I was being pulled upwards toward the ceiling tiles. The bent paperclips that the teacher had used to hang them from began to unhook from the ceiling, and they sling-shot straight in to my cheeks. *"Oww! they're biting my face!"* My screaming rivaled Brady's, and I'm sure upset the neighborhood dogs once again.

Frances stopped running and bent over to put her hands on her knees and to catch her breath. "I'm ok. Guys, I'm ok. I don't think it was anything. It just feels like string or something." Her voice was beginning to calm down and her breathing a little more focused. Franny's foot kicked Sally Singleton's Styrofoam sun. Frances picked it up and rolled the painted ball in her hand. "Yeah, I think it is some kind of art project."

"No! Whatever bit me was not an art project. It was sharp and had teeth." Brady insisted. "There was a web and a spider. I can still feel it burning my skin." Brady touched the tip of his nose.

I pulled the strings of monofilament off of my arms and started to collect myself. "I think that Frances is right. It feels like some kind of project to me too. This is just paper and string." I said. My cheeks still stung from the projectile paperclips, but I no longer thought that it was supernatural. I was finally able to free myself from Ms. Munoz's class projects and step safely away from the chaos. "I think we're going to be alright." I tried to reassure Brady and Frances.

"Why doesn't anyone ever believe me?" Brady said.

"I believe you." Frances told Brady. "I was just saying that whatever attacked *you* was not the same thing that must have attacked *me*. I must have just been not paying attention and ran into some kids art work. We will keep an eye on those bites of yours, and if we need to, get to the nurse's station for some first aid."

Now, if I would have said that, you could have heard the sarcasm dripping off every syllable of every word, but that wasn't the case with Frances. When she said it, she was being sincere. Franny knew as well as I did that the three of us had just ran into a bunch of group projects dangling from the ceiling, but she didn't say anything. You see, it was important to Brady that we believed that he had just been attacked for the second time that night. And because it was important to Brady, it was important to Frances too. Frances Maggie Lingersham had spent her whole life quietly in the corner being ignored, so she knew how important it was for Brady to be recognized, to be believed.

After blindly reaching out for each other in the absolute darkness, we were all able to untangle ourselves from Ms. Munoz's solar systems and reform our line of three. One hand plastered the walls and the other looped safely around each other's pants, we slowly and steadily inched our way to our homeroom door. It was decided that since we were so close, that maybe it wouldn't be such a bad idea after all to open it up and take a peek inside. Brady was right, maybe there might be something inside that we could use after all.

We had finally passed the other third grade classrooms and reached our fourth grade classroom door. Brady had once said that he knew our classroom by the smell. He said that you could smell the perfect blend of dry erase markers and orange oil wood polish from down the hall. Brady added that although most of the rooms smelled that way too, there was also a slight hint of the old lady perfume that Mrs. Anderson wore with a sense of pride. I loved the familiar feeling of the air conditioning pumping at full blast from under the door. Mrs. Anderson loved to leave the air conditioning on over the weekend, and the windows would be covered with wet dripping condensation when we walked in every Monday morning waiting to welcome you back to another wonderful week of learning. The students in her class could enjoy the feeling of a nice warm sweater from August until the end of May as long as they stayed in their seat. Frances simply said that she knew it was our classroom because of the impending sense of doom. Was she being dramatic? I am not too sure.

"Hold up." Frances said. She started to dig around in her pocket for the master keys.

"I know what I'm getting first." Brady said. "I left a Reese's Peanut Butter Cup in my desk. I'm starving."

"You do know that our next stop is the cafeteria, right?" I added.

Frances fumbled through the key ring trying to find one that would fit the lock. "Let me try this one." She said to herself. There wasn't one key that fit every door. No, it was more like one set of keys that if put in the right combination opened any door. "No, that wasn't it either. Just be patient."

Brady and I didn't say a word, but Franny thought that we must have been pressuring her in some way because she seemed very impatient. So the both of us looked at each other through the darkness and just stood there quietly as Frances flipped through key after key.

"I told you." Frances said and turned the key in the lock. Keep in mind that neither Brady nor I ever doubted that she could get the door open. "Now, be careful. We don't want to spend too much time in here, so let's just get in and out."

"I'm getting my Reese's." Brady said and made a b-line for his desk.

Now, to tell you the honest truth, I really didn't know what I should be looking for or what I should grab. I mean I have never been one of those students that needed to write stuff down or pass notes, so I figured that when it came to passing on information to the next group of unfortunate students who were in this same situation, that it would just be Frances that would do it. It was also too dark to grab a book to read. And it wasn't as if I had a first aid kit or a flashlight stashed away in my desk somewhere amongst my text books and crayons. So what did I do? I pulled the safety scissors from my supply box and shoved them into the back pocket of my jeans, then I grabbed a pencil and did the same thing. I thought to myself, glue stick? No, what would I need to stick together? Dry erase marker? No, that wouldn't do any good, and we weren't "responsible" enough to have a permanent marker. I have to admit that I was not very good at thinking on the fly.

"OK, let's go." Frances said in the dark corner of the classroom. Now, while Brady was getting a chocolate out of his desk and I was fumbling around my desk looking for school supplies, Frances was once again at least two steps ahead of us.

"Franny, what are you doing?" I said. I noticed that instead of heading to her desk, she went right for Mrs. Anderson's.

"She keeps this in her bottom desk drawer in case of a black out, and our school loses electricity." Franny said and held up a small pocket flashlight. She turned it on for just a fraction of a second to let the light shine. Her face lit up for a moment and the flash of brightness reflected off her cheek and her glasses. But before you could notice her smile, it was out again.

"You can't take that! She will kill you if she finds out that you went through her stuff!" Brady said, not bothering to lower his voice. But then he caught himself quickly and whispered, "Don't you remember anything about the line?" Brady pointed to the floor.

Ah yes, the line. Mrs. Anderson had this line. It was red duct tape that she had placed in a circumference about two feet away from her desk on all three sides. Because her chair was up against the wall, she only needed the tape on three sides creating a semicircle. She had carefully measured out from her desk in all directions a protective invisible barrier that kept all of the students in her class away from anything within reach. Imagine that line when you go to the bank in which every person calmly awaits his or her turn in line before being called up to the next teller's window. That was kind of the way it worked around Mrs. Anderson's desk.

Let's just say for the sake of argument that you had a question about a word problem that you were working on in class. Now, in a normal healthy classroom environment you could raise your hand quietly and the teacher would lovingly look over your shoulder and help you work through the problem until you understood how it was done. The teacher would walk away knowing that she had spread her mathematical knowledge, and you would walk away with a new-found love and appreciation for long division craftily disguised as a word problem. Win/Win.

Ah, but not so in Mrs. Anderson's fourth grade class. Let's say that you had the same question about the same word problem in her class. You would raise your hand and wait for the signal. This signal was usually a look of contempt and frustration followed by a head nod that told you to get up and come to her desk. If you were fortunate enough to get said nod, then you would approach the red duct tape taped to the floor. If you were deemed worthy, you could approach the desk with your paper. You had to make sure that you knew exactly what problem you needed help with, and never, ever turn the page around so she could read it. Mrs. Anderson could read upside down and found it insulting if you turned the page around so she could read it. After all, you were the one who needed the help. After a few sighs of disgust, she would reluctantly help you with your math. Mrs. Anderson would know that you were a failure as a student, and you would walk away ashamed of you ignorance. Lose/Lose.

"Do you think I care one little bit about some stupid red line?" Frances asked Brady.

"No, I guess not. It's just that if she finds out you went through her desk, you are going to be I so much trouble." Brady said. He was just doing his best to try to save Franny in his own simple way, I guess.

"We are in the church in the middle of the night without permission. I don't think borrowing a flashlight out of our teacher's desk is going to make much of a difference." Franny added.

"She has a good point there, Brady." I said.

"Are we about ready here?" Frances asked. Then she grabbed something else out of Mrs. Anderson's top desk drawer and slammed it shut. I couldn't quite make it out, but it didn't take me long into the night to figure out that while I was stashing my safety scissors into my cargo pants, Frances had grabbed something a little more substantial, our teacher's shears. They were long and very sharp. The kind where the black metal handle felt heavy in your hand. They were the type of scissors that actually made a "Shhht" noise when you opened and closed them.

"Aren't you going to grab something to write with?" I asked Franny.

"No, hopefully, if we do things right, I won't have to." She answered.

The three of us made a feeble attempt in the dark to try and put everything back to the way it was before we came in. Mrs. Anderson liked to have all of the chairs tucked under the desk before we all lined up to leave at the end of each day and nothing, I mean nothing, was to be on top because the custodians couldn't wipe down the desk each night if there was books and papers on it. But let me tell you a little secret. The custodians didn't come in at the end of each day to clean our room. Sure they emptied the trash and maybe vacuumed every other day or so but I know for a fact that they didn't do everything that Mrs. Anderson said they did.

You see, over in the corner of our classroom sat the pencil sharpener, and behind the pencil sharpener sat a roach. This roach, as I discovered, met its untimely death around let's say August 23rd. Now, according to Mrs. Anderson, the custodians came in at the end of each day to clean our room, and the way she made it sound, they did such a great job that even the smallest particle of dust was wiped clean. You could assemble top secret computers in our classroom at the end of the day. Of course she said this so that she could blame any mess that she found in the room on one of the students. So Charlie, the roach, (Yes, I named him.) sat in the corner of our room with all six legs fully extended just waiting to be recognized by one of the girls in class, so everyone could get a good scream. The deal was that no one ever did. It got to the point that I would pretend to sharpen my pencil just so I could routinely check on Charlie. For weeks he laid on his back unnoticed. After a month, I just came to the conclusion that he was our class pet. As of last Thursday, he was still there.

"Hurry up, Brady" Frances said. She held the keys in her hand ready to lock up the classroom.

"Ok, ok. Let me just do one thing real quick." Brady said and ran to Shane's desk.

He pulled out Shane's chair and began to rifle through his stuff. "What do you think you're doing?" I asked him. I squinted through the faint light of our windows to try and make out what exactly Brady's plans were.

"I just have to check something." Brady whispered and reached inside Shane's desk and pulled out Shane's school supply box. "I knew it! I deep down inside just knew it!" Brady held something in his hand, but he was too far away for me to make it out.

"What's that?" Frances and I asked pretty much at the same time.

"I'll tell you what this is." Brady answered and held the object high above his head. "This is my pen!" He said way too loudly.

I guess in all the excitement of recovering his pen, Brady forgot the part about being quiet and whispering when we could. But he sure was happy about finding that pen.

"Did Shane go to Dinosaur Park? I don't think so." Brady exclaimed.

You see, Brady *did* go to Dinosaur Park, and he spent part of his allowance on an official Dinosaur Park collectable pen. The same pen that he so proudly brought to school the next Monday, and the same pen that went "missing" by that afternoon.

"I knew he took it." Brady said. He checked the pen over the best he could in the dark for any sort of damage, after all it was a collectable. He took the pen putting it carefully in his pocket. When the pen went missing, Mrs. Anderson asked the class if anyone had taken Brady's "little" pen, of course no one had. That was the length of the investigation, but Brady always knew in the back of his head that Shane had taken it off his desk.

"Come on, let's go." Frances insisted.

"Ok, I'm ready. Pete, come on. Let's get out of here." Brady agreed walking out and trying to unwrap his candy at the same time.

With that, the three of us left Mrs. Anderson's classroom, and without saying another word, waited for Frances to lock the door behind us and lead the way. I don't know why we were waiting, because we all knew the way to the cafeteria from there, but Brady and I waited for Frances to take the lead. Brady followed closely behind Franny and then I followed behind Brady bringing up the rear. It was the way that we had traveled ever since Brady was touched in the stacks of paperwork, so it was unspoken that until something else happened, this was the order that we would be traveling in. Frances as the line leader, Brady in the middle, and as we called it in fourth grade, I was the caboose.

When we got to the end of the hall in front of Mr. Will's sixth grade classroom there was nowhere else to go but down. Frances stopped at the top of the staircase. "Here is what I know. We cannot and will not try and cut through the sanctuary to save time. No matter what you may see or hear, we need to stick together. Our only purpose right now is to get to the cafeteria. Do you understand me?"

"Sure thing boss." Brady said. His voice was a mix of sarcasm with a serious undertone.

"Peter?" Frances whispered.

"Huh?" I said. It wasn't that I didn't hear her. No, the reason I said "Huh" was because I was distracted by those intensely sharp metal scissors that Frances had pulled out of her back pocket as she was giving us her next little tidbit of information. She was holding them tightly in her hand, but not by the oddly shaped holes where you put your fingers. She was holding them just below that. The way that Frances was holding those scissors told me that Frances wasn't ready to cut, she was ready to stab.

"Did you hear a word I just said?" Franny asked.

"Yeah, yeah, I heard you. Get to the cafeteria." I repeated.

I hooked my index finger routinely around Brady's belt loop and motioned for him to do the same to Frances. Our three linked chain started down the stairs and toward the cafeteria.

# CHAPTER 8

Do fish need it to be dark in order for them to fall asleep? Do they need to swim inside that little under water castle to get a decent night's rest? I mean they don't have eyelids. So it's not like they can close their fish eyes and ignore the bright florescent light coming from overhead.

I have to share with you that our school had a pretty cool aquarium. I think that it was initially set up by some of the preschool teachers and room mothers to show the little ones about fish and stuff. But everyone, parents, students, and teachers loved it so much that the fish inside got bigger and bigger and a lot more colorful over the years. Before you knew it, the small aquarium was replaced with a slightly larger one and so on and so on until it was the main attraction of the preschool hallway.

When the three of us had gotten to the first floor the soft blue glow of the aquarium light filled the hall. The church decided to leave the light on all the time to give the hall a natural night light. It was welcoming to me to finally be able to see more than just a few inches in front us and not have that constant fear of bumping into something and breaking our noses. But while I was feeling relief that was not what Frances and Brady were feeling.

"Oh no!" Brady said in a loud whisper. He had apparently remembered that along with fumbling around in the dark, we were also supposed to be silent too. "The fish tank light is on! It's supposed to be dark!" Then he did something that to this day I still think was kind of strange. He crouched down the best he could and put his hands on his knees. Then when he was all hunched over, Brady waddled toward the aquarium. I am guessing that it was his very bad version of sneaking unnoticed. "We need to turn off the light!"

"The light!" was all that Franny said. She was quickly passed by Brady, the hunchback of St. Thomas. She too made her way as quickly as she could to the aquarium, but she just walked to it at fast pace like a normal person. The closer she got to the lights that filled the hallway and the aquarium, the brighter the glint of the blue light reflected on the sharp point off the shears still in her hand.

"Wait for me." I said and tried to catch up to them. If I am going to be honest with you then I have to admit that my walk was probably a mix of the fast paced walk of Franny and the crouched duck-like waddle of Brady.

When I came to a stop in front of the aquarium I was surprised to see that both Brady and Franny were just staring into the tank instead of pushing each other over trying to press the little button on the top of the tank that would blink the light off. Instead, they were both bending over looking into the tank, studying the inside. Brady had his hands on his knees as he bent down, and Frances had her hands on her hips. Mrs. Anderson's scissors pointed outward and rested in her hand as she did.

"What's going on? Why are you guys not turning off the light?" I asked in a whisper.

"Look, Peter." Frances said and pointed to the tank. "Where are all the fish?"

I looked into the tank and knew that the fish that inside were trained to come to the front glass and then swim to the surface of the aquarium. They were nowhere to be found. The fish always went to the top knowing that where there were people, there would be food. The oxygen bubbles floated and popped rapidly at the top in the far left hand corner of the tank making a soft steady burbling sound, but that was all of the movement I remember seeing.

"There they are!" Brady said excitedly. It was if he had won some kind of hidden fishy game. "They are all over there in the corner under that piece of corral."

"Where?" Frances asked and moved in so closely that her nose bumped the glass.

"Right there, look." Brady pointed to the large dark blue corral that formed an arch. "They are all right over there."

"I see them." I reaffirmed. And I did see them. I couldn't tell you how many fish were in the tank that night. One, because the number of fish in a preschool fish tank changed all the time, and two, all of the fish in the tank were cramped in tightly as closely as they could to each other. Multi-colored fish darted and dived into and over one another, and all of the fish were swimming the same direction. All of them were facing the glass at the back of the tank. I remember seeing smaller fish trying to squeeze themselves between the fins and gills of the larger fish. Small pebbles were being kicked up slightly and resettled on the rocky aquarium floor.

"Is that all of them?" I asked.

"Yeah, I think so. Why are they all doing that?" Brady questioned. "Why does it look like they are trying to hide or something?"

"I don't know." I said.

"That's not all of them." Frances said in a slow sad voice.

But it wasn't sadness. I looked at Franny's face in the azure light of the aquarium. Her eyes were wide and unblinking. But she wasn't looking under the corral at the crazy collection of fish like Brady and I were, instead she was totally and completely focused on the filter. Inside the clear tube that sucked up the gross fish poop water and spit out the clean semi-filtered water, there was a silver and green striped fish. I don't know enough about tropical fish to tell you what kind it was, but I know it wasn't the "Dory" or the "Nemo." And then I noticed what Frances was so wide eyed about. You see, it wasn't just the silver and green striped fish that had made its way up the pipe and had gotten stuck. Above him was a light blue one, and at the very top of the filter was another fish, a black one. Well, I should say half of a black fish. The tail of the little black fish had been chewed off leaving only a tiny spinal cord and head. And as I looked closer, the silver and green fish was still alive and nipping at the tail of the light blue one in front of him.

"It's as if nothing is going to stop it from getting to the top. Even if it has to eat the fish in front of him." Frances said in the same eerie monotone. Her eyes had still not blinked.

"Come on. We aren't here to look at the fish. We need to get to the cafeteria. We're almost there." I said. I leaned over the two of them and clicked off the light. The florescent tube blinked a few times and then stopped leaving the tank dark. The darkness broke the trance and both Brady and Frances collected themselves.

"You're right." Frances said, the look of determination returned to her face. She tucked the scissors into her back pocket once again and started walking toward the cafeteria.

"Wait for me." Brad said and rushed to catch up to Franny. When the three of us were walking together again, Brady turned back to me and whispered in the dark. "Hey Pete, what do you think those fish were trying to swim to?" he asked me.

I gave it some thought. "I don't think that they were trying to swim to anything, Brady. I think the question is 'What were they trying to swim away from?'"

Saying that out loud must have really scared everyone more than we were all willing to admit, because no one said anything, and we walked in absolute silence until we got to the cafeteria doors. The good news about the cafeteria's double doors was that they are never locked, and it was one of those doors that are designed to swing both in and out. This meant that Frances didn't have to stop and fumble through her pockets to pull out the keys.

Every step that we took echoed in the openness of the cafeteria. The only light in the huge space came through the widows to the concourse, and even most of that was blocked by the thickness of the oak trees. Frances's shoes clicked on the linoleum. Thank goodness Brady and I were wearing worn out sneakers. So other than the occasional squeak, we were pretty much silent.

The familiar smell of grease and junk food filled our noses. Usually the students could tell what was for lunch that day before their feet hit the bottom step, whether it was the spices of garlic and oregano in the spaghetti and meat sauce, or the cumin in the ground beef of the crispy tacos. Sometimes the line leader in our class couldn't help but announce to the rest of the line what was being served that day. Of course he or she was immediately punished by Mrs. Anderson for talking in line and sent to the end of the lunch line to be our new caboose.

"Do you guys want to wait here while I go into the kitchen, or do you want to come in with me?" Franny asked.

"I'm still hungry. One little Reese's Cup is not going to fill me up. Maybe the lunch ladies left something in one of the walk-in coolers for us to snack on or something." Brady said.

"Come to think of it, it that might be a good idea if we all found a little something to eat. It's going to be a long night. Why don't we all go in the kitchen? Brady and I will look around for the food, and you can look for whatever it is you think we might need." I suggested.

"Ok, let's go." Frances said and pushed open the door that separated the tables and chairs of the cafeteria from the kitchen.

None of us had ever been allowed into the kitchen area of the cafeteria before. The closest that we had ever gotten was just peeking over the cold aluminum railing. All any of the students were allowed to do was grab a plastic tray and a set of plastic utensils and slide it down the metal rails. Just like it a public school cafeteria, the lunch ladies would ask you what you wanted and then slop it down on a plate that had a half dozen little square and rectangular compartments. The trays were always bright primary colors, which never made sense to me because nothing is less appetizing than your Swedish meatballs swimming in gravy on a green tray background. But I digress.

"I don't know where anything is around here." Frances said and started to open every drawer she could find.

"I know were the walk-in coolers are. Let's see what we can find." Brady said and led me quickly to the back off the kitchen.

"Wait! Franny, what are you looking for exactly?" I asked before Brady could pull me away.

"That's right. I forgot. The lunch ladies leave them on that long magnet by the sink. I had almost forgotten about that." Frances said to herself, totally ignoring me. She began to make her way to the oversized sink.

Above the sink were three long strips of wood with three long magnetic strips attached to them where the cafeteria workers kept all of the sharp kitchen knives. The bright idea was that you are more likely to cut your finger searching through a drawer for just the right knife, so it is better to hang them by magnets above your head.

"I hope we find some cheese." Brady said. His voice getting more and more excited as we got closer and closer to the cooler doors. "I could really go for some cheese right about now."

I followed Brady to the walk-ins. The cold air blasted the two of us when he opened the door. There was a little 40 watt bulb that screwed into the wall right by the entry that did very little to light up the room. Our school's cafeteria workers were pretty good at making sure that everything inside was labeled properly with the contents and date on each and every box or container. The church obviously didn't want any problems with the state health inspectors.

I have seen enough television the first ten years of my life to know that it is a bad idea to let the door of any kitchen cooler or freezer close behind you, because you will get locked inside. Locked inside, usually meant that you had to bang on the door with both fist until either you invented some weird contraption to jimmy the lock, or a dog came to your rescue. I didn't have the MacGyver like skills or a dog, so I held the door of the walk-in open the best that I could with my ankle.

"I found the cheese." Brady said his breath visible in the cold. He balanced a box full of individually wrapped string cheese between his shoulder and the cold wire shelving. "I think that there are some pudding packs back here too. Pete, help me get this box down, will ya?"

So, of course, Brady was exactly a half step too deep inside the cooler for me to reach him. As I pushed the door to the cooler out extra wide hoping that it bought me just enough time to help Brady with the box and still get back in time to stop the door from closing with my ankle, we both heard Frances scream.

"What was that?" I yelled. But by the time I turned around from helping Brady, the door had shut behind me. I didn't react in time to help Brady with the box of pudding packs either. Franny's sudden high pitched scream startled him too, causing Brady to flip the box in the air causing all of the pudding packs to come raining down on his head and on the floor.

"That was Frances!" Brady said in a panic. He did his best to step over the broken packs, but instead slipped and tripped over dozens of chocolate and vanilla pudding cups.

We both heard another scream and then another followed by a series of crashing and banging. It sounded as if Frances was either pushing or being pushed into the stacks of pots and pans. So much for trying to be as quiet as we could.

"Franny!!" Brady and I yelled from inside the walk-in.

But there was no response from the other side of the thick, heavy freezer door. As Brady and I screamed to get out of there we could see our frosty breath filling the tiny room. Just like in every sit-com I had ever seen, we were trapped inside. Both of us were banging with our fist as hard as two fourth graders could bang against the frigid metal door. Both of us still yelling Frances's name. *"Frances!! Franny!! Open the door!!"* The cold made our hands, our cheeks, and our noses red. Brady's sneakers slipped and slid on the dessert covered floor.

And then, just as quickly as it started, it all stopped. There was no more screaming. We could no longer hear Franny's voice or any noise outside of the walk-in cooler for that matter. But what was even stranger than that, the door to the walk-in cooler opened. Now, I don't know if Brady noticed, because to this day he has never said anything about it, but it wasn't as if it just unlocked and opened. No, it was as if someone on the other side of the door pulled it open for us. In fact, at first I thought that maybe it was Frances on the other side of the thick door tugging at the handle and helping us get out.

"Franny" I yelled. My voice echoed throughout the kitchen. The room held a soft glow of light that shone from the walk-in cooler's tiny 40 watt bulb, but the heavy door shut slowly eclipsing Brady and me in darkness once again.

"Pete, are you ok?" Brady asked me. He was holding on to me the best he could because his Adidas still had a thin layer of chocolate and vanilla pudding on the soles. "Did you see Frances?"

"No, I didn't see anything. Open the door to the cooler real quick so we can look around." I said.

Brady pushed down on the handle and opened the door a crack to release the light. It seemed to work, because the kitchen part of the cafeteria filled with long shadows. It filled with shadows, but there was no sign of Frances.

"Hold the door open, Brady, and I will take a look around. Maybe Franny slipped and hit her head or something." I said.

So while Brady did his best to hold open the door to the walk-in cooler letting all of the cold air frost in a misty fog around him, I began to look for Franny. Deep down even then I knew that she didn't just slip and fall. When someone slips, they make a totally different set of sounds. There is kind of a "Woah!" and then a bump. What Brady and I heard on the other side of the cooler door was more like a fight. It was a series of bumps and crashes, and unless Frances slipped, got back up, and slipped again a few times, this was no accident.

"Frances. Franny?" I whispered. This time I was the one hunched over for no reason. "Franny, are you there?" I listened for any little noise that might be her.

"Anything Pete?" Brady asked.

"No, nothing yet." I turned and answered. Then I went back to searching, "Frances, say something." I begged. I froze in my steps when I saw the crimson colored knife on the floor, and the sharp pair of Mrs. Anderson's scissors next to them.

"Peter, where did you go? I can't see you anymore." Brady said.

"Don't worry about me. I'm here, just hold on." I said back. The reason that Brady couldn't see me was because I had to bend down behind the large island cutting block to pick up the knife. I knew that that is where Frances was heading, but I never actually saw her get there and pick a knife off of the magnet. Then I noticed that it wasn't just the one butcher's knife on the floor, but all of them. A huge meat cleaver followed by a few fillet knives were also thrown to the floor and scattered about. My mouth was open and my throat was dry. I remember that my breathing was shallow, and I couldn't seem to catch my breath. I picked up the butcher's knife with my pinky finger and my thumb. I carefully held it by the wooden handle.

"What is this?" I whispered to myself. Sure enough, I could feel that there was something warm and sticky on the blade and more on my hand now too as I gripped the handle. "Frances?" I whispered even softer. The words barely made it out of my mouth. I carefully placed the knife on the cutting block. I needed to wipe the sticky yet slick feeling off my hand. For a brief moment, I was no longer thinking about Frances. All I wanted was to get my hand clean again.

"Brady, get away from the cooler. Don't worry about anything, just get out of the kitchen." I said. I turned from the huge block of wood and towards the deep metal sinks. I placed my hands under the faucet and turned the water on hot. "I'm just washing my hands. I'll meet you right outside the door. Don't go anywhere." I said to him. My back was still turned.

"What happened? What about Frances? Did you find Franny?" Brady asked. And although he was asking questions, I knew he must have been listening to me, because the kitchen began to fill with blackness.

I could hear the fear and confusion in his voice. I didn't turn around. I just needed to get clean. The water burned my skin, but it was a good burn, a cleansing burn. When I physically couldn't take the pain any more I pulled my hands back and turned off the water with the tip of my elbow. I ripped a few paper towels from the rack and dried my hands until they couldn't get any drier. In the darkness, I couldn't tell if I had gotten all of the mess off of my hands, in fact I was pretty sure that I still had some under my fingernails. But it would have to do for now.

I know what you are thinking. Did you grab one of the knives? And yes, looking back on that moment I agree, it would have been a great idea, but you know what they say about hindsight. At the time, I just wanted to get out of there and find out what had happened to Frances.

"Come on, Brady. We need to get out of here." I said to him. Brady was waiting at the exit to the cafeteria leaning against the door. He was doing his best to try and scrape off the chocolate and vanilla pudding on his shoes by using the corner of the door frame.

"What about Frances?" Brady said, still a little out of breath. "We can't just leave her here. We need to stick together remember?"

"She's not here." I told him.

"What do you mean? How do you know that? How do you even know?" He asked. His questions were getting more and more frantic. I knew that if we didn't get out of that cafeteria soon, he would have ran back into the kitchen screaming for her, and that was not a good idea.

"I just do, Brady. I just do. Now, come on. We need to get out of the cafeteria." I said, pushing him out the door.

The hall was pitch black, so we had to use the wall as our guide. My goal was to get back to the fish tank and use the light to gather myself. Thank goodness that Brady sensed my panic and didn't question me too much on the way back to the aquarium. I fumbled in the dark to find the little red button on the aquarium light. Once I did, the blue glow shining throughout the water and the hall was a welcoming blanket. I pretty much tripped over myself trying to beat Brady to the safety of the light.

"I am so scared, Peter. What was all that about? We just left Frances all by herself back there. I thought that the plan was for all us to stick together?" Brady questioned. He put his hands on his knees and tried to catch his breath.

He wasn't alone. I was panting just as loudly as he was. If I could go back to that time, I think that the one thing that I would work on is my cardio. I thought that I was in pretty good shape back then. I mean I stayed pretty active. I played outside a few times a week, I tossed the ball in the backyard, my dad and I even went hiking a few times up in the nature trails right outside of our old hometown, and I was never the one that had to stop for a break. It was always my dad. I mean I knew that I was in better shape than Brady, but I was wheezing and just as much out of breath as he was.

"We had to get out of there. Whatever was in there took Franny." I told Brady between my panting.

"What do you mean 'took Franny'? How can you even know that?" Brady was not only afraid, but now he was getting upset at me.

"Look, Brady. I think Frances was going to get the knives while you and I got the food. At first she couldn't find them, so I saw her head to the big sinks by the wall. The knives were on the magnet that the cafeteria ladies keep hanging over them. When we got out of the cooler, I went over there and all of the knives were on the floor! All of them!" I told him.

I could tell by Brady's face as it glowed in the blue light of the aquarium that he wasn't sure what to believe and that he was still processing the information. He squinted for a bit and then closed his eyes completely. The only other time that I had ever seen him do this was during our weekly spelling test. Whenever Brady didn't know how to spell one of our words from the word list, he would concentrate really hard and then close his eyes to see if the word would magically visualize in his head. I could usually tell how many he missed on the test before he even turned it in to be graded.

"Ok, ok. Let me figure this out. Just because we heard a noise, and you saw a bunch of spilled knives on the floor doesn't mean that Frances isn't back deep in there somewhere." Brady said. "We need to back in there for her. We need to see if we can find her."

"We both know that all of the screaming and noises that we heard was her, Brady. She wasn't playing around, and she didn't just slip and fall. She was fighting something." I said. I stopped to judge the look on Brady's face. I wasn't sure that he could handle the rest, but I knew that I needed to tell him. "And I think that there was....was something on the floor."

"What?" Brady said. "What did you just say?"

He had heard me, but I said it again. "I think there was something nasty on the floor. I'm not saying that there was, I'm just saying that there was something wet, Brady. Lots of it. It was all over the floor and all over the knives. When I picked one up, it was all over my hand."

"Did it come from her?" he asked.

To tell you the truth, I hadn't even thought about it. This whole time I just assumed that it belonged to Frances. Maybe it was the sounds that she made when she was screaming. Maybe it was the way her voice sounded through the cold metal door.

"I don't know." I answered him.

"Then we don't know. We don't know if whatever you had all over your hand was from her." Brady said. "We have to go rescue her."

"Don't you think I want to do that? Don't you think that if there was any chance at all that Franny was back there, that I would want to get back to the cafeteria and get her? If she was back there, then why isn't she out here with us now? We weren't quiet about it. We ran out banging into everything we could screaming the whole way. Why didn't she answer or yell out when I called for her?" My voice sounded desperate and although it was cool in the hall, I could feel the sweat beading up on my forehead. How could I get Brady to understand that going back to the cafeteria was a bad idea?

"Maybe she couldn't answer us. Maybe she hit her head on something and was knocked out or something." Brady said.

I didn't want to stand there in the preschool hallway and debate the pros and cons of going back into the cafeteria to look for Frances, and thankfully I didn't have to, because we heard her voice. It was faint but we both heard it. It wasn't so much as a whisper as it was muffled words beyond the walls.

The look that Brady gave me was probably the same look that I was giving him. Our eyes were as wide as saucers and our jaws dropped. We had both heard the distinctive sounds of Frances coming from somewhere far away, and not from the direction of the cafeteria.

It was just seconds after that that the fish in the aquarium started to move. Brady later told me that his eyes were transfixed of the small school of tropicals fighting to get under one another. Every fish fighting not to be the one on top. Each one pushing the tiny brightly colored pebbles around and trying to get safely under the coral. But that was not what I was looking at, I was looking at the filter. The silver and green fish was biting and chomping at the tail of the light blue fish in front of him. The little blue fish was flailing about trying everything it could to move forward, but it was pinned between the remaining pieces of the black fish in front of him and the silver and green fish that was eating him alive.

"We need to find her." Brady said and started to head toward the staircase and back upstairs.

"Where are you going?" I asked. Franny's voice had come from down the preschool hallway, so why was Brady heading up the stairs.

"What do you mean, 'Where am I going'? I'm going up the stairs to go get Frances." Brady said and put his hand on the railing. "Aren't you coming?"

"Brady, the noise came from down there." I pointed down the preschool hallway.

"Are you crazy?" Brady asked. "It came from up there near the top of the stairs." Brady continued to say half way up the steps. "Now, come on."

"Brady, I'm not kidding. I know that it came from down the hall. Why are you going upstairs?" I asked.

"So what do we do?" Brady stood near the top step. Both of us were certain about where Franny's voice had come from. "We both can't be right." He said.

The two of us were at an impasse.

# CHAPTER 9

Most of the time I had to admit that I was kind of the boss around Brady. Sure he was bigger than me, but that didn't seem to make much of a difference. Whenever I had a plan or an idea, he usually went with it. On the other hand, if Brady had an idea or a plan, we would talk it out and debate it. I guess that he was a little more of a pushover than I was. That is the reason I was so surprised when Brady stood on that top step determined to get his way. He was not going to budge on the fact that he had heard Frances's voice at the top of the stairs and that going up there was the only way to save her.

"Peter, I know it came from up there." Brady said and pointed to the top of the stairs and down the hall.

Our group of three was down to two, so there was no way that I was going to let Brady head up there by himself. "Ok. Let's head up there and see what we can find, but if we don't see anything promise me that we will come down here and check too." I said.

"Ok, deal." Brady motioned for me to follow him up the stairs and back to the classrooms in which we came. I am embarrassed to admit it, but he even held out his belt loop so I could hold on as we made our way down the hall. I'm even more embarrassed to admit I took it.

Without any of us saying it out loud, we all would have agreed that Frances, since the moment the outside doors shut behind us and Shane and the others were nothing but a mocking memory, was our leader. So here Brady and I were without our leader literally walking around blind. As Frances walked up and down the stairwell without tripping once and flawlessly turning our little group around the corners, Brady led me up to the second floor like he was carrying an octopus in one hand while struggling with a rock in his shoe.

"Ouch!" I whispered. "Watch were you are going."

"This isn't as easy as I looks." He exclaimed. "It's not like I'm counting my steps, you know."

"Well stop banging me into the walls." I begged.

"We're almost there. I can feel it." Brady said and made another sharp right hand turn up the stairs.

When he did that the handrail poked me in the chest. "Ouch! Come on, man"

"Shh! We have to listen for her." As Brady said this, his pace slowed to almost nothing, and he leaned in forward.

He was right. I know for a fact that Franny's voice had come from the preschool hallway, but that didn't mean that while we were upstairs we shouldn't be quiet and listen for it again. The hall was just as dark as it had been the first time, but now with Frances missing it seemed worse. It seemed quieter. And for some reason the face of Pastor O'Leary and those beady eyes came into my head. It felt as if he was watching us. I don't know how he was doing it but even down that long dark hallway I was afraid to look behind me. I knew that if I did, I would come face to face with O'Creepy's eyes and that tissue paper thin smile of his.

"The keys." Brady turned and whispered.

"What?"

"The keys to everything. Frances had them in her pocket. Did she drop them on the floor?" Brady asked.

"You mean while I was picking up the stained butcher's knife, did I stop to look for the Mrs. Hanson's keys to everything? You mean did Frances, while she was being attacked and probably killed by who knows what, think to drop the keys so that you and I could find them and use them to unlock our homeroom?" Is what I wanted to say. Instead all I said was, "No."

Oh my, I just thought of something. That was the first time that night that I thought that Frances might not just be missing. That instead, she might be dead.

"Do you think that Mrs. Hanson has another set?" Brady asked.

"I doubt it. Why would anyone need two sets of keys that open everything? What are we even doing up here, Brady?" I asked back. I couldn't see his face, and he couldn't see mine. It was impossible to see, and there wasn't a single sound coming from upstairs. The whole thing just seemed like a waste of time. Where ever Frances was, she needed our help, and she wasn't getting it with us just standing around like two idiots in the dark.

Against my better judgement, I followed Brady back down our hallway towards Mrs. Anderson's door. Both of us were trying to be as silent as we could be hoping to hear Franny's voice again. If we could hear her, than that meant that we could save her.

"H-e-e-e-e-r-r-r-e" The noise came from under our classroom door. Brady and I were still a few doors away, but we both froze. I don't know how long we were still, but I broke the petrified silence when I walked to our classroom and reached out to touch the door.

"H-e-e-e-e-r-r-r-e" It repeated. I jerked my hand back suddenly almost popping Brady in the face. This time the voice sounded less like Frances.

I wasn't sure if Brady believed his own words, but he began to talk to our classroom door.

"Cut it out guys. We know it's you Elizabeth. Ha ha, very funny. You got us. You can come out now." Brady said to the closed door. He cupped his hands together in a cone and put his mouth to the crack in the door jam. The cold air from the air conditioning inside blasted his lips. "We can't get in there you know. We don't have a key." He said jokingly and jiggled the doorknob.

"Pete." Brady said turning to me, and although it was dark, I could almost see the tears of terror on his face. He turned the doorknob slowly and completely to the right. Mrs. Anderson's room was open.

The arctic air from inside hit me instantly as the door to our classroom opened. The blast of the cold air was much, much more intense than it had been just a few minutes, or was it hours, ago.

"Pete. I didn't do anything, I swear." Brady said.

"Shh! I know you didn't. Let's just listen and see if we can hear anything from inside." I whispered.

The two of us slowly crept into the room as quietly as we could. I don't know about him, and I can't speak for Brady, but there was a part of me that was hoping to hear Frances's voice again, and part of me that wasn't. Don't get me wrong. I wanted to save her, but I never wanted to hear that creepy "H-e-r-e" voice ever again.

"I know it came from in here, but where?" Brady asked.

It was true. I don't know what the two of us were expecting to see when we opened the door, but the dark classroom was exactly the way it had been when we had left it earlier. In fact, it wasn't until that moment in the darkness that I remembered that Franny had also grabbed that flashlight.

"Kind of look around and see if you can find anything that shows that Frances was around. I know her voice came from somewhere in here, so just listen." I said.

I saw Brady's head nod his agreement in the darkness. He tip-toed toward the rows of desk, and the tightly stuffed bookcase along the back wall. I, on the other hand, headed toward Mrs. Anderson's desk. The only sound that I remember hearing through the deafening quiet was the shuffle of our feet and my own breathing.

Mrs. Anderson's desk was always spotless. They say that a cluttered desk is a sign of genius. Well, our teacher's desk spoke for itself. I went around to the back, past the line of tape on the floor and around to her chair. Mrs. Anderson's oversized chair had wheels on the bottom so she could just kick out her feet and push herself away from her desk. That is when I thought that I saw something. It was just a very slight something, but it was there. It was a shift of shadows. In the small space between the part of the chair where Mrs. Anderson rested her back, and the seat cushion with the permanent indention of her butt, I know that I saw movement. And I'm not talking about one of those corner of your eye type of movements either. I was right there looking directly at the chair, and I think it was looking back at me. In fact, my plan was to sit down and open Mrs. Anderson's desk drawers to see if maybe she had another flashlight, or lighter, or something that might give us a little light. I didn't know who or what was hiding under our teacher's desk. So I did the only thing I could think of to do, I asked.

"Franny?" I whispered. No answer. So I tried again.

"Franny?" I said a little louder.

I must have said it louder than I had thought, because the only reaction I got was from Brady across the room. "What? Did you find her?" He said in a loud whisper.

Ok, ok, I admit that I jumped a bit when Brady called out. Startled, I looked up into the darkness in the general direction of Brady's shadow. "Shhh! There is something under her desk."

At that exact moment, whatever it was moved again. It looked as if it was shifting its weight. It looked as if it was trying to crawl deeper under the desk, into the uttermost corner. Now, I positively knew there was something there. At that particular moment I didn't care what a pile of scrap paper hidden in the library said about turning on the lights. I was willing to take the risk.

"Hide your eyes." I told Brady.

"What?" He responded.

But it was too late. I reached over Mrs. Anderson's desk the furthest that I possibly could, and with the tip of my fingers found the light switch. The classroom was blinded with row after row of florescent light. I lost my balance and leaned forward, catching myself on the desk with my hands. My eyes were clenched tightly to keep out the light, but to be honest, it was also to prevent myself from seeing whatever it was hiding under the desk.

"Argh! What are you doing?" Brady said from across the classroom. "Turn that off!"

"Not yet! There was something under the desk. That is what I was trying to tell you. Something moved." I told him. Now, I would have thought that when I said that there was something under the desk that maybe Brady would have come running over there to help me in case we had to pull Frances out from hiding in the corner. Brady did just the opposite. Not that I blamed him. After all, I didn't say some*one,* I said some*thing.* Brady took a quick step backwards causing him to bump into the oversized bookcase.

"What is it?" He asked. His voice was high and cracked.

I gulped and looked down between the back rest of our teacher's chair and the seat cushion. Mrs. Anderson's desk was too big and too deep to see the back even when I bent down a bit. The only way that I was going to be able to see it all is to move the chair out of the way and bend down all the way down to look.

"Shh!" I put my finger to my lips and motioned to Brady. With that, I slowly moved the chair backwards and out of the way. The legs of the chair screamed in pain squeaking and fighting to stay safely tucked into the darkness under the desk. How long had the classroom lights been on? I had no idea. Why did Frances have the only flashlight? Why wasn't Brady over here helping me? He was supposed to be my best friend. My mind was racing causing me to hold the chair more tightly. My knuckles were ivory white, but I knew that to be sure I would have to keep pulling and look for myself.

"Nothing." I whispered to myself. I bent down with more confidence, no longer afraid at what might be lurking under the teacher's desk. "Nothing." I repeated a bit louder so Brady could hear.

"She's not here is she?" Brady said defeated.

"I don't think so." I answered.

Brady went to the closet and opened it widely. There were stacks of textbooks and teacher's additions of the books that we kept in our desk. There were papers and printouts. There were boxes on the very top shelf labeled and filled with decorations to match whatever the next holiday may be. But, there was no Frances.

Brady closed the door of the closet until it clicked shut, and then said, "I heard her, Peter. I know that it was her voice, so why isn't she in here? Why was the door unlocked? What did you see, Pete? What's happening?"

Brady was on the verge of a break down. His eyes were welling quickly, and as if I didn't know it before, I knew then that with our leader, Frances, missing, I was going to have to pick up the slack. I was going to have to lead and take care of Brady. I was going to have to make sure we could get out of here.

"It's going to be alright, man. I heard her too, okay?" I said and pushed our teacher's chair back up under the desk. This time the legs didn't fight or scream, but instead slid under softly like a child slipping under the cool covers to go to sleep for the night. "Let's turn these lights out and get out of here as fast as we can."

I waited for Brady to return everything in the room to where it was before we came in to look around. I, on the other hand, was standing at the door with my finger on the light switch.

"Wait, I have an idea." Brady said. He ran to his desk and pulled out a piece of notebook paper. With his Dinosaur Land pen, he wrote something on it and then he went to Mrs. Anderson's desk a tore a small square of tape. Brady then ran towards me and stuck the tape at eye level on the outside of the classroom door. "I wrote a note. Even if Franny isn't here now, it doesn't mean that she won't come by later."

Maybe I was wrong about Brady. Maybe I wouldn't have to take care of him after all, but maybe instead, we would take care of each other.

"That's a great idea, Brady. But, what does it say?" I asked.

"Well, we always said that the best move all along was to set up our camp by the couches outside in the lobby by the adult Sunday school classes, right?

I told her that that is where we would be, and that after she reads this, she should head that way." Brady told me.

"Brady, you sir, are a genius." I joked.

I turned off the lights letting the room once again fill with darkness and silence. Then I followed him out the door. Brady waited for me in the hallway to close the door, and although we couldn't lock it, I jiggled the doorknob a bit just to check and see if it locked instantly behind us. It didn't.

The hallway was as black as pitch, but I didn't seem to mind as much anymore. I guess that I was getting used to all the darkness. It was actually comforting after that blinding exposure to the light. I guess Brady felt the same way, because he was no longer concerned with which of us walked down the hallway first, or for that matter if we were even locked together fingers in loops. It wasn't until we got to Mrs. Vasquez's first grade class that I thought of something. And the slimy thought that slipped under the crack of my mind whispered in Pastor O'Leary's voice. "What if whatever took Frances can read? Brady just told whatever killed Frances where you two would be, and better yet, that you aren't going anywhere." He finished this thought with a cackle.

"Stop it!" I told the voice in my head. "Frances isn't dead! She is just missing somewhere. She will find us, and we all will be just fine. It's got to be almost morning." The closer that we got to the end of the elementary school hallway, and the closer to the library, the louder the voice of O'Leary seemed to get.

O'Leary was no longer whispering. "You wrote it all down! Your best friend just wrote your death note! And you will never see the sun again! It's not even close to morning Ol' Petey boy!"

"We need to hurry." I told Brady. "I'm starting to hate this hall." Brady didn't ask why and didn't disagree. Instead he grabbed my shirt with one hand and let his finger glide lightly over the light blue painted walls. At a fast paced walk, we turned the corner. We were no longer on the school side of the church.

But before we were out of ear shot, I heard Pastor O'Leary one more time calling out to me. His voice was fading and echoing down the long empty hallway. "We have her now! You little girlfriend is ours. Franny is dead! Franny is dead. F-r-a-a-n-n-n-y is dead!" He said in a sing-song kind of way, getting louder so I could hear the last verse of the chorus before I was too far and the sound melted into the walls and into the floorboards.

This side of the St. Thomas was reserved less for St. Thomas Christian Academy and more for the members of the church, mostly the church elders. There was always coffee available complete with your choice of assorted creams and sugars on the long, thin counter by the walls, and if you were lucky enough and got there early, there were even glazed or chocolate doughnuts on Sunday mornings. Of course that is what other kids told me. Do you know how early you have to wake up on a Sunday morning to beat a gaggle of octogenarians to a pink box of Rally's Doughnuts? Because if you do, tell me, because I have never seen it. Some say that the first sets of great-grandparents have been seen on a Sunday morning as early as 6:00 am.

The couches were made with thick leather, and the pillows were soft and fluffy. Some of them had been hand embroidered by the Ladies Auxiliary. The moment that Brady and I saw them in the shadows, we both knew that we were going to be alright. This was the plan from the beginning, and it was Frances after all that had us wandering around in the deep dark corners of the church searching after things like knives and flashlights. No, this was a better plan. Just stay here and wait out the time.

"Do you think Franny will find us here?" Brady asked.

"Sure, why wouldn't she? You told her where we would be in your note, right?" I asked back.

Brady didn't answer me, but silently sat at the edge of one of the couches. And yes, I did notice that it was the one that I had picked for myself earlier in the week. I didn't mention that or O'Leary's eerie lullaby that he was singing to me on our way here. I figured that poor Brady had enough to deal with, and he was feeling pretty good about himself for thinking about that idea to leave the note for Franny.

"Yeah, I did." Brady finally answered, "It's just that I feel like we just left her all alone back there, first downstairs in the cafeteria kitchen, and now in our classroom. She has been pretty nice to us the whole time considering, and I don't want her to think that we just abandoned her." Brady confessed.

"We didn't leave her anywhere, Brady. She wasn't in the cafeteria or anywhere in the kitchen. I know she wasn't. I'm sure of it. Just like you know that something grabbed your ankle." Yeah, I know that was a low blow, but I also knew that saying it would work.

I continued, "I admit that I heard her voice in our class too, but she wasn't there. She wasn't anywhere. What were we supposed to do, start knocking down the walls? And what do you mean *considering*?" I asked.

"You know what I mean. Peter. We weren't exactly nice to her. None of us were." Brady confessed. "Did you even know she was going to be here tonight? Because I didn't, and if you did know, why didn't you say anything to me?" Brady finished.

"I didn't know." I answered.

"And do you know why we didn't know? Because we didn't ask. We didn't even think about the fact that maybe were weren't the only new kids and that maybe we wouldn't be the only ones that would be here tonight." Brady said.

What could I say? Brady was right. I never even asked around. I never thought that since Frances was being treated the same way that Brady and I were day in and day out, that maybe I should have talked to her about tonight before it actually happened. I know now that it would have definitely helped if we would have talked to and worked with Frances. Maybe things that night would have ended differently, better.

To ease my guilt, I told Brady, "I was never mean to Frances." I no longer felt close enough to call her Franny.

"Yeah, but we were never nice to her either, were we?" Though the thick shadows, I saw Brady's head lower slowly. "When you are all alone, not being nice and being mean sometimes feel like the same thing." he said.

The next few minutes were quiet as I am assuming that Brady was doing the same thing that I was doing. Both of us were going through every day since school had started. Both of us going over the last few months thinking that we could have done something, anything that would have helped make Frances not feel as if she was all alone at St. Thomas. We should have let her know that she had a friend.

Brady broke the silence this time. His voice was shallow and tear-filled. "There was this one day when Franny was coming out of the locker room, and she missed a button. You know, on her Polo shirt. Not that I was looking or anything. Anyway, I saw it right when she came back into the gym, before she sat on the bleachers. I didn't say anything. When the other girls came out they started to tease her. The started to laugh and giggle at first. I knew by the way they were pointing and pulling on their own shirts that they had noticed." Brady shared. He was quiet for a second or two. He just stared at his crossed legs across the overstuffed cushions, and he picked at the loose rubber strip on his sneaker. I thought that he was done talking, and then he continued, "I didn't say anything. I should have told her. I should have said something, anything."

Even through the darkness I could make out the tears running down Brady's cheeks. His sniffles were muffled by his sleeve. "It's ok, Brady." I said.

"No, it's not. It's never okay." He said. Brady put his fingers to his eyes, pinching them tightly. It was as if he thought that if he pinched hard enough the image would disappear. "I'm sorry, Franny."

I reached over as far as I could in the dark to lean in and touch Brady's shoulder. I just wanted him to know that I was there, and I understood. "I did the same thing. Well, not exactly the same thing." I said. It was my turn to confess.

Brady stood up in the dark and walked slowly and deliberately to the window. When he pulled back the dusty, forest green curtains, the moonlight was muddy, covered with a thick grey mist. The night sky let in no relief from the darkness. "If it's going to rain, I wish it would just do it already." He said to the window.

I wasn't sure if Brady had heard me. Looking back now, I am pretty sure that he did hear me, because he didn't stop me when I started, he just stood there and listened. You know what's funny? I don't even think I was telling the story to him to begin with, just like he wasn't really telling his story to me. So I just started talking.

"Frances wrote me a note once." I started. Brady didn't turn around but instead continued to stare out the window. I continued, "It was about a month ago. You see, I was reading this book. It was about this kid that finds a magic ring or something, and the ring grants wishes. Well anyway, it was during one of our silent reading times after lunch, and Frances gets up to go to the bookshelf to get herself a new book. As she walks by my desk, she drops a piece of paper in my lap."

This part of my story must have interested Brady enough to finally look away from the second story window. He let the curtains drop heavily back into place with a flop. The tiny flecks of dust floating in the shadows to settle themselves on the sill. It wasn't as if leaving the curtains open to let the moonlight in would have made much of a difference anyways. Brady sat down once again and let himself settle on the floor, the leather cushions of the couch supporting his back. "What did the note say?" He asked.

"Well, I jumped a bit. I mean my first thought was what if someone saw? What if someone thought it was a love note and that Frances Maggie Lingersham was my girlfriend?" I know, I know that is a terrible thing to think, but remember at the time we were in fourth grade. "The next thing I wondered was what the note said." I continued my confession to Brady and leaned forward.

"And?" Brady leaned in too, matching my intensity.

"That's just it, Brady. I unfolded the note under the safety of my library book and read it. All it said was, 'I read that one too. Do you like it?' and then under that it had those little boxes." I said.

"What little boxes?" Brady asked.

"You know. Those little boxes that you are supposed to check-off. There was a box for 'YES' and a box for 'NO'." I answered.

"So what did you do?" Brady asked again.

"What is the worst thing that I could have done?" I returned with a question of my own.

Brady thought about it for a second or two, and then answered. "Well, it sounds to me that she really liked that book. I mean if she was willing to write you a note about it and risk getting in trouble and everything." Brady said. He knew as well as everyone else in class that if you ever got caught passing notes in Mrs. Anderson's class it meant three days of no recess and the note went on the bulletin board. That was so everyone could read it. "So I guess the worst thing you could have done was check the 'NO' box." Brady answered.

He was wrong. "I didn't check the 'NO' box, or the 'YES' box. I did something much worse. I read the note and then crumbled it up into a ball. I threw it away." I told Brady. "I didn't even acknowledge that she wrote me. I just threw it away like trash."

"You're right. That is so much worse." Brady said.

"Thanks! Thanks for that." I said sarcastically. I wasn't mad at Brady or anything. I just didn't like being called out like that. "Sorry. I'm just saying that we all could have been a lot nicer to Frances. It wasn't just you, and it wasn't just me. It was all of us." I concluded.

I remember listening to the wind rattling the tree branches making them scrape the window as it picked up outside. I don't know if I was listening for Franny's footsteps or the sound of her voice, but I do remember the wind.

In the weeks of planning, I always pictured Brady and myself sitting with our little lanterns all aglow; both of us at the coffee table playing cards and drinking root beers. I would try and make Brady laugh until it came out of his nose and burned his nostrils. There was a time that I thought this whole night might actually be fun. I thought that maybe Shane and the rest of the guys would come out of hiding and join us. That was the big secret St. Thomas ritual. The whole thing was just a tradition of an unsupervised sleepover. But now, sitting in the darkness of the adult Bible study rooms, listening to the wind and Brady pick at his tennis shoe, it wasn't anything like that.

As I stared upward, my mouth was desert dry, and I had nothing to drink. And because I emptied my pockets, I didn't even have any loose change for the soda machine. My feet were hurting from all the walking, crawling, and moving around the three of us had done since we got inside the church. I guess I mean the two of us now. I was so exhausted, but there was no way that I could sleep or even close my eyes for a second. Part of me was afraid that if I did close my eyes that I would open them, and Brady would be gone. I would be all alone.

"Not *all* alone." O'Leary's voice whispered in my head. Where had he come from? Was he listening to our confessions the whole time? The sound of his words chilled my bones and put inch high goose bumps across my arms. Thank goodness that Brady started to speak to free me of O'Leary's trance. Brady's words recued me and chased O'Leary's away.

"What are we doing?" Brady asked.

"What do you mean? We are sitting here waiting to see if Frances can find her way back to us. It makes a lot more sense than us wandering around the whole church and school in the dark bumping into who-knows-what and listening to the walls." I answered.

"No, that's not what I meant." He replied.

I waited to see if he would continue. When he didn't, I stopped staring at the ceiling and propped myself up. "What do you mean then?" I asked.

"What are we doing here? In the middle of the night, I'm sitting on the floor. We haven't eaten anything. We lost Franny. Why are we even here?" Brady continued.

Before I could answer him, he went on, "Just because Shane and his stupid friends won't let us play with them, doesn't mean we have to do whatever they want us to." Brady was sitting up now, his body was no longer slouched over the dark brown leather. "It's the middle of the night, Peter. We broke the law just because a couple of guys in our class told us to. Why?"

But it was more than just that. I don't know if Brady understood, but even back then I did. I knew that it was much, much more than just Shane, and Darrick, and the others daring us to spend the night in the church. What about Mrs. Anderson and coach? The way that everyone had treated us since the first day of school was not normal. What about the notes hidden in the floorboards of the library that Frances had shown us? Shane and Darrick didn't put those there. No, this wasn't just some dare. As I thought about all of that, there was something else that Brady said that moved me.

"How do you know?" I asked him.

"Because I'm here, that's how I know." Brady's voice sounded angrier, but he continued, "I am here because I was bullied into being in here. I let myself get pushed around until I ended up on this couch in the church on a Saturday night." Brady said.

"No, that's not what I meant. How do you know it's the middle of the night?" I clarified.

"What do you mean?"

"I mean, how do you know what time it is? Is it 11:00? Midnight? Two o'clock in the morning? Have you even looked at a clock?" I answered.

Brady thought about it for a moment. "Well, there is that big clock with the Roman numbers that I can't read in the cafeteria, you know the one that hangs above the door. What about the little clock that Mrs. Anderson keeps on the corner of the desk? Oh, and there is one in the library in the preschool section right next to that sign that reads- *It's always time for a book*." he said.

"And did you bother to look at any of those?" I asked.

"No, I guess I didn't." Brady said. His voice had slowed just a bit as he began to calm himself down. My guess is that he was mentally going back through his mind to each of those moments to try and remember if he had looked at the time at any point at all during the night. "No, I didn't." he said again.

"Well, I did." I said to Brady. You see, one of the things that I failed to mention before was that when Brady and I were in our classroom looking around in the dark for Frances, and I was building up enough courage to look for the creature hiding under our teacher's desk, I had thought about picking up that clock on Mrs. Anderson's desk and using it as a weapon. I knew that that cheap little plastic clock that probably didn't weigh more than a half a pound, but the sharp corners would have come in handy. The thing about it was that when I went to reach for that dollar store clock, it wasn't there. I knew that it wasn't there. For some reason, I didn't tell Brady that it was missing. I guess there was still that part of me that wanted to protect him, or maybe I just didn't want him to think that I was going crazy.

"And? So, what time was it the last time that you checked?" Brady asked me.

"That's just it, Brady. I couldn't tell you. I don't remember what the clocks said. I have no idea what time it is, so how are we to know what time we are supposed to go down to the back doors and be let out of here? I have no idea how long Franny has been gone." I said back.

"She hasn't been gone long. It couldn't have been more than a couple of minutes." Brady tried to reassure me. He stopped and stood up. Through the shadows I saw him stretch out his arms as far as they would go and then stick his hands deep in his pockets. "I mean we have only been sitting here for a few minutes, right?"

And here is the weird thing about it, I couldn't even tell. I can't really explain it now, but at the time, with Brady and me sitting there in the darkness huddled around the thick leather couches and the smell of stale coffee in the air I couldn't tell him how long we had been sitting there, because I didn't know.

"Yeah, it has only been a few minutes. We just sat down here." I lied.

"That's what I thought." Brady lied back.

I have this little game that I play in my head. It started when I was first learning how to swim and I wanted to know how long I was holding my breath under the water. I would close my eyes and try and count to sixty. I would count, "One Mississippi- Two Mississippi- Three Mississippi" until I got to sixty. Then I would open my eyes and check the clock to see how close I had gotten to one minute. I had actually gotten pretty good at it. I was usually only a second or two off most of the time. I'm sure that psychiatrist have some fancy name for it now, but back then it was called counting in your head.

So I sat there in the dark watching Brady pace in slow deliberate circles around the coffee table. Every once in a while, I would hear him smack his knee on one of the sharp edges, followed by a slight groan. The whole time that he was doing that, I was counting in my head. "One Mississippi- Two Mississippi- Three Mississippi and so on." It took Brady about twenty Mississippi's to make his way around the table. So three times around the table equaled a minute. So, I counted, "One, two, three, four," but every time I tried to count Brady's laps, I would lose focus or my mind would wonder, and I would lose count and have to start all over again.

"I'm going." Brady said. He stopped his laps around the table and sat on the edge of the couch. He grabbed a long rectangular pillow with the words "Lamb of God" embroidered on the side and held it close to his chest.

"What do you mean? Where are you going?" I asked.

"It's my fault that Frances is out there somewhere. If I wasn't always thinking about my stomach and instead tried to help Franny, then she would be right here with us. We would have a stack of food, plenty to drink, a flashlight, and not to mention a few knives or something to protect ourselves. Right now, we are just sitting ducks." Brady replied.

Now, I just heard about a dozen things that Brady had just said that I thought were insane. There was no way to know how this night would have turned out if Brady had not wanted to head straight to the cooler for some snacks, but I had a strong feeling that it probably wouldn't have been much different than it was right now. But I decided not to go into all that with him. I decided instead to see if he was willing to listen to reason.

"We shouldn't split up. If we do, Franny will read the note you left her and come here, and we will be gone. We can't do that, man." I said.

"You can stay here if you want, but I'm tired of leaving Frances all alone." Brady continued, "She is out there, Peter. She needs us."

Keep in mind, that we had no idea if Frances was even alive. And as much as I hate to admit it even now, from the sounds that we heard, I had my doubts. What was it that O'Leary was singing before? "We have her now. We have your girlfriend."

Before I could stop him, Brady was heading down the halls toward the main staircase. Here was the strangest thing about it all. As he walked down the hallway, he stopped, turned completely around, and came back to the coffee table. Now, at first, I thought that maybe Brady had indeed come to his senses and changed his mind. But without saying a word, he reached out to the middle of the table and lifted the small glass bowl of long dead potpourri. Brady poured out the dust covered flakes of wood shavings and the dehydrated orange slices onto the table making a tiny pile. Although it was dark, with his right hand, I saw him lightly bounce the thick glass bowl in his hand to get a good comfortable feel of the weight. He gripped it firmly in the palm of his hand. But that wasn't the strange part. Brady reached out with his left hand and picked up the King James Version of the Bible that was sitting quietly under all that potpourri. So, with the Bible in his left hand and the thick glass bowl in his right, Brady walked back into the darkness of St. Thomas all alone.

# CHAPTER 10

Before I tell you what happened next I guess I should warn you. What I am about to tell you happened exactly as I am telling you, but I am not forcing you in any way to believe anything that I say. I am about to share some things that in the past have had a tendency to lose some people, and this is the part of my story where some people just can't stretch their minds around. In fact, I have no idea how much of this story you are believing so far anyway, but know that everything that I am sitting here today telling you is true. It really happened exactly the way I am saying it did.

As I told you, Frances was missing for who knows how long, and part of me thought that she wasn't missing at all, but was in fact dead. Brady, who was not only my best friend, but my only friend was fading in and out of fourth grade bravery. Now, he had turned his back on me and was heading down the hallway in the pitch black looking for Franny. Not to mention not having a clue where to turn next. So, there I was sitting alone on that leather couch. What was I supposed to do now? What would you have done?

"Where do you think you are going?" I shouted to Brady as he quickly began to disappear down the hall.

"I'm going back downstairs to look for Franny." Brady answered.

"I know, but where downstairs?"

"I think I will start in the one place that Franny said we shouldn't go." Brady said.

"Where is that?" I persisted for the third time. At least he had stopped walking away and was actually taking the time to calm down a bit and talk to me.

"The sanctuary." Brady said and then turned with his back to me once again. "Are you coming?"

I didn't really have a choice did I? What was I going to do, just sit in the dark while Brady went off to get himself hurt or worse? So I looked around the room to see if I could find something, anything that I might be able to use in case of an emergency. I mean if Brady was going to carry around that heavy glass bowl and a Bible, I figured that I might need something in my hands too.

There was that pile of old potpourri that Brady poured onto the table (worthless), couch cushions (even more worthless), and that was about it. Then I saw the rows of cabinets under the coffee maker. I opened the doors of the cabinets and blindly reached around for anything that I could find that might have some weight to it. I knocked over the Styrofoam coffee cups and a baggie full of those little brown stir sticks. Finally I found something that I thought that I could use. The custodians had gotten tired of hauling their tool boxes all around the church to this corner and that every time that they had to make any small repair, so they had gotten in the habit of stashing tools that they may need all around. There was always a screwdriver or a hammer hidden here and there. You just had to get lucky enough to find one. I dug my hand deeper to the back of the cabinet and felt the handle of the steel monkey wrench and knew instantly that it would be perfect. I pulled it out and, just to feel manly, I smacked it a few times in the palm of my hand.

"Hold on. I'm coming." I said to Brady. One way or another Brady was right. We couldn't just sit there. We were going out and look around to find Franny, and we weren't going to stop until we did.

So there we were. Brady and I equipped with whatever we could find and for some reason or another, heading down to the sanctuary. I had a million questions for Brady, starting with what pocket did he find all of this hidden courage all of a sudden? And ending with something like, what are we going to do if we get there and Franny isn't there? But instead of rocking the boat and upsetting whatever gentle balance Brady and insanity were battling, I decided to just follow along for now.

There were two ways to get to the sanctuary from where we were. There was the long way and the short way. Now, the short way would have made a lot more sense and would have saved us a lot of time. The problem with the short way was that neither Brady nor I had only really ever went that way once before. There was this back staircase that did this strange twisting wind around. I think that a long time ago there was a big add-on to that part of St. Thomas, probably as far back as the 1930's by the look of the decor. And it also looked like, in order to save money, the church members at the time decided not to tear down the old staircase, but instead decided to build the new additions around it. So as you made your way about halfway down the staircase, it seemed to stop suddenly and just plateau. There was a long step in the center of your decent that didn't go up or down. You had to take a few steps and round the corner just to get to the next step down. I know weird, right?

Mrs. Anderson never took our class around this back way for the fear that we would mess things up. She told our class that some parts of the church were for "adults" and "not meant for children's grubby hands." Ok, so I had to admit that I was not yet an adult, and come to think about it my hands are usually pretty grubby. So, I kind of got her point. The only reason that I even knew where the back staircase led was because of that time that a few of the sixth graders were trying to earn their leadership pin.

So there was this whole week where they were in charge of taking our class and a few others from one place to another. I was supposed to teach them responsibility and leadership. Now, normally leading us from one place to another wouldn't have made a difference to our class or Mrs. Anderson, but one Thursday, Mrs. Anderson was called into the principal's office for an important conference call on our way to chapel, so Nora Cain and Emily Ronce thought they would have a little fun.

"Do you babies want to see something cool?" they asked our line as we walked silently single file to the sanctuary.

We were *not* allowed to talk in line, but what were supposed to do, just stand there and be called a bunch of babies? And come on, what fourth grader would have said no to that? "No thank you. I'm not really into 'cool' things." Yeah, right. For that matter, what adult would have said no to that? So, because we knew that Mrs. Anderson had ears like a bat and could hear a cricket blink from a 1000 feet away, we all just nodded our heads.

Well, that was enough for Nora and Emily because they both smiled at one another and turned our snake-like line around from one direction to another. Before Gerald, our line leader, knew it, we were heading quickly and silently down the back stairway. There was an echo unlike any that I had ever heard before or since. Sure you could hear the clumping of our shoes on the steps, but the strange acoustics only seemed to pick up every other step. There was no natural rhythm to our walking. The result of which made it sound as if our class wasn't walking, but instead stumbling down the stairs.

"Stop!" Nora said. We all stopped and stared at her intensely. "Now, I don't want you babies to start whining to your mamas or to your witch of a teacher. So just shut your baby hole, or I will have Emily here shut it for you. Do you understand?" Nora said and made sure to gaze directly into every single one of our eyes. She never blinked once.

We all nodded. Even Shane and Darrick dared not to question a sixth grader.

"This is where it happened." Nora began. Her eyes followed the room and the winding staircase from top to bottom. "Isn't that right, Emily?"

"Yes, right here." Emily added. She was quickly catching on to whatever Nora had planned.

Nora shot Emily a glance and then continued. "Anyway. The body of the little girl is buried under these steps. They say it was an accident, but most people know it really wasn't." Nora's voice was barely above a whisper forcing all of us to lean in to hear her words. "They fixed the stairs the best they could, but they just couldn't get them to line up just right." She said and pointed to the long step in the center.

My whole class was looking around at the architecture trying to solve the unusual configuration of the staircase. The railing was lower than it should have been. The steps from one to another were uneven and almost caused you to trip. Even the echo was a little off. The more we looked around, the more the whole thing started to make sense. She had us now. Nora could have said anything, and we would have believed it.

"You see that part of the stairs that just goes flat for no reason?" She asked our entire class. "That there is where they say her dry bones still sit." Her eyes closed slowly and reverently as if she was going to stop and pray for the poor little nameless girl.

Thank God that when the line stopped, I was two steps behind that flat part of the staircase. Everyone in our class bent and twisted themselves around the staircase so they could look at the exact part of the stairwell that Nora Cain was talking about. Sure enough, it was Frances and another girl that were standing frozen directly over the long flat step, and directly over the little girl's corpse. Everyone looked at the long step and then looked up to see who was cursed enough to be standing directly over it. Now, forget the fact that half of the line had already stepped on it, and forget the fact that the second half of the line would still have to step on it to get across. The point was that if you were standing there during the story, it was ten times worse. I mean everyone knows that, right?

Emily shook her head slowly and then broke the dead quiet. "Nora, we need to get them to chapel time." Looking back on it now, I could have sworn that she was trying not to laugh.

"You're right. Let's go." She motioned to Gerald, signaling to him to get the line moving. "Remember, don't tell anyone about this." Nora warned us all with a smile. She and Emily nudged each other all the way to the sanctuary.

I did my best to lightly tip-toe over the long step that was the final resting place for what's-her-name. I think that everyone knows that the lighter the footwork, the less chance of the evil seeping through the cracks in the wood and attacking you.

I don't think that our fourth grade class was ever more attentive in chapel than on that day. Although all of our minds were not on the lessons or the worship songs, I can guarantee that we never prayed as hard as we did that day. I know I didn't.

But like I said, there were two ways to get to the sanctuary. The other way was the long way. That was the way that we knew, it was the way we always went every Thursday morning for our morning chapel time. Tonight it would take us at least three times as long to get to the sanctuary, and I wasn't too crazy about the darkness or the walk past the library again. Of course, that was probably a lot better than walking over the dead girl's body just to save some time.

"What did you find?" Brady asked.

I had half jogged and half ran down the hall to catch up to him in the darkness. I raised the monkey wrench up to show him, although I doubt he could see it in the black that was our hallway. "I got this." I slapped the weight of the tool in my hands a few times to show Brady that I knew exactly what to do with it if I needed. Of course, in reality I would have probably thrown it to the floor and ran away screaming like a three year old girl.

"That'll work." Brady said satisfied.

I have to admit that I felt a lot better about walking around in the dark now that I had something heavy in my hands. Something that I could use just in case we ran into something that didn't like the idea of us being there at night.

"Brady, what are we going to do when we get to the sanctuary? Neither one of us has the keys to get in." I asked.

"I'm not sure yet." Brady answered truthfully.

That's exactly what I was thinking. I knew that the reality of Brady and his new found courage would eventually hit a brick wall. The fact was that the best we could hope for when we got down there would be to get to the sanctuary doors and knock. And I am not really sure that I would want someone or something answering that door to tell you the truth.

"Don't worry, man. We will figure it out when we get there." He answered.

I didn't think we would in fact "figure it out," but I was kind of liking the new braver, manlier Brady, so I didn't want to do anything to upset him. So instead of doing anything to discourage him, I continued to walk closely behind him, letting Brady lead the way.

I felt my stomach tighten and my legs start to shake as we rounded the final corner on our walk back to the front of the library. For some reason, our paths always led us back this way, and I for one was getting tired of it. I wasn't sure if I should start talking in order to drown out the voice Pastor O'Leary, or if the fact that I was making sounds at all would wake him and get his attention. Listen to me. Wake him. How could I possibly wake him? He was a painting, and not a very good one at that. In the end I chose talking.

"Hey, Brady." I whispered. "I think that we are doing the right thing. I think we are going to be okay. I think that we can handle this on our own."

Brady stopped and turned to me in the darkness. "We aren't alone." he said.

That scared me to death. I stopped walking and began to look around the best I could to see if I could see anyone else in the hallway. I could just barely make out Brady's outline a few feet in front of me and the shadows of two chairs and a potted plant at the end of the hall. The tall indoor house plant stretched its leaves like grey tentacles that hugged the chairs beside it. No matter how tired I might have been, there was no way that I would have stopped and sat in either of those chairs. No, I would rather have stood all night long than feel the slow moving leaves of that plant creep around my neck.

"What do you mean? Did you see something? Was it Franny?" I asked Brady in a rapid series of questions.

"No, Peter. We are never completely alone. God is always with us." Brady smiled and said. He held up the Bible. "He will never leave you or forsake you, right?"

Just because I went to a private Christian school did not mean that I grew up in a church. I knew all the big stories. You know, Noah, Moses and the like. And of course, I knew all about Jesus. But this was different, Brady wasn't just quoting something that we all had to learn as part of our lessons. He was actually using it. He had grabbed that Bible off of the coffee table not to use as a weapon, but to actually open and read from if he needed. Ha, so I guess he was going to use it as a weapon in a way, right? A sword to be exact.

"Right, good point." I said. I mean what could I say? At the time I have to admit that I didn't really see how reading a story was going to come in handy.

Brady didn't catch the lack of optimism in my voice. Instead he just smiled back at me and turned around to head down the staircase. Now, I guess my eyes were finally getting adjusted to the darkness because although I did hold onto the back of Brady's shirt, I really didn't need to. The steps heading downstairs were becoming more natural to me. The same confidence could be said about Brady, because even with his hands full he was able to make it down the stairwell in the dark without stumbling and without having to grasp tightly to the railing.

When we got to the bottom of the stairs Brady turned to me and said, "Ok, so here is what I figure. We will try the main entrance doors to the sanctuary and if those are locked, which they probably are, we will go around the side."

"That sounds like a good idea." I replied.

The truth was it was not much of a master plan. I mean what else would we have tried after we tried the front door? Walk away and say, "Well, I tried"? No, we would walk around to the side of the sanctuary and try another door, but I was humoring him.

I remember that the closer that we got to the sanctuary, the colder it started to feel. It was like walking closer to an open window to keep the chill out, but there was no window in the middle of the church. It was October, and that meant a balance of wearing a light windbreaker on one day and a heavy coat the next. We were still a few weeks away from the first real Northern of the season. But for some reason, the way that the air changed so suddenly reminded me of that wind. That being said, this was the first time that I noticed a chill in the air since we had left Mrs. Anderson's classroom.

"Is it just me, or is it freezing?" I asked Brady.

"Huh? What did you say?" Brady said. He had been lost in some deep thought, and I must have broken him out of it.

"I said, are you cold? For some reason, I just got super cold." I repeated.

"Yeah, I guess I am. I didn't notice." Brady said, but as said this, we were interrupted by an ear piercing sound. A sound that I can still close my eyes and hear today. The doors, thick carved wood, to the sanctuary shook on their hinges.

*Bang! Bang! Bang!*

The two of us stood there perfectly frozen just a few short feet away from the sanctuary doors. Whatever had made that noise was coming from just on the other side of those heavy doors. I couldn't tell by the sounds if something was trying to get in, or trying to get out.

"Stay away from the sanctuary." I whispered. Brady's face was so ghost white from the banging that came from the other side of the door that I could have sworn that he was glowing in the dark. Both of us were too petrified to move a muscle let alone be brave enough to grab for the handle of the door.

"That's what she said before she disappeared. Frances told us to stay away from the sanctuary." I said a little louder so Brady could hear me.

"Shh! It will hear you. I know what she said." Brady whispered to me. He put his finger to his lips to tell me to keep it down, and then pointed to the far left side of the sanctuary where the hallway seemed to curve. His hands still clutching the heavy glass bowl and the Bible.

I didn't have to ask him what he meant. There was no way that I was even going to try and open the main doors, and I guess Brady was thinking the same thing. Both of us tip-toed as silently as we could to the side of the sanctuary and around the corner. One the side of the sanctuary and just around the curved corner was the smaller side door that our pastor and other members of the church would use in order to come out directly onto the staging area. This door appeared on the outside to look like every other door down the long hallway, and although it was just as solid as the main entrance, it didn't have all of the fancy wood carvings that the main door had chiseled into it. The only reason that Brady and I even knew it existed was because of Larry the Lightening Bug.

About a month ago, there was a program at our school, and every grade from the littlest preschool class all the way through the sixth grade gathered in the sanctuary to listen to Larry the Lightening Bug talk about the importance of saving electricity. Come to find out later that this was a program that went to every school in town using some state grant that the electric company received. So Larry the Lightening Bug went out to every city in the area.

So there he was, Larry the Lightening Bug. He looked like a humongous neon yellow lightbulb with insect wings. There was a prerecorded song that Larry danced to as he pointed to the preschool kids in the first three rows. "Be bright! Turn out the light! It's all up to you!" the lyrics rang through the pews. It didn't take longer than the second verse before every kid above the second grade was bored to the point of tears.

"So remember kids. Whenever you leave the room, turn off the light." Larry repeated.

Most of the older grade school students in the back rows were too busy trying to figure out if Larry the Lightening Bug was really a girl or a boy under the costume. Most of the guys thought that the legs were too skinny for it to be a guy. While most of the girls thought that they would never get a girl to pretend to be a guy everywhere she went. Meanwhile up in the front rows, the preschool kids were hypnotized. They nodded in unison and utter amazement as the five foot six inch lightbulb told them what to do.

"Don't forget to strangle your little sister in her sleep tonight!" Larry the Lightening Bug could have said, and every one of them would have silently nodded their head in agreement. Instead Larry said, "Don't forget to only run full loads in the washing machine!" Keep in mind that these were kids starting about the age three, so it would have actually made more sense to tell them to strangle their siblings than to do a full load of wash, but whatever.

The whole painful program ended about forty five minutes later. And it just so happened that out of all the classes walking back to their classrooms, ours was the one walking right by that side door to the sanctuary as Larry had finished handing out his lightbulb stickers. The stickers were actually pretty cool. They said, "Lights On," but when you turned off the lights in the dark they would glow with the words "Lights Off." So anyways, there comes Larry waddling his way through the door, only instead of walking through the door, his huge bulbous head gets stuck in the door jam. Our whole class is in line trying not to crack up laughing or else face the wrath of Mrs. Anderson. Our principal, Mrs. Ramirez, and one of Larry's assistants run over to poor Larry as fast as they could and start pulling and tugging on his arms trying to break him free. The whole time Mrs. Anderson is staring at all of us with her hawk-like eyes just dying to swoop down and bust one of us smiling. Never once did she offer to help the lightening bug. Let me just say, that all of us found out that Larry the Lightening Bug was in fact a guy when he started using words that not only should you not say in front of a line of fourth graders, but also words you should probably not be saying in a church. That was when Mrs. Anderson marched our class back to our room double time pace, and also when we found out that that particular door leads directly to the sanctuary stage.

Since Brady's hands were full, I took it upon myself to try the knob. It turned with ease with a series of loud clicks. I have to admit that I was a bit surprised that it was unlocked, because it wasn't like we had been having the best of luck that evening.

"You ready?" I turned and asked Brady. I opened the door a crack as quietly as I could. The heavy door creaked and groaned as if it were an old man. I was listening for any sounds coming from inside that might indicate that Frances might be in there. I was also listening for any sounds that might indicate that I needed to slam that door shut, push over Brady, and make a mad dash as fast as my little legs could carry me down that pitch black hallway.

With one hand Brady held up the thick glass potpourri bowl, and in the other his Bible. "Yeah, let's go find Franny."

I guess that he was fine with letting me lead the way now. Because the next thing I knew, I was my turn to put my finger to my lips and this time let Brady know that we needed to keep quiet. So even though we had not read all of the notes and letters left in the walls of the library shelves, and contradicting Frances's warning, Brady and I entered the sanctuary making the biggest mistake so far that night.

# CHAPTER 11

First off, the staging area of the sanctuary was a lot larger than I thought it would be. When you are sitting in the vast open ocean of pews you can't really tell how big the stage is, or just how deep back it goes. Brady and I stood away from the side door letting it click itself shut, and moved more toward the center of the stage. We both felt naked and exposed to anything that may be in there with us, and I hated it. As we stood there silently about two feet away from each other, we both squinted into the darkness trying to let our eyes adjust to the chasm of a room. Both of us were too afraid to say a word, instead all we did was listen for the sounds of Frances, or anyone else.

I looked toward the left side of the sanctuary at the main entrance. The same double doors where that banging had come from. Nothing. I never wanted a flashlight more that night than I did right then at that moment. The last thing that I wanted to have to do was to walk off of the stage and all the way over there to get a closer look at those doors. But no matter how much I didn't want to get a closer look, part of me wanted to, no needed to, see what had made all that noise.

Brady reached over and gently tapped me on the shoulder. He looked me in the eyes and then pointed with two fingers to the floor. He mouthed the words "Stay here." Then he pointed to the stage floor by my feet.

"Where are you going?" I whispered. "We need to get down off of here."

Brady turned and whispered back to me, "Shh! I'm just going to go over there." He pointed to the microphone stand and the podium in the middle of the pulpit.

So he just left me there. I was standing near the middle of the stage fully exposed and now alone. The only way that I could have been more vulnerable would have been if I was actually naked. Hey Brady, do the words "Sitting Duck" mean anything to you?

As awkwardly and stealthily as possible, Brady hunched himself over and hid behind the pulpit. The large oak podium was used week in and week out by our pastor to share message after message of both God 's love and God 's anger, but right now it was being used by Brady as what I could only describe as a protective shield. He rested his Bible on the top of the podium and with just his arm showing, pulled down the microphone that was securely fastened to the upper right hand corner. He tapped it a few times making sure that it was on, letting the magnified thumping echo bounce throughout the room.

"We know you are in here! We both heard you knocking on the door! All we want is our friend back! Let her go, and there won't be any trouble!" Brady said. His voice was loud and rang off the side walls and ricochet off the thick wooden doors on the sides and the stained glass images in the back of the empty sanctuary.

"What are you doing?" I shouted!

"We are not here to hurt you! Just give us back our friend!" Brady's voice filled the room. He was no longer shyly hiding behind the podium. Instead he was standing behind it with one hand grasping the side, and the other waving the potpourri bowl.

"What are you doing?" I repeated. Only this time I lowered my voice letting it become a forced whisper. "Are you crazy?"

Bait! Brady, the only friend that I had in this stupid school, was using me for what could only be described as bait. Sure, it was his voice in the microphone, but it was my body standing on the stage fully exposed like that goat in "Jurassic Park."

"It's ok. I have a plan." Brady whispered back to me, but of course his whisper was picked up by the microphone. So that meant that if anyone or anything was in the sanctuary with us, it had just heard everything that Brady had just said. Not only that, I think I could guess what Brady's brilliant plan was. When whatever was out there in the room with us came forward to eat me, Brady was going to hit it over the head with potpourri.

So what would you have done? I will tell you what I did. I ran! That's right, I ran right towards Brady! I had to stop him somehow, and I couldn't think of anything else that might do it. So, I dove toward his legs to try and take him down before whatever was out there decided to answer Brady's challenges.

"Stop!" I yelled as we hit the floor. "What are you trying to do, get us killed?"

"I know what I'm doing, Pete." Brady said.

We were both on the ground. I had my arms around Brady's legs, and struggling to still grip the wrench at the same time. Brady wiggled and pushed to break free of my grasp, but unfortunately the thick glass bowl didn't survive the tackle. Both of us watched it roll and wobble down the steps and across the sanctuary floor. It stopped abruptly with a loud smack. The two pieces rolled in opposite directions each heading under a different set of pews.

"Thanks, Pete." Brady said sarcastically. He was clearly upset. He stood up and straightened out his clothes.

"I'm sorry, man. We don't know what made that noise, or what happened to Franny for that matter." I whispered. I helped Brady fix his shirt and handed him the Bible. "I just don't think that that was the best way to find out." I finished.

"I'm just tired, Peter. I'm tired of just waiting for whatever it is out there to come out. I'm just tired of feeling like a fool out here and just waiting for one of us to be next. I just wanted to take it to them instead. I'm sorry that I didn't tell you." Brady's voice began to calm down. "We're cool, right?"

"Yeah, don't sweat it." I reassured him.

The two of us walked down the center steps together. Whatever had made all of that loud banging sound at the door was not interested in Brady's little tirade and let the two of us calm down without an incident.

"I think we need to check out that door." I told Brady.

"That is a great idea. Whatever made that noise was bound to leave some sort of marks or something." Brady replied. "I mean he almost tore the thing off of its hinges."

Now, the shortest distance between two points is a straight line, so the best move for Brady and I to make would be to walk directly down the center of the steps and halfway down the aisle. Then we could take a sharp turn to the left, but in order to do that we would have to walk by almost every single pew and therefore be open to anything that happened to be waiting for us in the darkness. Thank goodness that the two of us still had some kinds of weapons.

Brady clutched the Bible in both hands and held it tightly against his chest. I, on the other hand, carried the heavy metal wrench like a club ready to swing it at anything and anyone that would dare jump out of the shadows.

"You take the left side and I will take the right. If you see anything, I mean *anything*, let me know." I said to Brady.

"Ok, but remember we are here to find Frances." He reminded me.

"True, but we are still going to have to deal with whatever made that noise and took her in the first place." I remarked.

I could tell by Brady's reaction that that didn't sit too well with him. He loved the idea of playing the hero and rescuing the princess. It was the slaying the dragon that Brady had a problem with. But still, he held his side of the deal, and we slowly and steadily started down the aisle towards the grand entrance to the sanctuary.

"What do you think made that noise?" Brady asked.

We were only a few steps into our journey, and I could already tell that his imagination was getting the best of him. The last thing that I needed was for Brady to start describing all of the creepy crawling creatures that could be lurking in the darkness. So, I didn't answer.

"Whatever it was it sounded big... ... and mad. I think it wanted to get out of here." Brady added.

"I think whatever it was banging on that door just wanted to scare us." I replied.

"Well, it worked." Brady said.

We were about half way to the door now. No Mans Land. There was no turning back. I could start to see the brass handles to the double doors giving off a dull shine in the shadows. The wooden carvings began to define themselves.

"What was that?" Brady said suddenly.

I turned to my left to try and see if I could find out what Brady was talking about, but there was nothing but endless rows of hunter green cushioned pews. Brady cautiously reached out his hand and touched the worn out felt.

"It was right here. It was sitting right here in the corner of this pew." Brady said and patted the seat cushion. "It was curled up like a kitten. When it saw me, it fell off the edge and ran under it." Brady said. He slowly peeked underneath the seats.

To my surprise, Brady wasn't afraid. If I had seen anything move at all, I would have jumped out of my skin.

"Maybe it was a rat." I said. I am not sure that made him feel any better.

"No, it didn't have a tail, and I saw its eyes. They were blue." Brady said without turning and looking at me. He was fascinated by whatever he had seen just a second ago.

"Maybe it was a cat or something. It probably just snuck in here somehow and found a place to sleep for the night. My neighbor used to have a cat that didn't have a tail. It got cut off by the garage door or something." I said trying to encourage him and at the same time convince myself that there had to be some logical explanation.

Now, I had no idea how a cat would have gotten into the church in the first place and not have been seen by either someone who worked here or by one of the hundreds of students. I also had no clue as to how the cat would have opened the fifty pound sanctuary doors. Not to mention the lack of any food or water in here. But hey, in the cold dark spooky sanctuary it was going to be a cat, because I don't think my fourth grade heart could take it being anything else. All I knew was that I was gripping my wrench a lot tighter.

With a quickened pace Brady set forth toward the sanctuary doors. He had seen whatever it was there was to see in here, and he was no longer afraid. Determined, he tucked the Bible under his arm and pulled on the brass handles of the sanctuary doors. The heavy doors pulled a bit in his favor, and gave about an inch or two but not much more.

"See, it was locked the whole time. We couldn't have gotten in from this way even if we wanted to." I said to Brady.

Brady slowly traced his fingers along the deep grooves of the dark wood. He let the smoothness and the subtle etchings guide his hand. His silence scared me. Brady was never quiet. It was actually one of the reasons that we had become friends in the first place. He was the one that first came up to me at the beginning of school and started talking. If it had been left up to me, I would probably have never said a word, and we would have never even met.

"Are you alright?" I asked him, breaking the quiet. "What are you doing?"

"It didn't want out." Brady said solemnly. He continued, "I thought that maybe it was Frances at the door, and that maybe she was scared or something. That was why she was pounding on the door like that. She had heard us heading her way to save her, and she was hoping that we would open the door." Brady took a deep breath and repeated, "But it didn't want out."

"What do you mean?" I asked. I couldn't figure out where Brady was going with this. "What didn't want out?"

He didn't say anything at all, instead he just looked at me without blinking as if it was up to me to figure it all out. When I couldn't make a guess, he flicked the deadbolt effortlessly with just two fingers unlocking the doors to the sanctuary. I am not kidding when I say that the door pretty much opened on its own.

"If it was Frances, she would have just opened it." Brady said. As if to emphasize the point, he flicked the deadbolt back and forth, locking and unlocking it over and over again. The steady clicking emphasizing his point each time. "It was banging on the door so we would run over here and open it. It wanted us to think that it was Frances and that we would just run over here and come inside. I bet the door was unlocked the whole time."

"But you just unlocked it. I saw you. If we would have tried the door, it would have been locked, Brady." I told him.

"No, it wouldn't have made a difference. Whatever took Frances would have opened it for us." He said.

Brady walked away from the double doors and sat on the corner of the closest pew. He rested his Bible on the seat beside him. I didn't know if I was supposed to go to him, or what I exactly I was supposed to say. So I didn't say a word and just quietly sat next to him.

"I don't know what to do now, Peter. This was my only idea, and it didn't work." Brady said. He sounded exhausted.

"Look, it was a good idea to come down here and look for Franny. So it didn't turn out, so what. At least now we know that she isn't in here, right?" I said as I put my hand on his shoulder to console him. "Let's just go back up to the place where we told Franny we would be. If I have learned anything about Franny, she is probably up there right now just waiting on us."

Before Brady could answer, we both heard the same thing coming from the front of the sanctuary. Someone was whispering very softly into the microphone. The entire stage was empty. The thin lights from the windows and dark shadows played with the shapes of everything on it. But there was one thing that I knew that happened when I tackled Brady to the ground to get him to stop talking. He had dropped the microphone on the ground. I remember the dead thump followed by the low pitched hum of the reverb. And when I squinted my eyes and looked closer, there it was still lying dead on the floor, its long cord trailing off into the nowhere like a long rat's tail.

I shrank down in my seat as far as I could go and peered over the pew in front of us. Hunched over, I motioned for Brady to do the same. He bent down silently, and we both listened as intently as we could.

"I can't make it out." Brady whispered to me.

"Shh! It sounds like Frances." I whispered back.

And it did sound like Frances, but not like just her just casually talking though a microphone. If that was the case her voice would have been booming throughout the sanctuary, bouncing off the walls and echoing off the ceiling. No, it sounded as if she was still too far away from it, and the microphone was just barely picking up where she used to be. Her voice was distant and sounded electric and mechanical. There was still no mistaking that it was her. But unfortunately, it was just almost impossible to figure out what she was trying to tell us.

"I'm not here. I'm not here." Brady said under his breath.

"What?" I asked.

"That's what it sounds like she is saying. 'Oh Peter, help us.' That's what she is saying." Brady repeated her words and buried his head to cover his ears the best that he could.

Brady reached over to the seat beside him and put the Bible on his lap. His legs were shaking so nervously hard by then that the book almost fell on the floor a few times. He would catch it at the last possible second, and pull it back in closer to his body, but his knees were moving so fast that it would quickly work its way down again and slip back down.

"I don't think that is what she is saying." I told him. You know how if someone tells you to listen to something it sounds like nothing but garbled words and static, but then after they tell you what to listen for, that is all you can hear. It's like if you look at one of those optical illusions, you can't see anything at all, but then someone says, "It's a rabbit, see!" then you see the rabbit and can't understand how you could have missed it? Well, that is the way it was that night with the sounds we heard coming from the microphone. We both knew it was Franny's voice, but we both heard different things. You see, I heard Frances saying, "I'm *in* here. I'm *in* here." over and over again into the dead microphone, but after Brady said, "I'm not here. I'm not here." that was all I could hear.

I didn't know which of us was right, but I was sure hoping it was me. "She is saying 'I'm *in* here', not 'I'm *not* here.'" I tried to convince Brady, and to be honest, I was also trying to convince myself.

Both of us were too afraid to peek over the pews in front of us to see if anyone was now standing on the stage. But in the end, I decided to be the man and do what had to be done. I told Brady to just stay there and not to move. I told him that I would be right back and for him to not be afraid. I told him that I would handle this. So, I grabbed my wrench as tightly as I could with both hands until I could feel my knuckles turn pale. The black rubber handle felt nice and firm in my hand, and the weight of the metal gave me confidence. I slapped it against my palm a few times, and then I stood up slowly.

Now, I can't remember if I had my eyes completely open or not. I couldn't tell you what I saw through all of that darkness even if I did have them all the way open. I do remember that they were open enough that I was looking down the aisle with determination, then with my head focused down toward the worn carpet, I ran as fast as I could toward the front of the sanctuary and towards the center of the stage. I wasn't worried about whatever made the loud banging on the double doors, or the strange catlike thing that Brady had seen napping out of the corner of his eye. It was my turn to stand up and be a man. It was my turn to be brave. I was starting to feel the way that Brady had just moments ago when he had lead us here in the first place. I was tired of being afraid, and I wanted some answers. But more importantly, I wanted Franny back.

I stood at the top of the steps overlooking the entire sanctuary. I stood there silently and listened as intently as I could hoping to hear Franny's voice again. That was when I remembered the microphone on the floor. There it was still on the ground in the exact place that Brady had dropped it. Although distant, that is where her voice had been coming from in the first place, but there was no one else around on the stage, there was nothing up there with me. I bent down to pick it up.

"Hello?" I said. The sound of my voice amplified and carried. "Is anyone out there? Can anyone hear me?" I heard my voice echo back to me as it passed over the rows of pews and bounce itself off the huge stained glass images on the back walls.

So, I waited for what felt like forever. The sound of my voice gave Brady enough confidence to raise his head. His hair was an island above the sea of pews. But other than that, there was nothing.

"France? Was that you? Can you hear me?" I said a little louder than before. "We're here for you!"

I listened to my last words once again bounce off the back of the sanctuary. Brady watched me silently. Even in the darkness I could make out the wide whites of his eyes. Every once in a while I could see the shadow of his head shifting first left and then right searching the empty room for any answers to my questioning.

"Brady! Do you see anything? Can you hear Frances from there?" I called. I could hardly see anything at all even though my eyes had adjusted to the shadows. Brady's head nodded slightly. Was that a "yes"? Was that a "no"? I just couldn't make it out. I just assumed that he was too afraid to yell out and answer me. His head moved in what looked like little circles. What was wrong with his neck? What was he doing?

"Brady, say something. Can you see Frances? I can't tell what you are trying to say." I held the microphone firmly to my lips, and I was getting more comfortable to the amplified sound of my voice. I squinted the best that I could and noticed that Brady's head still bobbed up and down and then side to side as if it was just balancing itself on his neck like a ball on the head of a pin.

"What is that supposed to mean?" I asked. Ok, this was just getting ridiculous, and now I was getting mad. Why wasn't Brady answering me? I know now that it was both fear and stress causing me to get so mad at Brady so quickly. At least that is what my last three therapist have said. But all I knew at the time was that I was tired of playing games.

I slid the microphone back into its little black plastic holder on the corner of the podium. It squealed and squeaked its disapproval of being once again constrained. I leaned into it to give Brady one last chance to answer me. "Brady it is way too dark in here to try and play your little game, so just tell me. Can you see Frances? Did you hear her?" My voice boomed into the microphone.

Nothing.

"Fine." I whispered to myself.

Still mumbling, I made my way back down the center aisle once again. This time I was in no hurry as I had been before. Brady's was still there, his head still rolled loosely around his shoulders.

"Cut it out, dude." I said.

Nothing.

I remember that I was about half way up the aisle on my way to Brady. He was still sitting stoic on the back pew when something ran across my foot. I jumped out of my skin and dropped the wrench just a few inches away from my shoes. My first thought was that a rat had scurried across the aisle, and my second was that maybe it wasn't a rat at all. Maybe it was Brady's little cat friend.

"Woah! What was that?" I screamed. With my heart racing a mile a minute, I bent down to pick up my wrench. I was amazed about how quickly it had become my security blanket. "Brady!" I shouted, "You will not guess what just happened. I think whatever was sleeping on the pew just ran right in front of me. It scared me out of my skin." I joked.

That part of the night was actually pretty funny. This whole night had us all nervously walking on egg shells, so that any little sudden movement had us all jumping and screaming like a bunch of little preschool babies. I felt pretty embarrassed by the whole thing to tell you the truth. I mean the whole building was over a hundred years old, so there was no telling what might have been living in those walls. What do they always say? It's not the one pest you do see, it's the dozen family members that you don't.

"Don't worry, Brady. If that thing comes at me again I will be ready." I said, and I beat the wrench on the corner of the wooden pew a few times for good measure.

Nothing.

"Did you hear what I said, Brady? I said I would give him a few smacks with this here wrench." I giggled and did my best mob enforcer accent.

Nothing.

"Brady?" I questioned.

His head was no longer peeking over the back of the seats. I couldn't see his hair bobbing and wobbling in the shadows anymore. Maybe he had just gotten spooked when I yelled and had ducked back under the seats. Maybe the stress was getting to him again. I took a few more steps quietly towards him, first one step then another. Each time I passed the next set of pews I would lightly tap the back with my wrench. My mouth went desert dry, and I could smell the electricity in the air, like burnt wires.

My legs wouldn't move. I was only three steps away from where he was, and I couldn't move. I also couldn't see him. I looked on the floor hoping to see his sneakers or some other part of him trying to get under the pews. Nothing. I licked my lips, and my dry mouth filled with the taste of copper pennies. I had to brace myself by holding on to the polished wood of the pews so I wouldn't fall over.

"B-B-B-rady?" I whispered. I could barely hear the sound of my own voice. So I tried again. "Brady?" I said softly.

Nothing.

I will never forget what happened next for as long as I live. I remember biting my bottom lip and taking the last three steps. The wrench felt so heavy in my hand that I couldn't lift it. It fell weighted at my side. My heart was pounding! I'm not talking beating in my chest. No, I'm saying that although I was only in the fourth grade, my heart felt like I was fifty years old, and I had just sprinted around the football field after drinking three cups of coffee. I could feel it pulsing red in my ears. It was the only thing in the silence of the sanctuary that I could hear.

When I had reached the pew in which Brady was sitting and waiting for me, every fiber in my being screamed for me to close my eyes, to not look. My hands were shaking when I slowly reached down. The hairs on my arm stood on end and started to burn. The combination of the electricity smell and my own burnt hair made me gag. I pulled away and looked at the empty space. Brady was gone.

This time wasn't like it was earlier in the cafeteria with Frances. With her I was locked in the cooler. At least Brady and I thought it was locked. I never actually saw what happened to her because I wasn't really there. But with Brady I was right there. I was in the room and saw him sitting there even as I was walking towards him. I saw his head moving until the very last moment. I only took my eyes off of him for a second, for half a second. And the only reason that I did was because of that thing that ran in front of me and over my shoes.

*"Brady!"* I screamed. I no longer cared about the volume of my voice. The tears were rolling down my cheeks too quickly to care. What reason

did I have to keep my voice down? Everything that I had had been taken from me. I was all alone.

"*Brady!* Where are you?" I screamed. I'm not too ashamed to admit it now, but at that moment I was a blubbering idiot. I could barely understand my own words through all of the drool and snot. I was scared and alone, and all I wanted was to be warm and safe at home under the cool blankets of my nice soft bed. I just wanted to get out of there, forget my bike and run as fast as I could all the way to my front door. Instead, my knees gave out, and I hit the floor.

I had never fainted before or since that night. And ideally, I would have been out all night and not awoken until the next morning, but I was not that lucky. But I knew by the way that I was lying there on the floor that I hadn't just slipped and fallen. I had lost time. The back of my head throbbed in pain, but thankfully when I touched it to see if I was bleeding, my hand came back dry. I painfully did my best to pull myself up. Every move I made was an effort, and every sound I made still echoed throughout the empty sanctuary.

"Hello?" I said.

My voice was weak, but at least I sounded like myself again. I wiped the slobber from my mouth with my sleeve and took another deep breath. The air no longer tasted of burnt wires and pennies. And for the first time since Brady and I had stepped foot into the sanctuary, I felt a sense of calming peace.

"Brady? Frances? Are you out there? Can you hear me?" I said. Deep down I knew that I wouldn't get an answer, but I had to try.

I picked up the wrench off of the carpet and began the long trek to the stage once again. My pace was quick, and I was determined to do what I needed to do. Nothing jumped in front of me, and nothing echoed through the microphone. I remember picking up the microphone out of its cradle and speaking very clearly.

"Brady, Frances, I walking out of here now. I don't know where you are or what is happening, but I do know that I shouldn't be in here. Frances, you were right. We should have never even walked in here in the first place. Brady, you were right. We should never have stopped looking for Franny. I'm going to fix this! I'm not going to give up until I fix this! Do you hear me out there? I will not stop until you give me back my friends!"

There were no more tears on my face, and my voice was strong. Once I decided to stop thinking about myself, everything that night changed. Well, I take that back. When I was standing on that stage listening to my voice amplified like a king, I thought that everything that night would change for the better, I couldn't have been further from the truth. But hey, I was just a kid, and I had seen way too many movies.

The microphone once again squeaked and squealed angrily, protesting being put back in its plastic restraints so quickly. I looked up at the dark stained glass of the sanctuary and smiled. I couldn't make out the scenes through the thin moonlight that shone through them, but I knew that even through the darkness they were there. After a deep breath or two, instead of walking down the steps and through the double doors, I left through the side door that Brady and I had come in. And what could only have been a few minutes of time, seemed like hours.

I was lost. There was no mysterious voice guiding me in the darkness as to what to do next. No map was written on the notes left behind in the library. I had no idea what had happened to Frances or Brady, so I did the only logical thing there was to do. I went to get myself a soda.

# CHAPTER 12

One of the coolest things about our church was that it offered free coffee and tea to new visitors. We had this one section that was right off of the sanctuary that was made to look like someone's living room. I guess the purpose behind it was to make the new people that can to visit feel comfortable. So we had what most of the students called the Starbucks. There was a couch and a few overstuffed chairs along with a coffee table or two. Along the back wall was a coffee maker complete with everything you would need to make yourself a monster cup of Joe. Do people still say that, Joe? There was also an inverted glass bulb that had a silver spout at the bottom. There were a few older ladies that would put fresh iced tea with lemon in it every Sunday morning so visitors could make themselves a nice glass after the service.

On the walls were Bible verses about being good friends and good neighbors. And in one corner, there was a cork bulletin board that kept every church member updated with whatever happened to be going on that month. Since this was October, most of the news was about the fears of the satanic Halloween, and the church's healthy and wholesome alternative, Trunk-or-Treat. Trunk-or-Treat was the exact same thing as trick-or-treating, but families just parked their cars backwards so the trunk faced out. Kids in costumes would go from car to car asking for free candy. Don't ask me how handing out candy from the rear of your SUV was any less evil than handing it out from your front door.

Now, what I failed to mention earlier was that this room was actually going to be my first choice as a place to hold up for the night, but I knew that Brady had really terrible allergies, and once said that just the smell of the coffee would kill him. He didn't think that he was allergic to the actual coffee bean, but he also didn't want to risk it. Personally, I like the smell of coffee way more than I like the taste.

I mean staying in that "Starbucks" would have been perfect. There was the exact same set up as was upstairs by the study rooms, but down here they had sodas. You see, along with the counter full of caffeinated drinks for the adults, there was also a Coke machine in the corner. Believe me, there was a lot of controversy throughout St. Thomas about whether or not to put a Coke machine in the visitor's center. Most of the arguing wasn't about the sugar laced sodas as much as it was about the way the big glowing rectangle made the room look cheap and gaudy.

What most kids didn't know was that if you and your family came to our church to check it out and stayed behind to head to the visitor's center afterwards, you could score yourself a free soda. The pastor and the rest of the church would never ever hand a little kid a hot coffee, and because the ladies didn't want little kids messing with and eventually breaking the glass bulb full of tea, they stashed a little red plastic box under the counter. The church didn't want the adults to get a free drink from the church, but then have to turn around and make them pay for a soda for the kids.

"Hello, and welcome to St. Thomas. We are so happy that you came to visit our church today. Would you and your family enjoy a beverage?" Pastor Martin would say with a smile.

"Why yes, I believe that my family and I would love something refreshing to drink. I do feel a bit parched." The father of the visiting family would remark. He would then pat his son on the head messing up his hair.

"Well in that case, you and your wife help yourself to some hot coffee and some homemade sweet tea." The pastor would say and wave a hand towards the beverage counter.

"Thank you so much. That is so very kind of you. What a wonderful church you have here. But what about junior here?" Father would inquire.

"Oh, I'm so sorry. We have a soda machine, so you could *buy* junior a Sprite for only a dollar." Pastor Martin would answer.

Ok, so maybe my imagination was a little off. The point was there is no way that the church is going to make junior's dad pay for his own drink. So what a few of the church elders did was hide that little red box in the cabinets under the counter. It was filled with loose change that Pastor Martin or anyone else could use to show visitors that our church was hospitable to children too. Just not their teeth.

The only reason that I even knew about it at all was because it wasn't but a few months ago that my family were the ones making their way to the visitor's center to shake hands with the pastor and possibly score a free drink. And although my mom politely declined the offer, I still got to see where they stashed the money when Mr. Looper one of the church deacons opened the cabinet and shuffled some quarters and dimes in his hand.

The other great thing about our church's visitor's center was the fact that it had no door. Oh yeah, this was another big controversy that made its way through the ranks of the church. Now, I had to admit that this time both sides of the argument had good points.

You see, this is the way it all worked out. There was one side of the argument that wanted there to not only be doors to the visitor's center, but also that those doors should be locked almost all the time. The argument was that if you were going to offer free coffee and free tea and soft warm places for people to sit and read, then no one would ever want to leave. In fact, some people in the congregation thought that if the place was too comfortable that the church members would be in there all the time and there would be no room for visitors to come in at all. They argued that old men would just sit in there all morning long sipping coffee and hang out. Then when some visitor did happen to stop by, he or she would think that they were in some important business meeting and walk away not wanting to disturb them. But in reality, the old men would be just sitting around talking about knee surgeries and sports.

The other good point that was made was that someone would come on in if there was no doors and steal stuff. Sure it might only be a few plastic cups and nondairy creamers, but the point was that that stuff adds up over time. Not to mention the two to three dollars' worth of coins hidden below deck.

The other side argued that the visitor's center shouldn't even have doors on it at all because Heaven forbid if someone was to come by during the week seeking salvation and a tea, and find that the doors to both may be locked. They brought up the point that we never know when Jesus will send someone through our doors, so we as a church should be always ready to receive them. I never quite understood that part because the church itself and the sanctuary had doors and locks. Not only that, but one whole side of St. Thomas was banned from having any visitors at all because no one is really even allowed into the school part of the church during school hours just to keep all the students safe. But for some reason access to coffee and tea should always be open and available.

So after several committees and multiple debates, the senior members of the church decided that it was just not worth the risk to have someone come in and find the room locked up like Fort Knox. That is why the room not only does not have locks, but it doesn't even have doors. Crazy hippies! (For the record, they had to replace the coffee maker four times in the first three years after it had been repeatedly stolen.)

With wrench in hand, I made my way into the room and to the coffee counter. The whole place had the wonderful aroma of coffee that had permeated itself into the cushions of the sofas. I remember not really being afraid in there until it was time to open the cabinet. I mean looking back, anything at all could have been lurking in the darkness behind the couches just waiting to pounce out and grab me by the throat. But at the time all I could think about was how dry my tongue was getting. Does stress do that?

The Formica countertop was smooth and cool as I ran my fingers across it. Most of the supplies for fresh coffee were depleted and not going to be replenished until early Sunday morning by whichever parishioner noticed it first. I reached over and let my fingers glide over the side of the smooth, clear glass tea dispenser that had been wiped crystal clean. I remember getting a thrill touching the taboo glass, the bulbous glass forbidden for children to touch. The huge bulb precariously teetered on its pedestal, and instantly I knew why it was not allowed to be touched by anyone under the age of thirty.

I was fully expecting something to jump at my face when I opened the cabinet door. My mind flashed to the thing sleeping furry and curled in a ball at the corner of the pew. I saw it jumping in surprised shock when Brady put his hand too close. I knew that I had seen the same cat-like creature run in front of us as we made our way down the aisle. I fully expected its blue eyes to be glowing back into mine when I opened the little door. But when I slowly and carefully opened the cabinet door nothing attacked me. The wrench was wet in my palm and sweat dripped down my cheeks. My fear had gotten the best of me.

I fumbled around in the dark cabinet knocking over towers of Styrofoam cups and boxes of stir sticks looking for the little red box. Now, the whole thing could have been over in just a matter of seconds, but I was still heeding Franny's warning about not turning on any extra lights. You could never be too careful, right?

"Oh, come on." I whispered to myself. I mean it had to be in there. Unless Shane or someone else had thought about it ahead of time and came up here and cleaned it out. That would be just like him to not only shove us in here for his own amusement, but also to steal money from a church. No, what am I saying? Shane wasn't like that at all. He was the leader of the fourth grade, but he wasn't mean. Not really. The more time that passes the more I realize that Shane wasn't really the bully that I made him out to be all those years ago.

Finally my fingers bumped the little box, and I heard the change jingling inside. "Yes!"

I took the box of quarters and dimes to the soda machine and began sifting through the change. The soft red and white glow from the sideways Coke symbol gave me just enough light. The quarters slipped in the slot one after another. Clunk-Clunk-Clunk-Clunk. The soda machine was a hungry rectangular monster eating coin after coin, and I loved feeding it. I have never heard anything more satisfying than the hard thump of the aluminum can as it hit the tray at the bottom.

*Pfshhhht!* The carbonation sang. I brought the cold Coke to my lips and drank deeply. The bubbles tickled my nose.

"Do you really think that you are helping your friends, Peter?" A voice whispered in my ear.

I screamed and dropped my can of Coke, spilling it all over my shoes. Whoever had said that was inches away from my ear. My flesh was covered in goosebumps and every hair stood on end. I swatted the space by my left ear like I was swatting a mosquito, as if somehow that would help make the sound go away. It was a good thing that I didn't swing my right hand instead because I was still holding the wrench, and would have knocked myself out.

I let the soda bleed itself out on my foot. I was too afraid to bend down and pick it up. All of the sudden the bright refreshing light from the sideways Coke symbol no longer seemed so friendly and inviting, instead it turned everything it illuminated a dark crimson.

"Who said that?" I asked absolutely no one.

The only thing that I heard reply was the low electric hum of the cold soda machine. I gripped my wrench tighter and tighter in my hands as I bent down ever so carefully to try and salvage what was left of my drink. The Coke can was sticky, and I took the last remaining sip.

"Hello! I heard you. I don't know who said that, but I will find my friends. Do you hear me?" I said to the empty room. I was doing a lot of talking to myself lately.

In order to gather my nerves and catch my breath, I had a seat on the edge of the couch. My knees were shaking so loudly that I am sure that I could hear them. My hands were shaking even more than my knees. I had thought about maybe getting some more change out of the little red box and buying myself another Coke, but in the end I decided against it.

Something was trying to communicate with us. What us? I was the only one left. My little group of Three Musketeers was down to only one, me. And the more and more that I thought about it, the more I was thinking that the sounds that Brady and I had heard when we first made our way down here was not Frances at all. I started to think that someone or something had been playing with us from the very beginning. I decided at that moment that I was not going to jump and scare myself the next time it tried to speak to me. As hard as it was going to be, I would not try and overreact the next time it called.

What was that Bible story that our class had learned a few weeks ago during our school's chapel time? There was a kid, and God kept talking to him every time the kid went to sleep. That kid kept popping up over the covers and asking if anyone around was calling his name. And every time he was told, "No, go back to bed." After like the third time of hearing a voice call to him from his bedroom, someone finally told to just lie there quietly in the bed and just listen. It worked. He just relaxed and listened to what God had to say. That was going to be my plan too, although I had no doubt in my mind that whoever it was that was trying to get my attention was not God.

I didn't have to wait long. Before I knew it, I could hear a voice. It was very, very distant at first, a whispered whisper. But unlike the last time, I didn't overreact and start screaming. Instead I pretended to sip from my empty soda can and acted as if I did not hear. Sure enough, it worked! The whispers became louder, and then they came in a little louder still. This time

I could tell that it was more than one voice having some kind of conversation. The sounds were coming from more than one person.

I struggled to make out what they were saying. Although it was still very distant I could hear someone saying. "Do you think he can hear us?" the first voice was asking in desperation.

"Do you think he knows how close he is to finding us?" The second asked in turn.

The voices were still so faint, so far away that I remember moving my head in and angling my ears like a dog listening to a call whistle. The first voice sounded higher like that of a female, the second not much lower, but still sounded male. I carefully put my sticky can of soda down on the tiny round table to my right and pretended not to pay attention to the conversation.

"We need to speak louder if we want him to be able to hear us at all. We might not get another chance at this. The vail is so thin now." The male voice said.

"This is as loud as I dare get. They might hear me." The female replied back to him.

"We have to make sure he can hear us if we ever want to get out of here." The male replied soon after.

"Oh, I just can't hold it in any longer. This might be our last hope." the female voice started. "Help us, Peter." The girl's voice said. Only this time it was louder than before.

"Maybe if we try together." The boy suggested.

The two voices came together as one, "Peter! Can you hear us?" This time it was at full voice. It sounded as if they were right there beside me sitting on the soft couches across from me. The two of them were no longer whispering.

It took everything in my power not to answer them. I wanted to say "Yes! I can hear you! I'm right here!," but there was also a part of me that wanted to start screaming "This is insane!" and start waving my wrench around like some kind of ancient club. Instead, I did neither of those two things. I sat there quietly and let the two of them continue their conversation.

"It's no use. He can't hear us." Her voice was small again returning to a distant whisper.

"We tried. We will just have to try something else. We can't give up, Franny." The boy said trying to console her.

Wait, what was it that he had just said? What did he say at the end? Did he say "Franny"? It wasn't just any girl's voice calling out my name in the nothingness of the room, it was a girl that I knew. And not only that, it was Frances! That had to mean that the boy's voice that I heard wasn't a stranger at all. That had to be the sound of my best friend! Why had I not been able to identify them at first? The sounds must have been too distant, too muffled somehow for me to make them out.

I was so excited, but I didn't want to scare them away. And from what they had said earlier, they were not alone. Someone or something else was with them. And whatever that was, they did not want to raise its attention. So, I took the wrench and placed it gently across my lap. I leaned back into the center cushions of the couch. Even though my insides were tumbling like a cement mixer and I was as nervous as I had ever been that night, on the outside I wanted to at least give the appearance of not caring. Finally when I thought that my breathing was calm and my heart rate had slowed a bit, I decided to answer them.

"I can hear you." I said as calmly as I possibly could.

I waited. Nothing. Maybe I had waited too long. What if they were gone? Maybe I should have shouted out their names and begged them to give me a clue, any clue that could help me save them and help us get through this night. Man, how could I have ever been so stupid? Before I could say anything else, she answered.

"Peter? Is that you?" Franny asked.

My pulse quickened, and my mouth went dry. The sugar from the Coke just burned my throat and made me even more thirsty. I caught myself breathing faster and faster through my mouth instead of my nose. I took a long deep breath and answered her.

"Yes, I can hear you Frances." I said. My heart was beating through my chest as I leaned forward ever so slightly.

"Hee-hee-hee. Yes, finally! Oh Peter, I'm so happy." Frances's voice was full of relief but still sounded miles away.

I waited to see if she was going to say anything else. I could hear her talking to someone, but I couldn't make out the words. She was still too far away.

"Is Brady with you?" I asked her.

"What? Oh, oh yes… …and no! He is here too, but so far away. Come quickly. You have to save us, Peter." She answered.

This was it. Things were finally starting to go the right way for the first time tonight. I was getting so tired of just running around the church and bumping into walls. I was tired of stumbling around the school half blind and without any sense of purpose. My new plan was simple. I was going to find Frances and Brady, find the doors to the outside, and get out of this place. I didn't care what Shane, or Elizabeth, or anyone else in my class thought about us "new kids" anymore. I just wanted to get my friends and get out of here. I just wanted for this night to be over.

"Can you see me?" I said and for some reason looked up towards the ceiling. "Where do you want me to go? Frances?" I grabbed my wrench and slowly stood up.

It was Brady's voice that I heard this time. "No, no. We can't see you. We are lost in here. You have to find us. It's so very hot, Peter. So wet, so hot." He sounded weak.

Where in the building could they be? I thought about all of the places in the church that we hadn't been yet. The problem with that line of thinking was that there were hundreds of doors that I had never opened, so there could be at least that many possibilities.

Brady had said that wherever they were it was hot and wet. If it was hot and wet where they were being kept that meant that they could only be in a few places around St. Thomas. My mind went first back to the kitchen. Maybe Frances hadn't been taken from there in the first place. Maybe Brady was right when he said that we shouldn't have ran out of there so quickly. If Frances had been in the cafeteria stashed away somewhere, we owed it to her to have at least checked out every corner before I made us run out. Now, I would have to go back to the start and look all over again. But on the other hand, Brady had only been a foot or two away when he disappeared, so how could he be in the cafeteria?

*"What if that wasn't Brady you saw sitting in the back of the sanctuary?"* A voice that sounded a little bit like mine and a little bit like O'Leary's whispered in my head. My fearful subconscious was beginning to mix with O'Leary's evil words.

Of course it was Brady. I was sitting right beside him and only left him there for a second. I went straight up to the center of the stage. I mean I saw him looking at me when I was up there. He moved his head when I asked him questions. I mean it was just plain silly to think that it wasn't him sitting there.

*"You didn't see his face."* The voice seemed to say with a grin.

While it was true that the sanctuary was very dark, and I really couldn't make out anything past the first two or three rows. I know I saw Brady in the back of the room. He was definitely back there sitting on the last pew watching me as I made my way to the stage.

"You saw someone in the back of the sanctuary. But he didn't say a word, did he?" The voice, now solely O'Leary's, was growing more and more confident.

No, I wasn't going to let myself get caught up in all that. I was just going to tell myself that it had been my friend Brady the whole time, and that is all there was to it. At least now, knowing what I know, I can say that, but the truth was much, much more disturbing.

Where else could they have been taken that might have been? Brady said it was hot and wet where they were being held. So if they were not in the kitchen where they washed all the dishes and pots, which could only mean that they were in the boys' or girls' locker rooms off of the gymnasium. The elementary students were not allowed to use the shower areas, but the upperclassmen were required to shower after their athletics class. If you have ever been a fourth grade boy, you know that one of the most terrifying things in your immediate future is knowing that you will have to be naked in front of your classmates in just two short years. If you think that fourth grade bullies can be tough, they are nothing compared to a locker room full of awkward puberty. But because our gym time was right after the middle school, the locker room was still hot and steamy with a combination of hot water, teenage sweat, and too much Axe deodorant spray.

Brady had said that he and Frances were together. I could hear them talking to each other, so what if they weren't in the boys' locker room? What if they were in the girls' locker room? This thought brought on a whole new set of fears that I had yet to have that night. I would rather be stuffed in a gym locker with a used jock strap in my mouth, than set even one tiny toe in the girls' locker room. And I know if I were to take a survey of all my fellow male classmates in Mrs. Anderson's fourth grade class, I would not be in the minority on this one. After everything that we had had to go through so far this night it would be just fitting that I would have to make my way through the entire church and then back through the school just to end up end the girls' locker room. "Is that what this is all about?" I said aloud.

"Hurry, Peter." Franny's voice broke my thoughts like glass. "It's so hot down here."

There was one more place that I can't believe I didn't think about until I heard Franny's voice say something very specific. She had said the words, "down here." That could only mean one thing. They were not being held in the cafeteria, or the locker rooms. They were in the basement. To be more exact, they were in the boiler room.

# CHAPTER 13

I know you have seen all of those horror movies where the killer is lurking in the darkest corners of the boiler room. Well thank goodness, that as a nine year old, my parents had done a really good job of sheltering me from the likes of Wes Craven, and the melted face of Freddy Kruger. But that didn't mean that I thought the boiler room was any less creepy.

There was a door in the far corner of the church that we students never went near. For one reason, it was nowhere close to the classrooms or the school part of the church. So that meant that on your average day, there was no real reason to be on that side of the building or anywhere near that door. The other reason that the students never went by that door was because that is where the custodians would hang out and try to escape during their breaks.

For the most part the custodians were always supposed to always look busy. You know, walk around with a broom or a mop and look as if they were right in the middle of some major cleaning project. If they did this, both the church staff and more importantly the old ladies of the church wouldn't have any reason to question why they were "just standing around the halls watching the carpet grow." But every now and then they were allowed fifteen minutes or so to just hang out and take a break. This meant going down to the boiler room.

A few of the custodians had set up an old rusting aluminum card table a couple of those cheap fold-out chairs that had been left out in the rain so long that their green paint had flaked away and replaced by copper colored rust. They would go down there to sneak a smoke and talk about "those stinking Dallas Cowboys" that had blown another game on the television the night before. I'm also sure there were a few ribbings about which of the guys had struck out the weekend before with whatever girl they were dating.

The boiler room was always steamy hot and reeked of a wonderful combination of cigarettes, turpentine, and industrial cleaners. Sure, it probably wasn't the best place in the building to store shelf after shelf of flammable liquid, but this was before there were things like OSHA breathing down your neck and regular fire inspections. The guys would half sit and half balance on those broken down chairs with the cigarette smoke rising just inches away from who knows what might ignite.

I forgot to tell you how I knew all of this. Like I said, it wasn't one of those places that we fourth graders would regularly hang out. But that was also before our classmate Sally Hale almost died.

You see, Sally Hale was allergic to almost everything. If our class went outside for recess or we went outside for PE, Sally would have to put on her raincoat and mittens. She would also have a floppy sun hat covered with brightly painted sunflowers that was supposed to protect her from the brutal rays of the sun. That's right. Sally Hale was allergic to the *sun*. How anyone can make it to the fourth grade allergic to the sun is still a mystery. But that wasn't all. She was also allergic to peanuts, eggs, pork, bee stings, shellfish, and the color red. Yes, you heard correctly. She was allergic to the color red. Ok, Sally could touch the color red, but she couldn't eat it.

So of course everyone in class had to get to the bottom of that mystery. I mean what shades of red could she eat? What would happen if she did eat anything red? I think it was about the second or third week of school when all of us in Mrs. Anderson's class found out all about Sally's sad affliction.

"Can you eat an apple?" Shane asked her one day in the cafeteria. Well that one question started an avalanche of others.

"What if it's a green apple?" Brady followed up.

"What about hamburgers? I mean it started off red, but then you cook it and it changes to like a brownish grey." Someone else asked.

Now, I thought that those were all really good questions, but instead of just answering them, Sally started to cry. And I don't have to tell you that there is nothing on this earth worse than a crying girl. People will do just about anything to stop a girl from crying. First her eyes started to turn red (I have to admit that I thought that might have been an allergic reaction to just questions about the color red.), then they started to get watery, and the next thing our class knew, Sally was bawling.

Shocked, everyone's eyes grew to the size of large circles and no one wanted to be called out by Mrs. Anderson for making Sally cry, so everyone buried there head down pretending to look for something buried in the back of their lunch box, or looked around the cafeteria at anything but her. The object was to try and ignore her. They all went back to eating their lunch as fast as they could, because no one wanted to take the fall for making Sally Hale cry. A few of the teachers made a mad dash across the cafeteria upon hearing the noise to make sure that Sally wasn't hurt.

"What about the color pink?" Brady asked not quite picking up on the severity of the situation.

Before we knew it, Mrs. Anderson had grabbed Shane by the earlobe and Sally by the wrist and was dragging them both down the hallway. Our class could only assume that their next stop would be the principal's office. The rest of the lunch period was spent in awkward silence.

About a week later, Mrs. Anderson reluctantly helped Brady's mom, Mrs. Heath, pass out Spiderman cupcakes. It was Brady's birthday, and his mom dropped off a big box of cupcakes with different images of Spiderman or the Green Goblin on them. This was part of a little class party for all of us to enjoy at the end of the day. That was kind of the rule. You were only allowed to bring sweets for your birthday if you agreed to hand them out at the end of the day. That was so that you would go home all hyped up on sugar, and the teachers wouldn't have to deal with you.

So there we all were sitting at our desk all awaiting our cupcakes afraid to move or make a sound. Yes, even when we were supposed to be having a birthday party it was terrible dictatorship. "*The fun will begin now!*" I could hear Mrs. Anderson say. Ok, maybe that is a slight exaggeration, but not much of one. So much for Brady's class party. That is when Derrick had an idea.

"Let's give her this one." Darrick said and held out a Spiderman cupcake.

Brady's mom really went all out on those cupcakes. They weren't the ones that I was used to from the local Super Store bakery. No way, these were the fancy handmade cupcakes made by Angela's Cakery. Each and every individual cupcake was different from the last. Some of them had Spiderman's mask, others had just a web. For the Green Goblin, some had the evil smile of the Goblin, while others had a close up of the jack-o-lantern bombs that he uses. All in all, they were some of the best looking most beautiful cupcakes that I had ever seen, and as a guy that is not easy for me to say.

"Let's see what happens." Darrick continued. The cupcake he was holding was an image of Spiderman's web shooters. Although most of the picture on top was grey and blue, if you looked closely enough to the details you could make out a thin red line that traced the entire image.

Shane agreed, "Ok, hand it to me."

Darrick instead of handing the cupcakes down the row the way that he was supposed to, gave the web shooter cupcake to Shane who sat across from him. Shane placed it at the corner of his desk and held on to it for a bit. After two more cupcakes headed down the row, he looked at Darrick and winked. The thin red lined cupcake passed behind Shane to Brenton who in turn passed it behind him to Sally.

"We still have so much to do before the end of the day class, so eat your snack quickly." Mrs. Anderson said.

Mrs. Heath almost made a remark about how birthdays only come around once a year, but after noticing the stern and serious look across Mrs. Anderson's face, she decided against it. Meanwhile as everyone was gorging themselves on birthday cupcakes, Shane and Darrick were only nibbling on theirs, and carefully watching Sally to see if she would explode!

"She's taking a bite." Shane whispered.

Sally chomped away at her cupcake. She let the icing kiss the tip of her nose as she took bite after delicious bite.

"Nothing's happening." Darrick whispered back.

I remember first noticing Sally grip her stomach and then she started to turn green. I didn't claim to know how allergies work, but this was unlike anything that I had ever seen before. Sally Hale was punching her own stomach. Punch after punch Sally balled up her hand and hit herself in the gut a little harder each time.

"Help! It hurts! My stomach hurts!" Sally started screaming.

Now, everyone in class was watching her reaction and starting to get really scared. My first thought was that if your stomach hurts then you should probably stop punching yourself in the gut.

"*I'm getting sick!*" Sally said right before she blew chunks.

Everyone jumped horrified out of their school chairs trying to get as far as they could away from poor Sally Hale. We all started screaming and running around the room. We had a monthly fire drill so we would know exactly what to do in case of a fire, but we never even once had covered a barf drill. Mrs. Anderson did the best job she could to keep the class under control, but was a lost cause. Most of the girls in class tried to make it to the door so they could get out of there and make a run for it. A few of the girls who had a little more self-control went into mother mode and grabbed the tissue box off of the supply desk and the trashcan from the corner of the classroom to catch what they could, but this was going to be like trying to cork a fire hydrant. Some of the boys jumped on to their chairs and screamed like the girls, and others did everything they could to keep from laughing.

"Oh my! Someone help her. Oh the poor baby!" Brady's mom screamed. She ran over to Sally and tried to do anything she could to help.

*"Stop!!!!"* Mrs. Anderson yelled.

The entire classroom froze, including Mrs. Heath. Later, some of the second graders told us that they could hear Mrs. Anderson bellowing all the way down the hallway through their door.

"Every single student will sit down in their chairs and not say a single word." Mrs. Anderson said calmly.

Very quietly and slowly our class made it back to their seats. Most of us had dropped our fancy Angela's Cakery Spiderman specialty cupcake half eaten on the floor, and the few kids in class left that still held it in their hands only had to look at the wet mess or just get a whiff of the sugary chunks Sally had sprayed on the carpet before walking to the garbage to throw theirs away.

"M-M-Mrs. A-A-nderson? My chair has stuff on it." Brenton raised his hand to say.

She took a look at the rainbow mess dripping down his chair. "Fine, you can sit in the corner until we get this mess cleaned up."

With the class now seated quietly, and Sally now just silently sobbing in her seat everything was status quo. She had apparently gotten rid of every ounce of red frosting. It was out of her system, and it looked as if she was going to make it through. Well everything was status quo with the exception of Brady's mom who was still in shock, but still managing to gather her purse and hand our teacher the bag of Spiderman party favors to give out after the bell rang.

"Brenton since you have nowhere to sit, and Peter since you look as if you are ready to be sick too, why don't you two find a custodian to clean this situation up. And be quick about it." Mrs. Anderson said.

You didn't have to tell either one of us twice. We would do just about anything to get away from that smell. "Yes, ma'am" We said together. Brenton and I jumped out of our seats and ran down the hall.

Now, finding a custodian in our church is much, much harder than finding Jesus. If you want to get Jesus's attention all you have to do is ask, but in order to find a custodian, well that usually takes a little detective work.

"You go down that hall and I will go down this one." Brenton said as he rounded the corner to the left.

"Ok, that sounds good." I answered, but I have to admit that my pace was a little slower, because I was still trying not to throw up.

Less than two minutes later we were both standing outside the library without any custodial help. That could only mean one thing.

"Smoke break!" We both said at once.

Brenton and I ran down the stairs skipping as many as we dared without breaking an ankle. Although we weren't caught running the halls, we both figured that it would have been alright if we were on the count of this being an emergency and all. As we rounded the last corner on our way to the boiler room, we were stopped by Vice Principal Arnett.

"And just what has two fourth graders running through the halls of St. Thomas as if they were on fire? Come to think of it, if the halls were on fire you two are old enough to know the drills and shouldn't be running down here anyway. So?" Mr. Arnett said with very little authority in his voice. Picture Barney Fife without the confidence, and you would have our Vice Principal.

"We were looking for a janitor. Sally got sick." Brenton said.

"That's right. We were having a party in our room, and she threw up. Ok, not really a party, but cupcakes and stuff." I stammered. The thought of Mrs. Anderson allowing us to have a party in the classroom meant that she might get in trouble, so I tried to backtrack. "Well, you see it was Brady's birthday coming up, and his mom brought the class some Spiderman cupcakes, and not those cheap kind either, but those from like one of those fancy cupcake stores."

"Stop! I get it. Go get a custodian, and I will head up there and check it out for myself." Mr. Arnett said.

"Oh no, that's ok. We got it all covered now. There is no reason to go all the way up there. It's all over." I said trying to discourage him.

Well it didn't take much to talk him out of confronting both a smelly pile of cupcake barf and worse, Mrs. Anderson. "Yes, you two boys seem to have it all covered. No more running in the halls. You hear me?" He finished.

"Yes sir!" Brenton and I answered, and then we both fast walked ourselves to the boiler room.

Let the record show that when Brenton and I got to the door to the boiler room both of the custodians did their best to hide their cigarettes. And that was also the first time that I had ever had a chance to see what was behind that door. That was the first time that I saw the aluminum chairs and the tiny table. I wasn't sure exactly what the huge pipes that snaked and twisted behind them did exactly, or where exactly they might have went. I also noticed how hot it was in there. Both of the custodians were sweating and had a white terrycloth towel that they would use to wipe their brows whenever they would bead up.

"Yes, gentlemen. How may we help you this fine afternoon?" Jerry our tall skinny janitor said. He was clearly mocking us.

"Stop it, J. Can't you see there is some type of emergency? Go on young'uns, what brings you down to our humble abode?" Curtis the older, over weight janitor said. He waved his hand outward as if welcoming us inside the Grand Hall of the Custodial Palace, rather than the tight boiler room. And although his words sounded as if he was more on our side, there was something about his tone that made it sound as if he was making fun of us too.

"One of the girls, Sally, got sick, and Mrs. Anderson sent us to find you guys cuz we need help cleaning it up. Do you know who Sally is? Anyway, we need help in our room." Brenton said. His words came fast, so the two of them would understand just how dire the situation was.

I didn't say anything. My eyes had followed Curtis's short chubby hand, and I was taking in all of the strange and wonderful things on the shelves behind them. There were cans of paint in colors that I recognized throughout the church, and next to that was everything you would need to paint the entire church including drop cloths and painter's tape. There were cans of different sized nails and bolts. One rusted out can was labeled "electric," and I had no idea what you could fit in a can that small. But the one thing that really stuck out the most was a big white plastic spray bottle complete with a long white tube that stuck out of the top and ended with a green and red trigger. One the side of the bottle was the word "Caution," and on the other were the words "Rat Killa" written in messy, black Sharpie. There was a picture of a poorly hand-drawn rat with little x's for eyes.

"Isn't that right, Peter?" Brenton asked.

"What?" I asked. I had been temporarily hypnotized by the cartoon dead rat, but Brenton had broken the spell. "Yeah, yeah what he said."

"So, come on." Brenton motion for Jerry and Curtis to follow him.

"I need to get a few things first. Tell that w…Tell your teacher that I am on my way, and that the both of us will be up there shortly." Jerry told Brenton.

Brenton shook his head as if to say, "Well, I tried." Then without waiting for me to follow, he headed down the hallway and back toward the stairs.

"Does that stuff really work?" I asked pointing to the bottle of rat poison.

"Don't see any rats around here do you?" Jerry remarked. He grabbed a few rags off of the shelf and a spray can of some type of all-purpose cleaner. He didn't know it yet, but he was going to need a lot more than that to clean up after Sally Hale.

Curtis mocked reaching in his holster and pointed his fingers like a pistol, and then he aimed them in the one of the dark corners of the boiler room. "Every time." Curtis said as he pulled the imaginary triggers and shot his imaginary ammo and then slowly stood up relieving the ever grateful aluminum chair.

So here I was back again in front of that same door feeling the warm steam seeping in though the other side. I wasn't a hundred percent sure that this was where I was supposed to be, but both Frances and Brady had said that it was hot and wet wherever they were being held. I didn't question at the time how I was able to hear their voices echoing from the other side of the church, and maybe looking back I should have. All I knew at that moment was that I wanted more than anything to find my friends, and this was the only real clue that I had. I was just thankful that O'Leary and his creepy cat friend left me alone, and didn't give me any trouble on the way down. I guess if I was thinking, I should have questioned that too.

The door to the boiler room was locked. I didn't know why I was surprised about that. There were a lot of things in there that the church probably didn't want just anybody to be able to get to. Not only were there all of those paints, poisons, and chemicals, but the floors because of the condensation were extremely slippery all the time. All St. Thomas needed was to have some old lady slip and break a hip trying to get a bottle of Pine Sol off of the top shelf. Also that is where the circuit breakers to the entire building were including both the church side and the school side.

So I had a choice, I could either try to get that door open and get to Franny and Brady who needed me on the other side, or I could walk away and try to look for them somewhere else. It really wasn't much of a choice at all. I had faith that my friends were on the other side of that door. Ha ha, it's funny saying that out loud now because, I didn't think that I had faith in anything other than my brother Aiden waking me up in the middle of the night with his crying.

"Brady? Franny? Are you in there?" I said and put my ear to the door. "The door is locked. See if you can open it from your side." I whispered through the crack of the doorframe.

I didn't want whatever it was that put them in there in the first place to know that I was there and ready to get them out. That was when I realized something, and the lightbulb in my head clicked. "Duh, if Brady and Frances could open the door from their side, they wouldn't need me on this side trying to get the two of them out." I said to myself.

I directed my words to the boiler room door. "Ok, if you can hear me, back away from the doorway. It's locked, so I'm doing to have to ram it." I whispered again.

Now, keep in mind that I was nine. And not only did I weigh less than a hundred pounds soaking wet, but also I had never "rammed" anything in my life. But I wasn't going to let any of those minor details deter me from trying. So, I pushed a little on the door while turning the knob back and forth just to make sure one last time that it was locked and that there was no other way that this door was going to be opened other than brute force.

Nothing.

"Ok guys. Here I go." I said. I took a few steps backwards and grabbing my elbow leaned my whole body towards the door. Should I aim for the center? Should I aim towards the doorknob? How would I know? I had seen dozens of movies where the hero knocks in a door, but for the life of me I couldn't remember the trick of how they did it.

I took a deep breath. "Peter, you got this." I said to myself. I took off as fast as I could with the limited space that I had in the hallway. And exactly what you think would have happened, happened. I bounced off the locked, boiler-room door with a loud and painful *thud*!

Wincing in pain, I listened through the door to check if Brady or Frances heard me and were somehow coming to my aid. There was not a sound. I had to try again. This time I would aim more for the doorknob where the actual lock may be.

"Ok, back up again. I'm going to give this one more try." I said to the locked door.

Taking an even deeper breath, because I knew how much it was going to hurt this time around, I braced myself for impact. I had thought about maybe switching arms, but why have two sore shoulders.

*Thud!*

I pushed on the door and twisted the knob again to see if it would turn. It was still locked tight. So far the stupid door was winning 2-0. If I couldn't get through the door, then what was the use of even trying to save them? Frustrated, I kicked the door as hard as I could. And of course, it creaked open a few tiny inches. I had probably loosened it when I hit it with my shoulder. At least that is what I told myself to feel a bit better about the deep steady throbbing in my arm.

"Hello?" I said.

My voice echoed around the tiny room. But unlike in the humongous sanctuary where my voice bounced forever, joyfully off of the walls, stained glass, and rows and rows of pews, in the boiler room my echo escaped but then was eaten quickly. I could hear my little "Hello" ricochet off the thick twisted pipes. It was instantly absorbed in the exposed dirty pink insulation shoved into the grooves of the wooden framed walls.

"Brady? Frances? Come on out." I said. I took a few cautious steps into the boiler room. I could immediately feel the heat of the hot water heaters form beads of sweat on my arms and my cheeks. My nostrils filled instantly with chemicals and steam. "Guys. I'm here. I got the door open. You can come out now."

One step became two. I passed the tiny table and chairs that Curtis and Jerry had used as they were sharing a smoke and last night's gossip. Every step I took was damp and melted the dried pudding making my shoes slip. I couldn't see more than a few feet inside the room. First, because it was a mess with piles and piles of rags, mops, buckets, and who knows what else that was stashed in this catch-all corner of the church. Second, because although it didn't work out too well for Frances, I was still taking her no lights advice to heart.

I carefully felt my way around the right hand side of the boiler room. Like a makeshift braille, I used my fingertips to feel the warm damp walls and the plywood shelves. Luckily I had had lots of practice feeling my way around with my eyes closed in line on the way to the library. I was always careful as I moved my fingers lightly over every invisible object, knowing that there were probably a million things that I could cut my fingertips on if I didn't watch myself.

Whoever had taken my friends probably had them tied up and gagged somewhere, so that was probably the reason that Brady and Frances didn't come running when I busted the door open. If they were tied up and gagged in the corner of the boiler room, it was going to be almost impossible to find them without any lights. So although I didn't want to do it, I didn't think that I had much of a choice but to turn on a light, even if was just for a second or two.

"Ok, guys. I don't know if you can hear me or not, but you might want to cover your eyes. I'm going to turn on the lights for just a second to see if I can find you. I want you to move around if you can. Ok, here I go." And with that announcement, I flicked on the light switch.

I should have warned myself too. Although the bulb was only a 60 watt, it filled the front of the boiler room with instant light that blinded me more than it helped me. I shut my eyes to keep out the light, and then slowly squinted them open just enough so I could find my friends.

Huge silver and grey pipes ran in all directions like the legs of an obese metal spider. The maze of pipes and tubes ran across the room and through the walls. I was relieved to see the green flecked aluminum chairs folded and leaning against the bricks. The dusty, dirty shelves were still filled with cans and containers. And there was their king, "Rat Killa," sitting proudly in the center. The only things that I didn't see around the room anywhere were Frances and Brady.

They had to be here. They had to be somewhere in this room. There was no way that I had gotten all of this wrong. There was no way that I had went through all of this for nothing. They were supposed to be sitting in the corner, tied together, with filthy rags sticking half out of their mouths. They were supposed to be overjoyed with tears of relief in their eyes when I came in like a hero and recued them.

"Brady, where are you? Franny? You can come out now. I'm here. It's safe." I whispered.

I knew that I needed to turn the light off soon. The longer it was on the more danger I was going to be in. But I also couldn't turn off that bulb until I found Frances and Brady, or until I knew beyond a shadow of a doubt that they were not anywhere in here. I was not going to run out afraid like I had done earlier in the cafeteria.

There was a rustling sound coming from the corner of the room. Behind what had to be the main heating system for the entire church there was a noise. I remember bending down as much as I could trying not to let my hands touch the disgustingly slimy floor to try and look around the wall-sized enclosure. If the metal pipes were the legs of the spider, then they must have been tied somewhere behind the bulging, sweating abdomen.

"Brady? Is that you?" I wanted to move closer, but the rubber soles of my sneakers were melted to the floor. I mean they weren't actually melted, but my legs were lead, and there was no way that they would let me move any closer to whatever was making that noise behind the boiler.

The rustling sound didn't stop at the sound of my voice. In fact, after it heard me talking it seemed to be getting even more worked up. I wished that I could had at least seen Brady's shoes sticking out from around the corner, or maybe the top of Frances's hair so I could be certain that it was them. But then I heard something else.

"Mmmrrrph," garbled the dark indistinguishable shape from behind the boiler.

"Hello? Franny? Is that you?" I squeamishly replied.

The sound coming from behind the boiler sounded like a girl's voice.

What was I being so afraid of? It had to be them, and here I was too scared to help. As much as my legs protested, I took another step closer. They must have heard me, because as soon as I did another sound appeared.

"Mmmrrrph. Rrruurrggh," the sound answered me.

Gathering up every ounce of courage that I had left inside, I took the last three steps until I was just inches away from the edge of the darkness. I could just barely make out the old boxes and rags, rusted out cans and buckets all barely sticking out from the army green rubber tarp. And was that a Brady's shoulder leaning against the exposed pink fiberglass insulation that lined the walls?

"Don't worry guys. I got ya." I said. I pulled back the rubber tarp with all the strength that I could, and the tarp replied with a loud *fwap*!

My heart jumped into my chest. There was no Brady. No Frances. At least not on the part of the wall that I could now see. The cardboard boxes oozed from the corners with a crimson red slime. The black rags hung wet and bundled with the same goo. Nothing was moving.

"Mmmrrrrph. Rrruuurrggh," It said again from the protected part that was still covered by the tarp.

I guess that I wasn't strong enough or close enough to pull the entire rubber tarp off on my first try. I had no choice but to get in there even closer and try it again. I bent down and grabbed the wet corner of the green-grey tarp. Again, I pulled as hard as I could, but it was still stuck on something. I pulled again and again, each time with more confidence. The thing felt so heavy in my hands that I did everything that I could just to hold on to it. It was no use, there was no way to get a good grip on it. The heat from the room covered everything with a humid film. The only way that I was going to be able to tug the whole thing off on my next pull would be to get a better grip. That meant that I would have to let go of the wrench and grab it with both hands.

The nonslip handle of the wrench stuck fast to my palm. I bent down carefully and leaned the wrench against my ankle. If I had to let it go, I still wanted to have the feeling of that security beside me. I took a deep breath and with my entire fourth grade frame, yanked as hard as I could.

The rubber tarp slipped out of my hands, and I ended up falling backwards and smacking down hard on my tailbone. I wasn't sure what that tarp was stuck on before, but I knew it wasn't budging. That was when I saw the hand.

The army tarp wasn't snagged on something. Someone was holding the other end and pulling back trying to prevent me from exposing it. I don't know if I was supposed to see the tiny hand, but I did. It must have been because I had fallen straight backwards and ended up on my butt, but because I was now sitting on the floor, I saw the hand.

"Brady? Is that you? What are you doing, man?" I asked. I dusted myself off, and stood back up. "Come on, man. Stop horsing around, and let's get out of here."

Something shifted itself under the tarp as if it was trying to get away from me. As if it was scared of me. Whatever had taken Brady and Frances had done quite a number on them if they were so afraid that they were trying to avoid me. I grabbed the wrench firmly in my hand again.

"I'm not kidding, man." I said. The thing shifted again. "Brady, is that you?"

As if to respond to my question, the ashen hand curled itself into a tiny fist around the corner of the tarp and held on tightly. Its nails were as black as the darkness behind it. "Grrrurrrggh," It almost purred.

"Ok, here is the deal, Brady. I'm going to give you one last chance to come out of there and stop fooling around. If you don't come out on the count of three, I'm going to smack you as hard as I can with this wrench. Do you hear me?" I warned him. I was tired of playing games, and I just wanted to get out of there.

I waited. I could still hear the thing in the corner growling and purring. There was no laughing or snickering as if they were trying to play a trick on me. The small hand curled itself into a tighter ball as if gripping and preparing itself for an attack.

"One."

My eyes, too afraid to blink, were starting to sting with the salty, dirty sweat dripping off my brow and into my eyes. My tongue was once again twenty grit sandpaper, and the back of my throat burned of turpentine fumes.

"Two."

I could feel the tiny beads of sweat multiplying on my upper lip. The wrench started to tremble a bit in my hand, so I gripped it with both my right and my left just to keep from dropping it on the floor. Half of me knew that I should kill the lights just to be on the safe side, while the other half of me wanted more lights, too afraid of what would be lurking in the darkness. Whatever was under the tarp was still there. I had no choice.

"Three!"

I dove across the slick rubber tarp towards the lump in the corner. The skinny, grey hand immediately disappeared as I repeatedly swung the wrench. Over and over again I struck each strange bulge under the thick cover. All of my fear and pent up aggression came pouring out of me. I am not too ashamed to admit it now, but I cried. Not little tears either, but I was sobbing. Screaming and crying I hit the tarp until my arm was worn out and tired. The wrench was so heavy in my hand that I could no longer lift it. It fell to the floor of the boiler room with a dead thud.

I rolled myself to the side and off the pile. My shirt was dirty and drenched in sweat. I squinted through my tears to see if anything moved. Although it was slight, I saw something underneath the worn tarp slowly undulate and pulse. And then the tarp collapsed leaving nothing behind. The once lumpy canvas was now smooth and slick on the boiler room floor. I didn't know what to think anymore. My head hurt, and my whole body was worn out. All of the adrenaline in my body had drained in an instant. And then it occurred to me. What if it was my friends after all, and I had been too afraid to look under the tarp, too afraid to just pull it back and save them? And now just as quickly as they had disappeared the first time, they were once again gone.

"Brady?" I struggled, "Frances?"

As much as I hated it, I was going to have to lift the cover off of what was once mounds of rubber to see what was underneath. I needed to see what was under it just to make sure that it was in fact nothingness and wasn't what was left of Frances or Brady.

That is when I did something on my own that I had never done without being asked by one of the teachers here at St. Thomas. I prayed. "Dear God, please don't let this be Brady and Franny. And God, please let them be alright."

Now, came the hard part. I was still half sitting and half laying on the floor, but I still managed to pull the heavy Army tarp off of the boxes and other equipment piled behind the boiler. It was not Brady and Frances lying on the floor beside me. I knew that there was something under that heavy tarp when I was swinging my wrench, but now there was nothing underneath it. The only stain was that of paint that had long ago dried in an awkward circle.

I felt my heart jump out of my chest and into my throat. Instinctively, my body did the same, and I jumped out of the way of the crumpled tarp and I got to my feet the best that I could.

Half stumbling, I was able to reach down and pick up the wrench, and I instantly felt better having that security in my hand. I had imagined so many terrible things moving under that tarp before it went limp. Was the strange hand that I knew that I saw from a creature? Was there some beast living and hiding in the church boiler room? Maybe it was the hand of Brady reaching up for help and then being mercifully saved at the last second as I launched into my tirade.

"Oh my, what have I done?" I whispered to myself. "I had a chance to save him and I blew it. I was too afraid to help him."

I guess God did answer my first solo prayer. I had prayed that Brady and Frances weren't under the tarp, and they weren't. But whatever that thing was that moved and grabbed the corner, it was definitely not from God. And that was when I noticed that the edges of the once still tarp was beginning to move once again. Whatever it was was still alive and now trying to crawl itself towards me.

*"Aaaahh!"* I screamed as the long thin fingers of the creature tried to wrap themselves around my shoelaces. I had thought about beating the thing again and crushing those thin knuckles with the business end of the wrench. But as grotesque as it was, it was also pitiful and suffering. The hand looked as if it was in pain and needed more help and sympathy than it did a beating. I had to put this thing out of its misery, but there was no way that I could hit it again.

I ran to the shelf and pulled down the plastic bottle of poison. The words "Rat Killa" stared back at me. Looking back, I am not sure if it was more humane than just hitting it over and over again with the wrench, but at the time the only thing that I could think about was what Curtis the custodian had said a little over a month ago when I asked if that stuff worked.

"Every time"

I pumped the primer on the top of the bottle repeatedly until I could feel it resisting. I remember trying to balance both the wrench and the little plastic trigger in my sweaty hand. The thin white tube connecting the rat poison and the trigger kept getting tangled around my wrist. But the suffering thing in the corner was gaining strength, so I needed to act fast.

The first spray from the bottle was thin and missed the thing under the tarp by at least two feet. It screeched and squealed from under the thick blanket. The poison had rolled down the uneven floor, and finally reached the thin fingers of the monster. The fingers reeled back quickly and hid under the tarp once again. I didn't even feel the tears rolling down my cheeks. I was crying, sympathizing with the pain and sorrow that whatever was under there was feeling. All it wanted was help, but it didn't belong here. Not here in the boiler room, not here at the church, and probably not even here in this realm of existence.

"R*rrhhheeee!!!*" The creature screamed and begged. Its long human arms reached out to me hoping that I would relieve the pain, but I was too petrified with fear. The boney fingertips were nothing more than black nails trying to grab on to anything within its reach.

I sprayed it again and again. Each time that I did, the thing behind the boiler reacted by trying to curl itself up tighter and tighter. When the poison had reduced itself to just a trickle, I put the bottle down and studied the thing that was now just hiding. But the worst part was the smell. The smell was a mix of rancid meat and fine burnt hair. It filled my lungs that were already struggling to breathe past the steam and poison.

"Hey? Are you still alive?" I asked. Grabbing a mop handle, I poked it a few times. The tip of the wooden mop handle sunk deeply into the empty tarp. I could feel the hard concrete floor beneath it. "Gross." I said and threw the mop on the floor beside the now empty "Rat Killa."

The room was quiet once again, and the mysterious tarp was now just a wet bundle on the floor. I grabbed my trusty wrench and shoved it deep into the back pocket of my cargo pants. Right before I turned out the light to the boiler room and shut the door, I thought about Curtis.

"Every time."

# CHAPTER 14

I guess in reality I should have been more bothered and disturbed about what had just happened in the boiler room. I mean don't get me wrong, I was definitely traumatized. I remember my hands shaking so hard I could barely turn the doorknob to close the boiler room door. And on top of that, apparently when I kicked the door open in the first place, I broke the lock. So the door really didn't shut the way that it did before.

Not to mention that my only lead as to where Brady and Frances were was now totally gone. I started to wonder if that was even them to start with. Why would they somehow all of a sudden be able to psychically call me all the way down into the boiler room and then if they could do all that, not be in there when I did get in? And instead it was just all some weird trick to lead me to whatever that thing was in there playing hide-and-go-seek in the corner.

"How did you like meeting my little friend?" a voice said. I couldn't even tell you where that voice was coming from. Was it coming from behind me? To my left? To my right? The answer was "Yes," it seemed to be coming from all those places at once.

It was also a voice that unfortunately I was beginning to recognize all too well. O'Leary's smile from his portrait in the library came into my head like a migraine. I mean there I was filthy, covered in cold sweat and custodial dust. My feet and the back of my pants were wet with the condensation from the boiler room floor. The chill from the cold air made my goosebumps crawl to attention. I didn't know how much more of this I could take, and now O'Leary had to come in with his snappy comments. I stood fast holding the wrench in my hand like a mighty warrior's weapon once again. I had already taken down that mysterious lump in the boiler room, so a creepy picture of a pastor should be no trouble at all, right?

"What do you mean?" I asked him. I waited quietly for a second or two to see if he would reply. When he didn't, I shouted again.

"What do you mean by little friend? What do you think that this is, O'Leary, some kind of sick game?" I yelled toward the ceiling. If O'Leary wanted to talk, then fine let's talk.

"Of course, Petey. This is all one big game. But here is the good news my son. You are winning!" His voice hissed. Afterwards he let out another ear piercing laugh. I covered my ears, but I could still hear him though the thin slits between my fingers.

Wait, could O'Leary hear my thoughts? I didn't say any of that out loud, did I? I couldn't remember. To this day I still am not sure if I was actually talking to myself out loud, or if the whole thing was just a conversation that I was having in my head.

"What did you do with my friends?" I screamed.

"You don't have any friends. You are all alone little Petey." he answered. I could tell by the tone in his voice that O'Leary was enjoying every second of this. He had been waiting all night to get me alone and talk to me, to torture me with his words of hatred and doubt. Now, that I was finally by myself and he had taken everything away from me, he was finally getting his opportunity.

I waved the heavy metal wrench in the air like a club and threatened to take the fight to him. "Stop telling me what I have and what I don't have. Stop playing these stupid games, and tell me how to get my friends back." I didn't know where all of this bravado was coming from, but I was not going to back down now. "Come on. I'm not afraid of you and your sick twisted pets. I'm not afraid of your creepy voice either. So, you can just stop all of this and tell me what I want to know!"

"So brave, are we? Just like His Son. He was a brave one too, but you aren't Him." O'Leary said with a snarl in his voice. "Not even close." He finished with a laugh that shook me down to my soul.

This wasn't working, and I wasn't getting anywhere with him. He was enjoying playing with me. The air around me was freezing cold causing the hair on my arms to stand on end. I don't know if I felt that way because I had just come out of the boiler room where the air was so thick and humid to the cool air conditioned hall of the church, or was it something else. I do remember that it was so cold that I could see my own breath as I spoke. So,

I guess I was speaking out loud and not just having that conversation in my head after all.

First the weird cat-like thing sleeping in the pews of the sanctuary, and then whatever that was hiding scared under that thick Army tarp. Pets, that it is what I had called that half-human thing that had just been hiding under the tarp, and that I beat down with a custodian's wrench and finished off with rat poison. Where had those things O'Leary had sent come from? Had I just killed some monster from who knows where? Part of me wanted to run back into the boiler room and look at it one last time just to verify that there was no way that thing could have come from anywhere other than a dark pit deep below. Part of me needed to see it again now that O'Leary had pretty much told me that he was the one who had sent it to me. It was like an optical illusion that you couldn't quite see until someone tells you where to look. Part of me wanted to go back and see it all for myself.

I didn't go and take a look back. I couldn't. I think that even after all this time, if the government agents were to tell me that they had caught one of those things, and it was on the aluminum table in some hidden military facility, I would still be too scared to walk in there and take a peek. I know what I saw that night and as long as I live I will never ever want to see it again. So instead of heading back down to the boiler room, I gripped the wrench as tightly as I could and walked down the dark corridor as far away from the memory of that creature as I could.

My first stop was the water fountain by the stairwell. From the first time that I had taken a sip, I had always loved the taste of the cool, clear water that came out of the porcelain white water fountains. The beautifully carved bowls were sprinkled and almost hidden here and there throughout the church and each one was decorated slightly differently from the others. If you just went up to one and took a drink, you probably wouldn't even notice the details. But I noticed that the one by the gymnasium had little fish along the sides and the spout in which the water came out looked like one of the fish was spitting the water in the air. That is kind of gross now that I think about it. But the one upstairs by our classroom was slightly different. Instead of little fish, this one had vines and bunches of grapes carved into the porcelain. The one outside of the boiler room and just down the hall was finely decorated with sea shells.

The collection of the church's detailed porcelain drinking fountains must have been at least fifty years old, but the water that poured out of each of them was always cold and sweet. They all looked as if they were built into part of the walls and hardly stuck out into the hallway at all. All of the kids in fourth grade thought they were pretty cool because you were in essence sticking your head in the wall every time you took a drink.

The best time to enjoy the fountains was right after recess. But I could have really used a drink because, right now my mouth was sticky dry, and my tongue was a sandpaper weight at the bottom that tasted of dirty sweat. I could feel every sweet drop of the water from the fountain refresh me from within as I gulped it down. I didn't realize how thirsty I was until I had that steady flow of water save me from the tip of my lips to the bottom of my stomach. But isn't that the way it always is with that sort of thing. You never know how much you truly needed something until you finally get it.

"Brady, Frances, I know that you are somewhere inside this church. Don't worry I am going to find you. I won't give up until I do." I said to myself. The problem was I didn't know where to start looking. I was right back in the same place that I was before I had been drawn to the boiler room. Ha, I guess with the weird whispers coming from what I could only assume was Brady and Frances that I was drawn down there, wasn't I? I had never thought about it like that before, but I guess without telling me directly, they were guiding me down below to them.

The most logical thing to do would be to try and make my way back to the library. From there, I could pull out those pages of scrap paper and maybe find out something that could help me find my way to them. That would be the Frances way to do something. Plan it all out. Quietly do the research needed to find my friends, taking important notes the whole time, and then go about it all step by step executing each part. There were a few things wrong with this plan. First of all, I'm not Frances. I could look at all of those little scraps of paper all night long, and it wouldn't bring me any closer to finding my friends. Although Mrs. Anderson did everything she could to hide the fact, Franny was the smartest kid in our class. I was probably second to last. Sorry Gerald Spanning.

Second, the clues that Frances had found in the library were directly under the picture of Pastor O'Leary. There was no way that I wanted to be alone in a room with that image again. It was hard enough the first time in the library when the three of us were still together. I could feel my pulse racing at just the thought of being in there alone.

The next most logical thing to do is the "WWBD" ideology. This was also known as the "What Would Brady Do?" method of thinking. I had walked into St Thomas Academy everyday thinking that I was the strongest and bravest of the three of us, but after all that had happened so far, I was neither. So my thinking was that if Brady were in my shoes, he would go back to the cafeteria and start at the beginning. It would not only give him another chance to look over the places in the kitchen where we had heard all that noise and where Frances had gone missing, but also another chance to get something to eat. Clues and snacks was definitely the way Brady would have thought.

There were just a few things wrong with this plan too. I was not brave. So even if I made it all the way down to the cafeteria by myself and managed to find my way back to the kitchen, what would I be looking for? I wasn't going to just pick up a butcher's knife and start hacking my way through the church slaying demon after demon. After all, this was way before video games gave every preteen the courage to go into any situation ready to kill. But I think the most important thing keeping me from being as brave as I needed to be was the way that the knives had been scattered across the worn wooden floor of the kitchen. You see, Brady didn't have a chance to see all of that chaos. I had quickly grabbed him and went running out of there as fast as I could, so of course he was brave and ready to take on whatever took Frances. Also, I wasn't sure if Brady was hearing the voice of one of the creepy pastors whispering in his ear all night? As far as I knew, the answer to that question was "no."

Between Frances disappearing in the cafeteria leaving nothing but screams and a mess on the kitchen floor, and the way that I had just turned my head in the sanctuary for less than a second and Brady vanishing, it seemed that every option seemed like a bad one. That was when I saw Brady's Bible.

I had been walking in somewhat of a haze just trying to gather my thoughts and figure out what my next move was going to be when out of the corner of my eye I saw his Bible. Don't ask me how I knew that in a building full of Bibles, I knew that this one was his. Don't ask me how I saw it in the complete darkness of the halls. I just did. I told myself at the time that it was probably because my eyes were getting adjusted to the light. I was probably slowly turning into one of those blind newts that live in the cracks and crevasses of caves so long that they no longer need to use their eyes to get around in the dark. Of course now if you were to ask me how I saw that Bible I would have a different answer.

"Brady?" I whispered, my breath still visible.

I figured that if his Bible was there, that maybe he wouldn't be too far behind. I remember picking it up, and the spine of the book was still warm from where Brady had held it tight. That made me wonder if the broken glass bowl that he had held and then dropped in his other hand was around there too.

"Brady? Are you there?" my whisper dared to get a little louder.

I squinted in the darkness of the hallway, but couldn't see anything else. Beside and all around me was nothing but emptiness. The only familiar object was another poster on the wall advertising the upcoming "Trunk-or-Treat." Maybe Brady had dropped his Bible running away from that creature in the boiler room. I needed light. Part of me wanted to see if there was any clues on the floor that might help me figure out what had happened here, like the ones I was still trying to piece together that I had found in the kitchen where Frances had disappeared. God, *I hope that Brady was able to fight back. Give him the strength to at least do that.* I had done it again without even recognizing it, my second prayer.

Some of the pages of the Bible that I had found were torn loose and stuck out like jagged teeth. I guess I didn't notice it at first from far off, but when I stood up and held it in my hand I could feel the page after page that had been torn out and haphazardly replaced. Now, I really needed a light to see what had happened to the book, but there was no way that I was going to turn on the lights in the hall. I just needed a little light not much to see what had happened to the pages of Brady's Bible. I didn't have a flashlight handy, but I had the next best thing.

One of the great things about our school was that they hated for the preschoolers to have to walk anywhere, so they put all of their classrooms as closely together as possible. In fact the little kids didn't really have to toddle very far to get to anything except the gymnasium, and they only went there twice a week. Therefore, if I could make it towards the cafeteria and then eventually the preschool classes, then I could use the light of the fish aquarium to check out Brady's book. Since I had decided to head down to the cafeteria anyway, I could use the soft blue light of the aquarium to decipher what Brady had left for me.

I made my way down the hallway once again with one hand on the wall and the other on the Bible. My wrench was tucked securely into the back pocket of my cargo pants. Hundreds of shadows along the way played games with my head, scurrying in the corners of my eyes always just out of sight.

I had no idea what time it was getting to be, but it felt to me as if I had been there roaming the halls of St. Thomas for days. I would have never admitted to anyone in my class, but back in fourth grade I had to be in bed and under the covers by nine o'clock. While others in my class bragged about staying up until ten, or watching the ball game until they fell asleep, I was sawing logs. My mom and dad told me over and over again that getting a good night's sleep was as important as eating right and exercising. Of course they usually said it when we were sitting in front of the television splitting a pepperoni and sausage pizza. But never the less, when nine o'clock rolled around, I was under the covers ready for bed. So I should have been dead tired. I should have been sound asleep in a little ball or something curled up on one of those overstuffed leather couches in the adult prayer center. Instead, I couldn't have been more alert.

The light of the aquarium was off just as we had left it before. I could still hear the slow steady bubbles burbling their way to the surface. I hadn't realized just how quiet the night had become since my little excursion in the boiler room. I turned the thin black knob on the back of the aquarium's lid letting the light flicker slowly at first and then faster until the whole hall was filled with the soft shimmering blue of florescent water. The fish inside the tank, temporarily blinded by the light, shook a bit at first and then quickly swam over each other once again trying to hide in the twisted maze of the coral and to safety under the rainbow colored plastic castle. The translucent air tube in the corner still strained to suck in the dirty water. Its opening now semi-clogged with the train of half eaten tiny tropical fish corpses.

I used the blue light of the aquarium to try and make out whatever it was that Brady had written out. The light was dull and barely made the pages legible. Not only that, but it looked as if Brady had written everything down on his knee using a blunt nub of a pencil and not his Dinosaur Land pen.

"Pete" was the only thing written on the first torn page of Brady's Bible.

I couldn't quiet see what he had written on the next few pages. My shadow seemed to cover the Bible, and no matter which way I twisted and turned I couldn't get the angle right. The only thing that seemed to work was kneeling down on my knees and hunching over. When I did this, the aquarium light filled each torn out page with waves of beautifully shimmering blue. It reminded me of Brady's face in the light of the stained glass window by the entry's spiral staircase.

"Peter" the second legible page read.

The next three ripped pages were either my name over and over again, or random scribbling that I couldn't figure out. Brady was right handed, but his handwriting over the Bible scripture was mangled and messy. It was as if he was writing with his left hand instead. Let me put it this way, if Mrs. Anderson had seen it, she would have handed it right back without a word, and Brady would be writing the whole thing over. Mrs. Anderson made it clear to the class more than once that she is not fluent in "Chicken Scratch."

I was just about to give up on the whole thing when I ran across something different. Way different.

"Entr hr" the beginning read. Then almost written directly over that read the word, "*No!*" There was a scribbling of mazes and arrows that continued from one torn page to the next. The whole thing was written quickly. It seemed as if Brady was trying to write it on the run, and then sometimes the lines were crossed out again with the word "*No!*" over them.

"P- This is sfe." was drawn from a torn page of Exodus in what looked like a cross between dark green water colors and then traced over again in a purple crayon. Brady had circled what looked like a staircase, but which one?

"Ths way. Don't lok dwn." his crayon instructions read. The purple crayon was smeared with what I first thought was just water, but now I am thinking that the way it dotted the page, it might have been Brady's tears. I held this fragmented page of Leviticus toward the still reflective blue light of the aquarium.

That was the way that it went for page after page. Each of them written in a different way, some in ink, some with pencil, some charcoal, some of the pages were written in things that I would rather not have guessed. Some of pages of Brady's Bible had so much written on them that I couldn't make any of it out. It was just words and pictures drawn on top of other words and pictures. Other pages had just a single word or two. There was no order to any of it either. The pages of the Bible itself were scrambled and not in their correct order, and I thought that even if I could have put them in order, it wouldn't have helped much.

I took what seemed forever looking at each page under the dim light of the aquarium. Finally, I thought that I had figured it all out. These pages in front of me might not have been just a series of random words and drawings after all. It was as if I was staring too closely at a puzzle, and I needed to step away to get the larger image. Brady wasn't just scribbling on the pages of the Bible that he had picked up. He had a purpose.

This was a map. The words were instructions. More specifically, it was instructions meant for me. The penciled in lines and boxes were rooms and hallways. The more I looked, the more I started to recognize parts of the church and school. Maybe Brady didn't drop this trying to fend off some creature from Hades. Maybe he had left this for me to find. Was it a way to Frances? Was this where they were being kept? And how was he able to even get this to me in the first place? Where did he get all of the different stuff to write with? For that matter, how on Earth did he have time to write it all down? This would have taken hours and hours of work to get all of this information down. He hadn't been missing for that long. Had he? These questions and a thousand more came into my head at once.

"Brady, thanks man. I needed this." I said aloud and closed the Bible.

Part of one of the pages said "Enter here" at least that is what I was able to make out. But then over that was written the word "No." So although I was pretty sure that the place that Brady had drawn was the entrance to the gym, I had to look for somewhere else.

I remembered another page that had "P-This is sfe" written across the top. That had to have meant, "Peter, this is safe." so I scrambled through the torn pages of the Old Testament to see if I could remember where I had put it. I knew it was one of the earlier books, but for the life of me I couldn't remember which one.

Now, I am much better than I was back in fourth grade when it came to knowing the books of the Bible. Believe me, there is a song that teaches every Christian school kid the books of the Bible, and you will learn them whether you want to learn them or not. I mean it has been years, and I can still hum the first verse or two: "Genesis, Exodus, Leviticus, Numbers, and Deu-ter-onomy." The tune still rings in my head.

There it was filed snugly in the pages of Leviticus. Brady's words minus a vowel or two. "P-This is sfe"

I held up the page the best that I could up to the blue of the aquarium light. The tiny bubbles popping on the surface of the water made the shadows on the thin page bounce and swim like tropical fish. Maybe not the fish in this particular aquarium though.

The words that Brady had written down pointed to a series of boxes, one inside the other, each one smaller than the last. Inside that third little square was a circle in burnt red. The map looked to be back pointing me back to the school cafeteria. I recognized the way he had drawn out a few of the long rectangular tables and a few of the chairs. The map was not just taking me back to the cafeteria, but back in the kitchen. That was definitely not a safe place. Brady must have been out of his mind. How could the place where all of this started to go south be thought of as a "safe" place? But Brady's copper red circle had not just focused on the kitchen of the legendary, "Home of the Band-Aid Chili," he had circled the little corner of his drawing, and inside that dark circle was a crudely drawn cross. I knew were Brady was sending me. It was a place that I had already been once tonight. It wasn't the cafeteria or the kitchen itself that Brady was telling me was my new little safe haven. No, it was the walk-in cooler.

# Chapter 15

I tip-toed the best that I could past the wet and sticky stains on the kitchen floor, but every careful step still echoed in the emptiness. The thin smear had started on one side of the room next to the now vacant rack of knives, and although I didn't notice it beforehand, lead out past the large bathtub sized sinks all the way to the doorway. There was still a mix of aromas in the room, the smell of Friday's lunch of corndogs with tater tots and Clorox bleach permeated the air. The only lights in the kitchen came from the blinking 12:00 on the microwave and the pilot lights of the gas stove.

I wanted to stop for just a second or two and look for something I might be able to use to defend myself that was maybe a little better than the handyman's wrench in my back pocket. Brady had said that this place was supposed to be safe, but just as insurance it would be nice to have a big sharp knife. But I tell you that although there were plenty to choose from scattered about along the wooden floorboards, I just couldn't do it. I mean all of them were still just lying there untouched all over the floor of our cafeteria's kitchen. Some of them were still spotted with what, I wasn't even going to begin to guess.

"Come on, Peter. Be a man." I told myself.

So I picked up one of the smaller ones. I guessed the cooks at our school just used it for peeling potatoes or carrots or something like that because the blade on the one I picked up was only a few inches long and very thin. I also remembering choosing that one because it was one of the few pieces on the floor that looked clean and didn't have any signs of stickiness on it. If Franny was hurt or worse somewhere, I didn't want to be carrying around a knife that might have been use to....well you know.

"I can't." I whispered and shook my head in fourth grade shame.

I carefully put the knife back on the magnetic board above the sinks. The Bible that Brady had left for me to find and the wrench in my back pocket were going to have to be enough for me. There was just some invisible line that I wasn't quite willing to cross, at least not yet anyways.

The door to the walk-in cooler was just as heavy as it was the first time that Brady and I had opened it. The floor was still slick with a dull rainbow of pudding cups. The dim light bulb flickered on and mixed with the rush of warm air, casting a cold hazy fog over all of the chilled cardboard boxes of plastic wrapped meats and vacuum sealed vegetables. On the back racks were rows and rows of half pint sized chocolate milks.

Brady had written down that this place was safe, but he didn't tell me what I was supposed to do when I got here. Also, there was no way that I could look around this cooler and not have the heavy door slam behind me. I assume that the ladies that do all of our cooking for school lunches don't have a problem with being in the forty degree cooler with the three inch thick door shut behind them, but the way my night was going, there was no way that I wanted to take that risk. There had to be some way to keep the door open while I figured out what Brady wanted me to do in there. So I looked around and did the best that I could considering the floor was already covered with a slick coating of pudding cups.

"Come on....come on." I grunted under my breath. I was able to kick the almost completely frozen box of assorted chicken parts (I swear to you that that was what was written on the side of the box on a bright yellow sticker, "Assorted Chicken Parts") to the door with no problem, but the hardest part was trying to wedge it in just the right way so it wouldn't just slide right out. The bottom of the frozen chicken box was getting wet and folding under its own weight with the more and more pudding cups that it slid across.

I kicked it with the tip of my toes, but every time that I thought that I almost had it, the stupid thing would slip off the corner, and the door would shut. And every time, I would have to stop the heavy door with my shoulder to keep it from slamming closed again. There was no choice. I had to just let it go and have faith that everything would be alright.

*Ok,* God. *Here it goes.*

And now what was quickly becoming a habit, I prayed to the heavens above that everything would be alright when the door did shut behind me. The door thankfully didn't slam shut but instead clicked twice. The first let me know that the door was closed and the second to let me know that not even the cold air filling the room would be escaping. *No air.* I turned the knob a half turn just to make sure that it wasn't locked (It wasn't.), and if I needed to make a quick escape, I would be able to high tail it out of there.

So there I was in my frigid walk-in tomb. The light bulb above was barely giving off enough light to read the labels, and I was quickly starting to get really really cold. I cupped my handed and blew in the warm air to keep my fingers from tingling with the chill. And as far as I could tell by looking around, there was nothing from Brady or Frances in the cooler that could help me out.

I pushed a few of the lighter smaller boxes from one side of the walk-in to the other trying to figure out why Brady had sent me here in the first place, and what exactly made this place so safe. I didn't know how much longer I was going to be able to withstand the coldness, and I was just about to give up. That was when I saw the symbol.

One the back wall near the corner of the walk-in cooler there was a small symbol scratched into the aluminum. The last time that I was at the church and brave enough to look around the kitchen, it was still there, but that was years and years ago. I am not sure how the etching in the wall was done at all, because I tried once to scratch just a straight line with the edge of my keys into that aluminum and came up short, but there in the top most corner was a circle and a cross.

"That doesn't look right. What is that?" my breath clouded in front of me with each word.

As far as I knew, that little marking could have been there forever, or even Evercool, the company that makes walk-in coolers could have put it there as some kind of quality symbol. But I knew, some part of me just knew, that that wasn't the case. That marking looked new. It looked like the image that Brady had tried in vain to draw in the torn pages of his Bible. Brady or Frances had put that there for me to find.

I traced the etching slowly with my nearly frozen fingers. "What does this mean, Brady? Why did you put it here?"

*Boom! Scritch! Boom! Scritch!*

From right outside the cooler door I heard something walking around the kitchen. I could tell by the sounds coming from right on the other side that whatever it was, it was too big to be either Brady or Frances. It was also too big to be another of those creature that O'Leary had sent to nap in the pews or cower in the corners of church boiler rooms. No, whatever it was sounded as if it was too big for the room. I could hear it bumping into stainless steel carts sending them rolling across the kitchen, and I could hear the beast struggling to make its way around the kitchen area of our cafeteria, squeezing its way closer. Pots and pans came crashing down around it like a Teflon avalanche. Each one bouncing off the floor causing culinary cymbals.

My little investigation in the back of the nearly freezing cooler kicked into high gear the moment I heard the noises from the other side. I still had to be as quiet as I could be and also try and manage to figure out what Brady's message had meant. The cold steel knob on the cooler door began its slow counterclockwise twist. I just knew that I had been too loud, and it had heard me fumbling around. Was this thing just outside the door one of the reasons that Franny wanted us to be silent as we wandered around in the dark? Well whatever it was, it had found what it was looking for, and was coming inside.

"Come on." I said. With my right hand I was pushing and tracing the symbol, and with my left I was trying to knock down as many boxes of frozen food as I could off of the shelves within my reach. Piles of pink frozen hamburger patties and bag after bag of crinkle cut French fries fell at my feet. Before I knew it, I was ankle deep in next week's lunch menu, but I didn't care. I just wanted as many obstacles as I could between me and whatever it was on the other side of that door.

I traced the circle a few times and then the cross. I tried pushing on it. Just when I was about to give up all together I pounded on it as hard as I could with my frozen fist. Thousands of tiny needles stung my palm with each frozen smack. Nothing seemed to be working, but then I noticed that I was looking in the wrong place the whole time.

"What is this?" I saw that the back wall of the Evercool walk-in cooler was open just a crack. I slid my hand in the crack that I had made pulling the wall sized door toward me. Now, I wished that I hadn't dumped all of those boxes on the floor, because all that I had done was create a wedge that prevented the door from opening.

Meanwhile, the main door to the cooler was opening at about the same time. The cold air whooshed out of the room, and I could just barely through the fog, make out what looked to be a long grey tentacle.

"That is why it had such a hard time opening the door." I said, my words being pulled away from me and toward the monster in the frosty air.

The thing fumbled and stumbled again trying to make its way through the tight doorway. Now, keep in mind that Brady and I could stand side by side at the entrance to that thing, but this monster was so large that I never even saw the whole body. Its blubbery walrus-like form undulated as hard as it could to make it inside. I still remember its slimy, slick tentacles pulling against the doorframe.

I was frozen in place. My heart was racing but for the life of me I could not get myself to bend over and pick up the Bible, or for that matter, the wrench that had fallen on the wet floor. My hands felt slick with a combination of perspiration and humidity. I needed to snap out of it and get moving, but I couldn't. It was the sound that it made that finally got me going.

*Ssslllluuurrrggg!*

The creature sounded as if it was struggling and having a hard time breathing in the cold air around it. I don't remember seeing a true face on the beast. I mean there was no real facial features like eyes or a nose that I could identify. There was a mouth, or should I say a beak. I once got on the computer and tried to find anything that I thought might even slightly resemble what I had seen that night. I never really found anything that matched, but I do remember thinking that the razor sharp beak looked a lot like the mouth of one of those giant squids. Which made sense to me, because that thing looked as if it was not only having a hard time moving around on land, but maybe wasn't even supposed to be out of the water.

The sea creature wasn't giving up, even though the blast of cold air seemed to be slowing it down. Was this the thing that grabbed Frances? Was this the thing that Frances had tried to fight off with all of those knives? I had no idea, but I did know that I needed to get out of there. And despite what Brady had written on that Bible page, I didn't feel safe at all.

I pushed one more time against the solid metal door, and I could just reach in up to my elbow. There was no way that I was going to be able to get that hidden door open before one of those dripping tentacles would reach me.

God, *I can't do this on my own. I just need a little help getting this stupid door open.*

Ok, so maybe this praying thing was becoming a real habit. But I didn't think at the time I was ready to let go of the wrench just yet.

The long tentacles stretched out and over each other like snakes. Each time reaching a bit closer to me than before. The tipped over boxes of French fries and burger patties that were my make shift barrier were now being tossed aside. The wire racks with stacks of food were yanked from the walls. Not only was the monster getting closer and closer to me, but also it was getting angry and cold. And worse than that, it was ready to take the whole situation out on me as if the whole thing was my fault.

I had no choice but to somehow sandwich my body between the ever so slim crack that I had made in the doorway. I bit down on my lower lip and pushed on it until I thought that the veins in my neck would pop.

It moved!

It was just a hair, but I could feel it move. I tried again. It moved another quarter inch. The first tentacle slithered closer and touched the tip of my sneaker. I did all I could, but I could only get my arm in up to my shoulder. There was no way that I would be able to get away in time. The creature had touched my shoe, and that gave it the incentive that it needed to continue towards me. Its tentacles moved faster and faster now excited by the prospect of finally catching its prey. The dim lightbulb above was almost completely eclipsed by the blob-like body now wedged in the entrance.

"No way! You ain't getting me! You aren't even real!" I screamed at the monster. But if he wasn't real, then was the thing in the boiler room real? What about Frances and Brady? If this wasn't real, then where were they?

"It's real, and it is sooooo hungry. Hungry for you, Petey." O'Leary chuckled. The words echoed throughout the metal cooler and in my head.

That was the push and the incentive that I needed. My knuckles whitened and my fingers screamed in cold pain as I pushed the door open enough to finally slip through. All I saw was darkness, but the dark unknown was better than the evil heading toward me.

I crawled on my hands and knees to the floor and as quickly and carefully as I could, I reached into the Evercool to grab my Bible and the custodian's wrench before that thing got any closer. The Bible's once wonderful brown leather cover was caked in goo and frozen breadcrumbs from whatever had spilled on it. I yanked the book into the blackness of the hall, and then went for the wrench. A long thin tentacle grabbed the business end of the tool at the same time that I gripped the handle. What happened next could only be described as a macabre tug-o-war. The harder that I pulled, the harder the tentacle pulled back.

"Give me that wrench!" I grunted through a clenched jaw.

My feet were propped up against the wall for leverage, but it did no good. There was just no way that that the fourth grade me was going to out pull and out tug a beast that must have weighed tons. In fact, I doubt I could out pull that thing today. So needless to say, that was the moment when I lost the wrench. My only hope now was to somehow get that door closed behind me.

I stood up and shifted both my weight and my attention to doing just that. I didn't realize how sore I was until I stood up. I never have and never will claim to be the most physically fit guy, but I was putting my body through the wringer that night. My body whole ached, but I mustered all the strength that I could and used my shoulder to push the door closed. It creaked a bit at first (the door, not my shoulder), but to my surprise, it closed without too much of a fight. So there I was temporarily safe from the octopus-like creature on the other side of the walk-in cooler, but now in a pitch black hallway that shouldn't even have existed. I really didn't have much of a choice, so I started walking down the hall and into the unknown.

The walls were slick with a cool condensation. I could feel the slime on my fingers and taste its mustiness on my tongue as I tried to feel my way blindly to wherever this dark distant tunnel leading me. I thought that I knew what dark was before, but the halls of St. Thomas were nothing compared to this. Imagine closing your eyes. Now, close them tighter, and now tighter still. Now, close them the way a toddler does, to the point it starts to hurt if you don't open them soon. I had always heard of the saying "so dark you can't see your hand in front of your face," but this was the first time in my life that I actually had a chance to try it.

I started with one hand on the wall and with the other I held out the Bible right in front of my face. Nothing. I pulled it within just a few inches of my nose, and I still couldn't make it out. In fact, I smelled the cover of the old leather and what I thought may have been yogurt before I ever saw anything. The book touched the tip of my nose before I saw the rectangular shape.

"Ha, well what do you know? It's true." I thought to myself.

The whole night was so absurd. I couldn't help but laugh at the fact that I was actually checking an old idiom to see if it was true. My slight grin turned into full blown laughter.

"Peter, my man, you are cracking up. You are going crazy in here. The next thing you know it will be raining cats and dogs!" I thought to myself, and started laughing until my sides hurt, and my back was wet with the mildew that covered the old bricks. I would have probably stayed in the dank dark nothingness just laughing the rest of the night away if it wasn't for O'Leary.

"Petey, you didn't really think you were safe, did you?" he whispered from behind me.

Even in the most remote part of the church, he had managed to find me. I moved as quickly as I could down the dark hidden corridor. I had to get away from the sound of his voice and the thing on the other side of the hidden cooler door.

"That's it, Petey. Run! Run as fast as you can, but you will never find them. They're dead, Petey. They're both dead." O'Creepy cackled.

It was true. I hadn't even noticed it before, but I was running. I couldn't see a thing a thing in front of me as I bounced like a pinball from one wall to the other, and on top of that, the thick rancid smell of black mold and slime was making it harder and harder for me to breathe. But as long as O'Leary was whispering in my ear, I wasn't going to stop moving.

My lungs were burning, and my heartbeat echoed throughout the stone chamber. I had to stop to catch my breath, even if it was just for a second or two. I just couldn't keep up that pace. Not only all that, but the soles of my shoes were wet which caused my feet to slip out from under me after each step. I finally stopped and put my grimy hands on my knees to bend down and collect myself.

"What are you going to do now, Petey? Left or right?" O'Leary's voice chuckled with anticipation.

The creepy pastor was right. Before I was able to reach out with my hands and touch both sides of the tunnel at once, but now I could only feel the slick smooth bricks on my right. Carefully, I took one step to my left and then another and finally, I felt the brick wall. I had come to a fork in the road. Ha, another idiom. Surprised I didn't think of it at the time.

"Oh Petey, you need some help don't you? Well, how about a clue? One tunnel leads to your friend, Brady, and the other one leads, well… … to my friend."

O'Leary was helping me now? I had a choice to make, and I'm not talking about left or right. I had to choose whether or not I was going to listen to him. Pastor Martin told us one Wednesday during chapel time that the devil was also known as the Prince of Lies. I wasn't sure if I had ever come face to face with the devil, but I did know that O'Leary was the closest thing to the devil in this church. So needless to say, I wasn't keen on taking any of his advice or directions. How was I going to pick the right path? I gulped, and took a few steps forward down the pathway to my right.

"Yes, Petey. Good choice. Good choice. That is the path I would have chosen myself. I can almost hear dear old Brady now. Can't you?" O'Leary said the moment I took my first step.

Great. Of course the second he said that I was going down the right path, I froze. I had to rethink this thing. If O'Leary wanted me to go to the right and that is what I was doing, did that mean I was heading toward Brady or something worse? Prince of Lies, right?

"You want me to go to the right?" I echoed through the pitch blackness of the cool stone tunnel.

Nothing.

I started to second guess myself. Maybe he knows that I know that he is lying. Maybe he is just tricking me. But if he knows I know, then wouldn't he send me down the wrong path and tell me it was the right one? I didn't know any more. The whole thing was making my head hurt. With just a few words, O'Leary had confused me and stopped me in my tracks. I mean would either one of these tunnels lead me to Brady? But I had to do something. So I took a few more steps. I had chosen the right path and no matter what he said, I was sticking to it.

"Okay, Petey ol' chum, I can't do this to you. You have been through enough. You are going down the wrong path. Go ahead and turn around before you get lost forever here in the darkness." O'Leary's voice sounded softer, like an old friend.

But I tell you that although I was scared and didn't know what to do, I didn't turn around. Half of me was tearing at my soul to listen him and to just turn around. My heartbeat was still pounding like a jackhammer in my fourth grade chest. The only thing that I knew I could do at that moment was to just keep walking forward. Why was O'Leary telling me to turn around? Was he trying to trick me before? Or was he trying to trick me now? I just kept moving forward.

"*Stop!!* If you don't stop right now, I will kill your friend Brady. Do you hear what I am saying, Peter? I will slit his fat throat until nothing comes out but strawberry jelly! *Turn around!*" O'Leary screamed.

I had never heard O'Leary that upset. "I thought he was already dead." I said to myself as I tried to catch what was left of my breath. Once again I stopped and put my hands on my knees and listened for his voice again.

When he said nothing, I replied. "You are nothing but a liar!"

Although I couldn't see anything, I kept my head down and pushed myself to move onward. I no longer had to hold on to the wall for support. Now, that I think about it, both of my hands were too busy clutching the Bible. Cool.

"You will pay for this Peter Alan Gentry! And so will everyone you love!" he screeched.

I ran and I ran. The darkness of the tunnel seemed endless, and I don't know if I had stopped because I finally ran out of breath, or I had ran out of tunnel. But the passageway stopped abruptly. The rounded walls of the final few feet were like a period at the end of a long sentence. I had hit the end, and there was nothing. I was exhausted, and my clothes felt heavy and weighted on my shoulders. The idea of walking all that way back through the dank musty darkness back to O'Leary and whatever that tentacled creature was lurking at the other end was more than I thought I could take. He had lied again. There was no Brady and Frances at the end of this hidden passage, and there was no "Friend of O'Leary" either. Just another slimy, damp wall covered in ancient bricks. At least that was what I thought at first.

I could see my shoes. It didn't quiet register at first, but I could see the tips of my sneakers. Sure enough there were tiny shadows bouncing off of the cobblestone that lined the floor of the chamber. A light literally at the end of the tunnel.

This wasn't the end. That light had to be coming from somewhere. There was a door somewhere along the back wall. I did the best that I could to feel around for some kind of way to get the door open, but all I felt was the same slick cool surface. I could feel the grooves of each brick, but nothing that felt like an opening. So, I put my fingers at the base of the door. The thin golden light shone on my fingertips as I traced the outline. I remember being careful not to put my fingers under the door completely. There was still no telling if there might be something on the other side, and there was no way I was going to take any chances.

Although I lost it a few times, there was definitely a pattern. One line solid line of grout went from the light coming from under the door straight up the bricks. I reached up and followed it as far as I could, but it went on higher than I could reach on my tip toes. My hands were already filthy so I didn't mind pushing and pulling on the wall to see if I could get it to move. And just like the entrance in the back of the walk-in cooler, this heavy door began to slowly and reluctantly give. The sounds of stone scraping on stone filled the chamber with gritty echoes. Where the doorway in the back of the Evercool was icy cold and slick and caused my hands to slip and my shoes to slide, this door was like sticking your hand down the kitchen sink. The bricks were slimy, and I really didn't want to know what was oozing between my fingers. But I knew that what I was doing was working because the harder that I pushed, the more light I could see.

I was almost able to get my arm through the crack. But would that have been a smart thing to do? So far, if there was something in there, it wasn't making any effort to get at me. I mean nothing had tried to grab my hand or help me get the door open. I was so afraid that a long sticky octopus tentacle was going to grab my arm and yank me through the door. It would have been just like O'Leary to lead me down a dark hidden tunnel that does nothing but circles around back to the creature in the kitchen. But nothing grabbed me, so I slowly and timidly pushed my arm through as far as it would go. My already dirty shirt picked up another layer of filth up to my collarbone.

Still nothing from the other side. So with one last heave, I opened the door just enough to get inside. I picked up my Bible and walked in.

There on a tiny cot was Brady. His long greasy hair was matted down in front of his face blocking his eyes. The torn fabric of his shirt matched the rips in the cot. He looked dead. Maybe that was the reason that he didn't jump up and help me open the door. Had I come all of this way just to find my best friend's body?

"Brady, is that you? Are you ok?" I said and very carefully touched the cuff of his jeans that drooped over the side of the metal cot. I could already feel the tears welling in my eyes.

The laces of his shoes were missing. They had been taken out of his tennis shoes and now they looped around a beam in the center of the room.

"Oh my, Brady. Tell me you didn't do it."

But I could tell that Brady's attempt to kill himself had been unsuccessful because the laces had broken under his weight. Why would he do that? What had been so bad that he would want to take his own life?

"Brady? Don't be dead. It's me, Peter." I pleaded to his lifeless body.

I leaned over and nudged him by his shoulders. I could feel his shoulder bones under his loose skin. What had happened to him? I rattled the cot this time with another more aggressive shake. He still wasn't moving, and I couldn't tell if he was even breathing or not. But there was no way that I was just going to turn around and leave my best friend there in some dungeon. I wasn't leaving Brady behind, dead or not. I would carry him back if I had to.

His leg moved first and then his arm. Brady was still alive! I balanced myself at the edge of his cot and tried to slowly help him sit up. He was very groggy and very tired. His sunken cheeks looked hungry and dry cracked lips were dehydrated. But he was alive, and that was all that mattered at the moment.

"Pete?" he said to me in a voice barely above a sigh.

"Yeah Brady, it's me. I've come to take you out of here. Everything's going to be alright." I answered.

"Why did it take you so long to find me? I left you so many clues." Brady said in the same dry whisper.

"What are you talking about, Brady? I came as fast as I could. It's only been a few minutes. I found the clue you left for me. I came in through the back of the cooler." I was puzzled, but I tried to reassure him.

Brady looked at me with deep shallow eyes. "Peter, it's been months."

# CHAPTER 16

I didn't understand what Brady was talking about. He did look as if he had been kept in that room for longer than a few minutes. The way his cheeks were sunken in, the length of his hair, and the fact that it looked as if he had lost a lot of weight in just that little amount of time made me not question him, at least for the moment. But it was more than that. There was a sense of desperation and loss in his voice. It sounded as if I had in some way disappointed him, and he had long ago given up on me ever coming for him.

I looked up at Brady's dirty shoelaces still knotted together and dangling from the beam in the center of the room.

"Come on. Let's get out of here." I said and picked up Brady. I let him lean his weak frame against mine, and I held him up on my shoulder taking as much of his weight that my small frame could hold. His knees buckled out from under him a few times, but after a step or two, he was already feeling a bit stronger.

I remember noticing the large steel door on the opposite wall of where his cot laid, and I could see the scratch marks around the edges where Brady had tried to open it. At least I assumed that the marks were made by him. It reminded me more of those doors you see in a hospital room, you know the ones that you have to push that big round button on the wall to get it to open. It looked more like that than to the doors to a church. The lower corners where it had been kicked repeatedly, and the area around the doorknob was a dingy scratched white.

"We can't go back the way that I came in. We have to try and get that door open." I told him.

"You can't. I tried." his whispered. His voice wasn't here with us, but off somewhere deep in space.

"Well, maybe the both of us working together can get that thing open." I said. I grabbed at the rusted doorknob and gave it a twist. It wasn't that it was frozen and didn't move, but just the opposite, all it did was spin. I couldn't seem get a decent grip on it at all. My fingers kept slipping, and I soon found out why there were so many scratch marks around the cracks.

"You can't. I tried." Brady repeated in the same zombie-like trance.

"Brady, snap out of it, man. I can't do this by myself. You have to get over here and help me out." I pleaded. Although Brady, with a little help from the wall, was standing now on his own, that was about all he was able to do. I felt horrible about asking him to help me, because the guy could hardly stand, but I wasn't lying when I said that I needed his help.

I half pushed and half walked him closer to the door. All I needed him to do was try. I had already opened two nearly impossible doors tonight, so I had real confidence going into this one, especially if I could get Brady to help me out.

"You can't. I tried." he repeated.

Poor Brady. His eyes were glazed as he looked past me and peered at the walls behind me. Whatever he had been going through all of this time must have been a hundred times worse than any boiler room tarp creature or kitchen cooler squid monster from hades. He was gone, somewhere else, and I prayed that after I got him out of this situation, he would come back to me. But for now, we had to concentrate on getting out of that cell.

"Look." I said, "Just put your hands here" I held his hands in mine and helped him grasp the doorknob with both hands. "There you go. Now, all you have to do is pull. Do you hear me, Brady? When I count to three, pull as hard as you can. Understand?"

"I tried." Brady said. He stared without blinking at the rusted doorknob.

Hey, at least he didn't say, "You can't. I tried." I dug my already sore and grimy fingers in the crack of the thick industrial door. The tips of my fingers ached.

"One!"

I couldn't tell if Brady was pulling on the knob yet or not, but at least he hadn't let go.

"Two!"

Brady's head started to bobble and weave. He was doing a weird figure eight with his neck. He still held on to the knob, but it looked as if he was getting dizzy from standing so long. It must have been a combination of the malnutrition and dehydration that was causing him to almost faint.

"Come on, Brady, we're almost there!" I said trying to encourage him.

Brady's eyes froze, and his head turned to the attention of the metal legs of the worn Army cot. No, it wasn't the cot he was staring at, it was the Bible that I had placed on the floor beside it when I had sat down next to him. I must have forgotten to pick it up. His eyes widened, and he smiled a black and yellow smile.

"Three!" I yelled.

But it was too late. Brady let go of the doorknob and fell to his knees. As he was trying to frantically crawl his way to the Bible, I fell tailbone first onto the concrete floor. Brady gripped the Bible and brought it to his chest like Smegal holding his "Precious" ring.

"Ouch, Brady! That hurt! What was that all about?" I said and stumbled to my knees. "What are you trying to do, kill me?"

But he wasn't paying any attention to me. He sat on the floor crossed legged in a tight ball flipping through the pages of the torn bible. It didn't look as if he was looking for anything in particular, but more like he was just taking comfort in the feeling of having it in his hands.

What I didn't notice because I was too busy being tripped up by Brady was that the door was now open. Not only was the door open, but it flew open as if it wasn't locked, jammed, or even closed all the way. That was why I went flying through the air and nearly broke my butt bone in the fall. I can be honest with you and tell you that my tailbone still aches sometimes if the rain is coming in from the west. I couldn't for the life of me figure out why Brady didn't just open the door and walk out of this room a long time ago, or why he kept insisting to me that it was useless to even try.

"Brady, look." I said and nudged him toward the open door. The door is open, and now we can get out of there. "It wasn't even that hard, so come on. Grab that Bible and let's get out of here before someone or something shows up to try and stop us." I continued and grabbed him by the arm. Thank you God that he was as weak as he was and didn't put up too much of a fight. He was just relieved and excited to be getting out of that tiny prison, and although I had only been in there with Brady for a few minutes, so was I.

If the first tunnel was dungeon-like with its dark slimy wet brick walls and its cobblestone floor, than this hallway was just the opposite. My eyes were almost blinded as I walked through squinting my way down. Overhead was row after eye piercing row of bright white florescent lighting. I wasn't more than five feet tall, and I could easily reach up and touch the warm bulbs. The walls were lined with white subway tiles. Even the floor looked as if it was once painted white before a worn path of concrete left the center grey and exposed.

Brady held on to the Bible with one hand and to my arm with the other, keeping his eyes shut the entire time. I guided us around one corner and then another. Our breathing was staggered and echoed off of the tiles. This path was longer than the one that had led me to Brady. In fact, it was longer than it should have been. Even with its snake-like twist and turns, the whole tunnel seemed longer than the church itself.

Our fourth grade class along with a few others once had to run the circumference of the whole St. Thomas property for P.E. Which meant we had to start from one long fence line in the front of the school, run around the chapel, and finally make our way back around the track that took up most of the back part of the property. This blinding maze of tiles and lights that Brady and I were traveling seemed much much longer than that. There was even twice when I just couldn't go on any longer, and we had to stop. I had to catch my breath before heading forward once again.

"Brady, don't worry. It can't be too much longer. This tunnel has to end soon." I reassured him the first time that we stopped. The tiles on the walls were blindingly bright, and the whole hallway smelled of bleach. Brady didn't say a word, but just leaned his worn and tired body against the wall.

"I have to stop, but just for a second or two. Let me catch my breath. I think I see the end of this thing." I said much later the second time we stopped. I didn't really see the end of the white hallway, but I just couldn't tell Brady that. Not that he ever said anything in response. He just kept holding on tightly to both me and the Bible.

The pockets of my dirty cargo pants weighed heavy around my legs and my shoes felt like lead weights around my ankles, but I knew that we had to keep moving. Was this what Brady meant when he said that he tried to get out? Maybe he didn't mean the door to his dungeon, but this overly bright never ending hallway. Was this some kind of sick trick that O'Leary was playing on us?

After a few more stops and what seemed like an eternity, I saw the end. "I see it!" This time I wasn't lying to Brady. I could just make out something at the end of the hall. I couldn't tell what it was, but only that it was different. "There, do you see it? We just have a bit further." I reassured him.

As we got closer and closer I could feel the excitement in Brady's steps. Although he hadn't said anything since we came through the door, I could feel the hope in his stride as we got closer to the end of the tunnel. I was no longer dragging him along. He was still holding on to me, sure, but now we were running together.

I still couldn't tell what exactly we were running towards. At that point I didn't care if it was a hundred squid monsters. I just wanted to be out of that hallway, and away from all of that light. There was something about the way it didn't just shine on me, but in some way the light seemed to shine through me. There was just a sense of exposure that I couldn't put my finger on. The whole night I didn't feel dirty inside or out, not truly dirty until I was under that light. And it wasn't like a soft glow of the afternoon sun. No, more like the lights you see as you look up from the gurney right before the drugs set in, and you go under the knife. Whatever was ahead if us was just the opposite. Ahead of us was dark. After the way my night had been going, the last thing that I thought I would have wanted was the dark, but I couldn't wait to get out of this tunnel and all of that light.

There was a familiar smell in the air. A horribly wonderful combination of mothballs and rubbing alcohol. The closer that we got to the dark opening at the end of the hall, the stronger and stronger I could smell it burning in my nostrils.

"Do you smell that, Brady? You know what that means, right?" I said.

Sure I was out of breath, and my lungs felt as if I had daggers poking me through my side, but I was overjoyed. For the first time in a long time I finally felt as if I had some control as what was happening to us. I knew where the tunnel had led us.

"Yes." Brady answered.

He answered me! Brady wasn't a basket case after all. It was the first thing that he had said to me since we left that tiny cell of a room. Maybe the further away that we got from where he was being kept, the better he was feeling. At least that is what I was hoping. All I really cared about was that Brady, my best friend was coming back to me. He was finally talking.

"Yes, Brady, yes!" I tried to encourage him even more. We were almost to our destination, and I could already feel the cold air blasting around my ankles. "Just a little more. Come on, man."

I knew how that bunch of kids coming back from Narnia in that book that my third grade teacher, Mrs. Pendleton, read to us must have felt. There was that sense that everything was going to be okay. That you were finally safe and finally home. Only instead of pushing our way through racks and racks of big, thick, politically incorrect, fur coats and heavy winter jackets, Brady and I pushed our way through boxes of rolled math and science posters and stacks of labeled school supplies.

The familiar smell of mothballs came from the boxes that Mrs. Anderson had over-filled with shepherd's Christmas costumes for the annual pageant where the fourth graders always played the shepherds watching their fields by night, and the Easter parade that each grade participated in where the grades walked up and down the hallways of the Heavenly Gates Retirement Home waving their palm branches. Mrs. Anderson was against both events, but she said that if we had to participate the least we could do was not parade around with holes in our pants. Hence the mothballs.

As for the rubbing alcohol, well let me just say that Mrs. Anderson's ankles got mighty sore at the end of the day whenever our class had to climb up and down the stairs a few extra times. So she would always keep a plastic bottle of Sweet Relief rubbing alcohol in the bottom drawer of her desk and try to apply it discretely during afternoon quiet reading time. She was actually pretty good at hiding it too until one time that in the middle of the dead silence Shane dropped his library book "on accident" and made her jump up out of her seat, and spill half of a bottle of the stuff onto the carpet.

"Made it!" I said and grabbed onto the back shelves of Mrs. Anderson's closet. I looked back, and Brady was smiling. "I told you that I would save you."

"Made it." Brady repeated quietly and smiled back.

I opened the closet door slowly and carefully and walked into our frigid classroom. Brady was still holding on to me, but after a few steps, let go and walked around the room by himself. But it was different for him than it was for me. You see, when I opened that door and walked through, I felt for the first time in that class a sense of that same coming home, that same sense of comfort that I mentioned earlier. There was just something wonderful about seeing all of our desk spotless and lined up in perfect rows. Each one had our chairs tucked neatly behind them. Even Mrs. Anderson's desk, usually a menacing monolith that represented trouble, seemed to be inviting me in.

I found my desk and pulled out my chair. I more collapsed than sat down. The cold and the darkness covered me like cool sheets on a hot summer night. I remembering closing my eyes and letting my body finally feel less tense, and I could feel all of my muscles relax. It was also the first time I had a chance to feel how badly my shoulder had been bruised trying to knock open that door. It throbbed lightly.

But like I said, it was different for Brady. For him it was like looking at the ocean for the first time, or maybe looking into the Grand Canyon. Although it was dark, I could still see his eyes widen, and there was a look of astonishment on his face. He later told me that it was as if you had dreamt all of your life about something, someplace, and then walked through a door and there it was. Mrs. Anderson's fourth grade classroom was his paradise.

"It's all here. All of it is exactly like I remembered it." Brady said. He traced his fingertips along a few desk in one of the rows, and then did the same to three of the chairs.

"Of course it is, Brady. We were just here a few hours ago. It couldn't have been much longer than that." I told him.

He turned and looked at me.

"Look, Brady. Why don't you come over to your desk and have a seat for a bit? I know that I'm exhausted, so you must be too." I continued.

There was no way that he wasn't worn out. I mean he was barely able to stand just a few minutes ago, and then to have to run all that way. He should have been on the floor tired, or at least dead on his feet. But instead of taking my advice, Brady was still too astounded to be back in our homeroom class.

"Thirsty." Brady said more to himself, and then shuffled his feet over to the window.

The glass of the windows were covered in condensation, and the branches from the thick oaks outside made the lights and shadows dance. The strange thing that I noticed was that shadows were dancing in the same places as they were before when Frances had led the three of us down here the first time. That meant that the moon was in the exact same place in the sky as it was before. But that was impossible, wasn't it?

"Thirsty." he repeated. Then Brady took two of his fingers and touched the glass. He rubbed them slowly from the top of the window to almost the bottom. Brady stared at his wet fingertips and licked the water off of them. Then, his eyes and attention went from the glass to the short bookshelves under the now streaked windows.

"Brady, what are you doing? We can go to the water fountains. We can find you something to drink." I started to get up out of my chair.

"Thirsty." Brady said. He grabbed the teardrop shaped plastic misting bottle off of the shelf and began to slowly unscrew the top. Mrs. Anderson kept it there to water the potted plants that she had blooming on the window sill. The little green trigger spun around in slow circles. He loosened it completely and then gently pulled out the long clear tube that pulled the water through the gun. Brady carefully balanced the wet trigger returning it to the shelf. I sat there frozen and amazed. I mean I guess it was just water inside the bottle, but gross. I mean that had to be nasty sink water that had been sitting stagnate on that shelf for weeks.

"Oh Brady, come on. You don't have to drink that." I tried to say, but I was still mesmerized. Brady was slowly and steadily drinking all of the water out of the mister bottle. Ok, so maybe Brady wasn't a hundred percent back to normal.

"A few hours ago?" Brady stopped drinking and sat the plastic bottle down on Emma Talsey's desk.

"What?" I asked.

"What do you mean a few hours ago?" Brady's voice was sounding much better. The gravel in the back of his throat must have been washed out with that last drink of plant water.

"I mean that we were just here a few hours ago. We were just here earlier tonight. Don't tell me that you don't remember coming here with Frances." Brady winced at the sound of her name. "It was when we first came into the church. Remember, she grabbed the flashlight."

"Of course I remember, Peter." Brady said and pulled out a chair to finally sit down. "I'm not stupid."

"Of course, man. I didn't think that you were. It's just you are acting kind of weird." I replied carefully. Brady was obviously struggling with sanity, and

I didn't want to do anything that might push him over the edge. My best move was to just keep smiling and humor him until we could both figure out what was going on around here.

"I remember, okay? It's just that it wasn't earlier tonight. That was months ago, Pete." Brady said seriously. His eyes burned a hole in me. He meant every word. His body leaned against the wall and he began to speak to me, no more like he was pleading to me to help him understand.

"You left me." Brady continued and then paused. "You left the both of us. Months ago." With his last words, Brady voice once again faded, and he looked to the ground at the worn carpet. His voice filled with disappointment.

I sat there staring at Brady not knowing what to say. He was serious, dead serious. It was a mixed look of not just disappointment, but anger, and sadness. What was he talking about? Yes, he looked and acted as if he had been locked up and gone for much longer than just a few hours, but months? That was impossible.

I think it was almost three whole years ago from today that Brady and I were finally able to sit down and have a few drinks and talk about his time in that room. I don't have the time to go into those details, not that there were many. But I will tell you that he used some of the same words over and over again as we talked that night. No matter how hard I tried to pry some of the details of Brady's time in that cell, not just so I would have something to say to people like you, but also for myself as well. All he kept coming back to were the same two words "Nothing" and "Alone." But that night as we sat at our desks trying to recover from whatever it was that we had just been trying to get away from, I will never forget just how serious the look on Brady's face was.

"I'm sorry." was all I could think of to say to him. There was no use getting into an argument about how long he had been in there, or how long it took me to get to him. Neither of us had the energy.

The chill of the air being pumped out of the air conditioner felt nice on my fingertips and on my toes. The familiar smells of our classroom helped me settle down. And even in the darkness, I could make out the safe rectangular shapes of the desk and the bookcases, the posters on the walls and the computer center that Mrs. Anderson had set up in the corner. When I thought that Brady was ready, I asked him a question.

"You said 'both of us', Brady. Does that mean that you were in there with Franny?" I asked. "Is she alright? How can we get her?"

Brady stood up and went to the front of the room. He stood in front of the white board. Although we were never allowed to touch the Expo markers as per specific orders from Mrs., Anderson, Brady grabbed the red marker and made a small square in the middle of the board.

"This was me." Brady pointed to the square. "When things got really bad, he would come and open the door and take me here." Brady drew a long line from the red square straight down. He connected it to a long rectangle. But after drawing it, he shook his head and erased the rectangle with the ball of his hand and instead drew it again using a black marker. He divided the long rectangle into a dozen or so little blocks, so it looked like an egg carton.

"Who is 'he'?" I asked.

Brady didn't answer, but instead continued. "That is where I saw her. I don't know if she saw me, but I saw Frances." He pointed to the rows of little tiny squares inside of the rectangle and marked the square in the bottom right hand corner. "Although, I remember long ago that I got to talk to her. It was only for a second or two, but the vail was so thin. We thought we had a chance to get to you. But no matter how hard we tried, you just couldn't hear us. And then she was gone."

"No, Brady. I heard you! I heard every word! That is what brought me to you." my voice raced.

"I never heard from her again. Franny I miss you so much." Brady cried.

"Was she alright? How do we get to her?" I said and stood up excited ignoring his tears.

I walked to the white board and took the Expo from Brady's hand. I pointed to the same little square. "Brady, we have to get to her. Tell me where this is." I said and pounded dots on the square.

Brady took the black Expo marker from my hand and silently returned it into its little magnetic pocket in the corner of the board, and then he took out the blue one. He slowly walked across the room studying every step. He finally made his way back to the window where he had licked his fingers after getting them wet with the condensation. He squeaked opened the blue marker and drew a tiny dot on the glass. "This is us."

"There? I don't get it?" I said.

"Actually, not there, but I can't open the window. The dot really belongs on the other side of the glass." Brady put the cap back on the marker and walked back to the white board. "Don't you get it, Peter? We can't get to her. We aren't even close."

"Then how do we get close?" I demanded.

"He has her now. We can't go get her, and I can't go back there." Brady said shaking his head. His eyes got large and saucer like, but just as quickly he stopped looking at me and instead looked shamefully down at his feet.

Brady was really starting to make me mad. I mean I saved his butt, and all he did was complain that I took too long to get to him, and that now he was telling me that there was no way that he was even going to try and save Frances. Now, he was giving up. I mean I get it. The guy had been through something terrible. Something that I could never understand, but in my world all I knew was that this was still just spending one stinking night in St. Thomas.

I stood there in the dark inches away from Brady's face, and I am not afraid to tell you that I was so close to punching him. But even hungry and dehydrated, Brady was still much bigger than me. So instead of punching him, I got loud. "How dare you! Look at me!" I started in on him.

Brady looked up like a puppy that just got caught peeing on the rug. He was silent and on the verge of tears, but that didn't stop me. God knows my heart and how I wish I would have just given him a hug or something and told him that I was there for him. But like I said, I was mad and in fourth grade. All of my feelings of weakness and hopelessness of everything that had happened that night came gushing out of me like a firehose.

"Don't you dare cry on me! I don't care what you think. I ran as fast as I could. I killed a... ..... I-don't-know-what to get to you. It hasn't been months, it's been minutes, and if you can't handle that then you are just a little bed wetting baby!" I screamed in his face.

I found out later when I overheard Brady's mom and my mom talking at the kitchen table once that after this night Brady did wet the bed. I found out that even months after this night was over, Brady would still wake up covered in sweat, and his sheets soaked in urine. That was of course on the nights when he could even sleep at all.

Yeah, I stink. But I wasn't done making my best friend feel like dirt. "We need to find Frances! I found you, so don't give me this 'We can't'. We will find her, Brady." I was starting to calm down a bit. "We have to."

Brady should have punched me. He should have laid into me the way that I had laid into him, but like I said, there was nothing left inside of him. Instead he turned away from me and quietly sat down at his desk. Brady tucked in his chair and crossed his arms over his chest. The tears shimmered down his shallow cheeks, glowing in the moonlight.

"I tried to save her, Peter. For the longest time, I tried. That is what he wanted me to do. Each time I would get a little closer to her, but I was never able to reach her. And every single time he would laugh. He would laugh from the bottom of his gut until tears of joy ran down his face. But that wouldn't stop me from trying. I would try again and again, no matter how much he kept laughing at me." Brady said to me. He leaned in and put his elbows on his desk, and rested his chin in his hands. "You can't save her, Peter."

I grabbed the closest chair to Brady and turned it around. I remember straddling the seat and leaning my body against the back of the chair. "Then what should we do, Brady?" I wasn't mad anymore, and I still had no idea what or who he was talking about.

"Pray." Brady said. "That's all we can do. We can hide and pray for the morning to come. We can pray that this will all be over soon." He opened up the dirty, torn Bible and flipped blindly through the pages. It was still way too dark to read. Slowly he turned each page as if it were brand new as if he was afraid to rip the thin paper.

"Brady?" I said. He looked up at me from his book. "Is it almost over? Is it almost dawn?' I asked.

Brady sat quietly for what seemed like a long time in the silence of the room, but was probably no more than just a few seconds as if he was thinking. "No, Peter. It hasn't even started."

He wasn't guessing. He said it as if he knew how this terrible night would end, as if it were just some horrific movie that he had already seen, so he knew how it would wrap up. And although at first I felt pretty safe and sound back in our homeroom, now I felt as if I had to get out of there. I looked at the closet door. Had Brady left it open just a crack? I couldn't remember. Whomever Brady was talking about kept him in that dark dank cell and that meant that there was only one bright hallway separating us. And the more I thought about it, the more that wasn't far enough.

"Ok, Brady, but we need to get out of this classroom. We can't stay here.

Let's see if there is anything else we might need tucked in these desk or something, and then we can get out." I suggested.

Brady must have been thinking the same thing. He didn't question me, or say that it wasn't a good idea. Instead, he got up without saying a word and started to look around in the darkness to see if there was anything else that we should take out of there before we left. I quickly followed his lead and started looking around the classroom myself. To tell you the truth, I wasn't sure what we would find, but the first thing that I grabbed was one of our classroom Bibles off the bookshelf. If Brady's torn and ragged copy that he had found by the adult study rooms saved me before, I was hoping that a new one with a decent cover might even be better.

Brady grabbed a marker and an ink pen from his desk. We opened Mrs. Anderson's desk also just to see if there was anything worth pocketing. I guess my biggest score as a pack of salted peanuts and half of a Twix bar.

"Brady, do you think we might need these?" I questioned him as I held up a pair of scissors.

"No, but put these in your back pocket for later." Brady answered.

He held up a pair of paper sunglasses that folded to fit into a thin clear pocket found in the back of one of our class science flip books. They were the kind of glasses that you could use to look into a total eclipse without frying your eyeballs. Of course, whoever was the genius that included them in our fourth grade science book about space never figured that they would be completely useless when you put them on and looked at the pages of the book.

"What do I need those for? You can't even see out of them." I said to him as he handed me the glasses.

"Just trust me, Peter. You will know when to put them on." Brady said.

With that, the two of us left nothing but the frost of our last few breaths in the freezing classroom. Our pockets were full of school supplies and snacks for whatever may lie ahead. Brady seemed to know what we had to do and what tools we would need to do it, so of course I trusted him. I mean really, what choice did I have?

# CHAPTER 17

"You do know where you are going, right?" I questioned Brady.

He wasn't very talkative. You see, before Brady was lost in some cell deep inside an unknown part of St. Thomas, and I found him comatose in that cell just lying there on a torn-up army cot, he would talk your ear off if you gave him half a chance. In fact, there was more than once that I faked falling asleep as he was telling me a story about how his cat learned how to fetch a balled up piece of paper, or pretended that I was running late to something and had to cut our conversation about how his grandmother made the absolute best pumpkin pie in the world, anything, just so I could avoid listening to him drone on and on about nothing. But now as we both left our homeroom class, he was much more stoic.

The door to Mrs. Anderson's classroom shut with an extra loud bang, and the two of us jumped. For half a moment I wondered to myself if I was ever going to walk back in that classroom again. There was something in the sound of that door and the way that it had shut that made it all sound so final.

The both of us were getting way too familiar with the darkness that seemed to be in every corner of the church and the quietness of those pitch black hallways. Classroom after classroom seemed to zip by as we made our way down the hall, and for the first time that night I noticed that the air coming from under each door was different. Some, like Mrs. Pendleton's second grade classroom, seemed to radiate heat through the thin pane of glass in the door. While others, like Mrs. Anderson's blew chillingly cold. I mean I get it, the whole church is an old building, but there was nothing normal about the way each room's temperature was so dramatically different.

"I think that we should change first before we get inside." Brady said. With that, he headed towards the parts of the church that we students really never ventured. We were heading to some of those doors that I told you about earlier. You know the ones that just seemed to walk by and never opened.

Now, remember, I had no idea exactly where we were going, or what we were about to do. All I knew was that I had some really stale snacks getting squished in my pockets along with a pair of safety scissors and a pair of useless solar eclipse sunglasses. But like I said, for some reason I had great faith in Brady. So with my pockets full, I followed Brady.

"Brady, are you sure that you know what to do in order to get Franny back?" I questioned.

He didn't answer me. Instead, he stretched out his hand and felt along the long left hand side of the hallway. Brady would stop at each closed door and count out loud to himself.

"One." he whispered.

After a few more silent steps, he would stop and do it again. "One, two."

I was beginning to think that maybe Brady had forgotten about me, and didn't even know that I was following behind him anymore. Or for that matter, if he did know I was back there, I don't really think he cared that I was.

"One, two, three" he continued.

When he had gotten to about seven I couldn't take it anymore and tapped him on the shoulder. "Brady, do you need my help or anything? What are you counting for?" I asked.

He finally acknowledged my existence, "No, Pete, I'm fine. I am counting because I need to find the ninth door on the left. Inside it should have what we need to change."

See, here is the strange thing. I didn't even question that! I mean how could he possibly have known all of this? How could he have known that we had to count the doors and change clothes? Was it hidden somewhere? Was it written down on something? Did Brady find it while he spent all that time in that room? I would ask him about it from time to time, and he would always say roughly the same thing. "I don't know how I knew, Peter. I just did. And it all worked out, didn't it? I mean almost." But at that time, on that night, I just believed him and let him lead the way.

"Ok, Brady. I trust you." I said.

"Great! What number was I on? Was that last door the seventh, or was the next one supposed to be the seventh?" he said in a frustrated whisper.

"What? No, that was the seventh door. I heard you say seven." I said and shook my head reassuringly.

"Are you sure? We can't get it wrong. Bad things can find us if we get it wrong." Brady stressed.

"Yes, I'm sure." I said. No, I wasn't one hundred percent sure, but I wasn't going to tell Brady that. After all, I was the one that messed up his count in the first place.

"Ok, Peter. I trust *you*." Brady repeated my words back to me.

He put his arm out and touched the textured wall again. His hands slowly moving towards what we both were hoping was door number eight.

"One, two, three, four, five, six, seven, eight." Brady said under his breath. "Only one more to go."

"God, please let this next door be door number nine." I whispered a quick prayer.

"This should be it. When we get inside don't bother to take off your clothes, just put the robe on over it." Brady gave me the instructions as he carefully and quietly twisted the brass knob.

Inside the musty smelling room were row after row of bright white gowns. Even in the thin light of the moon through the only window, the baptismal robes seemed to glow angelically on the racks. They were each carefully hung on pearl silk hangers with little bows on the top. The light pink bows were for the women, and the dark green bows on the hangers were meant for the men. Not only were the robes separated by sex, but also by size. The ones closest to the door were smaller and meant for toddlers, and then it went all the way up to what I could only assume were reserved for the NBA.

"This is perfect. Try to find one that fits you and put it on. Hurry." Brady put his worn and torn Bible on a chair beside him and immediately began flipping through the robes. He spent the next few minutes trying to find one that would fit a used-to-be-kind-of-husky-but-had-now-lost-a-tremendous-amount-of-weight-because-he-was-imprisoned sized boy. I, on the other hand, just needed a child sized medium.

To my surprise, Brady was able to find one right away, but in contrast everyone that I tried on seemed to be wrong in one way or another. The first one had super long sleeves that hung way past my wrist. I looked like an albino sea lion.

"This is right." Brady said reassuringly. "This just feels like the right thing to do. I better write it all down." he said to himself. Brady reached into his pants pocket and pulled out a wad of crumpled notebook paper. "Ninth door on the left. Put on a robe." Brady continued to mumble to himself as he scribbled the instructions on the scrap of paper with the nub of his pencil.

I don't know who hung all of those robes, but the next three I tried on were way too small. I felt like Goldilocks. Too small, too big, and then finally, just right. The sleeves stopped just above my wrist and the length was a little past my waist. I helped Brady zip up the back of his and then he returned the favor.

There we were, Brady and I, in our white baptismal robes ready to take on whatever Brady had planned for us next. The problem with that was that I wasn't really sure that he knew exactly what to do next.

"Now what?" I asked.

"Well you see, the next part wasn't as clear. I knew that we had to get here and put these on." Brady said and held out his arms so his sleeves fell like the wings of a dove. "But the next part wasn't as clear." he repeated.

"So, we just walk around the church looking like a boys' choir?" I flapped my wings too. "Try and describe what you think you saw, and maybe I can help you figure it out." I suggested.

Brady picked up his Bible and sat on one of the forest green padded chairs and thought for a moment. "That's the thing, Pete. It was like I was on top of the sanctuary looking down on the whole room, but instead of rows and rows of pews, all I saw was….." Brady began and then his voice trailed off.

"What did you see, man?" I said. I could tell by the tone of his voice that whatever Brady was trying to remember seemed to hurt him. He was struggling, but not because he couldn't remember, but because he *could*, and that memory was scaring him to death.

There was again a smell of mothballs. Only this time it was mixed with the aroma of stale linen that filled the room, and I longed for that cold chilled air of Mrs. Anderson's room as my back started to get sticky with sweat. I could tell by the beads building on Brady's forehead that he was feeling hot too.

"I… I think it was a special place. I don't know how I know, but it was a place that was not here or there, somewhere in between. It was a place for people who were stuck." Brady said. He didn't say it to be over dramatic or to scare me for some kind of dramatic effect. I am telling you that to this day, if I think about it, I can still hear the somber tone of his voice. Brady was serious.

He continued. "It was black and grey. And there was smoke coming from the black made my eyes water and burn. The back of my throat felt as if it was on fire. There was screaming and crying, Peter. So much screaming and so much pain was coming from so deep that I swear I couldn't see a thing. My eyes burned so much." Tears ran down Brady's cheeks and down his chin.

I wasn't really sure what to do. I mean I was only in fourth grade for goodness sake, and my best friend just got finished telling me about what could only be described as some kind of purgatory.

"I'm sure that wasn't it. It was probably just one of O'Leary's tricks to try and scare you." I tried to reassure him.

"Who?" Brady asked.

"Oh, no one." I said and sat down beside him. "Is what you saw the way back to Frances? Is this all going to give us a chance to find her and get out of this place?" I changed the subject.

"I think so. I remember hearing her. She was very far away, but she was there."

My mind went back to the images of squares, rectangles, and long winding pathways that Brady had drawn on the white board in our class. I remembered the way that he walked so quietly to the window and the *thunk* sound as his finger pointed to the thick pane of glass. That had to be where Frances was now, on the other side of that glass.

"Then that is where we are going." I told Brady. "Frances would go for us." There was no doubt in my mind that if the situation was reversed, she would have too.

"You're right, Pete." Brady said and stood up.

I would say that the whole thing came off as pretty manly and brave, but when he stood up he was very careful to straighten up and smooth out the creases in his robe. Which looked a little bit too much like a long flowing skirt in the moonlight.

"We need to get back to the sanctuary." Brady said and led us out the door.

The huge wooden doors that fought so hard to keep us out the first time opened without a struggle. It was strange how quickly all of this was becoming comfortable. From the faint glow of the stained glass windows to the velvet cushions on the pews, it all felt familiar. Earlier in the evening the room felt vast and foreign, a forest of dark corners and shadows. But now as Brady and I walked down the center isle I was no longer afraid to take the next step. Our white cotton baptismal robes swished and swayed gently as we walked. I had no idea where we were heading, so I let Brady lead the way.

Attached to the back side of every pew was a tiny little shelf that held a few donated Bibles and a hymnal or two. Only the older people in the church ever bothered to open them when the pastor told the congregation what page to turn to in order to sing along. Most people just mumbled the words until they got to the chorus, or read them off of the big screens that were set up high above our heads in each corner of the sanctuary. As my attention swayed from the backs of the pews to the steps we took as we got closer and closer to the stage in front, I noticed the way that the shadows played against the lights and made the oversized cross in the center of the stage seem to look as if it was coming at you. It was a wonderful 3-D effect. I bet that when they put it up there they had no idea that it looked that way in the middle of the night. It was all so beautiful, what with the wooden cross above, and the multicolored stained glass, and the rows and rows padded seats, and little shelves of Bibles a few questions came to mind. How could Brady have seen what he said that he had seen in a place like this? How could he have seen all of that blackness and evil? Wasn't a place like this supposed to be holy ground?

"We have to go back up there." Brady said and pointed to the stage. His long white wings fluttering as he pointed. "I don't know why just yet, but when we get up there we will know."

I watched Brady trudge his way to the steps of the stage being careful not to trip over the long gown. His whole body seemed so much smaller than it was before. His heels popped out of his shoes as he took each step, and although he was wearing a belt, he still had to pull up his jeans through his robe to keep it from falling.

"What am I supposed to be looking for?" I questioned. I was still whispering, although I had no idea why. It seemed kind of pointless now, after all we had seen everything there was to see. And whatever was out there hiding in the shadows surely knew we were there.

There were no cat-like creatures sleeping on the seats and nothing scurrying under our feet as far as I knew. The only sound came from Brady and me making our way to the huge wooden cross that hung above the stage.

Brady was the first to get to the top step and on to the stage. He immediately began to spin around slowly with his eyes darting from one corner of the sanctuary to the other. I might not have known what to be looking for, but it looked as if he did.

"It's got to be here. It just has to be here." Brady kept repeating. By the time I got up to the stage and near the podium, Brady was already excited and running back down again.

"Where are you going now?" I asked.

"I'll be back. Just stay there. I need to get something." Brady insisted.

So there I was, exposed. The last time that I was up there alone Brady disappeared right before my eyes, so you can imagine that I wasn't too keen on him running off again. I stood at the top of the steps squinting into the darkness waiting for Brady to return with the dark oak cross hovering behind me by a few thin wires, and the huge stained glass image of Christ shining dimly at the far end of the sanctuary. Where was Brady going?

I didn't have to wait long. Brady came sprinting back to me with the nub of his pencil in one hand and a Visitor's Information Card in the other. You see, the VIC was what Pastor Martin would ask new people to fill out so the church would have a record of their visit. It sounds sweet enough, but like my dad would say, *that's how they get you.* And although he was joking, there was a bit of truth to it.

"I have to write this out. It's right there. See it?" Brady had his arms outstretched across the top of the podium so he could write whatever he had planned. The long white sleeves of his robe hung over the sides of the information card and would occasionally get in his way to the point that he would have to brush them off with frustration. "I'm just not a very good drawer."

Now, as an adult, I know there is no such word as "drawer," but as a fourth grader in Mrs. Anderson's class with Brady sitting not too far away, I knew exactly what he meant. Once when our class had to draw a picture of everyone in our family for a Family Tree project, I'm not kidding when I say that when the projects were displayed in the halls of the church more than one mom looked at Brady's picture and said, "Bless his sweet heart." Which is code for, "That kid must be mentally slow."

"Brady, what happened to your pen? You know the one from Dinosaur Land?" I asked.

"I had to use it. I had to try and get the lock open." Brady answered. "But the cheap thing just snapped in half. I should have just let Shane keep it." he finished without looking up from his project.

"Come on Brady, don't worry about it." I said hoping to make him feel better. I watched his fingers move franticly across the VIC. "What are you doing? What do you see out there that we have to write down?" I asked.

Brady finished his drawing and shoved the VIC into his pocket along with the nubby pencil. "It's right there." Brady said and pointed to the opposite wall high above the stained glass.

I strained my eyes to look through the darkness. "What are you talking about? We can't just break the glass and get out. That is like some sacred image or something, and besides, what about Frances? We can't leave without her." I stressed.

"No, not there." Brady pointed to the wall of glass. "There!" This time his hand raised up enough that I knew what we was talking about. Brady was talking about the baptismal. Not the one we used now, but the one that they used to use ages ago before closing it up.

A long time before Brady and I were part of the history of St. Thomas, they used to make a really big deal about being baptized. So the congregation collected money for years in order to build a wonderful and unique place to baptize people for everyone to see. They also must have thought that the higher to the heavens that they built it the closer they would be to God.

There was what can only be described as this large porcelain tub that was ordered from some small town in Italy that I can't pronounce. Anyways, it was bought with donations, and then after being hand carved, it was carefully shipped overseas. The tub was then tenderly raised twenty five feet or so above the sanctuary so when anyone new had accepted Jesus Christ as their personal Savior, everyone in the congregation could bare witness. Now if that person happened to be too small to climb the twenty-five foot ladder to the baptismal, well that tot was just hoisted up bucket-brigade style to the top until he or she reached the Promised Land.

There was only one problem that the forefathers of St. Thomas failed to recognize. When you are twenty five feet above the congregation, the only thing the congregation can see from the comfort of their pews is the porcelain white bottom of the tub and the little claws at the bottom of each leg. The pastor would have to yell to the people below what was happening, and everyone would just have to take his word for it. It wasn't long before a new pastor was brought in and the tub from above was drained of its soul cleansing waters, never to be used again.

"What are you talking about? We can't go up there!" I told him. "Are you telling me Frances is up there in that tub?"

"Not exactly, but we need to get up there." Brady answered. "Come on."

Now, I knew what Brady was writing down on that Visitor's Information Card. He was telling whoever might get around to reading it that after you go and put on a long white nightgown, make your way to the bathtub hanging in the back of the sanctuary. I don't know if after reading what Brady had written if they would have done it, but honestly, what choice did I have?

"Wow! It's a lot higher up there than I thought. It just doesn't look that high up from way back there, does it?" Brady said as he looked straight up the ladder to the bottom of the tub.

The homemade ladder was really just a series of 2x4's hammered together and then hammered again to the wall. And it didn't look as if it had been maintained and mended over the years. Brady and I were actually lucky that we could see anything at all. The way that the light form the stained glass light played off of the walls and the tub gave us just enough light to see the top. I guess that in the light of day it must have been beautiful. It would have been as if you were climbing Jacob's ladder itself to get to heaven.

As Brady took the first few delicate steps, I realized that he wasn't carrying his Bible anymore. I knew that his hands were full when he was scribbling down instructions, but I just assumed that he had crammed the Bible in his back pocket. The thing was pretty ragged. But now that he was climbing up the steps and his butt was three inches away, I couldn't help but notice.

"Brady?" I asked.

He stopped on the third rung and looked down at me over his shoulder. “What?” he whispered. I guess we were back to whispering.

“Where did your Bible go? I thought you still had it with you.” I asked.

Brady froze for half a second. “It’s in the changing room. I must have put it down for just a second to put the robe on. Oh man, oh man!” Brady took a step down.

“Should we go back and get it?” I suggested. I did a quick pat on my back pocket and felt the large lump of the Bible that I had stashed.

“No, it’s too late.” He remarked.

When I think back about how the whole night laid itself out now, I don’t know why we didn’t just go back and get another Bible from one of the pews. In fact we should have grabbed handfuls of books to take up there with us. For some reason I understood what Brady was saying. At that moment and at that exact time, he was right. As we stood at the base of the 2x4 ladder on our way to the top, we had in fact come too far to turn around now.

“Don’t worry. You probably won’t need it.” I said trying to encourage him.

And for the first time since Brady was in that cell staring into the nothingness, he became stoic and comatose again. Under his breath he whispered something so softly that I couldn’t make it out. I don’t even think it was meant for me to hear in the first place.

“What did you say, Brady?” I asked.

“Yeah, I will.” he repeated. Brady gripped the next rung of the 2x4 ladder and looked up to the top again. He began the slow assent to the top. One slow step after another, Brady was almost half way up to the top before I had enough guts to put my pudding and gunk encrusted shoe on the first rung and take that first step.

The board immediately creaked painfully under my weight. Years of non-use had made the boards lazy. Much later when the police tried to use the ladder to get to the top to take a good look into the tub, they had to use a set of harnesses and strap themselves to the closest support beams to keep themselves safe, and to keep the ladder from crumbling under their own weight. I guess it was the happy fact that in fourth grade I couldn’t have weighed more than sixty-five pounds soaking wet. That is what kept me from falling over two stories to the ground below.

When I looked up, I could hear Brady more than I could see him. His body, although thinner, still blocked the little amount of moonlight that fought its way into the room. The bottom of his long baptismal robe flapped along with his sleeves against the ladder. He was never in the best of shape before, but now I could hear him struggling to get to the top.

"We're almost there." Brady said. He gripped the side of the ladder with his elbow and looked down to me. "I'm almost to the bottom of the tub. I can feel the pipes. We need to get inside."

As Brady looked down to me, and I strained to look up, I knew that we were going to have to climb into the thing, but in the back of my head I was in denial. Ok, so what if we get all the way up there and climb inside? Then what? We would still be two kids in blouses in an old tub suspended way too high over the sanctuary.

Each time I took the next step up each rung of the ladder I could feel the crunching of broken snacks in my left pocket and the poke of the safety scissors in my right pocket. I had lost or had to abandon almost everything that I had collected along my way that night. More than once as I made my way to the top, I remember that I had to stop and shove the Bible deeper in my back pocket just to keep it from falling out.

*You probably won't need it. Yeah, I will.*

Step after step, rung after rung, I tried not to look up, but just take every step and every rung one at a time. I was about to look up again, when I heard Brady's voice again, but this time it sounded a little different. The only way that I can describe it is that it sounded more distant than it should have.

"I'm in!" Brady said. In my determination to keep climbing, I didn't even hear Brady get to the top of the ladder and flip himself inside the huge Italian porcelain tub. "Watch out. The ladder is pretty bad when you get up here. I almost munched it and fell. Just use the right side, and you should be alright." Brady loudly whispered his instructions down to me.

Like I said before, Brady was not the most fit and athletic kid in fourth grade, to be honest that was probably Shane, but Brady had me beat when it came to climbing that ladder in the dark. I don't know if you can sweat through your sneakers, but my feet were slick and seemed to slide off every new rung. Finally, I felt Brady reach out and grab my arm.

"I've got you. Just kinda hoist yourself up on the lip right there." Brady pulled me up towards him as he spoke.

"No problem." I grunted as he pulled.

I asked around and found out later that a long time ago there was a platform built around the top of the 2x4 ladder that the pastor and the Christian-to-be would stand on before getting into the water. That made a lot of sense to me, because there was no way that the pastor and the would-be saved wouldn't have been able to do anything more gracefully than Brady and I just did trying to get into the tub. And if the thing was full of water at the time, the water would have splashed out, and everyone below us would have been re-baptized whether they wanted to be or not.

"Thanks." I said and used the edge of the white porcelain to pull myself up the last few inches.

My young back ached, and my thighs hurt from climbing and from having a dull pair of scissors in my pocket jabbing me, but I was here. Our robes hung low on our sweaty bodies, and the sleeves no longer looked like the wings of a spring dove, but instead reminded me of the toilet paper that hung from the trees on Saturday morning when your house was attacked by drunk and crazy teenagers the night before.

I looked over at Brady, and he didn't look much better than I did. "So, we're up here. What do we do now?" I asked.

# Chapter 18

"This is right. This is where I saw her." Brady said. He looked over the edge of the baptismal at the vast sanctuary below. The pulpit seemed small and distant in the darkness.

"Where you saw Frances?" I asked.

"Yes, I was up here, and she was over there." Brady pointed to the wooden cross that hung by thin wires on the other side of the room.

"What do you mean? When did you see her?" I asked him. The whole thing was very confusing. As far as I knew, Frances had never even been in here with us. When was Brady and Frances climbing around?

"Every day, I saw her when I tried to close my eyes and go to sleep. I saw her every time I closed my eyes and make everything back to the way it was before. I saw her every time that I prayed to Jesus that you would come and save us." Brady said. "But she isn't here now."

I shifted my weight carefully to look over the edge of the tub and around the sanctuary the best that I could, but the light from the stained glass wasn't enough to make out any details. The room was more shadow than light.

"We have to get her to come out. She must be afraid. They must have her so scared." Brady's voice was compassionate and quivered on the verge of tears.

I put my hands to my face and cupped my voice. "Frances, it's us, Brady and Peter! We are here for you! You can come out now!"

"What are you doing?" Brady said in a loud whisper. "Are you crazy? Not like that. He can hear you."

I figured that Brady must have been referring to Pastor O'Leary, and Brady was right. It was a stupid move. All we needed was to be stuck up there when a huge squid demon or one of those hairless cats came in to the sanctuary. We would have nowhere to go. But to tell you the truth, I could handle dealing either of them before I could deal with O'Leary and that sinister laugh of his.

"Sorry." I apologized.

"Do you still have that Bible?" Brady asked.

I pulled the book from my oversized back pocket and handed it to Brady. He flipped it over in his hands and started to rummage through the folded pages. Frantically, he looked through the scripture. I didn't know what he was looking for, so I didn't know how much help I could have been. But, there were a few verses that I knew and after hearing the "Books of the Bible" song dozens of times in music class, I could pretty much find my way around.

"Brady, what are you looking for?" I asked.

"Light. I am trying to find anything that has the word 'light' in it. I need that verse about light." Brady said. "It's too dark where she is. She needs light."

Neither of us were what I would call fourth grade biblical scholars, but we did have religion class every day and chapel once a week, so we weren't totally lost. Also this was my first year in a Christian school, but Brady had been the new kid in at least four different private schools since kindergarten.

I felt helpless, as he flipped through the pages. I knew there was something about lamps, but that was about it. I had no clue where to find it. "What about the light on my feet?" I suggested.

"Good one. Thanks, Pete. I know that one." Brady smiled at me and said. He opened the Bible to the middle. "It's somewhere in Psalms."

As I watched Brady open the Bible and thumb his way blindly through the pages to find the chapter and verse that he needed from the book of Psalms, I just had to ask, "How is reading about light going to help Franny see her way back to the sanctuary and back here to us?"

But Brady didn't even look up to acknowledge me. He was on a mission and getting closer and closer to finding what he needed. The excitement in his voice reflected it.

"Twenty-three, no that's not it. 110? No, come on, Brady think. Lamp on my feet." he said to himself.

That was when I remember first seeing it roll in. It was small at first like a low fog. The pews looked as if they were floating amongst the clouds. As Brady was preoccupied desperately looking through the Bible for just the right words, the sanctuary was slowly filling with a thick grey fog. But there was something hiding inside. Every once in a while, I could just make out a thin arm reaching for the cushioned seats. Long dark grey tentacles would wrap around the forearm or the elbow just as it started to get a grip on the pews. Then it would pull it back into the nothingness. Thin, almost translucent limbs struggled over and over again fruitlessly trying to get free.

"Brady." His name came out like more of a squeak than a sound. "It's coming. Look down. God help us, Brady please hurry."

Brady was lost in his own little world. He was no longer engulfed in an oversized bathtub. He was no longer hovering over the sanctuary. He was lost in the pages of that book. Even as the slow fog crept its way past the rows of pews and over the first few steps of the staging area, Brady's concentration could not be broken.

"Yes! I found it. It was waiting for me right here the whole time. All I had to do was find it." Brady said triumphantly. He opened the Bible to Psalms 119 verse 105.

I think it must have been more from his memory than actually Brady reading the words, because I could barely make out the letters in the dark, but Brady had no problem at all reciting the scripture. He held the Bible open and traced the words with his index finger as he read.

"Your word is a lamp for my feet and a light on my path." Brady read the words aloud and looked up waiting to see the results.

Nothing was happening. I shouldn't say that. Something was happening all right. The thick fog started that now engulfed the floor of the sanctuary began to swirl in places all around the room. The bottom of the pews were almost completely covered now, as was the first four steps of the pulpit. From the center of each miniature whirlpool I could just make out the limbs of both women and men reaching and grasping more frantically than they were just moments ago.

"I don't think it's working the way you want it to, Brady." I said. "All you are doing is making them mad."

I should have known that that meant it was in fact working the way that he wanted. But Brady wasn't looking at the pool of smoke and fog that now covered the first few feet of the room. He wasn't looking at the multiple sets of tentacles that worked to keep anyone from reaching the surface. Instead, he was looking directly across from us at the huge cross that hung above the stage.

"Yes, yes it is. Look!" Brady pointed to the cross. "A lamp for my feet and a light for my path. Do you hear me? That is from the Bible!" Brady was no longer trying to be quiet. He raised the Bible high in his hands like a Southern Baptist preacher at an old fashion church revival.

I didn't know who Brady was talking to and getting so angry with as he shouted out scripture, but I could see what he was talking about. Across the sanctuary, on the far side of the room, was something. There was someone on the cross trying to crawl their way to the top. It was much too dark to see anything in any detail, and the only reason that I even saw anything at all was because Brady was pointing at it, and telling me where to look.

"Wait. I know another one." Brady said and brought the Bible to his chest to start flipping through it once again. "Here. Take this!" And with that Brady began to read again.

I couldn't tell what book of the Bible Brady had found, but I knew by the way he was holding it that the chapter and verse must have come from somewhere in the New Testament. He balanced the book in his right hand and started to once again trace the words as he read.

"I am the light of the world! Do you hear that? The light of the whole world! Whoever walks with me will not walk in darkness but have light of life." Brady repeated the verses with confidence. "That's from John! You remember John, don't you?"

That really made the things hiding in the fog angry. For the first time, I could hear the sounds of moaning and the pain coming from below the surface. Whatever was pulling them back in the fog and away from the pews was no longer just tugging them back gently anymore. No, it was yanking them back into the abyss. And there was a smell that reached even twenty five feet into the air and into the baptismal tub high above them. I really don't know how to describe it. It smelled like fatty meat left out in the summer sun. But not just that, there was also the smell of matches that had just been blown out. The odor was almost an after taste.

"Look! Look!" Brady was dangerously jumping up and down in the baptismal. The whole thing rocked on rusted nuts and bolts. I could hear the homemade ladder creak under us after each jump.

"Woah! Settle down. You are going to make this whole thing fall if you aren't careful. What? What am I supposed to be looking at?" I asked Brady.

"Frances!" Brady said. He closed the Bible and used it to point across the sanctuary.

I couldn't believe my eyes. There she was. Although I could barely make it out, I could still recognize the grandma sweater that she always wore. It looked ragged and torn, but for that matter so did Frances. She was straddling the bottom of the cross and trying to make her way to the center where the two boards met. Her hair, usually frizzy, was slick and pasted against her skin.

Below us the fog was alive with anger and resentment. There were no longer long decrepit arms reaching through the swirls trying to get away. They had been overcome. I noticed on the corner of one of the pews sat a cat. The cat like creature had patches of its orange fur missing, and the tail was red, raw and much much too long. The tip of it dangled in the misty floor below. When our eyes met I saw the twin reflected blue mirrors of its eyes. Whatever was in the depths of the fog was even too much for him.

Brady had contained himself long enough to stop jumping. "Look, Pete. There she is. We have to get to her." He said.

"How? There is no way to get to the other side of the sanctuary without getting down and running through that." I said and pointed straight down.

It must have been the first time that he looked down at the sanctuary floor, because I could almost hear his heart drop. And at the same time that he looked down, he must have noticed the smell. If it was bad before, then it was ten times worse now. The rancid meat had not only sat in the heat of the summer sun, but was starting to bloat.

Once when I was five, there was a local cat that used to terrorize the neighborhood. Even the neighborhood dogs would cross the street if they saw that cat coming. Then one day when I went out to ride my bike, I saw the gray and white stripped cat on the side of the road. Apparently, the thing had fallen asleep in the gutter of the street and got itself ran over. Well, it was gross, but for the most part it looked as if it was just sleeping there on the side of the road. If it wasn't for the small thin trail of blood coming from the corner of its mouth, I would have thought just that. Now, you would think that the owner of the house would have come outside, and seen the dead cat, and thought "Gross, I'm going to have to clean that up." Then reluctantly grabbed a shovel to dispose of the beast of Albany Street.

Well, three days later the cat was still lying in the gutter. Only now the legs were sticking obscenely up in the air and the stomach was bloated. The cat looked like a furry balloon. And the thing started to smell too. By the fifth day, I had to ride my bike on the other side of the street just to avoid the stench. By the next weekend I went outside and to my surprise there was no stink. The terror of the neighborhood had passed the point of rot. I had to dare myself to look, but there he was thin, just matted fur over brittle bones. I will never know why the owner of the house didn't throw the cat away, or at least call someone to pick it up.

"Oh Pete, it's terrible." Brady said and buried his nose into his long white sleeve. "What is that smell?"

"I am pretty sure it is coming from down there. Now how are we going to get to Franny?" I asked.

"Light for my feet. Light for my feet." Brady repeated. Each time that he did, the floor of the sanctuary seemed to stir more angrily.

"Frances! Can you hear me?" I shouted over the pool of smoke and bitterness below us. I no longer cared about keeping my voice down so things couldn't hear me, or about keeping myself under control. We had finally made our way to Frances, and I was not going to let her go.

Her head looked up over the plane of the cross, but she said nothing.

"She can hear us, Pete. She can hear us!" Brady said to me. He must have agreed that the time for secrets and whispers were over. Then he turned back to Frances, "We are coming for you! Just hold on to the cross! Don't let go! It's the only way!"

There was no way that Brady and I could just climb down the 2x4 ladder and just walk down the aisle. There was also no way to get from where we were in the porcelain baptismal two stories off the ground to the other side of the sanctuary without touching the floor below. We were stuck.

"We can't get to her. There is no way." I told Brady.

"We can and we will. We got this far didn't we. As long as we have this," Brady held the Bible up over his shoulder. "Then we can get to Frances."

Talk about irony. The second that Brady waved the Bible up over his head, the voice that I had been hearing all night startled him. Pastor O'Leary's voice whispered and hissed off the walls. It swirled around the room like the fog below. It scared Brady enough that he fell back and lost his balance. His white robe got entangled in mine as we both struggled to remain standing and not come toppling out of the tub.

Brady's words, "As long as we have this." were still in the air floating in a word bubble above us when Brady fell into my arms. He reached for the side of the tub to catch himself, and when he did, the Bible in his hand fell into the mist and grey below.

"Oh, no! What are we going to do now?" Brady looked over the side. Tears were already starting to form from the corners of his eyes. "We're going to lose."

Where the Bible had fallen to the sanctuary floor the fog and the things lurking within it separated. There was a perfect circle of forest green carpet and the edge of a pew exposed now. An invisible barrier was keeping the fog from creeping back in. And in the center of this perfectly clear opening was the Bible that Brady had dropped. I would tell you that nothing could get through it, but that wasn't true. All around the circle were fingertips. Thin grey fingertips reached for the book in the center. Long painted nails and bony fingers with wedding rings and jewelry still dangling from them stretched as far as they could to get to it. But no matter how hard they tried, nothing could reach. The sounds of agony no longer sounded like a slow moan, but were now excited at the possibility of redemption.

"Yesssssss" O'Leary hissed into the room. "You will lose. You were always going to lose."

His voice seemed to be coming from nowhere and everywhere all at once. I had heard his lies all night long so I knew not to listen to him, but this was all new to Brady.

"Who are you? Leave us alone!" Brady shouted.

"It's O'Leary. He is the one that has been doing all of this to us. He is the one that took you and Frances. He's the one that sent all of those things. He is the one that is doing all of this." I frantically tried to explain to Brady. I pointed to the floor and the swirling fog. "Look, we need to figure out a way to get to Frances."

Frances across the sanctuary seemingly miles away was still holding on to the cross the best that she could, but by the looks of it she didn't have much more time before she would come sliding off. She looked too weak to hold on much longer.

Brady didn't know how to react. His bravery ended the second that the Bible went over the edge. He no longer had a plan. "No, that is not the one that took me. That is not the one that would come to my cell." Brady said. He was making his way to the edge of the baptismal tub and to the wooden ladder.

"What are you talking about? Of course that's him." I insisted.

"No, Peter, the voice is all wrong. The one that took me was much smaller. His voice was like nails on a chalkboard. It hurt to hear him speak. This O'Leary is not the one I saw when it took me." Brady had hoisted himself over the lip of the baptismal and was already down the first three rungs.

"Brady, what are you doing? Did you see those things? There is no way to get to her. Whatever is down there will pull you under the fog before you even get a chance to start running to her." I pleaded. I remember grabbing his wrist. I remember that I was not only trying to hold him there with my words, but also I was physically trying to hold him back too.

"Did you see what happened when the Bible hit the floor? They can't go near it, Pete. They're afraid of it." Brady said. His voice was excited. "You just have to have faith." He said and broke the grip that I had on his wrist, and headed once again down the fragile ladder.

As he descended the stairs I yelled down to him. "You're crazy!"

Brady looked up at me and smiled. "Yeah, but that's what they always say before everything comes out right."

From twenty five feet in the air all I could see was the top of Brady's head as he made his way to the bottom rungs of the ladder. I could still hear the creaks of each board as he shifted his weight from the right hand side to the left. I was afraid to move or even breathe for the fear that I might bring unwanted attention to him. I don't know what was going through Brady's mind, because he never told me. But I can tell you what was going through mine. "That kid's going to die."

I could tell that Brady had made it to the bottom because there was a cloud of smoke kicked up around his knees every time that he took a step. From the top of the ladder I couldn't make out much of the details in the darkness, but the faint light that did make its way through gave me a clue that at least Brady had made it that far. But instead of heading down the main aisle toward the stage and more importantly toward Frances, Brady turned left down the first long set of pews that he came to. Now where on Earth was he going?

"Where is your friend, Peter?" O'Leary's voice echoed throughout the sanctuary. "Don't tell me he is going to rescue your girlfriend. How could you just stand in that bloated bathtub like a fool and let him take your girl like that? Be a man, Peter."

The thing about it was that I wasn't a man. I was nine. For that matter, so was Brady. That was the thing about O'Leary, if you just reacted to the first thing that he said you could get yourself in trouble. In fact, he was relying on the fact that you would. But if you stopped for a minute and thought about what he was saying, you could figure him out. Sure, Frances was my friend, and for the record she was a girl. But before that night, I hadn't said more than a few words to her all year. I am not proud to say it, but I ignored her like everyone else in Mrs. Anderson's class.

"Hey, Pete! I made it." Brady looked up and shouted.

As far as I could tell, sometimes Brady could hear O'Leary's voice and sometimes he couldn't. You have to believe me when I say that his nasty words were out there, and they were real. I know it wasn't just in my head. Brady had heard O'Leary talking to us just seconds ago, but now he acted as if he couldn't hear a word that he had just said.

I figured it out. Brady was heading down the closest pew to the left to get his hands on another Bible. That was why the fog had only risen a few feet above the ground. In the back of every pew was that Bible tucked into that little shelf. The fog and whatever was slithering around in it could only get so far before getting sent back. The Bibles in the pews were keeping them under control. But the problem with the way that that was working was the fact that Brady was still knee deep in in the grey fog. His legs below his knees were not being protected.

"Brady! Listen to me carefully. You need to hurry. You need to get up on top of the seats. Jump up on the cushions as fast as you can. The ground isn't safe." I said as loudly as I could trying to warn him.

Brady attention shifted as he looked down at the thick grey swirling around his knees. He was no longer safe in the heights of the baptismal. He was now literally knee deep in the muck. "Aaah! It touched me. Someone just touched my leg!" Brady shouted. He immediately started to high step his way to the pews. "A hand! A hand!" He kept shouting.

"Don't worry about the hands. Worry about the other stuff!" I shouted down to him.

Brady looked up at me. "What do you mean 'other stuff'? They are trying to pull me under!"

"Trust me. They aren't trying to pull you down. They are trying to pull themselves up!" I yelled.

I don't know how I knew that. Maybe it was the way that I saw them reaching skywards before, or the way that the long slime cover tentacles kept pulling them back under the fog. But I think that more than any of that was the moans and the cries for help that I had heard from even deeper inside. I just knew that the pain that I heard was coming from the same ones reaching for the Bible and trying to get out.

Brady reached down into the fog and pulled loose the tight grasp of a pair of skeletal fingers that were wrapping around his ankles. He was almost to the rows of pews and the Bibles when a long black tentacle wrapped him around the waist and yanked him under. The fog plumbed upwards in a mini explosion and then the room was dead quiet. The fog settled in again. Even the cat-like creature that was perched in the corner was nowhere to be found.

"Brady!" I yelled over and over into the nothingness.

"What are you going to do now, Petey?" O'Leary said in a sarcastically worried tone. Then he began to laugh. A laugh that was cold, and filled the entire sanctuary with an eerie chill.

"Noooooo!" Frances screamed from the cross.

I jerked my head up toward the cross surprised at the sudden sound, and saw Frances dangling from the center where the two boards met. Her thin arm was reaching out to where Brady had once stood in the mist. I was also startled because it was the first thing that I had heard her say since she had disappeared. I'm not saying that I could see her crying from the other side of the sanctuary, but somehow by the sounds of her screams, I knew that she was. I am not too proud to admit that when Brady went under that fog, so was I.

I was once again frozen in place. Brady was gone, sucked under the fog surrounding the floor of the sanctuary, and there was no way that I could make my way to Frances now. I wanted to yell out to her to let her know that everything was going to be alright and that I could somehow make it across the room to get to her. I wanted to yell out to Brady that although he might be under the thick grey fog, I was on my way down, and I would be there to pull him out. But instead, I stood there frozen and speechless. For years I told myself that it wasn't my fault that all of that had happening to us and that I was just a stupid kid. But now I'm not too sure. I think that if I was in exactly the same situation today, I would still be that frozen fourth grader twenty five feet above the ground unable to move or scream.

"Now's your chance, Petey." O'Leary said. His voice filled the sanctuary and was ringing with joy and excitement. He almost sounded giddy. "See, I helped you out. Your competition is gone. Now you have the girl all to yourself. All you have to do is go get her."

"Shut up! Just shut up!" I screamed at O'Leary. Then I turned my attention to the space on the ground that Brady had just stood seconds ago. I strained to look through the darkness and the thick soup of fog to see if I could spot any part of my best friend. I saw something. I wasn't sure what it was, but there was something moving just beneath the surface.

As I made my way to the ladder, I thought I heard Frances from the other side of the room. Her voice was faint, and if it weren't for the fact that the sanctuary was dead silent, I don't think that I would have been able to hear her at all. I carefully flung my leg over the side of the imported baptismal and tried my best to balance myself on the right side, the safe side, of the 2x4's. This time I knew it was her voice that I heard; I knew that Frances was talking to me.

"Peter, be careful. Don't look down. Have faith. Be quiet." were the words that I remember hearing. I know that someone, maybe Frances, maybe someone else, was sharing so much more, but those are the only words that I could make out.

I buried my head into the rungs of the ladder and held on tightly with the pit of my elbows. "Franny, I hear you, and I am coming for you. Just hold on to that cross as tightly as you can. Have faith Franny, I'm coming." I yelled.

"That's it, Petey my man. You are my hero. Your mighty quest is almost complete! You have made your way through the castle, defeated the monster, and overcome your enemy. Now all you need to do is claim the damsel in distress." Once again I could hear the excitement and eagerness in O'Leary's voice. I could also hear something dark and sinister behind it.

I stopped for just a moment when the bottoms of my shoes fell into the thickness of the fog. There were still probably two more rungs to go before

I was completely down, but I had not yet fully entered into the abyss. *This is it, Peter. You can do this. Remember, you are never alone. Dear* God, *give me the strength, and be my light.* I said to myself. This was the first night that I had made it a habit talking to my God, but it was comforting in a way that I can't explain. I am proud to say that I have talked to Him every night since. I took a deep breath and lowered myself down the last two steps of the rickety ladder. Before I realized it, I was off the wooden steps and knee deep into the fog of the sanctuary. One way or another I was going to make it to Frances.

I have told Brady this a number of times over the years, but it was a good thing that he went down first, because I would have had no idea what to do once I had gotten down to the bottom of the ladder. He actually had a great idea in going toward the Bibles right away. The problem with his plan was that Brady had never played Hot Lava.

Do you know about the game that I am talking about? For some unknown reason, the carpet and the tile floor in your house has become hot lava and thank goodness, the couch and all of its cushions are resistant to heat. As a kid you have to get from one side of the room to the other without touching the floor. If you accidently slipped and your feet touched the ground, you were burned to a crisp. I was the master. I could get from my living room couch, across the dining room table and chairs, across the kitchen floor (via alternating sofa cushions), to the refrigerator for a soda and never scorch a sock along the way.

Although the floor of the sanctuary wasn't hot lava, the premises would work pretty much the same way. So the second that I made it off the ladder, I jumped to the closest pew. The imaginary hot lava that flowed through my living room never actually jumped up to grab you and pull you in, but the same could not be said for the things grasping blindly in the fog below me. My first jump was almost my last when I felt someone or something brush the rubbery sole of my sneakers. What was it that Frances had said, "Don't look down."? That was a good idea, because I didn't want to know what had almost grabbed me and pulled me under.

"That's my boy! Go get 'em, cowboy!" O'Leary laughed, his words taunting me.

"I thought that I was a brave knight. Now I'm a cowboy? You can't even keep your lies straight anymore, can you?" I replied.

As I balanced myself on the long velvet seat cushions of the pews, I could still hear Frances calling out to me. She was weak and barely able to grasp to the cross for dear life, but she was still trying to help me. "Don't talk to him. He likes it when you talk back. It gives him strength and power here." Frances's thin voice said from atop the cross.

"Hang on, Frances." I took two Bibles out of the seats in front of me and threw them on the floor between me and the next set of pews.

Just as before when Brady had accidentally dropped his Bible, the area around it cleared in a perfect circle. I was hoping that I would have been able to see a trace of Brady once the fog had cleared. Unfortunately, Brady was nowhere to be found. I thought for sure that I was close enough to where he had been taken to be able to grab him and pull him up, but I was too slow, and now he was gone.

Just as before, thin hands dared to reach into the tiny clearing to try and touch the Bible in the middle. But just as before, their reach was falling just short. I centered myself the best that I could on the pew and then jumped on to the first Bible. I hop-scotched from the cover of one Bible to the other and then quickly to the pews in front of them. I could tell you now that it went as perfectly as I had planned, but I still have a tiny scar on my shin that would say otherwise. The second Bible stepping stone slipped out from under me. Not enough to cause me to fall, but just enough for me to come up three inches short of my goal and bang my shin against the hard wooden side of the pew.

I rested tired and weary against the back of the seat. I remember being extra careful not to let any part of my body fall into the sea of mist swirling and undulating just two inches below me. I knew from thousands of afternoons in my living room that any part of you could fall into the "hot lava" if you weren't careful enough.

I looked up to the distant image of Frances. "How do you know that talking to O'Leary gives him strength?" I shouted to Frances. Although it didn't feel like it, I must have been making my way closer to the cross and closer to Frances. I no longer felt as if I had to scream at the top of my lungs across the vast openness of the sanctuary in order for her to hear me. And when she answered me, I knew that it was true.

Because although I was scared, I talked to him, and Brady didn't." Frances answered. Her voice sounded almost sad. It was as if she was remembering something faint and distant in the darkest corner of her memories. "That is why he took me away, because I asked him questions. He called me special. I wanted to talk to him. I wanted to know more. Brady, on the other hand, was too afraid to talk, so O'Leary left him alone. He kept him there in that room forever."

After listening to what Frances and Brady had been through, I felt so sorry for them. I knew that if I could somehow get to Frances, then she and I could find Brady and then somehow get out of there. For the second time that night I thought about how long we had been there in the church. There was no way that the sun wasn't coming up soon. It had to have been hours since we were locked in St. Thomas. But what had Brady said before? He had been locked in that cell for days, maybe even months before I found him. Even though that was clearly impossible, for Brady it had been true. And before he disappeared under the puff of grey fog, he surely looked like it.

"I didn't know that the whole time that I was talking to O'Leary, I was feeding him. I had no idea." Frances faded.

I knew I only had a few more seconds before Frances would lose her grip on that cross and fall hard and fast to the stage floor below. So here is what I did. Still using the "Hot Lava" method, I threw one Bible after another in front of me until I had a makeshift stepping stone path of God 's holy word. Each time I did, the fog cleared quickly and I was able to jump closer and closer to Frances. I balanced myself on the arms of the pews each time I felt myself tipping one way or the other.

"Do you think that your little jumping game is going to work?" O'Leary chimed in. "Come on, Petey. You know that I could just say.....*Boo!* Hahaha!" O'Leary laughed from his belly when I lost my balance and almost fell face first into the fog.

But I tell you that I had never in my life concentrated so much on one specific thing. My mind only thought about the next carefully planned jump, the next Bible sitting in the next cleared circle, the next safe landing that would bring me closer to her. But there was something that I heard in O'Leary's words that I hadn't heard before. For the first time since he had invaded my thoughts and had made this night the nightmare that it was, I heard fear in his voice.

I was finally able to get myself to the last clear row of pews before the open chasm that lead to the stage. But now I was in a no man's land, the front row of the sanctuary. With rock concerts and carnival rides people would physically run each other over just to be near the front, but that wasn't the case on Sunday mornings in church. You would think that everyone would want to be as close as they could to the pastor's message, the cross, and everything that the church had to offer on any given Sunday. After all, the closer to the front row, the closer to God.

Now, I know that most people have "their seat" when it comes to Sunday morning, and Whoa to the poor innocent Christian who would dare to sit in "their seat," but some people just have a tough time waking up that early on the weekend and tend to come in a bit later than others. There could be a packed house at St. Thomas, and the only row left open with prime seating available would be the front row. People would just lean against the stained glass along the back wall rather than sit up in front. I've seen it happen. I once saw a sign outside a small black and white church in the middle of East Texas that read, "Get here early. Still good seats in the back."

Despite Frances's warnings, I spoke once again to the nothingness of the room hoping O'Leary was listening. "I don't get it, O'Leary. I don't understand how you can even be in here!" I yelled to the ceiling. "This is supposed to be God 's house. How is all of this even here?" I said and pointed to the thick grey covering the floor.

Frances adjusted herself slowly and carefully on the crux of the huge wooden cross. I could tell by the way she was barely holding on that she didn't have much time before she would slip. She was looking weak, so I knew that I had to do something quickly. The acidic smell in the room was burning the deepest part of my nostrils and making my eyes water. But the worst part of the whole situation was the fact that I didn't have any more Bibles within my reach. That must have been one of the reasons that no one liked to sit in the front row, no Bibles available in the seat in front of you. You were on your own.

"Don't talk to him, Peter." Frances warned.

I couldn't help myself. I had heard what I thought was fear in his voice for the first time, and I felt as if it would have been my only opportunity to strike. Frances had been right all night long, but for the life of me, I just had to know why he was here.

"Well, what's the matter, O'Leary? Cat's got your tongue? Tell me. Why are you here? How did you even get in the sanctuary?" I said again pretending not to hear Frances's warning.

"Fine, Petey. You want to know how I got into this beautiful house of God. I was invited." O'Leary said with a sour hint in his voice. "That's right, my boy. Every Sunday you people open the big double doors of the church and just invite me right inside, so one day I just decided to stay."

I didn't understand then what he was trying to say at the time my nine year old brain just couldn't comprehend it, but now that I am much older, I think that maybe I do. He continued.

"You people come in here thinking that you are all high and mighty. You think you are all better than the ones just outside that door, or even better than the ones that sit around you, but you are not. God may not be able to look upon your sin, but I wallow in it." I could tell by O'Leary's voice that he had been dying to tell me this all night. There was something in the way that he was sharing with me that made me think that he wanted me to know.

"What do you mean? The people that come here to this church are Christians. You can't touch them." I told O'Leary. At the time I wasn't a hundred percent sure that was right, but it sounded like something that I had heard once.

"Not all of them. So many of you people come in lost and alone. They carry in with them so much delicious sin. What do you think happens to all of that sin when they don't ask for forgiveness, and instead sit there quietly listening and thinking to themselves that they are not worthy of Him? And you people don't even try and talk to them. You just sit there ignoring their pain, and thinking 'someone else will take care of their needs'." O'Leary said smugly.

As a kid I was confused, I didn't really quiet understand what he was saying. What was he talking about? Everyone who came into church loved God and loved everyone else around them, didn't they? But as an adult, I now know exactly what he was telling me that night. The seats every Sunday are filled with pain and need, and unfortunately, most of the time no one steps up to help. I mean how else could I possibly sit here today and explain how that much evil had gotten into St. Thomas? As bad as O'Leary was, I can't help but think that there were millions of others just like him in churches all around the world. Creatures waiting for us to fail and then feeding off the sin.

That is when I noticed that there was no fog on the stage or around the pulpit. The cross and the baptismal were also clear. That is why although the unsaved might have been filling the pews, the fog couldn't rise above God 's word. I looked at Frances hanging by a thin cob-web. Frances only had seconds before she would lose her last remaining strength and come crashing to the ground at bone breaking speed.

She must have seen the look of desperation in my eyes and known what I was thinking, because she barely managed to whisper, "No, Peter. Don't do it. It's too late for me. Save Brady."

I knew that if I ran as fast as I could, I could make it through the last remaining few feet of nothingness and make it to the steps of the stage. Four maybe five steps in the fog was all I would need to get there. *How many did Brady need?* I couldn't doubt myself any longer. *Dear* God, *help me get to that cross.* I prayed. And with that, I took off running.

# Chapter 19

There is this game that we used to play at recess. I don't think it had an official name, but the object of the game was pretty simple. You had to try and get as far as you could from one side of the playground to the other using only three steps. After you were done with your three steps, you would take a rock that you were holding in your hand and then when your turn was over, you would put the rock in the dirt by the edge of your tennis shoe to mark your place. The kid that had stretched the furthest in just three steps would win. Now, I know what you are thinking, "That's stupid. The kid with the longest legs would always win." But the thing is, that's not always true. You see, it wasn't about who had the longest legs, it was about who could bend.

That is why it was one of the only games on the playground that the boys and the girls loved to play together. The guys liked to show off, and the girls loved to win. It was also the reason it was twice as embarrassing when Brice Olson split his pants right down the middle trying to beat the all-time record. (He came up about three inches short.)

Now, Brady and I never really got to play along with the rest of the kids in class, but we did try our two man version of it on our own on the other side of the playground. I was pretty good at it, and I am sure that if Shane, Darrick, or any of the others had asked me to join them, I would have held my own.

That game is what was going through my mind as I took the longest steps of my life trying to make it past the front row of pews and to the bottom steps of the stage. It had only taken a brief second for a long greasy tentacle to pull Brady under the fog. And from what I could tell, the things under the fog were just as active now that I was down here as they were then when Brady had made his attempt. I don't remember if I was looking down into the thick grey around my feet, or if I was focused on Frances. All I remember was O'Leary's voice ringing throughout the sanctuary as I ran.

"That's my boy! Go for it young man! Here he comes Frances, your knight in shining armor! *Ha-ha-ha*!" O'Leary was mocking me and laughing hysterically at my attempt to make it to the stage.

And with O'Leary's laughter still ringing in the air, she fell.

I could tell by the sound that it wasn't good. Frances's body bounced slightly and then laid in a silent heap on the floor near the podium. I used every ounce of strength that I had to leap to the last step of the stage. Long black tentacles curled around my ankles and up my thighs. Screams and moans echoed throughout the sanctuary. I wasn't sure if the voices below the fog were angry because I had made it, or if in some eerie way they were cheering me on.

I punched and kicked as hard as I could to get the creatures to loosen their grip, but they were too strong. I knew right then and there that that was it. I was going to die. I was going to be pulled under the thick and eerie fog just as Brady had been, with nothing left to remember me by but a small puff of smoke. But then I looked over at Frances lying there, nothing left of her but a tiny pile of rags and sticks, and that gave me the strength that I needed to get free. I twisted my entire body like an alligator wrestling its prey. I rolled in the same direction of the dark tentacles that surrounded my feet making the grip around them unbearably tighter. But it worked, the thing hidden in the shadows and fog couldn't stand the pain either and finally had to let go. The moment that I was free of the monster's grasp, I ran to Frances.

I had never seen a dead body before. Well, I take that back. I had seen my Uncle Walter for just a second in his suit laying in a coffin at his funeral. I didn't really know my uncle, but my dad made me go out of respect. My mom on the other hand, didn't think it was a good idea. Too morbid. I think mom was right. Kids shouldn't see a dead body until they are at least twenty five. I tossed and turned for more than a week after that funeral. I kept getting woken up by images of my dead Uncle Walter screaming from under the dirt, "I'm not dead! Dig me out!"

But I knew the moment that I tried to pick her up and hold her in my arms that Frances was dead. Her arms were thin, limp twigs, and her legs were even thinner. One of her shoes had come off in the fall and laid just a few feet away. I put her down as gently as I could. I crossed her arms over her sweater, and slipped her shoe softly back on her foot. The quiet girl that no one ever talked to, including myself, was quiet again, but now it was too late. I thought about all of the times that I should have talked to her, and all of the opportunities that passed when I should have been nicer to her and stood up for her when no one else would. But now that I am an adult, and this is the mature me talking, I would hope that thing would have been different between us. Unfortunately, I believe the fourth grade me would have done things that exact same way that it happened. Too scared to do anything but try to blend in and not be the next victim.

"Franny?" I whispered. I picked her up slightly and rested her head against my chest. She was so light. I brushed her curly brown hair back out of her face, being extra careful to make sure that it framed her face just right. The thin quiet lids of her eyes made it look as if she was just sleeping. I leaned in until my lips were almost touching her soft cheek.

"Franny?" I repeated. Nothing.

His wicked voice pierced the quiet moment like a knife. "What are you crying about? You prayed to your God that you would get to the cross, and you did. You didn't think that it was all going to work out the way that *you* wanted it to, did you?" O'Leary said smugly.

"Leave me alone! Just leave us all alone!" I screamed until my voice echoed off stained glass in the back of the sanctuary. Tears that were once burned my eyes because of the putrid stench in the room were now replaced by salty tears of sorrow. I remember sobbing. Why couldn't she have just held on a minute longer?

"Think about this, Petey, my boy. Her last thought before she fell was 'Why didn't he save me?' You failed her, Peter." O'Leary's mocked Frances's voice, but his words rang true to the core of my heart.

I placed her frail, broken body on the floor. Frances was dead, and Brady was nowhere to be found. I had never felt so helpless or alone. The thick fog still lingered on the floor of the sanctuary, and the sounds of suffering still filled the room like a static. I knew what I had to do. I had to somehow find Brady and get us out of there. I was able to find him once for goodness sake, so I knew that I could do it again. And once I found him, if at all possible, I needed to get rid of O'Leary.

That's when I saw something on the cross above me.

Frances had hung something in the crux of the cross before she fell. It looked from several feet below to be a strip of cloth of some kind, but in the darkness of the room, it was hard to make it out. It could have been nothing, and maybe she had just ripped a strip of her sweater on the way down. The only way that I was going to be able to know for sure was by getting up there and getting that piece of whatever it was down. I had really no other option. And I definitely knew I was on the right track when I heard O'Leary start to panic. I had to see for myself what it was Frances had put up there.

"That's it, Petey. It's over. Give up. You gave it your best shot. You can't blame a kid for trying, can you." O'Leary said, but I could hear just the slightest hint of fear and for the first time vulnerability as he spoke those words.

I ignored him and looked around for any possible way to get up there to the cross. The heavy wooden cross must have weighed tons and have been lifted up there with a crane. There was no way to get from the stage of the sanctuary to the cross, because the only thing that seemed to be holding it up were thin wires attached to the walls behind it. But despite it being impossible high, somehow Frances had made it up there. Somehow even though she was barely able to move her weaken bones, she had made it up there to hug that cross. So I had to find my own way up there no matter what it took.

The whole time I was up there in the pulpit of the sanctuary I remember O'Leary constantly taunting me, planting doubt after doubt in my head.

"Do you think you are any different from the thousands that have sat in this room before you? Do you think you are special in some way?" He hissed. "So much delicious sin. So many wonderful sinners afraid to surrender themselves to Him. No one willing to help. All waiting in marvelous shame for me to guide them."

I wasn't a strong believer back then. Truth be told, there probably isn't a whole lot of nine year olds that are. So it didn't take much for his poisonous words to take root. I tried my hardest to ignore O'Leary and instead focus on getting to that cross. I pushed with my already throbbing shoulder and knocked over the podium with a loud crash that echoed throughout the sanctuary. That was followed by the screeching of the microphone when it cracked out of its plastic holder and bounced off the ground. The things squirming in the fog hated the sound of the microphone's reverb, because when the high pitched electric squeal rang from one end of the room to the other, they screamed in an agonistic response.

"What do you think you are doing there, Petey? So many smarter, older, better kids than you have tried to escape and have failed, so what makes you think that you won't just follow them down that same path? Even your girlfriend couldn't win." O'Leary said.

His words were needles in my soul. I was doing my best to ignore his voice, but deep down inside I knew that he was right. What did I believe anyway? All those hours of school listening to story after story about God 's Son, and did I really think that somehow I was a stronger believer than the others that had failed. Even Brady was a stronger Christian than me, and look how that ended.

"Yes, she couldn't win, so you killed her! Didn't you?" He said in a tone that echoed off the pews and ricocheted off the stained glass images in the far reaches of the sanctuary.

I could hear behind all of that hatred the hint of desperation in O'Leary's voice. That was one of the only two things giving me hope. The other was the plan that I had to get to whatever Frances had left for me up on that cross.

I jumped on the toppled podium, and although it only raised me about a foot off of the ground, it was enough to make a difference. The thin steel wires that held the cross were bolted securely to the wall behind it. Now that the podium made me a foot taller, I could see how it was all connected. I didn't have to make it to the cross all at once, all I had to do was make it to the wires that held it up.

As hard as I could, I bent over and pushed the podium up against the back wall. The whole time I could hear behind me the long black tentacles of the creatures in the fog as they pulled the more and more aggressive hands away from the bottom steps. It was as if the poor people being held back knew what I was trying to do with that podium, and they were excited and actually cheering for me to succeed. They wanted me to get to that cross. They wanted me to win. Where these the fallen ones that O'Leary was talking about?

"And how exactly do you think this is going to help Brady?" O'Leary questioned, "Your pal had to be the hero, because you didn't have the guts. And now, because you were a chicken, he's gone."

I could feel his words crawling under my skin. He was trying everything that he could to take my focus away from what I was doing. Every part of my fourth grade mind wanted to yell back at him. *"She's not my girlfriend! It's not my fault!"* But I didn't. Instead, I reached up as high as I could to grab the thin stainless steel wire bolted securely to the wall.

I'm telling you that there is no way that I could have reached the cross on my own, but I knew that I could, if I tried hard enough, maybe get myself a little closer to it. So here is what I did. Even standing on the podium, I still couldn't reach the wire, but I had a crazy plan.

I had seen on one of those comedy shows that come on in the afternoon when everyone is home from school a part where these two guys were locked in a jail cell and couldn't reach the key that was hung just out of their reach on a little peg board. So the guys took off their belts and used it as a whip to knock the key off the peg board and then when the keys had fallen to the ground, they slowly drug the keys towards them. So I didn't need to reach the wire, all I had to do was use my belt to bring that wire closer to me. I mean if it was on afternoon television it had to be true, right?

I slid my belt out from around each of the loops of my cargo pants and was ready to use it as a whip, but even if I did happen to hit the wire with the buckle of my belt, it wouldn't be with enough force to make any difference. I began to think to myself that this plan wasn't going to work out the way it had in my imagination. I was starting to doubt myself.

That was when I looked down at Frances's body silently resting on the floor of the stage just a few feet away. I had crossed her arms and shut her eyes, so now it looked as if she was just sleeping. But I knew that she was never ever going to wake up from this nap. O'Leary was right all along, I was weak, and that is why she was lying there.

O'Leary must have seen me somehow looking at Frances's silent body and could feel my doubt filling my heart, and so he once again tried to pounce on it. "So beautiful. Isn't she, Petey? I can't believe you let her die. At least she won't be alone for long. Brady will be joining her soon. Such a shame. Isn't it my boy?" O'Leary mocked my sorrow with every word.

I swung my belt around my head like a lasso. I had heard everything that O'Leary had said, and it burned. My vision was blurred from the thousands of tears and the strong sulfur stench in the air, but I couldn't give up. There was something deep in my heart telling me that God doesn't give us anything that we cannot handle. And at the time, I wasn't even sure if deep down I believed it. I was weak, and I couldn't hold in my anger or my words any longer; I just had to say something back to him. I couldn't just listen silently to all of that hateful venom that O'Leary was spitting into my ears and not do anything. So I screamed back at him.

*"Stop! You are nothing! Do you hear me? Nothing! This is all your fault! Not mine!"* My voice was hoarse and tired. I wanted to sound bigger, so much bigger than my small nine year old body.

O'Leary didn't say anything back to me. He didn't have to say anything at all. His high pitched laughter was more than enough. He cackled until the things in the fog squirmed under the pews. Each of them hiding from their master. He finished his hideous laughing with a few small giggles as if he was trying to control himself.

All of his mocking fueled my anger. With one final desperate leap I threw my belt over the thin steel wire. And then with both hands I yanked down as hard as I could. My feet left the floor, and all of my weight was dangling by my belt strap. My legs were kicking violently underneath me. But it was enough. The bolt pulled itself from the drywall, and when it did, I went crashing to the floor. That was enough to get O'Leary worked up again, and the helpless ones under the fog something to start cheering about.

"Yesssss. Pullll the crosssss down. Have it come crassssshhhing down." O'Leary's voice had changed. He no longer sounded like the mad man that had tormented me since the beginning of this crazy night in St. Thomas, now he sounded more like a serpent. But not just any serpent, a huge python. His voice was still deep and gravelly, but now there was a sick slow hiss in his words. He sounded as if his face drooped below itself as if he was having some kind of a stroke. He was struggling to get the words out.

The cross had fallen slightly, but not completely. Whoever put it in and secured it to the wall must have been a much better engineer than the guy who installed the bathtub baptismal. Two support wires still hung the cross a few feet above the ground, but it had fallen enough so I could start climbing.

The un-sanded wood was rough and rustic on my hands and I could feel tiny splinters trying to get though my skin as I shimmied up. That was when I remembered the pair of safety scissors in my pocket. I had to protect my hands in some way, or there was no way that I would be able to make it up to the top of that cross. The edges of the scissors were dull, but I knew that all I would need is a thin strip of cloth to wrap around my palms. So I took the safety scissors and tried to cut into the white robe that hung like rags down to my waist. It took a while for the scissors to get going, but the old material cut easily once I got past the thick edging. I wrapped the white strips around each of my palms a few times and began my ascent.

The fog surrounding the floor of the sanctuary ebbed and flowed in dark grey waves with every move I made toward the center of that cross and the smell of sulfur burned the back of my throat. There was more than once that I thought my grip would slip through the wrappings, and I just knew I was going to fall just like Frances had fallen. But the funny thing was that the harder and tighter that I hung on, the easier the climb seemed to be.

I must have been a few feet up above the stage and on my way to the center of the cross when I saw him. Through the thick fog I saw Brady. Don't ask me how I knew it was him. I tell myself that it was because all of the other arms and fingers reaching skyward were all grey and ashen. They were the limbs of the dead and desperate. They had spent eternity waiting for someone to save them, to pull them out, but it was too late for them. I told myself that Brady's arm was thicker than those around it and not as skeletal as the others. And both of those reasons were true, but it was neither of those things that helped me identify Brady's outreached arm among all of those engulfed in the fog. Now that I am older, and dare I say wiser, I know that there was something more out there. There was someone more showing me the way. Guiding me.

The problem was that I was dangling about three feet above the stage and working my way up to the center of the cross. Did I dare give up my quest and climb down and save him? Did I even dare to yell out his name and bring any attention to the fact that I saw him? I wanted Brady to know that I was there, but I didn't want O'Leary to know. Thankfully, O'Leary solved that problem for me.

"There he issss. Your little friend issss sssssooo close." O'Leary sounded as if he had not recovered from that stroke. His voice was deeper, to the point it rattled the rows of padded pews and the Bibles stored safely in the backs of the seats in front of them. "He belongssss to me now, Peter. Join him."

"Brady." I whispered. I did the only thing I knew I had to do. I had to keep making my way up to the crux of the cross. I had to find out what Frances had left dangling for me. If in fact it was anything at all.

I was almost to the center of the cross. I kept one eye on Brady's hand,

and the other on the sliver of red cloth. The way the shadows played in the moving mist, I would, every once in a while, lose sight of him. But every time I would start to panic, I would see a few of his fingers break through again. Brady wasn't giving up, so neither was I.

"Peter! It'sssss no use! Fall like the otherssss. The fallen are sssoooo deliciousss. *Fall*!" O'Leary's voice boomed. The last word he had spoken had almost caused me to lose my grip. I caught myself once again and looked down at Frances. Frances's poor and fragile body rocked from one side to the other upon hearing O'Leary's voice. Her hands fell to her side, no longer crossed across her chest. His slurred echo shook the multi-colored stained glass windows. A few of the Bibles fell from their seats and bounced from the velvet cushions to the floor below. And each time, a complete and perfect circle opened around it. I clenched to the cross for dear life. My arms and legs burned, and I started to understand why Frances couldn't hold on any longer and finally just had to let go. Every tiny muscle in my young body was screaming for me to do the same.

"God, give me strength." I said aloud. Yeah, I know. Now I was praying out loud, but it gave me the strength that I needed to get to the center of that cross and to that thin red strip of cloth that I just knew Franny had left there for me to find.

I had no idea what was scribbled on the thin ribbon, but there was something written on the cloth, and it was in Frances's handwriting. The problem was that I couldn't read it. When I opened the tiny strip, the words inside glowed a blinding white. The light coming from the writing was like looking into the sun. As I gripped to the cross with all my might, I folded the ribbon to protect my eyes. If only I had sunglasses. Wait! I did have sunglasses. With one arm I locked myself to the rough wood of the cross, and with the other I reached into my pocket to pull out the eclipse glasses that Brady had convinced me to carry. After almost dropping them twice, I slipped them on my soaked tear stained face.

The writing on the cloth still glowed bright through the glasses, but at least now I could look at it without blinding myself. The words were so beautiful. The problem was, I couldn't make it out. It looked to my fourth grade eyes to be written in some kind of code, or maybe it was written backwards. But the moment that I grabbed it and tried to slowly pronounce the words, O'Leary let me know that he was *not* happy.

*"Fall! Give yourssssself to me!"* He screeched.

There was more that he said, so much more, but I couldn't make it out. Partly because he was in real pain now. He was struggling to get the words out, and I could hear it in him. But another reason that I couldn't make out what he was trying to say was because O'Leary was no longer speaking English. His words were a mix of English and gibberish in long dead languages. I have tried to remember some of the phrases and words over the many years, but I could never quite pinpoint what he was saying. But in his rant, he gave me an idea.

The words the Frances had found scribbled down on that red cloth weren't written backwards. It just wasn't written in English. "E Tenebris In Lucem," I tried to sound out the phrase in nothing more than a quiet whisper.

When I saw the reaction below to my words, I tried to read them again through the shade of my paper glasses. Only this time, I read them louder and with more confidence. "E Tenebris In Lucem" I had no idea what those words meant, but O'Leary and his minions hated them, and that was enough for me.

My arms were Jell-O and about to give out. I could feel myself sweating through my robe and in return, slipping down the cross. I just had to hold on a little while longer. "God, hold me!" I screamed.

Meanwhile, the ground was breaking lose below me, literally. The grey swirls of fog turned black. Like a thousand tiny violent thunderstorms swirling around the base of the sanctuary. As I gripped as tightly as I could to the cross, I could hear the screams of the lost souls pleading for help and mercy, but it was too late for them. No help was coming. The ebony tentacles curling around every desperate body told me that there was no hope. But through all of that chaos, I kept my eyes on Brady. Sure, I was hanging on by a thread above the insanity below, but he was inside it.

O'Leary was yelling now, but not always to me. Sometimes I could understand his rants. *"Peter! You will not win!"* He directed his words to me. But other times I knew that he was no longer talking to me. *"My lord, I beseech you!"* But most of the time, I couldn't tell what he was saying. His dark black words were foreign and slurred.

As a scholar, I know now what I was repeating over and over that night in October. As I was dangling from the cross with Frances silent below me and Brady struggling under the otherworldly fog, I read the words she had left for me. "E Tenebris In Lucem, In Darkness, Light."

But at that moment of time as I dangled, barely hanging to the cross, I had no idea what the words meant that I was reading. I just repeated them over and over again chanting them like a prayer. And as I did, it hurt O'Leary like nothing else could. So I repeated them, because it was the only thing I knew to do that was having any effect. It was the only thing that was working.

That's when I slipped.

I felt it first start to give in my arms. I was looking towards Brady and repeating the words that Frances had found written for me over and over again, and I guess that I had forgotten that even though O'Leary was obviously hurting and in pain, I still had to manage to hang on. I took my attention away from the cross for just a split second, and my arms gave out.

"E Tenebris In Lucem" I said one last time as the crimson cloth slipped out of my hands. I had instinctively wrapped my arms around the cross to keep from falling, and when I did, my eclipse glasses slid off the end of my nose and drifted like an autumn leaf to the ground below. My legs were no longer dangling below me and thankfully still wrapped around the base of the cross, so when my arms finally gave out, I hung there upside down like a bat, unable to pull myself up. I didn't have the upper body strength, and I knew that if I fell from that height I was either going to break my arm, my neck, or both. Cold sweat dripped from the tip of my chin into my already red and watering eyes. The stirring creatures below me made the rotted meat stench rise and burn in my nostrils.

"*Yesssss!* Come to my sssssside." O'Leary pleaded.

But the thing was, we both knew that it was over for him. We both knew that I didn't need that strip of cloth anymore. I just needed the words that were written on them. "E Tenebris In Lucem" I whispered. And then my legs gave out too.

I know that you won't believe me. Most people, as much as they want to believe it, are still trying to come to terms with their own spiritual blindness and struggle with this part of my story. You see, as my nine year old body was falling to the floor to what was certain to be my doom, someone caught me. I remember that my eyes were as closed as tightly as they could be. I was bracing myself for the hit that was coming, because I knew that when I did hit the ground I would break, and then my body would roll down the steps and into the black pools of swirling fog. The long ebony tentacles would be reaching out and waiting for me. But I didn't happen that way. I fell softly. You see, when I say that I fell softly off of that cross it wasn't like falling on a pile of feathery pillows or like falling into a fluffy cloud, it was like falling out from a tree branch and being caught in your father's arms.

As soon as I was placed safely down, I opened my eyes. It was just a tiny crack at first, but then my eyes were wonderfully and fully opened. The once thick grey fog began to fade into the carpet. The once never ending black swirls of smoke were now quickly becoming thin wisp of white. There were no signs of the creatures that just seconds ago wrapped themselves around every pew. And it took me a few minutes to realize that even the reeking smell of burning flesh was gone. The sanctuary felt exactly the way that it should have, it felt like home. My knees could no longer hold up my weak and fragile frame, so I fell to them and began to weep. But I wasn't weeping tears of sadness, but relief. And as I did, the stained glass windows filled the room with a fabulous river of colors that washed over me.

Meanwhile, Frances's lifeless body was still and motionless. There lied a little girl that should have spent the last few months being one of my best friends, but instead, because I was afraid of what others might think of me, was a fragile shell that I never really had a chance to know. She is still one of my greatest regrets. I went to Frances and placed her back gently on the stage and crossed her arms once again over her chest. My tears leaked down my cheeks.

I looked out into the once dark and silent sanctuary that was now slowly being filled with the lights of the new dawn. The beautiful stained glass continued to bounce rainbows where there was moments ago just shadows. "E Tenebris In Lucem."

Out of the corner of my eye I saw Brady. "Brady?" I called out. With my shoes filled with lead, I stumbled tired down the few steps to the body lying curled on the floor. I just knew at that moment that I had lost him too. He was rolled over on his side with his back to me, so I couldn't see his face.

"Brady?" I cautiously said again.

"Peter?" Brady's voice was faint, but I knew it was his.

I carefully rolled him over on his back and wiped the mix of tears and snot from his face. "Yeah, Brady. It's me, Peter. You are going to be okay." I know that with both of us being nine year old boys it wasn't the coolest thing to do, but I held him tightly in my arms until he was ready to move again.

I could bore you with how we made it to the back doors of the school. But to tell you the truth, nothing really happened. The early Saturday morning sun was out, so the halls of St. Thomas had filled with natural light. The walk that Brady and I shared on the way toward the double doors was silent. There was a few times that we had to stop for a minute or two, and I had to hold him up, and more than once he did have to grab my belt loop as we went down the stairs.

Oh wait, there is one thing that happened along the way.

As we were making our way to the exit, Brady stopped me by grabbing my shoulders and looking me square in the eyes. "We have to stop by the library." Brady said.

"Why?" I asked.

He pulled his baptismal robe to the side and reached into the pocket of his jeans. He pulled out a hand full of little wads of scrap paper. On them Brady had written down his notes and a map. "For the next time."

My God, I questioned. How many times had this happened before? How many different little pieces of paper and pages from books had the three of us laid out on that table? A dozen? Two dozen? I didn't ask and really I didn't want to know. The thought of it all was just too much. So without conversation, Brady and I made the long and silent walk back to the library and pulled back the little wooden panel that sat underneath the shelves. Brady shoved his notes beside the others and snapped the board back in place. Neither one of us looking up at the portrait of Pastor O'Leary.

"God, let this help someone else the way it helped us." Brady prayed.

"Amen" I answered.

# CHAPTER 20

As I look at the clock, I realize that I'm running out of time, and I need to go soon, so let me wrap this up. And I guess out of respect I will start with Frances. The first set of paramedics that stepped foot in St. Thomas found her body exactly where we told them she would be. Officially, they reported her death as an accidental fall. And I guess technically, that is right. And although I was scolded by more than one adult for touching the body, they understood that I was just a stupid kid and had probably seen one too many television shows where they cross the victim's hands across their chest.

As far as I know, they never did explain how she had lost that much weight in under twelve hours. Frances wasn't a small child, but when they picked her up and carried her off, the emergency technician said she felt hollow like a bird. And although Brady and I were both sitting far away under one of the big Oak trees, I can still picture the way Franny's arms hung at her side like broken wings. The two of us were dirty and our baptismal robes hung like rags around us. A policeman wrapped us in a blanket and tried to keep us warm in the early morning cool of an October dawn. Brady and I answered the officer's questions as straight forward as we could.

I had also heard through rumors that Frances's parents tried to sue St. Thomas, but because we had broken into the church which was considered trespassing, and the cause of death was ruled an accidental fall, they really didn't have much of an argument. They moved to somewhere outside of Cleveland, Ohio within a year of her death. In fact, I can only remember maybe once or twice since Frances's funeral that I have talked to her mom and dad.

If you look carefully through the old St. Thomas Christian Academy yearbook, you will find pictures of Frances walking alone, or in the background playing around all of the rest of Mrs. Anderson's class, but the truth was she was never part of our class. We never let her. And truth be told, I'm not even sure if asked if she would have wanted to be part of our class. Sometimes I think she was just happy being herself, a watcher. But here is something that I do know about Frances Maggie Lingersham. On that night, in St. Thomas church and school, on a chilly October evening, she was there every step of the way for Brady and me. She was our best friend, and I wouldn't be here today, doing what I do, if it wasn't for her.

Like I said, Frances will always be one of my biggest regrets. I regret not being able to get to know her. I regret not standing up for her when no one else would. And when she did reach out to me, I was too ashamed to do anything but disappoint her. I think that all she ever wanted to be was accepted, and I couldn't even give her that. I'm sorry, Franny.

I still pray for her soul, and when I do, tears fill my eyes when I hear Him whisper, "She is home, Peter, and she is safe."

As for Brady, I still talk to him from time to time. He works up near Dallas doing the bookkeeping for some oil company. He has long ago gained all that weight back, and then some. Whenever he is in town, he looks me up, and we share a dinner and catch up. We cut into big juicy steaks and talk about his family. He has a beautiful wife and two little red-headed girls. Cute as a button they are. And Brady isn't shy about sharing pictures.

He doesn't like to talk about that night in St. Thomas, and I don't blame him. He says that he has a hard time remembering anything past our time together slipping on pudding cups in the walk-in cooler, but I don't believe him. I think he remembers everything, and that is why he doesn't like to talk about it. In my heart I believe that I saw a small part of the afterlife that night, but Brady, Brady was in it. I can only imagine what he must have seen, and what he must have been through. So instead, we talk about the Dallas Cowboys, or depending on the time of year, the Houston Astros. It's just good to see his face from time to time, and know that I am not alone.

There was one time though that he said something that stuck with me. We had just finished our dinner, and we were waiting on the check, when he shared something that he had not only been holding on to throughout the entire dinner, but probably since that night that it all happened.

"We got it right, Pete. Sure, we tell ourselves that everything that we read and study is true, but really it all comes down to faith. But Peter, I'm telling you that we got it right." Brady told me. He was quiet and pulled gently to straighten the napkin folded across his legs.

"What's that, Brady? What did we get right?" I asked him.

Brady looked up from his lap and stared into my eyes. "All of it." Then he crossed his hands in front of himself and put his fist to his chin. "We got all of it right, and it is so beautiful. Better than we ever imagined."

Part of me wanted him to explain, but I could tell by the way he changed the subject back to the Cowboy's playoff chances that he was done.

Other than that, we exchange Christmas cards, and birthday cards, and that is about it.

His parents let him stay at St. Thomas to finish out the fourth grade tuition free. But in fifth grade, he transferred back into the public school system. I guess after all that he had been through, bullies are nothing. I stuck around St. Thomas until eighth grade, and then my dad took another job about an hour away, so we packed up and moved again. But for five years, Brady and I rode our bikes and stayed at each other's houses. We never talked about that night and what we had done, or what we had seen. And after a while, we stopped talking about Frances too. Instead we just got quiet.

St. Thomas didn't change. There were reports in the local papers about how three kids broke into the school and vandalized the sanctuary by tearing down the almost one ton cross that hovered above the pulpit. There was a mention or two about the tragedy of poor Frances Maggie Lingersham who had slipped and fallen to her death. The church issued a statement and even offered to have her service in the little chapel on the corner of the church's property. (Mr. and Mrs. Lingersham politely declined the invitation.) But for the most part other than a few whispers here and there that soon faded, everything was status quo for good old St. Thomas.

By Monday morning, Mrs. Anderson even had Frances's desk in the back of the classroom taken out and put into storage. It was as if she had never existed. Mrs. Anderson just kept teaching class as if it was just any other normal autumn Monday.

A few of the boys and girls in class stared at Brady and me all morning long, but they were all too afraid to say anything to us. It wasn't until Shane invited us to sit at his table with the rest of the guys during lunch almost a week later that things started to feel different, better. We were actually part of the group. Brady and I were now part of the fourth grade class.

There was another time that I remember sitting in the library a few days after that. I was working on a report about the Arctic Circle, when Ms. James came around to dust off the book shelves. As she dusted, the long wooden paneling underneath slipped and one of Brady's notes fell out onto the worn out green carpet. The librarian cautiously looked around the room and shoved his note back in with the rest of them. Then she snapped the panel back into place. She didn't notice that I had seen what she had done, but it was enough to tell me that she knew it was there.

Like I said, it's about time for me to go. It's almost 9:00 o'clock, and there are a handful of people out there waiting to hear what I have to say. But that is my testimony. That's how on one cool October night I literally fell into the arms of my Savior. It's how I came to Christ. It's all true, one hundred percent of it, but if you are like most people, you won't believe it all. You will just pick out the parts that suit you best, and I am okay with that.

"Pastor, it's about time to start." Mrs. Nola says as she politely pokes her head in the door.

"I hear the music, Joanne. I will be out in a moment." I answer.

That's my cue. I hope you will stay for the service. I think you might like the message. It's all about forgiveness.

CPSIA information can be obtained
at www.ICGtesting.com
Printed in the USA
LVOW10s0957190518
577803LV00001B/73/P